CHARLIE CARILLO

raising jake

KENSINGTON BOOKS
www.kensingtonbooks.com

KENSINGTON BOOKS are published by

Kensington Publishing Corp.
119 West 40th Street
New York, NY 10018

All Kensington titles, imprints, and distributed lines are available at special quantity discounts for bulk purchases for sales promotion, premiums, fund-raising, educational, or institutional use.

Special book excerpts or customized printings can also be created to fit specific needs. For details, write or phone the office of the Kensington Special Sales Manager: Kensington Publishing Corp., 119 West 40th Street, New York, NY 10018. Attn.: Special Sales Department. Phone: 1-800-221-2647.

Kensington and the K logo Reg. U.S. Pat. & TM Off.

ISBN-13: 978-0-7582-3504-6
ISBN-10: 0-7582-3504-6

First printing: September 2009
10 9 8 7 6 5 4 3 2 1

Printed in the United States of America

Fic.

To my one and only Kim—
A believer

My thanks to:

Tony Carillo, Cissy Carillo, Mary Carillo, Gina Carillo, Rafael Richardson-Carillo, Frank O'Mahony, Betty O'Mahony, Catherine Bohrsmann, James Bohrsmann, Felicity Rubinstein, Carol Pink, Malcolm Pink, Charles Lachman, Bill Hoffmann, Gary Goldstein, Kate Duffy, Audrey LaFehr, Anne Edelstein, Amy Schiffman, Krista Ingebretson, Peg Ashdown, Ivy Tillyer, Denise Lister-Fell and Simon Fell (aka "Dr. Fellenstein")

raising jake

CHAPTER ONE

It's the first phone call from my son's school that I've ever gotten at work, and of course I immediately think the worst. I'm a divorced father who catches glimpses of his seventeen-year-old son on weekends, snapshots of his life ever since I split from his mother, and suddenly my guts go into free fall with the knowledge that anything, absolutely anything could have happened to him. Failing grades. A drug habit. A fatal overdose. Whatever it is it's my fault, entirely my fault for not being around.

These jolly possibilities shoot through my brain in less time than it takes to sneeze. If they ever have a Guilt Olympics, I'll carry the torch at the opening ceremonies.

The caller identifies himself as the headmaster, and I can feel sweat breaking out along my hairline. This is the guy who writes letters to me and the rest of the parents, asking for contributions to fill in the "gaps" not covered by tuition payments. Those payments come to about twenty-four thousand dollars a year, two grand per month, including February, which has just twenty-eight days. I've always been proud of myself for never writing a contribution check, not once, not ever. I probably wouldn't have written the tuition checks, either, except that those payments are part of my divorce agreement, and if I miss one I'm in court, and as much as I hate writing a tuition check, it beats the hell out of writing a check to a lawyer.

That's not quite true. The truth is that unless my kid goes to private school, he'll wind up in a school where he has to pass through a metal detector every day, and who wants that for their child? Like so many parents trapped on the island of Manhattan, I do what I have to do, and tell myself that it's well worth the nightmares triggered by ever-deepening debt.

My mouth has gone dry. I have to lick my lips before daring to ask, "Is my son hurt?"

"Oh no! Nothing like that!" The guy chuckles apologetically. "Forgive me for frightening you, Mr. Sullivan."

Actually, this is just the jolt I need to burn the fuzz off a hangover I've been nursing all morning. Now, at least, I'm clear in the head. Nothing like a death scare to blow the pipes clean.

"Why are you calling?" I ask, nearly adding the word "Headmaster" to the sentence. It's a funny word, that one, the kind of word you'd sooner associate with leafy English boarding schools than you would a soot-stained brick building on the Upper West Side.

The headmaster clears his throat. "It's a matter I'd prefer to discuss in person. Could you come to my office at one p.m.?"

An hour from now. "That's not a great time for me, Headmaster."

"I thought maybe you could extend your lunch hour."

"I don't get a lunch hour. Look, his mother will be back in town on Monday. She's really the one who handles educational matters."

My son is obviously not in a life-and-death situation. It seems fair to pass this mysterious mess off to the ex, the one who selected and insisted upon this school in the first place.

"I'm afraid it can't wait," the headmaster says. "I feel I really must see one of Jacob's guardians today."

Guardians. He actually says *guardians*. That's a bad news word, if ever there was one. I start to sweat all over again. "What the hell did he do?"

"One p.m., then?"

"Yeah, all right, I'll be there."

He couldn't have picked a worse time for a meeting. The newspaper goes to press at 2:00 p.m., and the story I'm working on this particular day is a bit complicated, and so far I'm not getting anywhere with it.

The story is this: was that bottle of liquid Britney Spears was photographed swigging from during a stroll with her elaborately tattooed boyfriend a bottle of whiskey, as the editors of the *New York Star* would like to believe, or a bottle of ginseng, as Britney's publicist vows it was? Believe it or not, this is our third day covering this matter, and the bosses are eager to stretch it to a fourth. It's just an excuse to publish the photos over and over, but by now our excuses are starting to seem a little lame.

It's also a tightrope walk, legally speaking. The words have to be just right, all your "allegedlys" and "reportedlys" tucked in place, which is probably why the story goes to a crusty old rewrite man like me. I'm good at this shit, it both shames and thrills me to say. I can imply things without actually saying them. I can titillate without showing tits.

And now, suddenly, I've got to dump this hornet's nest into somebody else's lap so I can go and see the headmaster at a school I haven't set foot in for more than five years.

The day city editor is a prematurely balding Australian named Derek Slaughterchild, and I'm not looking forward to telling him I have to bolt with a deadline coming up. Slaughterchild is one of those guys who learned young that the way to move ahead in the tabloid news game is to go through the day with a pained, miserable look on your face, hang around long past your shift, and always be anxious. He believes that work done in a state of panic is better than anything achieved in a state of relaxation.

And that's pretty funny, because his father, a lovable alcoholic named Malcolm Slaughterchild, was his polar opposite. Malcolm was the day city editor back when I was a copyboy, nearly thirty years ago, and no matter what was happening I don't think his pulse rate ever changed. Moments after Hinckley shot Ronald Reagan, everyone in the newsroom was running around screaming, and as I handed the latest wire copy to Malcolm he took a deep breath, ran a hand through his thick, silvery hair and murmured, "This could alter my dinner plans."

Apparently such a temperament skips a generation. Malcolm and his ruined liver were dead and buried, his son was alive and miserable, and here I was, damn near fifty years old, screwing up my courage to ask for the afternoon off. Working for a tabloid newspaper is a little bit like being in high school forever. They scream your name when they want you and treat you like an untrustworthy child, and prom night never comes.

"Derek."

He looks up at me squinty-eyed, the light from the overhead fluorescents making his scalp gleam at the crown, where his hair is thinnest. "You wrapped up?"

"Not yet."

"We really need a new angle on this Britney bullshit, Sammy. Got to freshen it up, mate."

"Yeah, well, sadly for us, there wasn't a second photographer on the grassy knoll."

If he gets the Kennedy reference, his face doesn't show it. "What have you got, then?"

"Nothing."

"Mate."

"Derek, we broke the story. Then we broke Britney's denial. Then we went to the man on the street for his opinion. The only thing left to do is wait until she checks into rehab."

For the first time, he seems interested in something I have to say. "Is she checking into rehab?"

"I have no idea. But I don't think there's any way you can abuse ginseng, so I'd say it was unlikely."

Derek picks up the photo of Britney and stares at it like a man hoping to hear voices from above. Suddenly he says, "What about her body language?"

"Excuse me?"

"Her *body language*, mate." He runs a bony finger along the length of Britney's body. "The way she's positioned. Does it or does it not indicate whether she's drinking a health supplement, or whiskey?"

If you ever find yourself working for a tabloid publication, remember that it's important not to laugh at moments like these. You've got to take every editor's suggestion as seriously as Marie Curie took the tons and tons of dirt she boiled to get that one little teaspoon of radium. The only difference in the tabloid game is that you boil tons and tons of bullshit to get one little spoonful of dirt.

My heart is hammering away. I am actually afraid to ask this man for the afternoon off. I am ashamed of myself for being afraid to ask. I am angry at myself for being so cowardly about the whole thing.

And I'm gasping as if I've just run a hundred-yard dash.

Derek notices. "Are you all right, there, mate?"

I force myself to calm down, wondering where the tumor that's sure to be triggered by all this pent-up anxiety will strike me—lungs? Liver? Kidneys? Ten years from now, I'm going to die of cancer of the something-or-other because of my reluctance to ask for a few hours off in the middle of a workday. This is insane. I've just got to go ahead and do it.

"Thing of it is," I begin, fighting unsuccessfully to quell the quaking in my voice, "I'm going to have to hand the story off to somebody."

Derek's eyes narrow. "*Why* must you hand the story off?"

"I need to duck out of here for about two hours." I've picked a bad verb with "duck." It sounds like I mean to run out to the racetrack, but it's too late to worry about it now.

Derek is shaking his head. "I need a reason, mate."

I stare at him long and hard, this son of a man I liked very much, a man who used to bring little Derek to the newsroom when he was a toddler. He had a red fire engine that he'd roll back and forth along the floor, and once one of its rubber wheels came off its rim and rolled out of sight, so I got down on my hands and knees and found the little black doughnut under a desk and squeezed it back onto the rim, good as new. I handed the truck back to the teary four-year-old and urged him not to cry, because everything was okay, and the kid even thanked me for what I'd done, unbeknownst to anyone but the two of us.

And if someone had tapped me on the shoulder that day and told me that the cute kid in short pants would grow up to become my boss, busting my balls over a request to take a few hours off from work, who would have believed it?

Of course, there *is* a way out. I could tell Derek that it's an emergency of some kind involving my son, but I wouldn't even share my zip code with this man, much less a problem from my personal life. I'm actually suffering a miniature nervous breakdown here, having imagined everything up to and including my son's death, and all I want to do is get to his school and find out what the hell is going on.

"Derek," I manage to say, "just trust me. I have something important to do, so I'm going."

"No, you're not," he singsongs.

"I'm *not*?"

"Leave now and you're fired."

He says it flat out, no emphasis on the word "fired," no real emotion in his voice. He means what he says, and not only that, he's happy to say it. This has been building for months now, I suddenly realize. He knows I think he's a lousy editor, and he can taste my contempt for him. I guess he's grown tired of the taste.

I'm not exactly dealing from a position of strength. I'm one of the dinosaurs in the newsroom, older than most of the reporters by fifteen, twenty years. The paper has always been lousy, but there was a time when it was the *best* lousy thing around, funny and irreverent and occasionally even sympathetic to the plight of the little man. We used to do stories about honest cabbies who returned lost wallets. Now the only time we write about a cabbie is when he turns out to be a suspected terrorist, or when a celebrity stiffs him out of a tip or pukes in the backseat. Mostly we're up the asses of celebrities—following them, photographing them, trying to guess what they do with their genitals, and how often. It doesn't take much to become a celebrity anymore, so the field is huge, a cluster of idiotic young people either posing for the camera or pretending to dodge it.

Something in me snaps. Suddenly my fears are gone. All that's left is rage, but it's not a blind rage. In some weird way, this is exactly how I wanted it all to play out—me versus the asshole in charge.

I clear my throat and say, "You're going to fucking *fire* me, Derek?"

He's almost smug about it. He leans back in his chair and folds his hands together behind his head. "You heard what I said. If you want permission to go, I'll need a reason."

I think it's the word "permission" that does it. It's in the same league with "guardian." Suddenly the ridiculousness of it all comes into diamond-hard focus. I am literally embarrassed by the way I have spent my working life.

I want to bash Derek's face in. There hasn't been a newsroom punch-out since the old days, when boozing chain-smokers would mix it up and then buy each other drinks after hours. Now nobody smokes, and nobody fights. The reporters belong to gyms and exercise in spandex pants, to the barking commands of their personal trainers. When conflicts arise, they phone their lawyers. I know that if I touch Derek, I'll wind up in court. Enraged as I am, I remain sane enough to know I don't want to go to court, so I can't hit him.

All I can do is leave. In my head, I can hear the drumroll that precedes my next words.

"I'm going now, Derek."

"You're fired, Sullivan."

These are the words every man in the world is supposed to fear, right up there with "It's inoperable," but the first thing that hits me is the absurdity of the fact that this little weed should have the clout to speak such a sentence. A short, perfect sentence, noun-verb, bang-bang. Hemingway couldn't have put it more succinctly, and Derek Slaughterchild is no Hemingway.

I look at my hands, where I can feel a tingle of blood flooding to my fingers. Without realizing it I'd balled my hands into fists and loosened them at last at the words "You're fired," and what, I can't help wondering, would a body language expert have to say about *that*? ("Loose hands? Well, it's clear that deep down, you'd been clenching your fists for many, many years, and not until you were free of this miserable job did you finally relax. . . .")

I rub my hands together, push the blood along. "So that's it? That's all there is to it?"

"Give your notes to Hoffmann."

"There aren't any notes, asshole!"

I'm practically shouting. Derek picks up his phone and dials. "I'm calling security," he says, his voice suddenly gone shaky. "You've got five minutes to pack up."

I walk back to my desk, every eye in the newsroom on me. The only good thing is that a few years back, when the thrills had gone out of my job, I got rid of all the shit that had accumulated in and around my desk, so I have nothing to pack—no files, no personal effects, nothing. It's as if I always knew my departure would be sudden and ugly.

And I have no photographs to take off my cubicle walls, because I never hung any pictures here. I hate the whole idea of trying to turn the workplace into a little piece of home. This was never home, it was where I went to make money.

Until today.

Hoffmann is looking at me over the border between our cubicles, both fascinated and scared, as if getting fired might be contagious. He's about fifteen years younger than me, single and wild, a true cowboy of tabloid journalism. His blind quotes always sound as if they've been spoken by the same person, a person who sounds a lot like Hoffmann.

I put on my jacket, straighten my tie, tap on the partition separating me from Hoffmann. "Feel free to knock this down and make a duplex, Hoff."

"Are you really fired?"

"I am canned goods, man."

"Aren't you going to appeal it?"

"No."

Hoffmann extends a hand over the partition to shake with me. "I'm really sorry, Sammy."

"Water my plants, would you?"

"You don't have any plants."

"Good point," I say. "Good luck with the Britney story."

I walk to Derek's desk for the last time. His hands are trembling as he pretends to read the latest edition of the newspaper.

"Hey Derek—"

"Don't come any closer! Security will be here any minute to escort you to the sidewalk."

"Fuck security, I'll be gone before they get here. Listen to me, Derek."

He sighs with mock impatience as he looks up at me, feigning courage. "I'm listening."

"I'm sorry I fixed your fire engine that time."

He stares at me in genuine wonder. He doesn't remember the favor I did him, all those years ago. "Fire engine?"

"Never mind."

I flip him the bird and begin my final walk down the long hallway to the elevator. The walls are covered with framed front-page stories from years gone by, three or four of them written by yours truly, back in the days when my heart harbored something that resembled hope.

I have been a reporter at this newspaper longer than I have ever been anything else. I didn't love the place, and much of the time I didn't like it, but I did fit in here, and now I'll never be coming back. I guess I should be crying, but I'm not. I'm just numb over how such a momentous thing could happen so abruptly.

I don't know what my next move will be. For that reason I'm almost glad I have to go to my son's school, to find out what this fuss is all about.

Chapter Two

Being fired doesn't fully hit you until you leave the building, look around, and take your first breath as an unemployed person. I'm standing there on Sixth Avenue and Forty-sixth Street, and the sidewalks are jammed with people, and all I can think about is whether or not they have jobs. They're all in motion, and they all seem to have destinations. You know you're in trouble when you're jealous of strangers.

It's Friday, and Friday is a big day for firing people, if only for clerical purposes. I can't be alone in this fix. I don't *want* to be alone in this fix.

I head west and north, in the general direction of my son's school, my blood tingling as if it's been carbonated. The sidewalks are peppered with young people wearing Walkmans, or iPods, or whatever the hell they call the latest thing they need to ensure that they're amused every waking hour of the day. The sight both bothers and pleases me. On the one hand, these kids are missing out on the sidewalk sounds I've loved my whole life. On the other hand, it impairs their ability to concentrate and keeps them good and stupid, and a whole generation of stupid kids buys me another five years in the workforce. Or so I thought until today, when a stupid kid fired my rapidly aging ass.

I walk all the way to the school, and as I enter it the smell is exactly as I remembered, an all-boys' school smell, a testosterone and no-showers-after-gym-class odor. It hangs in the air like an arrogant, dangerous cologne, and I get the feeling that if a fertile woman walked in here and took a deep breath, she'd miss her next period.

On my way to the headmaster's office I pass a series of carved marble plaques featuring the names of all the school's headmasters, dating back to 1732.

Seventeen thirty-two! This place has certainly been around. Part of what you're shelling out for is its history, and right there at the bottom of the newest plaque is the name of the guy who phoned me, the latest keeper of the flame, etched into the marble: Peter Plymouth. How fitting that a guy named Plymouth should have his name carved into rock. His start date is carved in next to his name, with a dash next to it. When he dies, quits, or gets fired, a guy with a hammer and chisel will chip in his departure date. This has got to be the only school in Manhattan where part of the tuition fees go toward a stonecutter.

There's a secretary seated at a desk in front of the headmaster's office, a sixtyish, owl-shaped woman with her hair up in a tight gray bun. She's perfect for this place, the kind of woman no young male will lose valuable study time to over masturbatory fantasies.

I tell her who I am, explain that I have a one o'clock appointment. At the sound of my name her eyebrows go up, a clue to me that I'm in for some serious business. It happens to be one o'clock on the dot. She gestures at the closed door and says, "Go right in."

But I can't. Just being in a school setting has made me timid. I have to tap on the door first, and only when the voice from the other side tells me to come in am I able to do it.

It's a big room, with windows facing out on the branches of a

sycamore tree. Headmaster Peter Plymouth sits at a wide ma-
hogany desk with his back to the windows. He's wearing a dark
blue suit, a white shirt, and a black tie, and his long, bony body
seems to rise from his chair in sections, like a carpenter's ruler.
His hair is cut short, his face is unwrinkled, and his handshake is
hard and dry. He gestures for me to sit down before returning to
his own chair.

A lot had been made of this headmaster's appointment the
year before, because he'd graduated from the place twenty years
earlier, gone to Yale, and then begun an academic career that
took him from campus to campus all over the Northeast, with a
"year out" somewhere in the middle, when he got a grant to
write a book about Great Sailboat Races of the 1930s.

I know all this stuff because the school bombards my mailbox
with letters, keeping me abreast of this kind of news. I throw
out most of the mail without reading it, but there was something about the "Return of the Prodigal Son" memo that caught
my eye.

So now we're both seated, looking at each other. He's giving
me a bit of time to drink in the diplomas, the awards, the ribbons, and the sailing trophies that adorn his office. There's even
a ship in a bottle, right there on his desk.

"Well," he begins, "you have quite a son."

I have nothing to say in response to this. It means nothing—it
could be good, it could be bad. If this were a tennis match, he'd
have just served the ball into the net. I'm willing to sit and wait
for as long as I must for his second serve, which is even weaker
than the first.

"I'm sorry to drag you in here like this," he ventures. "I know
you're busy."

That would have been true an hour earlier, when I had a job,
the kind of job this man couldn't do in a million years. He's
never been in a newsroom full of frantic people, with editors

yelling for copy and copyboys rushing around and hysterical reporters using the word "fuck" as a noun, a verb, and even an adverb (i.e., "You are the fucking slowest copyboy in the world!").

No, Mr. Plymouth's pressure is a different kind of pressure, the pressure to get the boys placed in Ivy League colleges so the school can maintain its prestige and continue to have desperate parents clamoring to hurl their money at him.

"Don't apologize," I say. "Just tell me what's going on."

The headmaster opens his desk drawer and pulls out a couple of sheets of loose-leaf paper covered in jagged, spiky writing I immediately recognize as my son's.

"I'd like you to look at this," he says softly. "It's an essay your son composed yesterday in English class. It was a little exercise in spontaneous expression, assigned by Mr. Edmondson. The topic was 'The Cold Truth.' "

"The cold truth about *what?*"

"That was entirely up to the student. He could take the title and go any which way with it. I think you'll be interested in your son's choice."

He passes the pages to me. I take my time getting out my reading glasses, which I've only begun to wear after decades of squinting at the green glow of computer screens. I'm a little bit nervous, I'll admit, but at the same time it's a joy to read something that's actually been penned by a human hand for a change, however disturbing it might turn out to be.

THE COLD TRUTH
by Jacob Perez-Sullivan

You don't know it when you're a kid, because nobody tells you, but the key to life is being in the right clubs, pretty much from the time you start walking.

Nobody sells it to you that way—in fact, they try

to spin it the *other* way, so that it seems important to embrace and understand as many different kinds of people as you can in the course of your lifetime—but the truth is, that's not the truth.

Far from it. It's important to get into the right preschool, because this will naturally lead to the right elementary school, followed by the right high school, and then, of course, the right college.

The college is to this process what the orgasm is to the sex act. Anyone who makes it all the way through the other schools only to drop the ball when it comes to college has not understood the process. You don't belong to exclusionary groups all your life just to start mixing in with the general population at age eighteen. It makes a mockery of your entire life, not to mention the monumental waste of your parents' money.

The clubhouse life is a true commitment, made first by the parents and then by us, the students, by the time we're old enough to ride a two-wheeler. We get the point. Nobody has to spell it out for us. It's not a complicated or sophisticated strategy.

The saddest thing about the clubhouse life (there are many sad things, but we only have fifteen minutes to write this essay) is the fact that we only get to know each other. A school like ours is careful to stir the occasional African-American or Hispanic into the mix, but that's not for the benefit of those students, who are hand-picked for their apparent harmlessness.

No, those students are here so that the rest of us won't freak out every time we go to a cash machine and there's a member of a minority waiting behind us.

This is part of the clubhouse process—recognizing the fact that now and then, we must step outside the clubhouse, whether we like it or not. Step out, and then quickly step back in. And shut the door fast, lest an outsider follow you inside.

You're either in a good club, or you're in a bad club. The walls are there, whether you see them or not. It's all about the walls, and which side of the walls you're on.

That's the cold truth. It isn't pretty, and it isn't fair, but it's the cold truth. I can only hope the day will come when this sham just cannot go on, and the entire system collapses under the weight of its own bullshit. Maybe then, life will be fair.

When I finish reading the essay I continue holding the pages, just to stare at the symmetry of my son's handwriting. It's a beautiful thing. Nothing has been crossed out. It just flowed out of him, as if he'd been waiting all his young life to express these thoughts. And yet, according to the headmaster, he'd knocked it out just moments after getting the assignment in "spontaneous expression."

At last I look up at the headmaster, whose face is as blank as a blackboard on the first day of school.

"Quite an essay," he ventures. "Wouldn't you agree?"

"I certainly would."

"Naturally Mr. Edmondson was alarmed when he read it, and quite rightly he brought it to my attention."

"Alarmed?"

"Of course! This is clearly just a peek into something much more disturbing that your son is experiencing. It's the reason I called you here."

"You called me here because my ex-wife is out of town. I know I'm number two on the emergency phone call list."

"Mr. Sullivan, I hardly think this is the time to quibble over parental rivalries."

"Have you spoken with my son about this essay?"

His face darkens. "That's another reason I called you. Yes, I have spoken with him. Sometimes students do things like this in an attempt to be satirical. If that were the case, well, *fine*. We could all just laugh it off. But according to your son, he meant every word of it. Every single word."

"I'm sure he did."

"We gave him the chance to apologize, and he refused."

"Apologize for what?"

Mr. Plymouth's eyes widen. "Mr. Sullivan. Did you read the essay? He called this school a sham! He wants the entire system to collapse!"

"Under the weight of its own bullshit," I add helpfully.

"That's how he put it, yes. He wasn't exactly *subtle* about it."

"What did he say when you asked for an apology?"

"He said, and I quote, 'I wouldn't have written it if I didn't mean it.'"

"He saw through your game."

The headmaster falls back in his chair, as if he's just been hit in the chest with a medicine ball. He stares at me in wonder. "I beg your pardon?"

"I said, he saw through your game. You. This place." I gesture at the walls of his office. "He got to the guts of your game. He saw the Wizard of Oz, hiding behind the curtain. *That's* what's bothering you, Headmaster Plymouth."

CHAPTER THREE

The headmaster stares at me in openmouthed disbelief.

"This is not a game," he says evenly.

"Come on."

"Mr. Sullivan—"

"Listen, I know what it's like. I write for the *New York Star*, and every once in a while I'm interviewing somebody who can tell the angle I'm working, you know? He can tell I'm trying to get him to say something I need to make my story work, and he just won't give it to me. Happens maybe once every hundred interviews, and when it does it really stings, but what can you do? Not everybody's an idiot."

"We're going off on a bit of a tangent here—"

"No, we're not. This is the exact same thing we're talking about. When someone's wise to your racket, it can be very unsettling."

The headmaster nearly flinches at the word "racket." The thoughts spinning through his skull are are as obvious as the zipper headlines in Times Square. How he wishes he'd waited until Monday to deal with this matter, when the boy's mother will be back in town! Suddenly, his idea of an emergency is not such an emergency. The *real* emergency is me, here in his office, and now his problem is simple: how do I get rid of this guy?

"What we do here," he says, "can hardly be referred to as a *racket*."

"I would apologize for my choice of words, sir, but the selection of the right word at the right time just happens to be my business."

He lets out the tiniest of snorts. "Yes, well, for the *New York Star*."

Now he's stepped in it. His face flames up and he regrets what he's said, but it's too late. He's insulted a customer, and the customer is always right—and at this school, the customer is almost always white.

"Well, sir," I say, "you may not think highly of the product I help produce, but like it or not it's what makes it possible for my son to be educated within these hallowed halls."

He holds up his hands, palms out. "Forgive me."

"Forget it. I knew how you felt about it before we ever met. Not all of us get to write about sailboat races. Somebody's got to crank out the ugly stuff. That's just the way it is."

His face gets even redder. He's surprised that I know about his sailboat book. I don't look like the kind of parent who reads school bulletins.

He clears his throat and gets to his feet. This is a pretty good tactic on his part, I must admit. He's easily six inches taller than me, and what he wants is that rush he'll get from glowering down at me.

But it can only work if I stand up and go toe-to-toe with him. So I remain seated, gazing straight up into his remarkably hairless nostrils. He must use one of those rotary noise hair clippers.

He's in a bad spot. After a few moments he sighs, sits back down, and does the only thing left for him to do.

"What do you say we call your son in here?"

"I think that's a good idea."

He tells his secretary to send for my son, then drags a chair over and sets it so that the distances between all three chairs are equal. A perfect triangle. The loyalties could go any which way.

And then, silent as a sailboat, my son glides into the room.

I'm jolted by his appearance. I hadn't seen him over the past weekend, because the whole senior class had been taken on an overnight trip to the Catskill Mountains, and in the less than two weeks since I last saw him he's actually grown a beard. It's a fairly thick beard for a kid not yet eighteen years old, as black as coal and startling against his light complexion. His hair is nearly as dark as the beard, shoulder length and parted in the middle. Jake's dark features come from his mother, who's Spanish. That creamy white Irish skin comes from me. His sea-green eyes are anybody's guess.

Those eyes have a serenity I can only dream of for my blood-shot brown ones. He's wearing corduroy pants, a black shirt, and scuffed boots. The mandatory school tie hangs around his neck in a big, wide loop, as if he'd been condemned to death by a hangman who'd suddenly changed his mind and let him go. He's as slim as a jackrabbit and if he held out his arms and crossed his feet, you might just think him capable of changing water into wine.

As always, the sight of him makes my heart ache. How can he suddenly have a beard, this boy I remember with peach-fuzz cheeks? In the time his beard was growing in I was working late, or getting drunk, or watching old movies in the middle of the night. What was *he* doing, besides not shaving? Did he think about me even once during the two weeks I haven't seen him, not counting the pathetic "How's everything?" phone calls I make every day or two? It's just the latest in an endless series of gaps in our relationship. The gaps have jagged edges, and they bite right into my soul, if a fallen Catholic like me can be said to have a soul.

Jake doesn't seem surprised to see me. He looks at me and nods, not happy, not sad, and most amazingly, not nervous.

"Hey, Dad."

"Hello, Jake."

He turns to the headmaster and gestures at the empty chair. "Is this for me?"

"Yes, it is, Jacob. Please sit down."

Almost nobody calls him "Jacob." He's been "Jake" ever since he was a baby, but not to his mother, who chose the name and loathes the nickname. "Jake sounds like the name of a cardsharp," she always complained. In any case, Jacob-Jake sits in the chair, leans back and crosses his legs, the very poster child for Not a Worry in the World, Inc.

The headmaster, on the other hand, looks as if he could use a drink. "I was talking to your father about your essay."

"I figured, Mr. Plymouth."

"As I recall, you said you stand by what you've written."

"Yes, I do."

"And you're not sorry about what you've written?"

"Of course not."

"So what you've written here is how you truly feel about this school. You believe it to be a sham."

"Yes, totally."

"And you really would like to see the entire system collapse, as you say, under the weight of its own bullshit?"

Jake shrugs. "Well, it wouldn't bother me if it did."

My son is both abrupt and polite, an unusual combination. He stares at the headmaster, whose forehead, I now see, glistens with a light glaze of sweat. He turns to me and spreads his hands.

"You can see the position I'm in," he says. "Can't you?"

"It seems to me that *your* position is fine," I reply. "I'm a little more concerned about Jake's position."

Jake uncrosses his legs. "What *is* my position?"

The headmaster hesitates. "Well, Jacob. Unless you have a

change of heart about what you've expressed in this essay, I do not see how you can continue attending this school."

Jake doesn't exactly sit up straight, but he takes most of the slack out of his slouch. "You're expelling me?"

"That's what it would come to, yes."

"Whoa, whoa," I say, "hang on a second. Nobody got shot, nobody got stabbed here. A few opinions were expressed, that's all."

"This was *more* than just a few opinions, Mr. Sullivan. This was an indictment of the system that's worked at this school since 1732." He holds up Jake's essay. "With concepts this subversive, he becomes a potential threat to the rest of the student body."

"Oh, come *on*, man!" I say. "If anything this essay helps you *sell* the school's ideology!"

"I'm afraid we don't see it that way."

When a man is cornered, I've noticed, he'll often turn to the collective noun for comfort.

"If there's a 'we' involved in Jake's fate," I say, "I'd like to meet the people who compose it."

The headmaster is about to say something, but Jake speaks first.

"Subversive," he says, "is the very word they used throughout the McCarthy hearings. Funny we should be studying that in history class just now."

The headmaster doesn't much like being compared to Senator Joseph McCarthy, and my son clearly does not think much of the headmaster, who gazes at Jake for a moment before turning back to me.

"I am the final word on these matters," he says calmly. "The 'we' refers to those on the school board, with whom I confer on all key decisions. But the final decision is mine."

"And the key to everything is an apology from my son?"

"That's right. A *sincere* apology."

"Otherwise, he's out."

"I'm afraid so." He holds his hands up appeasingly. "No rush. Take the weekend and think things through."

What he means, really, is that we should let Jake's mother get involved in the matter, and she'll straighten it out to everyone's satisfaction. He's trying to buy time, but my son won't let him.

Jake gets to his feet. "You can have my apology right now," he begins. "I'm sorry, truly sorry, that a man in your position can be this frightened and freaked out by words on a page. I'm also sorry you dragged my father into this mess. He never liked this school in the first place, and not just because it's ridiculously expensive. Am I right, Dad?"

I lick my dry lips. "I've had some issues with it."

I'm sweating from places I never even knew I had. The headmaster's face looks as if it's been dusted with flour. He manages to force a slight smile as he says, "Is there anything else, Jacob?"

"Yes, sir. I just hope that somehow you manage to develop a sense of humor. But it's probably too late. It's not really the kind of thing you learn. You're pretty much born with it, or you're not."

The headmaster gets to his feet, which leaves me as the only one still sitting. "All right, Jacob," he says. "Go and clean out your locker."

There's the tiniest of grins on Jake's face, as if he's on the opposite side of a chessboard and just suckered his opponent into the very move he'd been hoping for. Slowly, oh so slowly, Jake reaches for the knot in his tie, undoes it, pulls it from around his neck, and tosses it on the headmaster's desk before walking out. A heartbeat later he pokes his head back in, looking only at me. Peter Plymouth no longer exists, as far as Jake is concerned.

"Meet you in front in five, Dad."

"Okay, Jake."

The headmaster picks up the tie, rolls it into a coil, and hands it to me, as solemnly as they hand folded flags to the mothers of dead soldiers. "I'm very sorry it had to happen this way, Mr. Sullivan."

I stick the coiled tie in my pocket. I'm obviously expected to leave the office, but I don't budge. We still have business to conduct, but Mr. Plymouth doesn't seem to realize this.

"What about my refund?"

"I'm sorry?"

"The tuition. The school year just started and you're kicking him out. You owe me my deposit, plus the first installment. I figure it's about seven grand."

His eyes widen in what appears to be genuine surprise. "Oh, no, no, no," he says. "That's not how it works, I'm afraid."

"You're *afraid*?"

"Mr. Sullivan, read your contract. The money is nonrefundable."

At last, it's time for me to get to *my* feet. I don't want to be looking up the man's nostrils at a time like this. "Do you actually think I'd let you kick my son out of this place *and* keep my money?"

"Mr. Sullivan—"

"Do you have any idea of how much I love money? I love money almost as much as this school does."

"We do not love money."

"You don't exactly *hate* it, do you?"

"The school takes the loss as well."

"The hell it does. The school year just started! Some poor slob on the waiting list will be here on Monday morning. When he gets here, give him this."

I take the coiled tie from my pocket and throw it at his chest. Now we've taken it up a notch. Technically, I've assaulted him, but even a tight-ass like Peter Plymouth would be too embarrassed to file charges against a man who's attacked him with a scrap of cotton-blend fabric.

In fact, he doesn't even flinch. He picks up the tie and puts it in his jacket pocket. "Again," he says, "I urge you to read your contract."

Suddenly he's oddly calm about the whole thing. He's such a Caucasian that it's almost laughable. In his head, it's all over. He figures he's got the law on his side, and that's that.

I breathe deeply, force myself to remain calm. It's time for me to roll out the heavy artillery.

"I'm not going to read the contract," I say. "But if I don't get my money back, you're going to be reading something you won't like very much."

"What exactly does that mean?"

God, am I glad I haven't told this man that I was fired an hour ago!

"It means that my newspaper has been sitting on a story about these 'rave-up' parties held at the homes of rich kids from schools like this one. Kids even younger than my son, boozing and drugging it up while their parents are away for the weekend, or running around Europe."

I pat my inner jacket pocket, where I still have my *New York Star* notebook. "I've got names and addresses. The police have been called more than once, and I've got details from a few emergency room reports, the kinds of details you never read about in the headmaster's monthly newsletter. For instance, did you know that one of the star players from your basketball team nearly flat-lined it at St. Luke's/Roosevelt after he swallowed Ec-stasy a few weeks ago? Best part is, he bought the drugs *in this building*, from a senior. An honor student, as I recall. But I'll have to check my notes to be sure."

I thought the headmaster had already turned as pale as he could, but I was wrong. Now he looks as if he's just donated a gal-lon of blood. He tries to lick his lips, and his tongue actually sticks to his lower lip.

"I don't believe you," he lies.

"Well, maybe you'll believe it when you read about it, and that phone on your desk starts ringing off the hook. Funny I should happen to have been the reporter assigned to check out this story, huh? I checked it out, all right, but I pissed on it to my bosses for the sake of my son. But that reason no longer exists. If I don't get my money back, the story runs in the *New York Star.* With pictures."

"Pictures?" The word leaps out of him as if he's been jabbed with a needle.

I nod solemnly. "These kids today have everything. Cell phones with digital cameras in them! Suddenly everybody's a photographer. Click, click. You throw 'em a few bucks, and they're happy to e-mail them over."

"Pictures of what?"

"Sixteen-year-olds being held upside down while beer from a keg is pumped into their mouths. Kids snorting something that isn't powdered sugar. Of course, we'll have to put bars across their eyes, because they're just kids. But some of them, Mr. Plymouth, are *your* kids."

"Was Jacob at these events?"

"Jake, as we both know, is no longer a student at this school. But I don't mind telling you that he wasn't there."

Of course he wasn't there. *Nobody* was there. I was making it all up as I went along. It's funny how imaginative you can get with that kind of money on the line.

Peter Plymouth slams his hand down hard on his desk, and for the first time, it dawns on me that I could be in physical danger. He's bigger and younger than me, and I know I'm pushing him in ways he's never been pushed.

He can take a poke at me if he wants, so long as I leave his office with a check. But he won't take a poke at me. He's hit his desk in frustration because I've beaten him, and he's not used to losing.

He pulls open one of his desk drawers, takes out a leather-bound book, opens it up, uncaps a fountain pen with a shaky hand and starts writing almost frantically, as if he's just had a great idea he doesn't want to forget. It only takes a few seconds, and when he's through he puffs on the page to dry the ink, then tears it out of the book and holds it out to me.

It's a check for seven thousand dollars and no cents. It's actually slightly higher than the total I've paid so far for Jake's senior year. I reach for the check, but he pulls it back, cocks his head, and narrows one eye at me.

"I assume I won't be reading anything disturbing in the *New York Star.*"

"Not from me you won't."

He hands over the check. "Good-bye, Mr. Sullivan."

I fold the check and slip it into my wallet. "I'll be back if it bounces."

"It won't bounce."

"Hand me Jake's essay, will you? I may have it framed."

He hands me the loose-leaf pages, which I carefully fold and slip inside my jacket pocket, next to my trusty notebook. I go to the door while Peter Plymouth returns to his chair. I turn to him one last time.

"You did the right thing here," I say, patting my wallet.

"Is that so?"

"Yes, it is. I can see why you're such a good sailor. The wind shifted, and you set your sails accordingly."

"Leave now or I'm phoning security."

I can't help laughing. "Funny, that's the second time today I've been threatened with security. Never knew I was such a dangerous person."

His secretary doesn't even glance at me as I go past her.

CHAPTER FOUR

Jake stands outside the building, leaning against the wall as if he's waiting for a bus he's in no particular hurry to catch. He's got all his stuff jammed into a lumpy blue laundry-type sack, which he adeptly shoulders like a merchant seaman. I try to take it from him as we head toward Broadway, but he insists he can carry it. I'm treating him like a little kid, even though he's bigger than me.

"I'm sorry about all this, Dad."

"Don't be sorry. It's not the end of the world."

"Mom won't like it."

This may be the understatement of the century. Jake's mother, Doris Perez (B.A., Wesleyan College; M.A., Yale University; Ph.D, Columbia University), will probably have to be coaxed in off a high ledge when she hears this news.

"Let's face it," I say. "Your mother will kill us when she finds out."

"Think so?"

"Jake. Have you and your mother *met*? Do you know how she feels about matters pertaining to formal education?"

"I have some idea."

"Well, then, I suggest we live it up in the little bit of time we have left. A last meal before we're executed." I point across the street. "Is that diner any good?"

"It's all right."

"Want to get a burger or something?"

"Burger'd be good."

We cross Broadway, and I wait until we reach the other side before saying, "By the way, I got fired today."

Jake stops walking. "You're kidding me!"

"No, it's true. Quite a day, huh?"

"Dad. I'm sorry."

"It's okay."

"Maybe we shouldn't eat out."

"Don't worry about it. I just got a seven thousand dollar refund from the school. We can have burgers and fries, if you like. Shit, you can even go nuts and order a milk shake. For once we're rolling in it, pally."

It's a typical Greek diner, with autographed glossy photos of soap opera actors nobody ever heard of grinning down on the brisk afternoon trade. Jake and I take a booth near the window. We order identically medium-rare cheeseburger platters with Cokes. People tend to eat poorly on the days they get bad news, I've noticed. I once sat in the kitchen of a woman whose husband had just been killed by a falling air conditioner (DEATH FROM THE SKY, read the front-page headline for my exclusive story), and in the course of a half-hour interview she chewed her way through an economy-sized bag of Cheetos and a box of Mallomars. She had not been happily married, but of course that particular detail never made it into print. (Unwritten tabloid rules: all widows grieve, and all guys who get killed by falling air conditioners were wonderful husbands.)

I watch my son eat. He doesn't wolf his food the way I do. He takes a bite of his burger and sets it back down on the plate, while I hang on to mine as if I'm afraid somebody might swipe it. He has a neat puddle of ketchup beside his fries, while I've Jackson

Pollocked the stuff all over my fries. I'm glad to see that one of us has a touch of class.

He chews and swallows. "Why did they fire you?"

"*They* didn't. One guy did. The day city editor."

"Why?"

"It doesn't really matter. We weren't getting along."

"How long have you been there?"

I need a moment to think about it. "Twenty-eight years." A shiver goes through me. "Almost twenty-nine. Would have been twenty-nine next month."

If I'd been a cop or a fireman, I'd be long retired, with a pension. As it is, I'm an ex-tabloid newspaperman, and I'm screwed. Jake knows it, too.

"God, I'm sorry, Dad."

"Like I said, don't worry about it. I'll get another job."

"Where?"

"Jake, you let me figure that out. Come on, eat up. We've got the whole day to figure things out. The whole weekend, actually, with your mother away."

I look out the window and see cars pulling up at the school, and kids piling into them. "Kind of early to be getting out of school, isn't it?"

"Friday dismissal," Jake says. "We always get out early on Fridays."

Somehow I never knew that. "Why?"

He shrugs. "So the rich kids' parents can get a head start on the way to their country homes and beat the traffic, I guess."

Jake has never had a country home. His mother lives on West Eighty-first Street, and my place is on West Ninety-third. Our joke is that during the hot weather he likes to stay with me, because it's a little cooler up north.

Suddenly two kids are standing at our booth, one tall and thin, the other short and chubby. Both carry book bags on their backs, and they're breathing hard, as if they'd run a long way to get here.

"Jake," the short one says, "what happened in Plymouth's office?"

"I'm out," Jake says flatly.

The two of them look at each other, eyes wide. "Man," the other boy says, "that *sucks*."

"I'll be all right," Jake says.

The tall one turns to me. "Are you Jake's father?"

I nod, but don't offer my hand. Somehow it doesn't seem like the right time for a handshake, and this is something these boys understand.

The tall one shakes his head in wonder. "Your son's essay *rocked*," he says. "Did you read it?"

"I sure did."

"Great shit," the short one says. "Really, *really* great shit." He thinks he's being bold, saying "shit" to an adult. This is the kind of kid whose idea of rebellion is wearing a baseball cap backward, or going to Colgate University instead of Yale, the way his father and grandfather and great-grandfather did.

Jake is smiling at them, the falsest smile I've ever seen him wear, but they don't know that. "You guys really liked my essay?"

"Oh, dude, it was *awesome*."

"Funny how neither of you mentioned that when Edmondson asked for comments."

Their faces fall. The tall one swallows, and his Adam's apple looks like a Ping-Pong ball lodged in his throat.

Jake laughs. "I'm just busting your chops," he says. "It's no big deal."

The boys seem relieved. The short one asks, "What are you gonna do, man? I mean, where are you gonna *go*?"

Jake shrugs. "Ask my father."

They turn their gaze to me. I take a sip of my Coke. "I have no idea," I say as cheerfully as I can. "Maybe I'll put him to work somewhere."

The boys laugh, then abruptly stop laughing. What at first seemed like a joke suddenly strikes them as a possibility both real and terrifying. You can quit school at age sixteen in New York City, but that's a concept that's never dawned on these kids. What with college and then graduate school or law school or med school, plus the "year out" here and there for the Peace Corps, or just to go backpacking across Europe, they could be crowding thirty before they're ready to go out there and turn a buck. That way, the gap between the start of a career and the maturation of a massive trust fund is only a few years.

I laugh out loud. "I'm just busting your chops," I say. "I'm not going to put Jake to work just yet. Truth is, I have to find myself a job first."

The two kids look at me, then at Jake, their mouths hanging open.

"He just got fired," Jake explains helpfully, almost cheerfully, and it's nearly balletic, the way they take identical steps backward, away from our booth. They have obviously been taught to stay away from losers, because losing is contagious. But they've also been taught to be polite, so they're in a little bit of a jam. I decide to let them off the hook.

"Well, fellows, it's been nice meeting you," I say, and it's just what they need to make their move. They tell me it's been nice meeting me, and then turn to Jake.

"Stay in touch, man," says the short one.

"You know where to find us," adds the tall one, and with that the two of them are gone, good-bye, out of there.

Jake takes a sip of his Coke. His former classmates pass the front window of the diner but don't look back for a final wave. It's dangerous to do that. Look at what happened to Lot's wife.

"Pair of assholes," Jake says, almost sympathetically. On another day I might have been stunned to hear my son speak this way, but not today. Foul language won't even crack the top ten list of this day's concerns.

"Why are they assholes?"

"I don't know, Dad. Maybe they were dropped on their heads when they were babies."

"No, what I meant was, what *makes* them assholes?"

"Coming in here and acting as if they care about me getting kicked out."

"They don't care?"

"Are you kidding? They're like people who slow down on the highway to look at a wreck. All they want is some juicy stuff to report back to the rest of the guys."

"You know, that's exactly the impression I got from them, but I didn't want to say anything."

"They're not complicated people, Dad. They'll just play the game for all it's worth, and get the jobs they're supposed to get, and marry the people they're supposed to marry. Then one day they'll die."

My son, the philosopher.

"And they'll be buried where they're supposed to be buried," I say. "You left that out."

"Good point, Dad."

"Listen, I want to know about this teacher, Edmondson. He's really the one who started this whole mess."

Jake rolls his eyes. "Edmondson's an old fart who's been there too long. He read what I wrote and he panicked. Don't be pissed off at him. He's just a frightened old man. He felt compelled to report what I'd written to Plymouth, another frightened man." Jake gestures in the direction of the school. "You'd be surprised at how much fear there is in that place."

"Fear?"

"Yeah, fear. Everybody's hanging from a thread, or they think they are. But look what happens when you cut the thread, Dad. You don't die. You don't even get sick. You go to a diner and have a burger and fries."

"Is that how it works?"

"Far as I can see."

For the first time, I'm getting a little angry with him. He's no longer in private school, but he's still got that private school mentality, where you're cocooned from the meteor shower that is the real world. It's time to slice open the cocoon.

"Let me tell you how *I* see it," I begin. "Right now I'm numb. But I have a feeling that when the numbness passes, I'm going to be scared."

Jake stares at me. "Scared of what?"

"Oh, you know, the usual mundane things. Making a living. Taking care of you. Little things like that."

"Don't worry about me. I can take care of myself."

"Is that so?"

"You'll see, Dad. Trust me."

"Trust you with what?"

"I've got a plan."

I laugh out loud. "You've been out of school for twenty minutes, and already you've got a *plan?*"

"It just came to me, in a flash. It's a pretty damn good plan, too."

"Jake. Don't screw around."

"I'm not!"

"All right, then. Care to share this great *plan* with me?"

"Not just yet, Dad. I'm still polishing it."

"Polishing the plan?"

"Yeah. I need a little time. And for the moment, I'd just like to enjoy my meal."

I'm dying to hear this plan, however ridiculous it might be, but I don't push him. We don't have much to say for the rest of the meal, which sits in my gut like lumps of lead. I finish eating before Jake does and I check the time. It's barely three o'clock, and there's no sign of any student life anywhere out on the street. They've all cleared off as if there's been a bomb scare.

"I won't ask you about your *big* plan," I say, "but have you got any plans for tonight?"

Jake shrugs. "I was going to see my girlfriend. I'm not sure she'll be my girlfriend anymore, after this."

This is a girl I've been hearing about without ever meeting. I have to wait for Jake to make the occasional remark about her and assemble the remarks into a human being, like an archaeologist trying to piece together a civilization from a few shards of pottery. All I know is that she goes to a private school on the Upper East Side, and they met at a party a few months ago.

"You think she'd break up with you because you got kicked out?"

"Let's just say it wouldn't amaze me."

"What's her name again?"

"Sarah. What's your girlfriend's name these days, Dad?"

"At the moment I don't have one."

"Yeah, right."

"It's the truth."

Actually, it's not the truth. For the past month or so I have been dating (if that's the right word, and I doubt that it is) a thirty-seven-year-old lawyer named Margie. Last night we got drunk together, and I remember her saying it would be nice to take a trip together, and suddenly I realize this has developed into a relationship of unspoken seriousness that has me uneasy. I rarely make it past the month mark with a woman, and my usual distance is actually more like three weeks. In matters of romance I'm a sprinter, even though I don't really have the legs for it anymore.

I have no intention of introducing Margie to Jake. He's met just two of the women I've dated since I split from his mother, and both times it was a mistake, so my policy since then has been to restrict myself mostly to midweek sex and keep the possibilities open for father-son activities on the weekends—possibilities that have been drying up, I've noticed, as Jake's relationship with Sarah has progressed. Lately all I've gotten is Saturday morning breakfast with the kid.

But this weekend is special. With his mother away I've got Jake sleeping over for two nights, so Margie is on hold until Monday. Margie said she understood, but her words didn't exactly match her narrowed eyes.

Jake finishes the last of his french fries. "Come on, Dad," he says. "Tell me her name."

"Whose name?"

"This woman you've been seeing."

I sigh, shake my head. "How did you know?"

"Your voice gets funny when you lie."

"It's nothing serious."

"Just tell me her name."

"Margie."

"You like her?"

"She's all right."

"Do you love her?"

This is amazing. Until now Jake has never, ever asked me a single question about my love life. Now, suddenly, I'm in the middle of an interrogation.

"It's too soon to tell," I say, and he looks at me as if he doesn't quite believe me.

"If you think it's too soon to tell," he says softly, "you're probably not in love with her."

I find this to be a stunning observation. I also know he's right. Why has it been so difficult for me to admit this to myself? Margie annoys me. She's loud and she's silly and she's bossy, or maybe the problem is that I'm somber and dark and stubborn. Either way, we are going nowhere. I'm going to have to deal with it, now that my son has opened my eyes.

Jake downs the rest of his Coke, wipes his mouth with a napkin. "I think you should have someone you can love, Dad. Maybe another wife."

I laugh out loud. It's a hell of a thing to say, and a hell of a time to say it. "Yeah, I'm a real catch. A guy crowding fifty, with no job."

"Come on."

"Listen, it's hard for people in my line of work. *Former* line of work."

"Why?"

"We get bored easily. We're sarcastic. We don't have a great outlook on humanity."

"Why not?"

"Why *not?* Look at the way the world is, son!"

"Yeah, but you were probably like that *before* you worked at the paper."

"Thanks a lot."

"Am I wrong? Tell me if I'm wrong."

I sigh, shrug. "I guess I've never had a great outlook on humanity."

"Why not? Did you have an unhappy childhood?"

"Hey, what the hell is this? *You* just got kicked out of school, and we're talking about *my* childhood? Why are we doing that?"

"Because I don't know anything about your childhood, Dad. Not one friggin' thing."

"This is hardly the time to discuss it!"

"All right, Dad. Whatever."

"I grew up in Queens. You knew that much, didn't you? I moved to Manhattan. Both my parents are dead. Happy?"

He holds a hand up. "Just forget it, Dad. I didn't mean to pry."

He picks up his Coke and takes a long pull on the straws. I rub my face with my hands, give his shoulder an awkward pat.

"Jake. I didn't mean to get nasty."

"If you don't want to talk about it, we won't talk about it."

"We were talking about newspapermen, and the way they look at the world. Problem is, we're convinced that *everybody's* working an angle. In the end we can only date each other, and that always turns out to be the worst thing of all."

"So who are you supposed to date?"

"A lot of newspapermen date waitresses. I don't know why. Maybe because they eat out a lot."

"Does that ever work out?"

"Not often. The waitresses want to be doing something else. You have to be willing to listen to their hopes and dreams. That gets a little grueling, at my age."

Just then, the waitress comes to clear away the dishes. She's a cute enough girl, closing in on thirty and a little thick at the ankles. When she turns to go I wink at Jake before calling her back.

"I'm sorry," I say. "I just had to ask—are you an actress?"

She blushes. "I'm trying to be one."

"Where'd I see you? Were you in a commercial or something?"

She nods happily. "I did the orange juice commercial. I'm the mother, pouring juice for the kids?"

"That's it, that's it! I *knew* I recognized you!"

"I'm rehearsing for a play now. The theater's my passion."

"Good for you!"

She tells us the wheres and whens of her off-off-off-off Broadway production, balancing our plates and glasses on her forearm all the while. She's practically floating on air when she walks away, as I've given legitimacy to the distant dream her family has certainly encouraged her to drop.

I turn to Jake. "See what I mean?"

"Did you actually see that commercial?"

"What commercial?"

He pats his hands together in mock applause. "Very good, Dad. You found a waitress who wants to be an actress. How rare."

We both laugh. It's my first real laugh of the day, and it feels good, like a swallow of coffee on a winter morning, or that moment when a hangover finally lets go and the cool, healing sweat breaks out on your forehead and you're ready to go out there and punch a cop. I feel something special coming. I don't know what it is, but it's coming, and I can't stop it, and I don't *want* to stop it.

And then, suddenly, I know what it is. Nearly eighteen years after his birth, I suspect that I am at long last going to get to know my son. And for better or worse, he is going to get to know me.

"Okay," I begin. "Here's *my* plan. Let's dump your sack at the apartment and figure out the weekend from there."

"Sounds good."

"I want to talk to you. I want you to talk to me. Let's talk about everything, and let's not be afraid of anything, all right? All that exists are tonight, Saturday, and Sunday."

"What about Monday?"

"For now I say, fuck Monday."

"Can we talk about your childhood?"

I roll my eyes, try to ignore the fact that my heart is suddenly beating faster than it should. "If you want. Don't expect to be thrilled, though. It was pretty dull, as childhoods go."

"I doubt that very much."

Jake smiles. He's got beautiful teeth, nicely spaced and white, teeth that didn't need braces and have cost me little more than cleaning bills all these years. That's one break I did catch. If Jake had needed braces, I probably would have had to hold up a few bodegas to pay the orthodontist.

Still aglow from believing she'd been recognized, the waitress drops off a check for $12.35, with a smiley face under the total and the words "Thank you!" I slap down a twenty and get up to leave.

"Hell of a tip," Jake says.

"She deserves it. Maybe it'll help her realize her dream. I'm all for dreams, especially the ones that don't come true."

"You're weird, Dad."

"I've heard that before."

The two of us walk out, floating in space like astronauts whose lifelines to the mother ship have snapped.

And just like that a tall, well-dressed black kid steps in front of Jake on the sidewalk, refusing to let him pass. "I've got to talk to you, Perez."

Jake calmly sets his bag on the sidewalk. "The name's Perez-*Sullivan*."

"Well, whatever your name is, we've got things to discuss before you disappear."

The kid speaks beautifully. He's actor-handsome and slightly taller than Jake, lean and muscular, tense as a tuning fork. I make a move toward them, but without even looking at me, Jake holds out a hand to keep me at bay. Then I notice that the black kid is wearing the school tie, and the whole thing becomes clear. He pokes Jake in the chest with his forefinger.

"See, I've got some *issues* with your *essay*. Let me ask you something, man. Do I look *harmless* to you?"

"Not in the least."

"Then why the hell did you say I was harmless?"

"I didn't. I said the school handpicked kids like you for their *apparent* harmlessness. You've got to pay attention to the adjective, Luther. It's vital to that sentence."

Luther eases back a step. Jake maintains his stance, as if they are still nose to nose. My son does not seem frightened or surprised in the least. This is disconcerting to Luther, who narrows his eyes.

"So what the hell *are* you saying?"

"I'm saying you fooled them, Luther. You're smarter than they are. Level with me. How do you feel about the people who run the school?"

Luther licks his lips. "I'm grateful for the opportunities I've had."

"Oh, come *on*, man! How do you feel about the people who make sure guys like you are always front and center for photo opportunities, whenever big shots come to visit? How do you feel about being trotted out like a show pony?"

Luther's eyes darken. "I fucking hate it."

"Well, I can understand that. But I wouldn't worry about it if I were you, Luther. Believe me, they don't know how you feel. You got 'em fooled. And I have a feeling you're going to fool them all the way into whatever college you choose."

"Hey, whoa, man. You listen to me. I work hard. I *bust* my ass."

"I know you do. You're going to get what you want. You play their game beautifully. I actually admire that, in a way. But I've had enough of the game. I just can't play it anymore."

Luther nods, purses his lips. "I hear you."

Jake extends his hand to Luther. "Good luck to you, man. Sorry you misunderstood what I wrote."

Luther's lips curl into a smile. He hesitates before shaking Jake's hand. "Man," he says, "I was going to punch you in the nose. And here I am now, shaking your hand."

"For what it's worth, Luther, I've always thought of you as an extremely fearsome individual. And for what it's worth, I'm not *disappearing*, I'm getting on with my life."

Luther laughs out loud, lets go of Jake's hand, and shakes his head. "Be cool, crazy man," he says, and then he's gone, before I can even introduce myself.

Jake picks up his bag, hoists it back onto his shoulder. "That was exciting, huh?"

"Jesus Christ, Jake, he was ready to clobber you!"

"Nah. Luther Johnson's got too much to lose. He's on a full scholarship, and he'd never do anything to jeopardize that. Not now, with Harvard and Princeton and Yale fighting to get him. He's a great student and a great athlete. Last thing his pristine record needs is an arrest on assault charges."

"Think that actually crossed his mind?"

"Of course it did. Believe me, Luther knows all about consequences. His father is serving fifteen years for manslaughter. Can we go home now, Dad?"

We drift along Broadway, heading north, making one stop at a bank so I can deposit Peter Plymouth's check. Once it clears, the grand total in my checking account will be $7,212.53. It's the most money I've ever had. For the moment, I allow myself to feel like a rich man. The moment will pass, I know, but not just yet. If nothing else, I'm learning how to appreciate The Moment. Not an easy thing for a fallen Catholic like me, trained as I was to believe that this life is really just a rehearsal for the afterlife.

When I come out of the bank Jake hoists his sack back onto his shoulder. "Hey, Dad," he says, "where's *your* stuff?"

"What stuff?"

"From your office. You gotta go back and get it?"

"There's nothing to take." I open my jacket to reveal the *New York Star* notebook jutting from my inside pocket. "Just this little souvenir to show for twenty-nine years on the job."

He stares at me and says, "You always knew they were going to fire you, didn't you?"

"Maybe. Maybe not. The one thing I *did* know is that in this life, endings come abruptly."

Jake nods. "I learned that one when you and Mom split."

My heart drops. Jake never, ever talks about this. He doesn't expect me to comment on it, or respond to it. But I do, and I surprise myself in the way I do it.

"I learned it when my mother died," I say softly.

"How old were you?"

"Your age."

Jake stops walking, sets the sack down, and stares at me. "Dad. I'm sorry."

"What are you sorry about? You knew my mother was dead."

"Yeah, but I didn't know you were so *young* when she died."

"I was young, all right. So was she. It was tough."

At last, we are talking about my childhood. It's a hell of a conversation to be having in broad daylight, in the middle of Broadway. This is the sort of thing people talk about in soft voices in the wee hours of the morning, just before the sun comes up. Jake is practically shouting at me, to be heard over the beeping alerts from a pastry delivery truck that's backing up.

"What did she die of?"

"Heart attack. I've told you this, haven't I?"

"Never! We've never talked about it!"

The beeping stops as the truck settles into a delivery bay. My heart is pounding. On top of everything else that's happening today, it seems ridiculous to be talking about a woman who died more than thirty years ago, but that's what we're doing, and I know that my son won't let it go.

"I thought you knew about my mother," I manage to say. Jake shakes his head.

"Dad," he says, "the truth is, you've hardly told me *anything* about your life. You don't like to leave many footprints, do you?"

"What the hell does *that* mean?"

"You travel light. You don't even have anything to pack up at work. One lousy notebook, after twenty-nine years! Look at all this crap I'm carrying, from just a few weeks in school!"

"Pick it up and let's get going."

This isn't going to be easy. Jake wants to know things, and I want to know things. Right now we're both holding our cards close to our chests, but it's early. Very early. We've got a whole weekend to get through, and anything can happen.

He manages to get the sack on his shoulder. It's obviously heavy and unwieldy.

"You need help with that?"

"I'm fine, Dad."

"I didn't mean to snap at you."

"Forget it. I just thought we were going to *talk* to each other, for once, and not be afraid of anything."

"We will, I swear. But let's get home first, okay?"

Jake doesn't want to take a cab, and he doesn't want to take turns carrying the sack. It's nearly a mile to my place and he carries it every step of the way, including the four rickety flights of stairs to my three-hundred-square-foot studio apartment.

CHAPTER FIVE

I'm hardly ever home at this hour, and for a moment I'm startled by the light. The rays of the sun are lasering through a narrow gap between two buildings across the street, splashing the place with a brightness I've never seen here. If the place were to go up for rent, this would be the hour to show it to prospective tenants.

It's not much but it's neat and clean, if only because it's too small to let it go sloppy. It would sink my soul to walk in and see laundry on the floor, or dishes in the sink, so before I leave for work each morning (Work? Remember work?) I always give it a once-over: wash the dishes, make the bed, hang the towels, sweep the kitchen floor. These are my stations of the cross, so to speak.

The room has a platform bed and a captain's bed, both of which I bought when my marriage broke up. Jake used to take the captain's bed whenever he slept over, but now I give him the bigger one, since he's grown to be taller and rangier than me. He sleeps spread wide, like a starfish, and I sleep fetal, so it works out.

It's a good thing I had a son. I can't imagine how the sleeping arrangements would have worked with a teenage daughter.

He sets his sack down and says, "You've got messages." The red light on my phone machine is winking away. I hit the button and an electronic voice informs me that I've got twenty-two messages.

I start listening to them. They're all from people at the newspaper, offering condolences and incredulity over what has happened. There's a pathetic rhythm to these calls, and about halfway through them I start deleting them after listening to just the first few words:

"I can't believe—"

"I'm so sorry—"

"No way they can—"

Jake laughs at what I'm doing. "Maybe you shouldn't do that," he suggests. "Some of them might be job offers."

"No such luck. All these people want is for me to call back with the gory details of what happened."

I continue deleting the messages after one or two words. Within minutes all the messages are gone, and the message machine light is back to its steady red glow as the electronic voice says, "You have listened to your last message."

I turn to my son. "Beer?"

"Why not?"

We've been drinking beer together for about a year. He's under age, of course, but all I'm trying to do is demystify alcohol for him. I take two Rolling Rocks from the refrigerator, toss one to him. He flops on the big bed, I flop on the little one. Upstairs, I hear the whine of a vacuum cleaner, a sound I've never heard here before. Like I said, I'm never home at this hour. We pop open the beers and take long gulps.

"Dad."

"I'm listening."

"I'm a little scared of how Mom is going to react."

"I thought you had a plan."

"I do, but I know she's going to flip out anyway."

"Maybe not. After all, this is a double punch, me losing my job and you getting kicked out of school. She might be too over-loaded to react at all."

I am full of shit, of course. What happened to me won't even amount to a blip on his mother's radar, except as to how it might affect my child support payments. She's always had contempt for my work but respect for the check, which puts her in the unique position of having to hope I hang on to a job that in her eyes benefits the world not even slightly.

A gleam catches my eye from the windowsill—it's the after-noon sun glinting off one of Jake's Little League Baseball tro-phies. There's also a basketball trophy and a couple of medals for running, hanging from ribbons on the wall. He was some athlete, my kid, but a few years ago he just lost interest in com-petitive sports, or so he said. These days it's just pickup soccer or basketball games after school—or as he puts it, "Nothing involv-ing a uniform."

Come to think of it, those games are gone, too. You can't do after-school sports if you're not in school.

I was never much of an athlete myself, so it always both puz-zled and delighted me to be the father of a star. There's a lot to it, hauling the kid to games and practices all over the place, and then one day it's all over and you can't help wondering if any of it meant anything.

"I can't believe you still have my trophies."

Apparently that gleam of light hit Jake in the eye, too.

"Of course I still have them. They've always been on the windowsill. What did you think I'd do, throw them away?"

"Of course not. I'm just a little surprised that they're still on display."

"Why?"

"It was a long time ago."

"Excuse me, but you're not even old enough to use the term 'a long time ago.' "

"Funny."

"Your 'long time ago' is my yesterday."

"It wasn't yesterday. I was ten years old when I won that base-ball trophy."

"Do you remember what it was for?"

"Baseball, I assume."

"Very good. But not just that. Look."

I get up and get the trophy. With my thumb I rub the dust off the little tarnished plate in front of the trophy, which says ROOKIE OF THE YEAR. I bring it to show Jake, who's now lying there with one hand behind his head and the other clenched around the Rolling Rock, which rests on his chest. His mother should see him now.

He squints to read it—Jesus, could he need glasses?—then grins and rolls his eyes.

"Rookie of the year. Yeah, I remember. I had such promise back then."

"You were a good player."

"I was all right."

"You were more than that."

"Dad. Calm down."

I put the trophy back in its place, return to the little bed. On a normal father-son weekend I wouldn't ask what I'm about to ask, but we said good-bye to normal hours ago.

"Jake," I say, "Why'd you quit?"

"Baseball?"

"All of it. All the sports."

I can feel my heart pounding. I'm going about it awkwardly, but you lose your subtle communication techniques when you're a divorced father. Back when I lived with Jake I knew what was going on in his life just by being there. The casual comment, the look on his face, the whatever it was that was bugging him even-tually came to light, and I could wait for it. That's the beauty of being there. You're a fisherman with all the time in the world, awaiting the tug on the line, the twitch of the pole.

But all that goes out the window when you get divorced and move out. You're not a fisherman anymore. You're a cop on a tight schedule, resorting to the least effective communication technique there is—good old Q & A.

Jake does not answer my question. I ask him again, softly this time: "Why'd you quit?"

He smiles at me in a strange way, a blend of pity and sympathy. "Is this part of your 'Let's talk about everything, let's not be afraid of anything' plan?"

"I don't know. Maybe."

"Because if it is . . ." He pauses, drains the last inch of beer down his throat. "If it is, I could use another beer."

I get us two more Rocks. It's not yet four o'clock in the afternoon, and my seventeen-year-old son and I are on our second round. In the little bit of time that we've been home, that magical narrow beam of light has begun to shrink with the turning of the world. Suddenly the light vanishes completely, and just like that the house is back to its old shadowy self.

Jake feels the jolt of it, too. He looks out the darkened window and says, "It's like an eclipse."

I hand him a fresh beer and return to the little bed. My hand is shaking so much that I almost chip a tooth, lifting my bottle to my lips. I've already asked my question twice, and I'm not going to ask it a third time. He knows what I'm waiting for, and at last he responds, at the end of a long, leisurely yawn.

"Well," Jake begins, "it's not as if it's because I was *afraid* to compete."

"I never thought you were. I saw every game you ever played, and you always wanted the ball."

"Yeah." He chuckles. "I wanted it too badly. Remember the time I stole the basketball from my own teammate?"

"Jesus, that was funny."

"He didn't think so. The coach didn't think so, either."

It actually happened, at a game on the Upper West Side. Jake was maybe twelve years old at the time, playing on a team with mostly black and Hispanic kids. It was a local league, a far cry from the white-bread private school team he also played for.

The star of the team was Eduardo, a lanky Puerto Rican who had all the tools—speed, shooting ability, the works. But he never passed the ball, ever, so once he had it his teammates might as well have sat on the bench and waited for him to do whatever the hell he planned to do.

Jake just got tired of it. One day, as Eduardo stood there bouncing the ball while glaring down five opponents, Jake slipped behind him, stole the ball, dribbled to the hoop, and scored a layup.

The whole gym exploded in applause and laughter. Eduardo stood stunned for a moment, then ran to Jake, fists flying. The ref and the coach grabbed him before he could land any punches, and then Eduardo was tossed from the game for unsportsmanlike conduct. In the history of that league, I'm sure it was the first and only time a kid ever got bounced from a game for unsportsmanlike conduct against a teammate.

I laugh out loud at the memory of it, and hoist my bottle toward Jake.

"Here's to Eduardo," I say, taking a pull. "Wonder whatever happened to that kid?"

"He's dead, Dad."

The shock of it hits me like a mallet to the back of my skull—shock over the news, shock over my son's casual tone.

"Dead!"

"Uh-huh."

"How?"

"He tried to hold up a bodega on 115th Street. He got into a shoot-out with the cops."

"When the hell was this?"

"About a year ago, I guess."

A year ago. That would have made him sixteen. A sixteen-year-old kid who used to play ball with my son gets shot dead during a holdup, and I don't know anything about it. Of course, we never would have reported it in the *New York Star*—not a Puerto Rican corpse north of Ninety-sixth Street. The only way I could ever know was through Jake, who'd never told me until now.

"I wish you'd told me back then."

"Why?"

It's a good question. Why? What was I going to do, attend the funeral? I didn't even know Eduardo's last name. All he ever was to me was a ball-hogging punch line to a funny story.

"I don't know why," I admit. "I just . . . Jesus! What else do you know about it?"

"Not much. From what I hear, he ignored the warnings to drop the gun and ran outside, firing away. So they had to shoot him."

"Jesus *Christ!*"

"What did you expect, Dad? That was Eduardo, all the way. He never gave up the ball. He wasn't about to give up the gun."

I stare at Jake, both awed and chilled by what he's just said. My son, I realize, is very smart. I always knew he could regurgitate what he'd learned from books and spit it back out on exams, but this is a new level of intelligence, and for some reason it's not a comfort to me. I would hate for him to think that I am stupid, and I wonder if he does. It's never occurred to me before. I've often wondered whether or not he liked me, but this is something new to ponder, something new to worry about. Just what I need.

"Dad," he says in the weary voice of one forced to explain something totally obvious, "you want to know why I stopped playing organized ball, right? It's because the coaches wreck the whole thing, the way they carry on. The yelling, the screaming . . .

I just couldn't listen to it anymore. Does that make any sense to you?"

"I'll have to take your word for it. I never had a coach."

Jake sits up straight on the bed, turns and looks at me. "You never had a coach? How is that possible?"

"I was never good enough to make any of the teams. And in the schoolyard games, it was always 'We got Sullivan.' "

"What the hell is that?"

"Two captains would choose up sides for kickball, or dodge-ball, or whatever, and I'd always be the last one left. That's when one of the captains would sigh and say, 'All right, we got Sullivan.' "

Whenever I tell that story to people I get laughs, and I expect one from Jake. Instead he is silent for a few moments before saying, "That really must have hurt, Dad."

I shrug. "You get over it in twenty years or so. Thirty years, tops." I'm shocked to find that my eyes are misting up. I blink back the tears, smile at Jake. "That's why I could never quite believe it, that I could be the father of a star athlete. Me, the guy they always chose last. And suddenly you just quit everything."

"I disappointed you."

"No, no, no. I just never understood why you did it, until now. Thank you for telling me."

Jake gets off the bed and comes over to me. He puts a hand on my shoulder, gives it a squeeze. "It's not like it was some aftershock from the divorce, in case that's what you were wondering."

It's exactly what I was wondering. "I appreciate that, Jake."

"You like to blame yourself for things, don't you, Dad?"

"It's not a question of liking it. It's just that I'm good at it."

"Well, give yourself a break on this one. I'm sorry I never told you about Eduardo. I thought I did. Maybe I found out about it on a weekday, and didn't see you until the weekend, and forgot about it in between, you know?"

The gaps, those fucking gaps. "Sure, Jake. That's probably what happened."

"Listen, Dad, as long as we're talking to each other, can I ask you to do something for me?"

It's the first time he's ever flat-out asked me to do something for him. I'm actually thrilled to hear the words, to feel that I'm needed in some way by my son. If he was about to ask me to be the getaway driver for a bank job he was pulling, I'd have gladly said yes.

"Name it," I say.

"Could you come with me to see my girlfriend?"

I'd sooner have expected him to ask me to knock over the bank.

"You want me to meet *Sarah*?" I ask in wonder.

"I just want you to come with me to see her," he says carefully. "It could get ugly."

I'm engulfed by a gulpy warmth. My son needs me with him. He *needs* me!

"Let's brush our teeth before we go," I suggest. "The last thing you need in a situation like this is beer breath. Where are we meeting her?"

"Just leave that to me," Jake says, flipping open his cell phone and hitting a speed-dial button. "I appreciate this, Dad, I really do. Hey, one other thing. Give me my essay, would you? I may need it."

CHAPTER SIX

We ride the crosstown bus through the park to the East Side, our teeth freshly brushed, our breaths minty from the Life Savers we've been sucking on. The bus we're on is a double bus, and we sit right at the axis, which creaks and shifts beneath our feet with every turn. We've always sat at the axis on crosstown buses, ever since Jake was a little kid. When the bus made sharp turns in those days I'd say, "Look, Jakey, the bus is breaking in half!" and he'd squeal with delight.

I turn to him. "Hey, Jake, do you remember—"

"You'd tell me the bus was breaking in half. Yeah, Dad, I remember."

"Oh."

He's a little too preoccupied for tender memories.

We're meeting Sarah at a Starbucks on Lexington Avenue. He's told her he has something important to talk about, but he hasn't told her about me coming along. He's remarkably calm, considering what may soon be happening.

I'm the one who's nervous. I'm actually jumpier now than I was a few hours ago, when I was losing my livelihood.

"You okay, Dad? You don't look so good."

"What are you going to say to this girl?"

"I'm just going to tell her about what happened today."

"And I'm coming with you because . . ."

"Because I asked you to. I don't think I've asked you to do too many things. If you don't want to do it, you can bail."

I'm a little stunned by this attack. "Hey. Nobody's *bailing*."

"All right, then, thank you."

"Know why you haven't asked me for things? Because I always took care of things before you had a chance to ask."

He nods. "There may be some truth to that."

"You're goddamn right there's some truth to that. Private school, summer vacations, cello lessons—"

"Dad, be fair. I didn't ask for *any* of it, and I didn't create the structure. I was born into it."

"At least you *had* a structure!"

Everybody on the bus is looking at me. I'm shouting without even realizing it. Jake is shocked, but not embarrassed.

"Dad. Chill."

"I'm sorry."

"What are you saying, that you didn't have a structure when you were a kid?"

"Oh, I had a structure all right. A fucking crazy structure."

His eyes widen. "Tell me about it."

"Not here, not now."

We ride in silence for a few moments. "Look, Dad, I need you to be calm for me. If you can't be calm, let me go by myself."

"I'll be calm. I promise. Whatever happens, I'll be calm."

We get off the bus and walk to the Starbucks. Jake sees her through the window and says, "She's early. That's funny, she's never early."

He waves to a girl in a pink blouse, seated alone at a window table for two. She's got blond hair braided into a pigtail that reaches to the center of her back. Her posture is perfect—spine straight and shoulders squared, as if she's ready to attempt a back dive off the high board. And when she sees Jake, her face lights up in what appears to be genuine delight. She blows him a kiss.

"Want me to wait out here?" I ask. Jake looks at me as if I'm an idiot partner in a robbery who's bungling the well-rehearsed caper before it even begins.

"We're going in together, Dad. Please, just play along."

I follow him inside. He plants a kiss on her cheek.

She's so beautiful it's almost painful to look at her. Her eyes are big and blue, and she's got a button nose and cheekbones that could cut diamonds. She rubs her face and says, "Ooh, Jake, that beard really *scratches!*"

"Sarah, I'd like you to meet my father."

She extends a hand. As we shake she says, "It's *so* good to meet you, sir."

"Call me Sammy."

I'm trying to appear both hip and fatherly, thinking hard of something to say, and the best I can do is, "What can I get for you guys?"

They both want lattes. For once I'm actually glad to be at Starbucks, glad to be someplace where the help moves as if they've been hit with tranquilizer darts. It'll give Jake and his girl a little private time. I don't get back to the table for a good five minutes, with lattes for them and a coffee for myself.

With surprising consideration, they've dragged a third chair over to this table meant for two. I sit down and see that they both seem relaxed. Obviously, the news of the day has not yet been reported. Sarah thanks me profusely, sips the latte, and lets out a small moan of pleasure.

"Ohhh, that just hits the spot," she says in a voice both girly and gravelly.

A funny thing is going on in the midst of everything else—I realize that I am jealous of my son. Never in my life have I ever been involved with anyone even remotely as beautiful as Sarah.

This is model beauty, but it's beyond that—she's also smart, and she seems to be crazy about my son.

No woman was ever crazy about me. All my life I've been involved with women I've known were wrong for me, women who looked wrong or moved wrong or even smelled wrong, in terms of their very scent—and all because I didn't have the patience or the whatever it is a person needs to persevere in that search for someone who'll knock your socks off simply by existing. You stop believing she's out there, and the cynicism that seeps into your soul after a lifetime in the tabloid newspaper game doesn't help, and half the time you've got a load on, so you learn to shut your eyes and just fuck what's in front of you, and be grateful for that.

And then one day your seventeen-year-old son shows you exactly how it's done, his very first time out of the gate. I can imagine them getting married one day, in a simple sunset ceremony at the edge of a lake, close friends and family only, and a barefoot girl playing the flute as Jake and Sarah read the vows they've written themselves . . .

Then Jake snaps me out of my totally ridiculous daydream by going ahead and pulling the trigger.

"Sarah," he casually begins, "I got kicked out of school today."

Sarah sits up even straighter than she'd already been sitting, which I wouldn't have thought was possible. "Jake. Is this a *joke*?"

"It's no joke. I'm out."

"Drugs?"

He laughs. "Come on. You know I don't do drugs."

This is a relief for me to hear. I figure it has to be the truth, if he's telling his girlfriend. But she certainly doesn't look relieved.

"Jake. Why?"

"I wrote an essay they didn't like."

"An essay? About what?"

He passes her the pages. "You might as well read it."

Sarah takes the pages and begins reading. She puts a hand to the nape of her neck, and those impossibly big eyes seem to grow even larger with each passing paragraph. She finishes with a gasp, an actual gasp. "Are you out of your *mind?*"

"I hope not."

"Jake! My *God!*"

"Didn't you like it?"

"Why didn't you just tell them you planned to blow up the school?"

"I don't want to blow up the school. It's valuable real estate."

She stares at him in wonder and exasperation, then turns to me. "What do you think of this, Mr. Sullivan?"

I swallow hard, look to Jake for guidance. His face is as blank as I've ever seen it. I don't know how he wants me to play it, so I decide to go with the truth.

I clear my throat. "Actually, I thought it was a hell of a good essay."

"You *did?!*"

"He made some excellent points, and it's a smooth read."

Sarah looks from me to Jake and back to me, trying to figure whether we've both gone insane, or if it's all a big gag of some kind. We're all going to share a big laugh, and then Jake's dad is going to spring for a nice meal at a tablecloth restaurant of her choice on the Upper East Side. *Oh, you guys! You had me going, there!* . . .

"It wasn't just the essay," Jake adds. "They actually threw me out because I wouldn't apologize."

"Why wouldn't you apologize?"

"I wasn't sorry."

Sarah hands the essay back to Jake, who folds it and sticks it in his hip pocket.

"Jacob Perez-Sullivan. You are such a *child*."

"I think it would have been childish to apologize."

"You realize, of course, that you've just squandered your entire future."

"You think?"

She lets out a shrieky noise, like a cat that's just had its tail stepped on, a noise that makes a few coffee drinkers turn around for a look.

"Come *on*," she says. "Get *real*. Do you know what this means? The Ivy League schools are *out*. And the whole second tier is probably out, too. Where are you going to go now, to a *state university*!"

"I can't even think about that stuff, unless I finish high school."

"Unless!"

"Well, yeah. I mean, technically, I'm a dropout."

"Oh my God, oh my *God*."

"Sarah." Jake reaches for her hand, but she pulls it away. "I didn't kill anyone. All I did was write something they didn't like. Can't you see? If I apologize for something l believe in, I'm a dead man."

She sits back, puts her hands to her temples. "Everything's *ruined*," she says, and the tears in her eyes appear to be real.

"Calm down," Jake says. "Nobody died."

"Your *future* just died!"

"Sarah—"

"Nantucket's *out*, I'm sure you realize."

"What?"

"I was going to invite you to our place in Nantucket next summer. Mom and Dad will never allow it now."

"Because I'm not in private school anymore?"

"Because you're not *serious*."

"Sarah. I am dead serious about what I wrote."

"You just *had* to do it, didn't you? Not that I'm surprised. Not with your . . ." She hesitates, thinks about it, and finally finds the right word . . .

"*. . . background.*"

The coffee in my mouth turns to acid. *I'm* Jake's background, and as Sarah says it she doesn't even bother looking at me.

Jake stares at her with a blend of amusement and disappointment. There's a sad grin on his face, the grin of a scientist whose lab rat has just confirmed his theory about how strenuous circumstances induce dreadful behavior.

But the experiment is not yet over. Calmly as a priest Jake says, "My background? You mean my dad, here?"

"Well, *yes*." And *still* she's not looking at me! "Working for that horrible rag. That's where your self-destructive attitude comes from, in case you wondered."

"I don't work for that horrible rag anymore," I say softly, trying to be helpful. At last she turns to look at me. Her face is now all but crimson with rage, and it highlights a slight bump on her nose I hadn't noticed before. She's not so perfect after all.

"I'm sorry I said that," she says, not sorry at all. "But I'm glad you don't work there anymore. It's a dreadful, fascist publication that caters to the lowest impulses in human beings."

Clearly, she's quoting one of her parents from a Park Avenue dinner table rant. "Anyway," she adds, "I think it's good that you quit."

"I didn't quit. They fired me today. Jake's out of school, and I'm out of work."

This is more than Sarah can take. Her family's idea of drama is when somebody parks the car on the street instead of tucking it into a nice safe garage. She's just found out that her boyfriend and his father are a pair of bums. She jumps to her feet as if a fire alarm has just sounded.

"I'm sorry, Jake." She shuts her eyes, holds up her hands. "I just . . . it's more than I can deal with. I'm sorry, but we're through."

Jake nods, but remains seated. "We *are* through, Sarah. You're right. But not because of this. We're through because last weekend you fucked Pete Hogan."

My stomach is in free fall. Sarah's mouth literally drops open.

She covers it with her hands as Jake continues speaking, calmly and slowly.

"Pete bragged about it. Didn't you think he would? Don't you know what he *is*? I go away one weekend, and look what happens."

"Jake. Please listen. Somebody put something in my drink. I never—"

"If you wanted to fuck Pete Hogan, all you had to do was tell me you wanted to fuck Pete Hogan. I'd have understood. Hell, his parents have a house on Martha's Vineyard. That's just a ferry ride from Nantucket, isn't it?"

"Jake, please let me—"

"Don't bother, Sarah. No point in trying to explain something so complicated to someone with my background. I'd never understand it."

He makes a shooing motion with his hand, as if to chase away a lazy fly. "Just go, Sarah. Leave."

Sarah knocks over what's left of her latte as she hurries away. Jake waits until she's nearly at the door, then yells her name. She stops where she is and turns to face him.

"*Your* father spends his life finding loopholes in the environmental laws so the companies that pay him can keep dumping their toxins in the rivers!" he shouts, loudly enough for every coffee drinker to hear. "That's *your* background, baby! Live with it! I'll take my background over yours any day!"

Sarah all but sprints out of Starbucks. I grab a wad of paper napkins and start soaking up what Sarah has spilled, amazed that it's still warm, that everything that's just happened took place in less time than it takes for a three-dollar latte to lose its heat.

Jake sits back and sips his latte, like a weary assassin after a successful but dull hit. "I'm glad that's out of the way," he says. "That's been bothering me all week."

"Who's Pete Hogan?"

"Nobody you need to know. Just some asshole. Thanks for being here, Dad."

"Jake, I'm sorry you've been hurt."

"I *was* hurt. Then I got over it. Then I got mad."

"I noticed. But you don't have to be over it. What I mean is, it's okay if you're still hurting."

Jake thinks it over for a second. "The hell with her," he says, but his eyes glisten with tears and his voice quakes as he says, "There's no loyalty, Dad. Why isn't anybody *loyal*?"

I don't know what to say, so I say nothing. I reach over to squeeze his shoulder, and he doesn't pull away. In fact, he startles me by turning to bury his face in my chest and hug me, hard and long. His sobs are silent, but he's sobbing, all right.

I shouldn't let the beard fool me. He's still just a boy, *my* boy, I say to myself as I hold him close and stroke his hair. It's been a long time since he's allowed me to do that, and I don't mind doing it. What I *do* mind is the way all those highly caffeinated people are staring at us.

"What the hell are you people looking at?" I all but bellow. "Go back to your overpriced beverages!"

They do just that, turning their faces away from Jake and me. I'm waiting for the manager to come over and ask us to leave, but it never happens. I can sit there at Starbucks and stroke my boy's hair for as long as I fucking well please.

CHAPTER SEVEN

I guess you could say that Jake was an accident, but you'd have to take it further than that and go all the way back to a series of circumstances that toppled like a row of dominoes toward the life we all now struggle through.

I met Jake's mother at a press event with a little bit of an intellectual crossover. It was the screening of a high-brow, low-budget film about some Puerto Rican poet whose name does not escape me, because I never had it trapped in the first place. Anyway, the *Star*'s movie reviewer had no intention of covering the screening, so he offered me his free pass to the film. I went because nothing better was happening that night. I was tired of chasing waitresses and copygirls, and figured this might be a way to fish in unexplored waters.

I was an awful person, glib and shallow, interested only in drunken good times and uncomplicated sex, if there is any such thing. I'm amazed that any woman had anything to do with me. I'd never really had a relationship before, nor was I interested in one. All I cared about was the next thrill, if only because it led to the thrill after that one. And it wasn't as if I was some kid—by this time, I was well past thirty. If a fortune-teller had told me that I was going to meet my future wife at this event, I'd have laughed in his face and demanded a refund. I wasn't in the market for a wife, then or ever.

The minute I got to the screening, I knew I'd made a mistake. It had drawn an intellectual-looking crowd, a lot of beards and bifocals—but what the hell, I was there already, and decided to give the movie a shot.

I fell asleep minutes after the lights went down—subtitles do that to me, I just can't help it—and when the lights came up I figured the night was a bust. I was going to go home but they'd set up a wine and cheese table in the lobby so that everybody could stand around and discuss what we'd just seen, and that's where I first set eyes on Doris Perez.

She had long dark hair that tumbled down her back like a basket of hastily dumped snakes, and she looked both bored and superior, an irresistible combination for a tabloid reporter eager for sex without courtship.

I struck up a conversation with her at the wine table, or maybe she struck it up with me. She was a professor in the Romance Languages Department at Columbia University, and she didn't think much of the film they'd just shown. Then she asked for my opinion of it.

"It was a little slow," I offered.

"That's amazing," Doris replied.

"What's amazing?"

"That you were able to watch it through your eyelids."

Okay, so now I knew she'd had her eye on me before I ever had mine on her.

"I don't know a lot about Puerto Rican poets," I admitted. "That's more like your specialty."

Her face grew dark. "I'm not Puerto Rican. I'm of Spanish descent."

"Have I insulted you?"

"I just want to make things clear."

"Well, let me make things clear, too. I'm not an academic, like the rest of this crowd. I'm a reporter for the *New York Star*."

She lost it. She literally put her head back and howled with laughter. I stood there and took it on the chin, determined that I was going to bed this broad, if only to make her lose control another way. When she stopped laughing she apologized, not meaning it, and went on to say that though she was not a *New York Star* reader she couldn't help but be assaulted by its noisy headlines every time she went to buy the *New York Times*.

"I'm sorry," she said, "but that's how I feel about it."

I urged her not to feel bad, that as far as I was concerned the last memorable person to come out of Columbia University was Lou Gehrig.

"Who's Lou Gehrig?" she asked.

It was my turn to laugh. "Are you kidding me?"

"I assure you, I am not."

"Greatest first baseman ever to play for the Yankees. Dropped out of Columbia to pursue a baseball career. They made a movie about it called *The Pride of the Yankees*. Now, *that* was a film. Not like this poet bullshit we just sat through."

"Where is this remarkable man now?"

"Long dead. He had a terrible illness. They named the disease after him. He was only thirty-eight years old."

"My age exactly. Perhaps I should be scared."

An older woman. Hmmm.

I told her not to worry, that academics never die young because it defeats the whole purpose of tenure. She forced a smile and asked me how old I was.

"Thirty-three. Bad age for guys. Jesus Christ. John Belushi."

"Who is John Belushi?"

For the next two hours we went at each other in a clash of ancient knowledge and popular culture, neither of us knowing anything the other knew, guzzling bad wine until the time came to clear out that theater.

We were both loaded. We piled into a cab and as soon as Doris gave the driver her address, we went at it in the backseat. I'm not a hump-in-public kind of person, but that time we came pretty close. The cabbie kept the meter running after we stopped, patient as a priest while Doris and I buttoned and zipped ourselves up. Then we raced up to her apartment to complete what we'd begun on the ride uptown.

It was nasty sex, I'm-better-than-you sex, take-that sex. In other words, it was excellent sex for first-time sex, so exhausting that I didn't have the strength to be annoyed when Doris wrapped herself around me before falling asleep.

I can't sleep like that. I gave her a few minutes to conk out all the way, then carefully disengaged myself from her grasp, got dressed, and tiptoed to the door. A pair of startled cats crisscrossed the living room, a cluttered place with floor-to-ceiling bookshelves against every wall. I was careful not to let the cats escape, and once outside I actually ran the mile or so to my apartment, though I was dead tired.

My feet must have known something that had not yet reached my brain. Flee, said the feet—flee before you get tangled up in something you'll regret.

I fled, but I came back the next night, and the night after that, if only to try and get the last word in a conflict with no end. Somehow, with nobody's consent, Doris and I became a couple, a "you say to-*may*-to, and I say to-*mah*-to" couple. I brought her to my world of knuckle-walking, side-of-the-mouth newspapermen, and she took me for supervised visits into the world of academic dinner parties, where people who'd actually died years earlier managed to show up to eat and drink, buoyed by tenure, the only force in the universe greater than death itself.

I wasn't having a good time. On the other hand, I wasn't having a bad time, either. That was the problem. We didn't fight— we grumbled. That's not such a good thing, because you never really blow your pipes clean the way you do with a knock-down, drag-out fight. So here I was, a man who'd never had a real relationship before, seriously involved for the first time with a woman who couldn't have been more wrong for me—all because we didn't have the steam to build up to a flashpoint fight.

It was maddening. It was frustrating. There seemed to be no legitimate way out. We mocked each other's worlds, little suspecting that we were actually mocking each other. That kind of thing never becomes evident until you're a few months into it and the sexual stuff has begun to lose steam.

It came to a head one night at one of those academic dinner parties. These things were always held in the book-lined homes of professors who were usually married to other professors. Doris was a rarity among her brethren, the academic who'd hooked up with a civilian. Often I was the only person at the table who didn't have a Ph.D, or wasn't angling to get one.

I was also the only one who turned out a complete product in the space of a day, day after day. The academics seemed to have weeks, months, even years to complete whatever the hell they were working on. They used semicolons and wrote sentences that went on as long and as senselessly as the Crusades. Nobody ever forced them to boil anything down to ten paragraphs. They didn't have to hit the mark, the way I did every time out.

They had grants, scholarships, endowments. They had six-month sabbaticals, yearlong sabbaticals. They taught three days a week, two days a week, once a week. They had off on Columbus Day, Martin Luther King Day, Veterans Day, Flag Day, Gay Pride Day, Doris Day Day . . . it wasn't exactly a killing pace, which is why their pensions were so damn important. They knew they were going to need extensive medical coverage for the endless ailments of people who live too long.

They could barely believe that Professor Perez was involved with a reporter from the *New York Star*. None of them actually admitted to *reading* the *Star*, of course—but like Doris, they did see those jaw-dropping headlines every time they went to buy the *New York Times*.

"Good Lord. Do you actually *work* there?"

The guy speaking to me was seated to my left at a table for eight in an overfurnished, overheated apartment on the Upper West Side. He was a white-haired fellow with the thickest glasses I'd ever seen and a vest that bunched up over his bulging belly. He always wore this vest and was known, behind his back, as The Vest.

He might have been sixty, and he might have been ninety. He was drinking a great deal of red wine but didn't seem to be getting especially drunk, so it was clear that he did this a lot. He taught contemporary American fiction at Columbia and he'd just buried his third wife, the only one of his wives he hadn't had to divorce. He looked as if he could be dead in an hour, but on the other hand he had tenure, which meant he could live long enough to marry two or three more times.

"Yes," I said to him, drinking Budweiser beer straight from the bottle, "I write for the *New York Star*."

"What's that like?"

"How do you mean?"

"Well, I mean . . ." His empty hands hovered in the air, like pudgy helicopters with no place to land. He let his hands drop, grabbed his wineglass, took a long swallow. "What I mean is, it's such a . . . *noisy* publication."

I had to laugh. I'd never heard anybody put it that way before. "Yeah, it *is* a noisy publication."

"All those horrible stories! The terrible things that happen to people!"

"What can I tell you? Terrible things happen every day."

"Yes, but—"

"But *what?*"

The Vest didn't like being challenged. He wasn't used to it. He couldn't intimidate me with a failing grade or the refusal of a recommendation, so he had no muscle over me. All he could do was clear his throat and drink more wine.

"It just seems so unnecessarily *cruel* at times," he said meekly.

That was a hot one, coming from him. Academics were capable of intracampus feuds and cruelties that would make a Mafioso lose his lunch.

I put a hand on The Vest's shoulder. "Hey, let's face it. Life is cruel."

"Yes, well . . . I must confess that those headlines *do* make me laugh."

"Yeah? You should see the ones that *don't* make it into print."

His eyes widened. "Really? Do you mean to say that there's such a thing as a headline that's *too offensive* for the *New York Star*?"

"Absolutely!" I swigged more beer, straight from the bottle. I was very deliberate about it, because I wanted Doris to see me do it. She was seated directly across from me, beside an ancient professor in a wheelchair who was plugged into an oxygen supply, the tubes running from a tank behind his wheelchair into each of his nostrils. Because of this guy nobody at the table was allowed to smoke, as he apparently had throughout the decades of his youth—three packs per day, unfiltered. Right now the old coot was fast asleep, so Doris had little to do but stare at me, glare at me.

Before we went to parties Doris always reminded me to drink beer from a glass, not a bottle—"We're not going to one of your bucket of blood saloons!"—and I always grudgingly obliged.

Not tonight. This was a special night. This was the night I was going to break up with Doris, once and for all, and I knew it would help me to trigger a fight to get the process rolling. I wanted her to throw the first punch. A cowardly strategy, but one that had proven extremely effective throughout my turbulent love life.

Doris called to me across the table, in a sickly sweet voice. "There's a glass in front of you, Samuel."

I grinned at her. "You can use it. I don't need it."

I took another swig from the bottle.

The Vest patted my arm impatiently. "Come, then, tell me."

"Tell you what?"

"Tell me a headline that didn't get printed because it was deemed too offensive."

"Well, a bunch of angry Hasidic Jews were threatening to block the runners in the New York City Marathon one year because the streets of Williamsburg needed paving. We had a photo of these guys standing side by side in the street, shoulder to shoulder, with their arms crossed. You ready for the headline?"

"Go ahead."

"Yidlock!"

"Ooooh," chuckled The Vest. "Ooh, that's good!"

I guzzled more beer and looked at Doris, who was now ignoring me, which is to say she was furious with me. We'd had six months of courtship, or whatever it was we were doing, and that was longer than I'd ever been monogamously involved with anyone—longer by five and a half months, to be precise. I didn't hate her but I didn't love her, and where does that leave you? What's the point? You look at somebody and you feel that hollow sense of free fall and you realize that the only thing to do is get yourself out, first of all, and then take it from there, even if there's no place to go from there. At least you're out.

"Excuse me," said a whispery female voice, and I turned to face the woman seated to my right. She was no more than twenty-two or twenty-three years old, with straight blond hair that rolled down her shoulders like avalanche snow. A mountain beauty, young and rough. Without looking at her feet I knew they had to be clad in sandals, even though it was the dead of winter, for this was the standard-issue footwear for the standard-issue graduate student, a must at any academic party.

"Excuse me," she repeated, "I couldn't help overhearing that you write for the *New York Star*."

"Guilty as charged."

"It shames me to say that I'm a big fan of the headlines." She giggled, her sky-blue eyes twinkling with shy mischief. By this time the oxygen gulper had awakened and was trying to converse with Doris, who continued to pretend to ignore me.

The graduate student offered her hand and introduced herself. I held her hand longer than I had to, and she was in no hurry to pull it away. She was an earnest plodder struggling toward that elusive Ph.D, and without doubt she was doing research for one of the professors at the table, and possibly having sex with him (or her) in exchange for being taken under their wing. Terrible things can happen to a person under a wing, where nobody can see you. . . .

I leaned back on my chair so I could speak with both The Vest and the grad student. This chair-leaning habit of mine was another of Doris's no-no's, but by this point I knew I was already in as much trouble as I could be in. The minute we got outside, I'd be getting it with both barrels. Good. Good. It was long overdue.

But first, I had a story to tell my two closet fans of *New York Star* headlines. I drained my beer, set the bottle on the table with a flourish.

"So," I began, "do you remember when Andy Warhol died some years back?"

"Certainly," said The Vest. "He was in the hospital!"

"That's right," I said. "Something went wrong after surgery, and he dropped dead."

"Yes, I remember it!"

"We had a headline that was all ready to go, set up in type and everything, but it was killed at the last minute, and I mean the *very* last minute. Are you ready for this?"

The Vest nodded with genuine eagerness. I turned to the graduate student. "Are you ready?"

She nodded uncertainly but enthusiastically. I took a deep breath, and did a drumroll on the tabletop with my fingertips. "Pop Goes the Warhol!"

The Vest threw his head back and howled with laughter. He knocked over his glass, and a river of red wine rolled across the table onto Doris's lap.

Doris jumped to her feet and glowered at me as if I'd planned it to happen exactly this way. She was interrupted by racking coughs from the guy in the wheelchair—she'd inadvertently yanked his oxygen hose loose. He struggled to breathe as Doris and three other dinner guests tried frantically to connect the hose back onto the tank.

The Vest kept laughing, totally unaware of the drama playing out right across from us.

"Pop goes the Warhol!" he roared. *"Priceless!"*

Doris finally got the hose back onto the tank. The old coot took deep breaths, and everybody settled back into their chairs. In the midst of this The Vest had passed out, his cheek to the tablecloth, a smile on his face. Through it all, the graduate student hadn't made a sound. At last she cleared her throat and leaned close to my ear.

"Who's Andy Warhol?" she whispered.

Doris dried herself as best she could with a napkin and told me to get our coats. Thirty seconds later we were out on the street on Upper Broadway, struggling into our coats as a light snow began to fall. She waited until she was buttoned up to the neck before opening fire.

"You complete *asshole.*"

"Didn't you have a good time tonight, Doris?"

"The things you do, merely to antagonize me!"

She began walking home. I stayed with her, shoulder to shoulder.

"Don't yell at me, yell at The Vest. He's the one who spilled wine all over you."

"You *pride* yourself on behaving like an ape, don't you?"

"Well, I don't know, Doris. Is an ape even *aware* that he's an ape? Can an ape feel pride? If he could, would he truly be an ape, or just an *imitation* of an ape?"

She glowered at me, and I couldn't help laughing.

"See how much I've learned from you, Doris? Six months ago I could never have come up with a bullshit analysis like that. Now it's second nature to me, after all these friggin' intellectual dinner parties."

Doris quickened her pace. It was easy to keep up with her. "Your hatred for women knows no bounds, does it?"

"Oh, I hate women now, is that it? I can't get along with you, so I *must* hate women."

"Your mother must have done some job on you."

"Shut up about my mother. You don't know anything about my mother."

"That's right, I don't. And I don't know anything about you, either. Nothing that matters, at any rate."

She was getting in some good shots, but that was all right. The angrier she was, the easier the breakup would be. She hugged herself against the cold, skidded on the sidewalk, and pushed me away when I moved to catch her.

"Why don't you just go back to the party, Samuel? Go back and fuck Leona."

"Who's Leona?"

"The little chippie you were flirting with."

"I wasn't flirting with her."

"The hell you weren't!"

"She doesn't even know who Andy Warhol was."

"As if that would stop you! I didn't know who Lou Gehrig was, and look at where *we've* wound up!"

"Yeah, Doris, just look at us." I grabbed her arm, brought her to a skidding halt, looked her right in the eye. "Are you happy, Doris? Tell me, are you happy?"

She stood and stared at me, her hair dusted with snowflakes in a way that made her look almost angelic. She sighed, shook her head, shrugged her shoulders. "What is it you want, Samuel? Obviously you've got some kind of plan."

It was time. I looked around, as if to fix the scene in memory. We were at Seventy-ninth Street and Broadway, and very few people were around. A skinny, bearded guy was walking a dachsund on a leash, the dog wrapped inside a plaid, tube-shaped sweater. Another lonely New Yorker, turning a pet into a partner to obsess over . . .

Doris waited for me to speak. The temperature had dropped severely since we'd left the party—it was cold, unbelievably cold. The snow was already sticking to the sidewalk like dust, with no wetness beneath it. There was an odd silence to the night, a silent but far from holy night. And then I spoke.

"I've had enough, Doris," I all but whispered. "I want to end this thing."

She continued staring at me and through me. Her eyes were steady but not tearful. She was waiting for more. I had a million complaints about Doris, but somehow, all I could think of was my own limitless list of flaws, and suddenly here they came, tumbling from my mouth.

"I'm a mess, Doris. I don't really know how to be in a relationship. I don't feel like half of a whole with you . . . I've never felt like half of a whole with *anyone.*" I swallowed, stamped my half-frozen feet. "You say I hate women . . . all I know is, I'm better off alone. That's what I want. That's what I've *always* wanted."

She took a deep breath, and it was all shivery when she let it out, staggered and stuttery. "Are you sure about this?"

"Yes, absolutely. I'm sorry. I should have just come out and said it, instead of behaving like an ass tonight."

Now at last came the tears. A nearby church bell gonged once, just once. It was one o'clock in the morning on a dark, desolate Sunday. Anybody in their right mind would have been home in bed, under the covers, but Doris and I stood there as if we meant to stay put until the sun rose. We should have had gloves and hats. We should have had scarves. We should have never met.

Doris held her arms out toward me, this complicated, tortured person with private pains of her own. What did I know about her? Her broken-English parents died when she'd begun her college studies, never appreciating her passion for higher education. She wangled a grant here, a scholarship there to make her way through with the rich kids. She cocooned herself within a fortress of books that would protect her from the cruel, ignorant world outside.

And I'd sneaked inside that fortress, not in a Trojan horse but in a Trojan condom. Now, at last, we had reached the final conflict. She took a step closer, arms still outstretched.

"Please hold me, Samuel."

I did as I was told. We held on to each other tightly, in what felt like the last embrace we would ever share. A crosstown bus stopped at the corner where we stood. The driver opened the doors for us, but I waved him off, and he seemed disappointed. He was all alone in that big double bus as he made his way emptily toward Central Park West.

Doris clung to me like a barnacle. I'd have to figure out my next move when she broke the embrace. Would we part forever right there, at the corner of Seventy-ninth and Broadway? Was I carrying the keys to my own apartment, or were they back at Doris's place, hanging on the hook beside the refrigerator? It would be awkward, going back with her now to get my keys, but then I realized that I'd have to go back there anyway to pick up my stuff—toothbrush, underwear, books. Maybe it would be better to do it this way, in one fell swoop. Everything I had would fit into a plastic supermarket shopping bag, no problem. By the time the sun rose, the break would be complete, with no need to see each other ever again.

I wanted to get moving toward whatever bleak and empty future awaited me, but I couldn't do that until Doris broke the embrace, and that wasn't happening. The snow was accumulating by this time, more than just a dusting. My hands hurt and my ears throbbed from the cold, but still Doris hung on, and then I felt her face move toward my ear in what I thought would be a farewell kiss on the cheek.

"Samuel," she breathed.

"Yeah, Doris?"

"I'm pregnant."

She said it flatly, matter-of-factly, like a government worker announcing the results of a lab test. I stared at her face and thought it seemed a little puffier than usual, a hormonal change brought about by developing life, the wiggle of the minnow within.

What could I say? I wasn't even sure I knew how to use language anymore. My entire vocabulary had been blown away by this news. Gradually the words reached my mouth, struggling like shipwreck survivors wading toward a beach. "How . . . far along are you?"

"About three months."

"Doris . . ."

I passed out right there on the corner. I don't know how she did it, but Doris hailed a cab, loaded me like luggage, and brought me to her place, where a couple of gallons of coffee brought me around to the reality of a scenario I'd never even imagined.

How could this have happened? A hole in the condom? A hole in the diaphragm? A hole in my head that got me into this fix in the first place?

"I'm keeping it," Doris announced. "No matter what you say, I'm keeping it."

"I didn't say anything!"

"But you're hoping I miscarry, aren't you?"

"Doris, for Christ's sake."

"I don't expect you to marry me."

This was something I hadn't even considered.

"Do you *want* to get married?" I ventured.

"Oh yes. I'm just *dying* to spend the rest of my life with a man who wants to be alone."

"Hey, Doris, come on. You like being alone, too."

"Do you have any feelings for me at *all*?"

"Of course I do!" I replied, not daring to ask her the same question.

She stared at me long and hard before saying, "Your medical plan is better than mine. It'd fill in the gaps mine doesn't cover."

It was a wedding proposal, admittedly a tough one to put to music, but there it was. I swallowed, nodded, sighed. "Let's do it, then, Doris."

"All right, we'll do it."

No rings, no getting down on one knee, no proclamations of love. There's more emotion at a driver's license renewal than there was on the night Doris and I decided to make it legal.

I married her, and she married me right back. It was a City Hall lunch break ceremony, a get-your-ass-on-my-superior-medical-plan-before-the-water-breaks ceremony. We didn't have a honeymoon. On our wedding night we sat in bed eating General Tso's chicken and vegetable lo mein while Doris read a biography of Octavio Paz and I watched *Animal House*.

Our marriage was under way.

Having never given any thought to being a husband or a father, I found it a little jarring to suddenly become the first thing and have the second thing looming.

I gave up my place and moved into hers, pretending not to hate cats. As I said, her parents were long dead, so at least I wouldn't be dealing with in-laws. If I was spooked by the idea of being married, I don't remember it. I'd probably have felt spooked if I'd married Doris and she *wasn't* pregnant. I embraced the concept that I had no choice. It was as if I'd been drafted, and there was an odd nobility in the fact that I wasn't dodging the draft to avoid the war of holy matrimony.

I sold the situation to myself. You ignore the sinking sensation in your heart and tell yourself that something is meant to be, something far bigger than either of the people involved in it. You tell yourself this is God's way of putting you on the right path, even if you don't believe in God, even if you don't believe in paths. Even Doris seemed to feel this way, and she, like so many of her academic brethren, was an agnostic.

I believed in God, all right, yet there were times when He really pissed me off.

But I liked Him fine the day my son was born. Ten fingers, ten toes, and a loud, lusty yell to announce his arrival into this Vale of Tears. Papoosed into a soft, snug blue blanket, Jacob looked both serene and annoyed, as if he were glad to be here despite the rocky nightlong voyage through his mother's birth canal. The nurse handed him to me, all seven pounds and twelve ounces of him, and this, I knew, was the Weight of the World I'd been hearing about all my life, cradled right there in my arms. There was a voice in my head, and it was my own voice, speaking six words of advice, or maybe it was a command: *you cannot be an asshole anymore.*

I did my best to heed those words. I'd like to think I still do, but I also like to think that I have a decent singing voice, despite the pained looks on people's faces on those rare drunken occasions when I break into song.

I wanted to get out of the city, or anyway, I thought I did. I had this idea of getting a house in upstate New York, with a big backyard and a rope swing for my son, and maybe a stream nearby for fishing. Jake would go to the local public school, and I'd work for the local newspaper, writing about early frosts and backyard bear sightings.

Doris wouldn't hear of it. At this point she was teaching just two days a week, so she could actually have commuted from this mythological country town, but she wouldn't even discuss the idea. We were staying in the city—case closed. In hindsight, Doris was right. Divorces are easier in cities, and Doris probably knew ours was coming even before I did.

In a lot of ways parenthood was easier for Doris and me because we weren't in love, so we didn't have to keep the flame of a relationship burning while we attended to our parental duties. We were two adults faced with the task of raising a child, or at least keeping him alive while he was in our care. I may never have been much of a husband, but I was always an excellent soldier.

I got up in the middle of the night to feed Jake, hold him, rock him. I changed his diapers at least as often as Doris did, and I was always happy to take him around the neighborhood in his stroller. Jake had a wide-open face and a sunburst of a smile he shined on anyone who looked at him. It always amazed me that two such contrary people could produce a child like that, a child who seemed to exist in a state of delight simply because he was alive. And it was amazing for me to see people smiling back at Jake as we moved up and down Broadway, hard-ass New Yorkers whose days were made better by the sight of this joyous kid.

Later on I did playgrounds. At that time I was working a night shift and didn't have to report to the newspaper until 2:00 p.m., so the mornings belonged to Jake and me. I'd be sitting on the bench with mothers and nannies, watching my two-year-old son navigate the incredibly perilous waters of the New York City playground.

It was a long fall from the monkey bars, there was always some semi-psychotic toddler who threw sand in kids' faces, and those *swings!* My *God!* How many times had Jake merrily wandered into the path of the swings only to have me yank him out of harm's way just a heartbeat before disaster?

For that matter, how many strangers' kids had I saved from certain concussions, and who the hell was supposed to be watching *them?!*

I was popular with the young mothers. They weren't used to the sight of a man who really knew the drill at a playground, and probably took me to be an unemployed loser with a deeply nurturing soul and a wife with a good job.

I learned more about females on the playground bench than I'd ever learned on bar stools. The way they spoke here was both matter-of-fact and sexy. One young mother in particular confided in me quite often. She had a toddling daughter and an infant son, and was in the middle of telling me about the trouble she and her husband were having with a downstairs neighbor's late-night loud music when she suddenly reached inside her blouse and pulled out a breast to suckle the boy.

She never broke stride in the telling of the tale, but there was so much blood pounding in my head that the rest of her story was inaudible to me. I just couldn't believe it—a beautiful, perfect young breast out there in the full light of morning. Not a hint of an effort to shield it from view as she plugged it into the greedy boy's mouth.

I managed to wrench my eyes from the sight of it as she carried on with her story, talking to me as if I were her best friend in the universe, and suddenly I realized that what I'd been hearing for years was true. You can buy them drinks, you can buy them cars, you can buy them houses, you can buy them the *world*, but it's all bullshit. Just listen to a woman. That's really all they ask, at least until it's time to get a car and a house.

Right there on that bench, I suddenly fell into a deep funk, and it took me a minute to figure out why. It was because I suspected that the only way I was ever going to see any woman's breasts (besides Doris's) was here on the playground, at feeding time. I was missing out—and worse, what I wanted was just inches from my mouth.

So close, and yet so far. It was all just a matter of time, and it broke my heart to look at my happy son up there on the swings, knowing that one day, he was going to be hit by the night train of divorce. No way to avoid it, unless Doris died, or I died.

I knew Doris wasn't going to die. The average academic lives longer than a Galápagos turtle, and she was no exception. If anyone was going to die, it was me.

Lots of newspapermen keel over before they hit the big five-oh, but you can't count on it. My health had always been good, and there was no sign of that changing. Of course, I could kill myself, but what would be a worse thing for Jake to live with—divorce, or a father who did himself in?

Clearly, there was only one way this was going to shake out. The clock was ticking for Doris and me. Someday that gleeful little boy was going to live through a divorce.

He doesn't suspect it yet, though. Just look at him, pumping his legs as he soars higher and higher!

"I'm going to the moon!" he shrieks to nobody in particular, and it doesn't matter if nobody believes it, because in his mind, Jake is already there.

Oh, Christ. What a beautiful child he is, and just look at his pathetic father, sitting on the bench all hunched over, as if he's on a bar stool at last call! Doesn't he know how lucky he is to have a boy like that? And who could believe that just minutes ago, the father of such a beautiful, gleeful boy could have been entertaining thoughts of suicide?

CHAPTER EIGHT

When Jake composes himself we leave the Starbucks and start walking west. It's clear to me that he's in no mood to board a bus, that he wants to walk all the way to my place, and that's fine by me. It's a beautiful evening, with just a taste of autumn in the air. The sun is low and orange as we walk toward it through the hills and valleys of Central Park.

"You okay, Jake?"

"Not bad," he says. "That thing with Sarah was hanging over my head, and now I've cleared the deck. I'm through with that school, and I'm through with her."

"Good way to look at it."

"It's hard to trust a woman, isn't it, Dad?"

"It's hard to trust *anybody.*"

"Did you ever trust anybody?"

"Not with anything that really counted."

"Did you trust Mom?"

Bull's-eye. "Well, sure."

Jake chuckles. "That wasn't very convincing, Dad."

"What do you want me to say?"

"How about the truth?"

"I trusted your mother with matters pertaining to your welfare."

Jake laughs out loud. "Jesus, Dad, have you been attending law school? What an answer!"

"Jake. Just ask what you *really* want to ask, all right?"

He stops walking, catches my elbow. "Did you ever love my mother?"

There's no way around this one. The truth will hurt, but a lie will kill him, and I want my son to live.

"No, Jake, I didn't," I say. "I'm sorry."

I feel as if I've just confessed to a murder, the murder of my son's spirit, but he's not crying, or even breathing hard. He's just nodding, as if to confirm his own thoughts. He releases my elbow and we resume walking.

"Funny," he says, "I found your wedding license in one of Mom's drawers a few weeks ago."

"You looked through her drawers?"

"I checked the date," he says, ignoring my question. "Six months before I was born."

"That's right."

"So you got married because she was pregnant."

"Yes, Jake, that is exactly what happened. It's hardly a new thing in this world."

"It's new to me."

We walk in silence for a minute or so. I reach out for Jake's shoulder but chicken out at the last second, letting my hand hover a moment before dropping it and shoving it in my pocket. I'm afraid that my touch will be more than he can bear, now that he knows the truth about his parents' marriage.

"I'm sorry, Jake."

"It's okay."

"Are you stunned?"

"Actually, I would have been stunned to hear that you loved her."

I'm glad we're in the park, walking on grass instead of pavement. In case one of us faints dead away from something the other says or asks, the injuries won't be too bad.

"Since when do you look through your mother's things?"

"I don't, usually. I had an impulse, and I followed it."

"What kind of impulse?"

"An impulse to know the truth."

"Jake. I just had one of those impulses myself."

"What about?"

"Well, your essay."

He rolls his eyes. "Are we still talking about my essay?"

"Just one thing about it. The bit where you said the right college was to the process what the orgasm is to the sex act."

"Did you like that line?"

"Very much, but I couldn't help wondering."

"Wondering what?"

"Wondering how you were able to write such a line with such . . . authority."

"You trying to ask me if I've been laid, Dad?"

"Yes, I . . . yes. That would sum it up nicely, in fact."

Our strides are just about identical as we plow westward, ever westward. Two joggers go panting past us, and the air is ripe with the lingering smell of hot dogs and pretzels, a smell that blends beautifully with the woodsy odors of nature that come alive in the park at the day's end.

Our feet are all but silent on the grass. The only sound is the distant wail of an ambulance, a sound that is to my son what the cry of an owl is to children growing up in the country.

When the sound of the ambulance fades to a whine he says softly, almost to himself, "I never slept with Sarah. But I had sex with Maya."

I'm about to press for details, but it seems that I'm supposed to know who Maya is. Suddenly it hits me, and I have to stop walking and put my hands on my knees to keep from falling.

"Maya the cleaning lady!"

"One and the same."

"Holy God."

"Take it easy, Father."

"Holy *shit!*"

"Dad. Please."

"You had sex with *Maya?*"

"Only once."

Maya the cleaning lady was a Czechoslovakian immigrant Doris had hired to iron clothes, wash windows, and swab the decks. When Jake was a toddler she was probably nineteen, maybe twenty, a slender, square-faced, flat-bellied girl who dreamed of becoming a fashion designer. While she worked toward that dream she toiled cleaning houses, and one of the sweetest things about Maya was the way she treated Jake. She squeezed his cheeks and tickled his ribs whenever she saw him, and even gave him a little feather duster so he could feel useful, following her around.

"My little helper!" she'd exclaim while hoisting him in the air, and then she'd rub noses with him in a way that made Jake giggle and made Maya's honey-blond ponytail flick from side to side like a horse's tail. When I saw that I couldn't help wondering what it might be like to grab that ponytail and ride Maya from behind, but I wasn't stupid enough to try and jump the cleaning lady. She remained a sweet fantasy, right up until this day my son speaks of her as a bittersweet reality.

Not bittersweet, exactly, but there's something sadly matter-of-fact about his tone of voice. Jake isn't ashamed of himself, but he isn't proud of himself, either. He's just telling me what's what, and only because I asked. And I'm not quite through asking.

"When?"

"A couple of months ago."

"Where?"

"In my room."

This staggers me. "In the middle of the day? What the hell were you doing home?"

"Teachers' conference. No school that day."

Fucking private schools, using any excuse to close the place! "Does your mother know?"

"Not unless Maya told her."

I wonder what Doris would think about it. She's a liberal, but she might not be this liberal. And the idea of her son fucking a grown woman who hasn't been to college could put Doris into a coma.

"Did she make the first move?"

Jake sighs. "Does it really matter, Dad? She'd just been dumped by her boyfriend. She was upset. I saw her crying, and I asked her what was wrong. We got to talking, and it just kind of . . . happened."

"Just the once?"

"Uh-huh."

"Was it awkward afterwards?"

"Not really. She put her clothes back on and waxed the kitchen floor. A true professional."

"Did you use a condom?"

"Of course!"

"You had them?"

"She did."

"Then it didn't just *happen,* Jake. A cleaning lady doesn't carry condoms. It's not something she packs up with the Ajax and the Lemon Pledge. She *planned* this thing."

"I honestly don't know if Maya is smart enough to plan something like that."

"Never underestimate a female."

Jake laughs, shakes his head. "Mom says you're a misogynist. Maybe she's right."

"Your mother calls me a misogynist?"

"Only when your name comes up."

"I do not hate women. I just believe a man should do all he can to defend himself against their wily, cunning ways."

"If Maya were wily and cunning, would she still be a cleaning lady?"

"All right, all right. I take it all back. She's a wonderful person who broke you in as nicely as it can be done."

"That's exactly right, Dad. She's also a lonely woman who needed to be held, and I was there to do it, and glad to do it."

I'm stunned by both his loyalty and his maturity, not to mention his next question.

"What was *your* first time like, Dad?"

"Terrifying and humiliating."

"Sorry to hear that."

"She was an older woman. She pretty much took me by the hand and had her way with me."

"It wasn't pleasant?"

"We both had our teeth clenched, as I recall. That's never a good sign."

"What was her name?"

"Fran. Short for Francine, I think, but I don't know for sure."

"She still alive?"

"How the hell should I know? It was a long time ago, right after . . ."

"Right after what?"

"After my mother died."

It's the first time I've connected *my* first time with my mother's death—out loud, anyway. Maybe my first no-hands sexual experience was an act of despair.

Jake stares at me with sympathetic eyes. "Was this back in your old neighborhood in Queens?"

"Yes, it was. She was what was known in those days as a 'divorcee.' Her husband had their kids for the weekend, and she came into Charlie's Bar for a drink, and I was there. To borrow a phrase from you, it just kind of . . . happened."

"How old were you?"

"Seventeen. Same as you."

"You were drinking in a bar when you were seventeen?"

"The legal age was eighteen back then, and I looked older than I was. And Charlie's Bar was a real dive, a bucket of blood. They served anybody who was old enough to walk in."

"How old was the woman?"

"I don't remember."

"Dad. Are we talking to each other, or not?"

"Thirty-three, maybe thirty-four."

"Holy shit, Dad! That's like the age gap between me and Maya! History really does repeat itself, doesn't it?"

"Not exactly. See, Fran was a barracuda. Maya is sweet. Maya used to carry you around on her shoulders when you were little. Do you remember that?"

"Vaguely."

"Well, I remember it distinctly. I was always amazed by how strong she was, a girl that slim."

"She's not slim anymore."

Oddly, weirdly, ridiculously, I feel my heart sink. "Maya's not slim?"

Jake shakes his head. "She's pretty stocky, Dad."

"You're kidding me."

"Her face is beautiful, though. She's kind."

"I can't believe she got fat."

Jake's face darkens. "Hey. Don't call her fat. I never said she was fat."

"I'm sorry! I'm just a little blown away by this! The last time I saw Maya she was as slim as a runway model!"

"Yeah, well, you've been away a long time, Dad."

All I can do is look at him. Yes, indeed, I *have* been away for a long, long time. I'm close enough to hear the whistle of breath through Jake's nostrils, but a canyon separates us.

Suddenly the sun is gone. A shiver goes through me. We pick up our pace, as if to warm up against the sudden chill.

"I assume Maya never made it as a fashion designer."

"Nope. Apparently she had a lot of trouble with the written work, so she gave it up. She's a cleaning lady. A cleaning lady with a broken heart, and broken dreams. That's why she looks old. Not because she got fat. Because she stopped dreaming."

"You may be right about that."

"I *know* I'm right about that."

When did *I* stop dreaming, and is it possible to start dreaming again? I suspect my son knows the answer to this question, but I'm afraid to ask him.

Then, suddenly, out of the blue, there's something I absolutely have to do, as soon as possible. I stop walking, grab Jake by the elbow. "Listen, kid, I need a favor."

"A favor?"

"I have to see Margie, and you've got to come with me."

Jake's eyes widen. "You sure you want me to go with you? I can wait at the house."

"No, no, no. I came with you to see Sarah, now you've got to come with me to see Margie. Give me your cell phone."

I refuse to carry a cell phone. This had been a sore point between me and Derek Slaughterchild. The last thing I want in life is to be reachable at all times. I'd sooner wear an ankle cuff that beeps every time you leave the house.

I call Margie, who's out someplace loud with laughter. It turns out to be a bar on the Upper West Side, where she's having drinks with the girls from her office. Not surprisingly, she's in a giggly state.

"You're interrupting my girlie night!" she says in mock anger.

"Yeah, I'm sorry about that," I say. "Listen, could we get a quick drink?"

"I thought you had your son tonight!"

"I do. He's with me."

"Oh my God, don't tell me I'm actually going to *meet* him!"

"Can we get that drink?"

"Come on over!" Margie says. "You know where I am!"

She hangs up without saying good-bye. I turn to Jake. "Do you mind doing this, kid? It won't take long."

"Ooh. That doesn't sound good, Dad."

"It won't be good, but it'll be brief. I've got to clear the deck, just like you did."

It takes us less than ten minutes to walk there. It's an old-fashioned joint, dark and high-ceilinged. We walk in together at the height of a raucous happy hour. Margie yells my name before I have a chance to pick her out of the crowd.

Not too many things in this world look as good as a blonde in black. Margie is rail-thin, and the black pants and jacket make her look even skinnier. She's had a few white wines, and as she approaches me she staggers and falls into my arms.

She tends to get drunk fast, because she doesn't eat. She *prides* herself on not eating. I once cooked dinner for Margie, chicken cutlets and mashed potatoes, and after she'd eaten a mouthful or two she lit up a cigarette and used her plate for an ashtray. I can still see the cigarette butt she jammed into the leftover mashed potatoes, angled like a sinking ocean liner just as it's about to plunge underwater forever. That was probably the moment I realized we were doomed.

But who am I kidding? We would have been doomed anyway, no matter how great a girl she was.

With my help, Margie struggles to her feet, kisses my cheek, and lets out a whoop. "Admit it, I make a great first impression, don't I?" She giggles, then formally extends a hand to Jake. "Hello, I'm Margie."

"Jake."

"My God, Sammy, you never told me he has a *beard!*"

"He didn't, the last time I saw him."

"Well, Jake, it's good to finally meet you."

How can someone I've been seeing for barely a month talk about how good it is to "finally" meet my son?

"Listen," I say, "it's loud in here. Can we go outside for a minute?"

"Great idea. Let me get my cigarettes."

She goes back to her table full of girlfriends, none of whom I've met. They look appraisingly at Jake and me, covering their mouths as they whisper to each other and laugh like mad.

Margie sighs as she steps outside, leans against the building, and lights up a Marlboro. "Do you smoke, Jake?"

"No, I don't."

"Good for you. Don't start, that's my advice. I know it'll be absolute *hell* for me when I have to stop."

And I know exactly when that will be—when she decides to get pregnant. As I mentioned, Margie is thirty-seven years old. Within a week of meeting her, she made it clear to me that one day not long from now, she wants to have a baby. Her biological clock is gonging away like Big Ben. She does not have time to waste, and the terrible truth is that I am a waste of time.

Margie inhales deeply and thoughtfully, really enjoying it, the way you enjoy something you know you are about to lose. She smiles at Jake, shaking her head in what appears to be wonder. "He certainly looks like you, under all that hair."

There's never a good time to pull the trigger. You just have to pull it.

"Margie," I say, "we can't do this anymore."

The cigarette in her mouth slants downward, just as I've seen it happen dozens of times to startled actors in the movies but never in real life, until now. She takes the cigarette and throws it toward the street. "What are you saying?"

"I'm saying that our relationship isn't going anywhere. I'm breaking up with you. I'm really sorry."

She's still leaning against the building. She puts a hand behind her back and pushes herself to a standing position on tottering legs. "I don't understand. Is this a *joke?*"

"I would never joke about this. You want things I don't want. You want to do things I've already done. There's no point in us being together."

She looks at Jake, the thing I've already done. It's hard to tell, but Margie appears to be more stunned than hurt. I'm hoping that's the case, and of course I'm wrong. She puts her hands over her face and starts to cry.

I stand there paralyzed, but Jake does not. He takes Margie in his arms like an old friend and strokes her hair. Margie puts her arms around Jake and cries on his shoulder.

"It's okay," he assures her. "You're going to be okay."

The other smokers outside the bar are staring at this oddest of scenes—a woman who's just been dumped by her middle-aged boyfriend being consoled by the boyfriend's teenage son, a kid she met five minutes earlier. Jake maintains the embrace until Margie pulls back. She holds him by the shoulders and asks, "How did a shit like your father ever have a wonderful son like you?"

"He's not a shit, Margie, he's just going through a troubled time. He likes you. That's why he doesn't want to waste your time."

"Is that right?"

Jake touches Margie's cheek. "Your dreams aren't his dreams. It's as simple as that."

At last Margie looks at me, then back at Jake. Her eyes shine with tears as she forces a smile. "Would you consider getting involved with an older woman, Jake?"

He smiles. "I have a feeling you'd be more than I could handle."

"Well, all I can say is, *somebody* raised you right. Your mother, I suspect." She kisses Jake on the cheek, turns to me. "I guess there's nothing to talk about."

"Not really, Margie."

"How can you be this *cold*?"

"I'm not cold, I'm numb. And I really am sorry."

She nods at me, her face all twisted in a kind of sour gratitude. In the big picture, I've done the right thing, but it's hard to appreciate the big picture when you're stuck in the misery of the little picture.

Margie clears her throat. "I'm going back to my friends, then." She wipes her eyes, tosses her hair, and shakes a finger in Jake's face. "*You*, young man. Please don't ever change the way you are." She kisses his hairy cheek, turns, and walks back inside without even looking at me.

Jake and I stand there for a moment on this sidewalk carpeted with countless cigarette butts, all spongy under our feet. Jake lets out a long, sad sigh.

"Okay, Dad? Are we even now?"

"We're even . . . Guess we've both got clear decks now, huh?"

"That's one way of looking at it."

"Let's walk."

I shouldn't feel good, but I do. There's a spring to my step and I almost feel like breaking into a run.

"This may sound bizarre to you, Jake, but it's actually kind of *refreshing*, not having a job or a girlfriend."

"It's not bad being a dropout without a girlfriend, either."

"Funny, I never even got to tell Margie that I got fired."

"Did you really like her, Dad?"

"Jake. Except for you, I honestly don't know if I really like anybody."

By the time we get home, that feeling of exhilaration has melted. We're both exhausted, and neither of us is hungry. It's barely eight o'clock, but we flop on the beds and fall asleep watching the Yankees game. Jake sleeps on his back, arms stretched wide, his breaths long and even. His brow is slightly knotted, as if he's conked out without quite resolving everything that's on his mind.

In the middle of the night I get up to cover Jake with a quilt, and at the touch of it he opens his eyes.

"You okay, Dad?"

"Just covering you. . . . You know, when you were born, I wanted to move to the country."

"You did?"

"It was just an idea I had."

"Mom would have hated it."

"That's why we didn't go."

"Think it would have been good?"

I stroke his forehead. "I don't know, buddy, I don't know. It would have been different."

"Don't agonize over it, Dad."

In the moonlight I see something over Jake's right eye, a whisper of a scar that I've somehow not noticed in daylight. I trace it with my finger.

Jake catches my wrist. "What are you doing?"

"You've got some kind of a scar here."

"Ah, I've had that my whole life."

"What are you talking about?"

"It's from the time I fell off the monkey bars."

"Come on. It's got to be from something else!"

"It isn't."

"You were four when that happened! How could you still have a scar?"

"I fell a long way. Don't you remember?"

I stroke his hair, sigh at the memory of it. "I remember, all right."

We were at a playground in Central Park on a beautiful autumn day, just Jake and me. He was a very good climber, with an apelike grip that enabled him to climb the monkey bars faster and higher than any of his friends.

He was so good at climbing that I became a little lackadaisical about watching him. Sure enough, it happened just as my attention waned. Down he went from the top of the bars, opening up a gash on his forehead that bled as if he'd been shot.

I carried him howling to the emergency room at St. Luke's/ Roosevelt Hospital, where a kindly old doctor applied a local anaesthetic before doing the needlework. Jake lay on his back the whole while, eyes tightly shut, his feet trembling in their little red sneakers. The anaesthetic didn't totally kill the pain, so Jake winced and moaned every time the needle went in, and I held his hand and told him to squeeze me as hard as he could.

I was crying, and trying not to let him see it. The doctor—eyeglasses perched on the tip of his nose, bald on top, squiggly gray curls tumbling over his ears—spoke soothingly as he worked.

"How did this happen?" he asked calmly.

"He fell off the monkey bars," I replied.

"Monkey bars! I didn't realize you were a monkey, young man!"

"I'm *not*," Jake breathed through tightly clenched teeth. "I'm a *boy*."

"Oh, I'm sorry. My mistake."

His fingers worked rapidly—it was hard to believe hands that fast could be connected to a voice that slow. He put the needle through for the final stitch. Jake let out a small cry and the doctor announced, "No more pain for you today! That's it, I'm afraid." He tied the stitch, dabbed the wound with an antiseptic solution, and put a bandage over it.

Jake released my hand. "Can I open my eyes, Daddy?"

"Yeah. It's all over, Jake."

He opened his eyes as if he didn't believe it. Then he looked at me and said, "Why are *you* crying, Daddy? *You* didn't get stitches!"

I wiped my eyes as the doctor and I both laughed out loud. The doctor pulled Jake up to a sitting position and held a mirror up to his face. "Okay, tough guy, take a look at yourself."

Jake smiled at his image. "Cool!"

"Yes, it *is* pretty cool, isn't it? Now listen to me. Don't touch the bandage, and don't get it wet. In about a week we'll take the stitches out, and it *will . . . not . . . hurt.* All right?"

He put his hand out like a lawyer to shake with Jake. "I'm sorry I mistook you for a monkey. You are clearly not a monkey. But you are not a bird, either, young man. You cannot fly, so please be careful up on those monkey bars."

He gave Jake a red lollipop, just like an old-time doctor. Then he turned to me and said, "You've got a brave kid there."

He shook hands with us and was gone.

We walked home slowly, very slowly, Jake savoring his lollipop without chewing it. Doris didn't yet know about what had happened. I was not looking forward to her reaction to this disaster, and neither was Jake.

But it was nice to hold hands as we walked. Jake had recently hit the age where he wouldn't hold my hand unless we were crossing a street, but in the wake of what had happened he needed my touch.

"Dad."

"Yeah, buddy?"

"Why can't I fly?"

He'd been wondering about it ever since the doctor told him he wasn't a bird.

"People can't fly. That's just the way it is."

"Why?"

"We're too heavy."

"Aren't birds heavy?"

"They have very light bones. We have heavy bones. Also, we have arms, not wings."

"Birds have wings!"

"That's right. Birds flap their wings, and that lifts them off the ground."

"Do birds get tired?"

"I don't know."

"If I had wings, could I fly?"

"I guess you could."

"I'm gonna get some wings."

By this time I was punchy, barely listening to what he was saying, preoccupied with the imminent conflict with Doris. She couldn't blame me any more than I was already blaming myself. I should have seen it coming. I should have caught him. I should have been there.

These were the very points she made as she embraced our son and lectured me over his shoulder.

A few weeks later I was startled to hear a loud thump from Jake's room. I went in and saw him crouched on the floor, having just jumped from his bed, an activity he'd been told not to do anymore for the sake of our poor downstairs neighbor, Mr. Mayhew. I was going to scold him for it, and then I noticed that his arms were sheathed inside matching blue spaghetti cartons, and his eyes were brimming with angry tears.

"They don't work, Dad!"

"What are you talking about?"

"My wings."

He held his arms out toward me. Jake had taken two empty Ronzoni spaghetti boxes and fashioned them into a pair of wings, which is to say he'd Scotch-taped a series of feathers along their edges—pigeon feathers mostly, but there was a lavender feather that may have come from a blue jay and a reddish feather that might have fallen from a cardinal. A cardinal on the Upper West Side?

"Jake. Where'd you get these feathers?"

"I found them in the park."

"You've been collecting them?"

"Yeah, but they don't *work*." He pulled the boxes from his arms, threw them to the floor, and dove into my arms for a hug. I sat on his bed, pulled him onto my lap.

"Buddy, buddy, I'm sorry." I stroked his hair, knowing that the stinging in the soles of his feet was one of life's bitterest lessons, and he was learning it early: what you *want* to do and what you *can* do are often two very different things.

"Why can't I fly?" Jake demanded, and from the tone of his voice it was clear he wasn't really asking me, he was asking God, which is odd, because between Doris and me Jake's religious training amounted to a big goose egg.

"Easy, buddy."

"It isn't fair! I have *wings*! I want to *fly*!"

"Jake, your wings are beautiful, but that doesn't mean you can fly! Lots of birds have wings, but they can't fly, either."

He was looking me right in the eye. "Really?"

"Sure! Chickens can't fly. Ostriches can't fly, either, and how about penguins? Remember those fat little penguins we saw in the zoo? They sure can't fly!"

"Yeah," Jake said, "but it's *different*."

"How's it different?"

"They don't *want* to fly, Dad."

He had me there. He got off my lap and stomped the spaghetti boxes flat. I let him get it all out of his system, but instead of fading, his rage seemed to be rising. He was jumping on the flattened cartons with both feet. It was only a matter of time before Mr. Mayhew phoned to complain.

"Jake! Whoa!"

I scooped him up, set him on the bed, and sat beside him. He was through crying, through feeling sorry for himself. Now he was just plain pissed off. I dared to put my arm across his shoulders, and he didn't shrug it away. I studied the scar on his forehead, which was already fading—the doctor had done a good job. You had to look hard to see the stitches, like six tiny whitecaps on an otherwise smooth sea. My son was a good healer, strong and healthy, and unhappier than I'd ever seen him.

"Listen to me, buddy, I know how you feel."

"No, you don't."

"Yes, I do. You're disappointed. Everybody gets disappointed."

"I don't care."

"Jake. Someday you will fly."

He narrowed his eyes, sat up straight. "I will?"

"Not the way you wanted to fly today. That's not going to happen. But someday something will happen that'll make you feel very, very happy. And when you're very, very happy, you'll feel as if your feet aren't touching the ground. You'll feel like you're flying."

He rubbed his nose. "Is that the truth?"

"I swear on my life."

"Did *you* ever feel like you were flying, Dad?"

It was a good question. Had I ever felt like I was flying? I'd felt as if my life was in free fall, but that's hardly the same thing. And if I *hadn't* felt like I was flying, how the hell did I know so much about it?

And then suddenly I realized I wasn't a liar after all. I knew what it was like to fly, as well as any man alive.

"Yeah, Jake, I did feel like I was flying, once. The day you were born, I flew like an eagle."

He smiled—Jesus, how good it was to see that smile, the smile I feared I might never see again on my boy's face! It was that rarest of moments for me as a parent, a moment I felt I'd handled in absolutely the right way, without a trace of a fuckup. I knew there wouldn't be many moments like this one, and that it called for a celebration. "Should we get an ice cream cone?"

"Yeah!"

"Okay, let's do that."

On the way out, Jake stuffed his spaghetti box wings into the trash.

"These wings are *stupid*," he announced.

"Oh no, they're not, buddy boy. They were a part of your beautiful dream, and dreams are never stupid."

Jake falls asleep while I'm stroking his hair. I return to my bed and stare out at the moon, thinking about the road not taken, the countless roads not taken.

I think about my own wings, my spiritual wings, and wonder whatever happened to them. One day you happen to look back at your shoulders and realize they've been clipped, before you ever even had a chance to flap them. There's a lot I haven't done and never will do, but maybe it'll be different for Jake. That's all I can hope for.

CHAPTER NINE

It's a little after eight in the morning when I open my eyes on my first full day as an unemployed man. It hits me all over again, like a crack across the face with a paddle, and it boils down to one thing—the paychecks have come to an end, while the bills have not.

I've had the same job for so long that I don't even know how to *begin* to look for work. The idea of going to another newspaper to crank out the same old shit is far from appealing, and the idea of becoming a flack for some public relations firm is even worse. That's as far as my imagination takes me this morning—a hack, or a flack. I'm qualified for nothing else. I'll probably have to buy a new suit for job interviews, and in some ways this seems like the worst thing of all. I hate suits. I hate shopping for clothes. I hate my life.

And what about my son's future? Just like that, the certainty and serenity of the next five years have been yanked out from under him. An easy senior year, followed by four years at a tranquil, leafy campus. Doris had been looking forward to visiting costly colleges with Jake all over the Northeast, taking their time selecting just the right one.

Now what?

It's as if Jake has just been jolted by the same thought. His eyes suddenly open, and for a moment he seems confused, the eternal confusion of a child of divorce, even after all these years. *Where am I, Mom's place or Dad's?* But it only lasts for a moment. He realizes where he is. He yawns, clears his throat, and kicks off the quilt. "We fell asleep with our clothes on."

"Yeah. At least we got our shoes off. You hungry, kid?"

"Starving. We didn't eat last night, did we?"

"We'll make up for it now."

I have all the stuff we need for breakfast—bacon, eggs, bread, butter. I'm always ready for Saturday morning, because Jake almost always has breakfast with me, and I insist upon making it. I want him to think of my house as a home, and I don't want him to think of his father as some pathetic loser who goes around with his thumb up his ass just because he hasn't got a woman looking after him. I figure it's the kind of thing I can't prove with words, so maybe the smell of frying bacon will do it for me.

While I'm cooking he goes to the bathroom and takes a leak, and it sounds like the force of a fire hose, strong enough to scratch the porcelain. Seventeen. Not a bad age. Prostate gland like an unripe grape.

He comes out and takes his usual seat at the table. I set a glass of orange juice in front of him. "Here. Start filling up your bladder again."

"You are obsessed with my pissing powers."

"Just a little jealous. You could rent yourself out, blasting barnacles off boats."

"I'll give it some thought, Dad. Wouldn't even need a high school diploma for that career, would I?"

I turn the bacon strips in the broiler pan. "That girlfriend of yours—"

"*Ex*-girlfriend."

"Right, ex-girlfriend. She was talking about the Ivy League schools, and the second tier. What the hell is the second tier?"

"One notch below Ivy. Duke. University of Michigan. William and Mary. Places like that."

"Good schools?"

"Good, but not good enough. Not when your parents lay out a hundred grand for a high school education."

"Where does Sarah want to go?"

"I don't know, and I don't really give a shit, Dad. I'm out of that game."

I scramble the eggs, pour them into a hot buttered pan. The smoke alarm goes off. It always does when I cook. Jake pulls it off the wall and pops out one of the batteries, killing the shrieking sound. "Was your mother's death a sudden thing?"

I knew we'd be getting back to this. Jake has been patient, letting the topic marinate overnight before coming back to it. I don't really have any more excuses. We've agreed to talk about all things. All I can do is stall it a little.

"Jake. Let me tell you something I've learned. *Everybody's* death is a sudden thing. Did you know that when Elvis died, not one newspaper in the country was ready with a standing obituary? Not one."

"I don't want to talk about Elvis, Dad. Please don't veer off the topic."

"What exactly is the topic?"

"My grandmother. I'm asking you something about my grandmother."

It's odd to hear my mother referred to by a word for something she never lived long enough to become.

"Was her death a shock? Or had she been sick for a long time?"

I have to answer him. "It was a shock. She hadn't been sick. She just . . . died."

Jake shakes his head. "Well, I guess that made it easy for her, but kind of rough on you and your father."

"That's exactly right. It was rough."

I'm scrambling eggs, keeping them moving around so they don't stick to the pan. It's good to have something to do with my trembling hands while discussing this particular matter. I'm hoping it's over, but it isn't.

"Was she home?"

"What?"

"Was she home when she died, or not?"

"What the hell are you asking *that* for?"

"What are you getting so upset about?"

"This doesn't happen to be one of my happiest memories."

"Whoa, whoa, Dad. We're supposed to be able to ask each other stuff, aren't we? Wasn't that the deal?"

"Yeah, that was the deal. So let me ask *you* something. Why did you stop playing the cello?"

It's as if I've just soaked him with a pail of ice water. Jake's shoulders harden, and his eyes narrow. "We weren't discussing the cello."

"We weren't discussing my mother, either."

"I'll tell you about the cello later."

"Swear?"

"Absolutely."

The cello mystery has been bugging me for three years. Jake began playing the instrument when he was seven and immediately displayed a genius for it, according to his cello instructor, who, it should be noted, charged a hundred and fifty dollars per lesson. (I once asked the instructor if that was his "genius" rate, and he responded with an ambivalent chuckle.) Jake actually played in a concert at Avery Fisher Music Hall when he was eleven years old, but then one day when he was fourteen he refused to play the cello anymore, and his mother wouldn't tell me why. I didn't save any money on the deal because the shrink Doris insisted on sending Jake to after he quit the cello also cost a hundred and fifty dollars per hour. Jump ball.

The bacon and eggs are done. I kill the flames and load the plates with food. Just as I set the plates down, the toast pops up. I have always been proud of my timing.

"So. Dad. Was she at home when she died, or not?"

For the first time in years, I feel the urge to give my son a smack. Instead, I answer his question. "No, goddamnit, she wasn't home."

"Where was she?"

"Out somewhere. I don't remember."

"How could you not remember a thing like that?"

"It was a long time ago, Jake. I don't remember where she dropped dead, all right?"

It's not all right, but he doesn't press it. We begin to eat. The food is good and hearty. Jake is silent. I am silent. We cannot go on like this.

"She loved bacon and eggs," I hear myself say.

Jake looks up from his food. "Your mother did?"

"Yeah. She loved good food. A true Italian girl. Great cook."

Jake sets his fork down. "Your mother was Italian?"

"You didn't know that?"

"I'm seventeen years old and *now* I'm finding out I'm part Italian!"

"I thought you knew."

"I assumed I was Irish from your side!"

"You are. But you're Italian, too, plus Spanish from your mother's side, as I'm sure you figured from the name 'Perez.' "

Jake looks pale. "I'm part Italian," he says, in a voice of wonder. "Jesus Christ, Dad, this would have been a nice thing to know about ten or fifteen years ago!"

"Why? You want to join the Mafia?"

"Don't kid around about it, Dad! This is my *history!*" he shouts, slamming the table with his fist. "It'd be nice to know where I came from! All my grandparents are dead, and I never even *met* them! You and Mom act as if you're Adam and Eve! The whole fucking world began when you two had me, and it ended when you split up!"

He's breathing hard, almost in tears. I reach for him, but he pulls away from me, covers his face with his hands. I never saw this problem coming, but now that it's out on the table, it seems obvious. Doris and I have fucked up royally.

Jake takes his hands away from his face. "I feel . . ."

"Jake?"

". . . like I came out of nowhere. My history is a mystery. How can I know who I am if I don't even know who *you* are?"

My heart is breaking. My boy is falling apart before my eyes. I get up and go around to the back of his chair to embrace him from behind, as if to keep him from exploding into a million pieces.

"What can I do?" I ask. "Tell me and I'll do it."

"Tell me things I don't know, Dad. Just *tell* me."

And then it comes to me, the thing to do, the *only* thing to do, a thing I should have done years ago. I never wanted to do it. I *still* don't want to do it. But suddenly, undeniably, the time to do it has come.

"I can do better than tell you about it, Jake. I can show you."

"*Show* me?"

"How'd you like to take a little ride today?"

I give him a final squeeze before breaking my embrace and returning to my chair. He's looking at me in wide-eyed anticipation, the way he did when he was little and I'd ask him if he wanted to go on the swings.

"Where are we going?"

"My old neighborhood. I'll show you where I grew up, where I went to school . . . everything. The fifty-cent tour, lunch included."

He wipes his eyes, forces a smile. "You'd really do that for me?"

"What do *you* think? Want to do it?"

"I'd love to. More than anything in the world."

"Well, wash the dishes and we'll go."

"Where?"

"Beautiful downtown Flushing, the garden spot of Queens. Hurry up, do those dishes. It's time for a long-overdue crash course in your ancestry."

Jake leaps to his feet, gathers the dishes, dumps them in the sink, turns on the water, and starts scrubbing.

"Road trip!" he exclaims.

"Yeah, that's right. We're going on a road trip."

The thought of it already has me trembling, but there's no backing out now. The road trip is on, and God only knows where it'll take us.

CHAPTER TEN

It's good to be in motion, if for no other reason than the fact that it makes you a moving target. Jake and I are in the borough of Queens, riding the Q-76 bus down Francis Lewis Boulevard.

I'm staring out the window at sights I haven't seen in nearly thirty years. Everything looks smaller and grayer than it used to, and the number of Asian businesses is startling. The bright red Chinese lettering on their signs seems to be the only real color around.

"What do you want to know about the cello?"

Seated beside me, Jake is looking out the window as he asks the question. I continue looking out the window as well. We both seem to instinctively realize that absence of eye contact will make this easier for us to talk about.

"You had real talent. Why'd you stop playing?"

"I wanted to switch to guitar. Wanted to play in a band with some guys from school."

"And?"

"And Mom wouldn't let me. She said I had a gift for playing the cello, and that it's wrong to waste a gift."

"Maybe you had a gift for the guitar as well. Maybe it's the *same* gift."

"That's what I said. Mom didn't want to hear about it. She said I had to stick with the cello."

A shiver goes through me, remembering the days when Doris used to try telling me what *I* had to do. "But you *didn't* stick with it."

"Well, no, I didn't."

I turn to look at him. "Jake. You going to tell me what happened, or what?"

He looks at me and sighs, a sound that seems to well up all the way from his ankles. "You remember the rooftop of our building? You used to take me up there to see the Fourth of July fireworks when I was little."

"Sure, I remember. What's that got to do with the cello?"

"One Saturday morning Mom wanted me to practice the cello for an hour. I'd had enough. I told her flat out that I didn't want to play the cello anymore. It was like she hadn't even heard what I said. She just kept insisting that I practice, because I was scheduled to play in a concert at Lincoln Center in a few weeks. I told her again that I didn't want to play the cello anymore, and she just rolled her eyes, like this was some kind of temporary anticello *phase* I was going through. Finally I agreed to practice, but only if I could go up on the roof to do it. She asked me why I'd want to do such a thing, but I ignored her. I just carried the cello up there, stuck it in a big metal garbage pail, squirted lighter fluid on it, and . . . lit a match."

He tells the tale without emphasis, as if he's a cop reading it off a police report, somebody else's act of madness. He's not smiling, but he's not frowning, either.

"Burned up pretty fast. Some kind of fruit wood, I think, and the strings made pinging sounds when they snapped. By the time Mom showed up, it was really roaring."

"Jesus Christ Almighty, she must have gone out of her mind!"

"No, she didn't. That was the best part. She wasn't angry, she was *scared*. I knew I had to make her afraid of me if I was ever going to get my way. She's an extremely determined person, as I'm sure you know."

I try to swallow, but my throat is dry. "Did the fire department show up?"

"No, no. The cello burned up in about five minutes, and all the ashes fell straight down into the garbage can. I was very careful about that. It's not like I was some crazy arsonist."

"Jake. My God. How could you *do* that?"

"It was the only way, Dad. You know what she can be like."

I sit back on the hard bus seat, dizzy and slightly nauseated. All Doris ever told me was that we were "discontinuing" the cello lessons because Jake was going through a "troubled" time. "That's why your mother sent you to the shrink?"

"Uh-huh."

"Was that any good?"

Jake shrugs. "The shrink wanted to know why I set the cello on fire. The simple answer would have been that I didn't want to set my mother on fire, but of course you can't say that, so we spent a few hours kicking around teenage angst and raging hormones and crap like that."

He ventures a smile at me. "I'm not crazy, you know. The cello was rented, and I knew Mom had taken the insurance policy on the rental, so it didn't cost you guys anything."

"Yeah? The shrink was a hundred and fifty a pop."

"Well, at least you didn't have to pay for any more cello lessons, Dad."

"I wish I could have paid for guitar lessons."

Jake shakes his head. "Nah. Wouldn't have been any point. The day I burned the cello was the day the music died."

My heart sinks. "Don't say that. It's not too late. If you want to play the guitar, you can play the guitar."

"Tell you the truth, Dad, I don't really know *what* I want anymore."

"I know how you feel."

This was all my fault. If I'd been around, he never would have had to burn the cello. Together we would have fought the good fight against his mother, and switched him over to the guitar. He might have liked it. He might have joined a band.

He might have been happy.

We're both jolted by the ringing of Jake's cell phone. He presses a caller ID button and his face goes pale. "Shit. It's Mom. What should I tell her?"

"Nothing."

"Maybe the school contacted her."

"If they could have contacted her, they'd have done that before they ever called me. Go ahead, answer it. I'm not here, by the way."

He takes a deep breath and answers the phone, sounding remarkably calm. "Hey, Mom. How's the conference going?"

He's not a bad actor. Most kids who've lived through a divorce can put on a pretty good show when they have to.

He rolls his eyes at me. "I'm on a bus," he tells her. "Just didn't feel like taking the subway. . . ."

Except for the crosstown bus Jake never rides buses, not counting those few weeks after 9/11 when everybody was convinced the subways were going to be bombed or anthraxed. We all felt safer riding buses, even though they were blowing up every other day in Israel.

"He's all right," I hear him say, and I realize Doris must have asked him how his father was. "She's fine," he says, and I realize she must have asked him about Sarah. "Not much," he says, and I know she's just asked him about his homework load for the weekend. Homework!

He tells her he loves her and clicks the phone shut. "Now we can both breathe a little easier," he says, grinning at me.

"Three lies in one phone call. Not bad."

"Well, the part about loving her is true. That should count for something."

"Do you love her?"

"Of course I do! She can't help the way she does things. And I'll tell you, she's a lot easier to get along with since I torched the cello."

"Jake. She'll be back tomorrow. We're going to have to deal with her, one way or another."

"You're the one who said, 'Fuck Monday.' "

"Yes, I did. But I never said, 'Fuck Sunday.' You just went from Ivy League shoo-in to high school dropout so fast, I'm surprised your ears didn't pop. Your mother doesn't even know it yet, but her wettest dream just went drier than the Sahara Desert. Please don't go kidding yourself that this can possibly go smoothly."

He stares at me. "I never kid myself," he says simply. "It doesn't pay off, does it?"

"No, it doesn't."

"Mom thought I was going to go the academic route, just like her."

"Don't knock it. Tenure. Summers off. A million holidays a year. Respect up the kazoo, especially as you get older."

"Thanks anyway. I'd join the army before I'd become a teacher. And believe me, I'm not about to join the army."

"Well, son, as long as we're talking this way it's my sad duty to inform you that someday, you will have to do *something* for a living. They taught you many wonderful things at that school, I'm sure, but the one lesson nobody seems to get around to is the one about the direct relationship between the need for money and the suffering that goes into getting it. Maybe they were saving it for last, but I tell you, it's a hell of a surprise to spring on people. Finding out there's no Santa Claus is nothing compared to this."

I pat him on the cheek, harder than necessary. He's a little surprised by the slap, and narrows his eyes at me for just a moment. "There's no Santa Claus?"

"Nope. Sorry, kid."

"Well, that's all right. Like I told you, I've got a plan. Have a little faith in your offspring, Father."

I get to my feet and push the tape that makes the bell ring. The bus glides to a stop. "We're here. Let's go."

There's nothing like a walk in the old neighborhood to remind you why you left and never came back. On the streets of Flushing we pass carpet-sized lawns protected by knee-high hedges. Behind them are houses that seemed to have been built by and for midgets, places that make you feel claustrophobic just to look at them. In the backyards they have their aboveground swimming pools, giant blue plastic teacups, and through the summer months they float on their backs on cloudy chlorinated water and wonder out loud how anybody can stand to live in Manhattan.

"First stop is my old school," I announce.

It takes less than five minutes to walk to Holy Cross High School, a big, gloomy place of yellow brick fronted by maple trees that don't seem to have grown much taller in all those years since I was last here. The patches of lawn are still bordered by short metal poles with chains looped between them. Jake follows me to the main entrance and stops at my side.

"Whoa, Dad. You went to *Catholic* school?"

"It was my mother's idea. Guess she wanted to save my soul. I'm not sure it worked."

There's a large crucifix hanging directly over the doorway, and the Jesus figure nailed to the cross is bigger than life-sized. It's made of some kind of weather-resistant metal, pitted and pocked by decades of rain and snow. It's a muscular Christ with a scowling face, as if He disapproves of every student who ever walked beneath him.

Jake can't stop staring at it. "Was that thing there when you went here?"

"Oh yeah."

"Pretty gruesome way to start the day, walking under that thing."

"Nothing like a good dose of guilt in the morning to get you going. . . . Do you know the story of the crucifixion?"

Jake laughs. "Dad. Are you *joking*?"

"I'm serious! I know I never told you about it, and your mother's no believer."

"I learned about it in school. World religion class, eighth grade. I think I got a B."

"What did they teach you?"

"That Jesus Christ died for mankind's sins, and He rose from the dead three days later."

I nodded. "That about wraps it up."

"Also that God is actually three beings—a father, a son, and a holy spirit. I never quite understood that."

"Nobody does. We all just acted like we did so the nuns wouldn't hit us with a yardstick."

Jake stares at the crucifix. I can barely stand to look at it, turn my gaze to the sidewalk. "The bravest kids in school used to throw snowballs at it."

"Oh, man," Jake laughs, "that took balls!"

"It sure did. But that's nothing, compared to what Paschal Tufano did. He climbed up there and stuck a cigarette in Jesus's mouth. And he was only a freshman at the time, a classmate of mine. Talk about balls."

Jake laughs. "Did he get caught?"

"He got caught, and he got expelled."

"You're kidding!"

"Swear to God. Many roads lead to expulsion, my son. You write a smart-ass essay, Paschal Tufano sticks a Marlboro in the mouth of the son of God. In the end, it's all the same."

I chuckle, thinking of Paschal, wondering what the hell ever became of him. Jake continues staring at the crucifix.

"Did you ever throw a snowball at it?"

"Never."

"Why not?"

"Because it would have been a sin, and at the time I was concerned with sins. Even *thinking* about chucking a snowball at the crucifix would have been a sin. That's what we were taught here. You don't have to actually do something bad. Even bad thoughts are sins."

Jake stares at me in wonder. "They taught you that?"

"They certainly did."

"That's unbelievable!"

"Now do you see why I never took you to church?"

"Did your parents believe in all this stuff?"

"My mother did. My father didn't."

"When did he die?"

"About five years after my mother, I guess."

"You *guess*? What did he die of?"

"He had a heart attack, too, Jake, and he died at home. *That* I remember. Okay?"

"Why are you getting nasty?"

"Jake. Please. All these questions ... I have to sit for a minute."

"Dad, are you all right?"

I'm far from all right. My shirt is damp with sweat and my head is pounding. I lick my upper lip and taste salt. "Thing is, Jake, I really can't stand the sight of a crucifix. Never could."

"Why? It's just a statue on a cross."

"It's a little more than that to me."

"Why?"

"Maybe I'll tell you later. Right now I just have to sit a minute, and be quiet."

I'm feeling dizzy, and the strength has left my legs. Taking me by the elbow, Jake helps me to a stoop across the street from the school, where we both sit down. Jake rubs my back in a circular motion.

"I'm sorry, Dad."

"Sorry about what?"

"Sorry that you're so . . . alone."

He's right. He's absolutely right. That is the perfect word for what I am.

And then, for the first time since the day I packed up and moved out on my wife and son, I begin to cry, and I mean hard. The tears are plopping on the cement between my feet, and I'm sobbing like a child, the child I haven't been for so very long.

It's an awful thing to do to Jake, but he's strong. He just keeps rubbing my back in the same circular motion.

"Hey, Dad. Come on. It'll be okay."

At last I start to calm down. The time has come to start telling him things, the things I have promised to tell him, things I've kept buried for so long that the graves no longer have headstones.

"Jake. There's something you should know about this school."

"You're not *enrolling* me here, are you?"

"No, no . . . Thing is, I never finished."

"What do you mean?"

My tongue is sticky. I try to swallow, but can't. "I dropped out in my senior year. I'm a high school dropout."

I sound like someone standing up at a meeting and declaring himself an alcoholic. Jake stops rubbing my back. His mind is totally blown.

"Dad. Jesus! *You're a high school dropout!*"

"It's something even your mother doesn't know about, and I'd like to keep it that way, all right?"

"I'll keep my mouth shut."

"Your mother has a Ph.D., so between us it sort of evens out for you."

"Why'd you drop out?"

"Let's just say I was going through a troubled time."

"Dad. You're *amazing!* No diploma, and you had a good career and everything!"

"I don't know if I'd go that far. Nobody ever asked to see a diploma at the *Star*, I can tell you that. All they wanted to know about was whether I could knock out fifteen paragraphs on a windswept fire in Canarsie in time for the bulldog edition."

"Well, I'm proud to be following in your footsteps."

"Ohhh my God, don't *say* that!"

I start crying all over again. Jake takes me in his arms, and actually rocks me back and forth. What a father-son weekend this is turning out to be! Jake has cried in my arms, and I've cried in his, and we're not even halfway through Saturday!

I feel as if I'm never going to be able to get to my feet again. I'll die right here on this stoop, across the street from the school where my formal education ground to a halt. I'm done, cooked, finished. It's going to take a miracle to get me back to the land of the living.

And then a miracle happens.

It's something I hear before I see, the loud, metallic snap of a lock across the street. The front door of the school is opening, a millimeter at a time, it seems, and then at last an ancient man steps outside, preceded by the broom he is clutching.

He's bent at the waist and cloaked in an old-fashioned priest's frock, a dresslike thing with buttons the size of gumdrops. His feet move like the feet of a child's windup robot, a shuffle step with minimal lifting, but he's moving with determination.

He lifts his goatlike head to regard Jake and me, long ears quivering, scant hair feathery atop his pink skull. His face is expressionless as he studies us through the biggest, thickest pair of eyeglasses I've ever seen. But he doesn't waste much time wondering who we could be. This man has a job to do. He clutches the broom in both hands, squares his shoulders, and begins sweeping yellow leaves toward the curb.

And then it hits me, and I all but fall to my knees over the splendor of the miracle before us.

"Oh my God," I say, more to myself than to Jake. "It's the Walking Holiday!"

His real name, I remember, is Father Brian Walls, and if I'd given him a thought over the past thirty years, it would have been about the certainty of his death soon after I left the school. But here he was, broom in his bony hands, doing what he'd done when I was a Holy Cross student—sweeping up the front of the school.

Jake senses the sanctity of the moment and whispers, "Why do you call him the Walking Holiday?"

"Because he was such an old man when I went to this school, we all figured we'd get a day off when he died."

"He sure screwed you, huh?"

"Yeah. Me and thousands of other guys since the class of 1974."

"How old is he?"

"I don't know. I don't think anybody knows. You'd have to saw him in half and count the rings, I think."

We watch him work. Father Walls is doing the best he can, but the leaves are not cooperating. Most of them resist the bite of the broom bristles, staying behind as he plows onward toward the curb. But it doesn't matter that he's doing a shitty job. What matters is that he's alive, he's out there, a man who's certainly within a whisper of his hundredth birthday, or maybe even past it and gunning for two hundred.

I'm gripped by a weirdly optimistic sensation, watching that old priest at work. Somehow, some way, my son is going to be all right, and so am I. I reach over and squeeze the back of Jake's neck.

"Let's walk," I say.

"Hang on, Dad. Maybe we should offer to help this guy sweep."

"No! That would *kill* him! Don't you get it? In his head, he's the only man in the world who can do it right. You take away his task, he might as well be dead."

Minutes later, Father Walls decides that his job is done, though he's managed to sweep a total of maybe a dozen leaves into the street. He shoulders the broom like a rifle and baby-steps his way back into the school. The door booms behind him with an echo that goes right through me.

"Okay, the show's over," I say. "Let's go."

I lead the way around the back of the school past the athletic field, where I heard the words "We Got Sullivan" innumerable times. It's a dirt field ringed by a running track, and the only person there is a fat kid in a full sweatsuit, puffing around the track in an obvious effort to lose weight.

"He shouldn't be doing that," Jake says. "He's too heavy. He'll wreck his knees."

"He'll find that out the hard way."

"No, he won't. Wait here."

Jake calls to the kid, who slows down to a waddle and meets Jake at the fence. Jake seems to be giving him serious advice, and then he says something that makes the kid laugh out loud. They high-five each other before the fat kid hobbles off to the showers. Jake returns to me with a grin on his face.

"What'd you tell him?"

"The truth. That he'll grind his knees into bonemeal if he keeps this up. Told him to use an exercise bike to drop some pounds before he starts running."

"He could have told you to go fuck yourself."

"That was a risk I was willing to take. Got to take some chances in life, Dad."

"What made him laugh?"

"I told him the girl he was trying to impress wasn't worth spending a lifetime in a wheelchair."

"He found that funny?"

"It's all in the delivery, Dad. Now come on. Show me where you lived. I want to see the house."

"It's the next stop on the tour," I say, but as it turns out we run into a bit of a detour on the way.

We walk a few blocks in the direction of my old house when suddenly my heart begins gonging away in my chest. Jake sees that something is wrong, and he's actually frightened by the way I'm breathing.

"You okay, Dad?"

"I just realized something."

"What's that?"

I point at a small brick house across the street from where we're standing, a house fronted by a ragged lawn and wildly overgrown privet hedges.

"Is that your old house? It looks abandoned!"

"No, that wasn't my house. . . ."

Should I tell him? Maybe not. And then it just bubbles out of me. "That's where I lost my virginity."

"No kidding?"

"I wouldn't kid about that."

CHAPTER ELEVEN

I was seventeen years old. My mother had been dead for a few months, and I was working for Napoli's World Famous Pizza, making endless deliveries on a bicycle. It was a big old clunker of a bike with fat balloon tires and crooked wheels and an oversized wire basket on the handlebars, big enough to hold six pies at a time.

Saturday night was always our biggest delivery night, and the night with the most problems. People were usually half in the bag when they called in their orders and often totally bombed by the time I arrived with their pies. Usually there was a party going on and they had to take up a collection to pay me, with a lot of stupid arguing over who owed what, and who still owed from the last time. I'd be standing there in the apartment hallway like an idiot while all this went on, but on the advice of old man Napoli I never handed over the pizza until I had the money. That was the surest way to get a door slammed in your face.

I was tired. Napoli made the best pies in Flushing and I'd been on the go nonstop since five thirty in the afternoon. Now it was past midnight, and this was my final delivery of the night—four sausage and pepperoni pies to the top story of a five-floor walk-up.

I could hear music and screaming and laughter from above as soon as they buzzed me into the vestibule. It was a shabby build-ing, the walls starved for paint, the linoleum floors crowded with banged-up baby carriages. An old lady on the second floor opened her door and glowered at me as I approached. She was obviously the closest thing this building had to a guard dog, and none too happy about the noise from above. She wore curlers and a hair net and she clutched at the lapels of her bathrobe to keep me from sneaking a peek at her withered breasts.

"Whaddya, bringin' 'em food at *this* hour?"

"Yes, ma'am."

"You tell them to pipe down!"

I ignored her, kept climbing, and paused to catch my breath at the door before knocking. I had to knock again, harder, to be heard above the racket. Suddenly it opened, and a fat, balding young guy with a cigar jammed into his mouth was grinning at me.

"Pizza's here!" he shouted. "Come on in, kid!"

I knew immediately that this was a bachelor party. I hated these things, knew I'd probably have to go through hell to get paid, but what could I do?

I followed him into a room so thick with smoke that I could hardly breathe. There were at least a dozen cigar smokers there, twenty-somethings with a smattering of thirty-somethings, all standing with their backs to me, shoulder to shoulder in a sloppy semicircle. Empty beer bottles were everywhere, and I looked in vain for a place to set the pizzas down. "Where do you want these?"

"In a minute, in a minute. First enjoy the show, kid."

"What show?"

He nudged one of the guys aside, pushed me into the gap. "This show!" he cried.

I blinked my watery eyes and saw a girl in a white cowboy hat, white skirt, and white boots dancing around a young man sprawled in a lounge chair, obviously the man due to marry in the morning. The men were whooping and yelling so loudly that they drowned out the stripper music coming from the girl's pathetic little boom box.

But the girl could hear it, or at least she pretended she could. She whirled and strutted and pointed an admonishing finger at the groom to be. It said MANDY in silver letters across the front of her hat, so the guys began chanting "Man-dee! Man-*dee!*"

Off came the halter top, off came the white skirt, and just like that Mandy stood naked before us, save for the hat and the boots.

This was the first naked woman I'd ever seen. I was unaware of the fact that I'd tightened my grip on the pizza boxes, hugging them as if they were a life raft. Mandy was blond haired and blue eyed, maybe two or three years older than me. She was dazzling but not beautiful, but the point was that she was *there*, in the flesh, almost within touching distance. I watched the rest of her blurry-fast routine, which ended with her blowing kisses to the crowd as she deftly picked her clothes up off the floor. She ducked into another room and within seconds she emerged wearing a trench coat that went all the way to her ankles. Without another word or gesture to the catcalling crowd, Mandy the stripper scooped up her little boom box and was gone. Obviously she'd been paid up front, unlike me.

"Ladies and gentlemen, Mandy has left the building!" said one of the guys, and they all laughed at that.

"Here, kid." The fat guy who'd let me in stuffed some bills into my shirt pocket, took the now-cold pies from me, and pointed at the front of my pants.

"Hey!" he said, "looks like somebody got a little excited here!"

I looked down. Streaks of pizza oil ran from my crotch to my thighs. I'd been squeezing those boxes even harder than I realized.

They exploded in laughter at the sight of me. I made the cardinal sin of not counting the money as I ran for the door and dashed down the stairs, thinking maybe I'd catch up to the stripper, half wanting it to happen, half fearing that it would.

But she was gone, and so was the delivery bike I'd left in front of the building. Somebody had stolen the fucking thing.

I couldn't believe it. That old clunker was such a hunk of junk that I couldn't even imagine anyone wanting to steal it, so I never bothered with the wheel lock that old man Napoli provided. The double bang of the stripper and the bicycle theft had me numb. I began the long walk back to Napoli's, wondering what I was going to tell him, wondering where the stripper had gone, wondering if "Mandy" was her real name and how often she stripped. I wondered if she had a real job as well, or if she was just a stripper. It was amazing to me that a woman could do something like that for money. I didn't think it was wrong, just amazing.

I took the money from my shirt pocket and counted it. The tab for the four pies had come to forty-eight bucks, and the guy had slipped me three twenties. Twelve bucks, the best tip I'd ever gotten. If the bike hadn't been stolen and my pants hadn't gotten fucked up, this would have been a hell of a good night.

Napoli was in a bad mood when I got back, eager to close up shop. He was about sixty years old, one of those lean, surly Italians whose eyes grew narrower with suspicion each and every year of his life. All those years of pulling pizza pies out of hot ovens didn't do much to improve his personality.

"Hey, Sammy. What'd you do, get lost?"

I wasn't about to tell him that I'd stopped to watch a stripper. "They took a long time to pay."

"Son of a bitch bastards." This was one of his favorite expressions.

I gave him two twenties and a ten from my wallet, and he gave back two dollars in change. I didn't want him knowing I'd gotten a twelve-dollar tip. It would hurt me the next time I was due for a raise. He gave me my weekly pay in cash, and then I had to tell him.

"Mr. Napoli—"

"Hey, your pants are all fucked up."

"I know."

"And you forgot to bring the bike inside."

I sighed, looked at the floor. "Somebody stole it."

"*Stole it?*"

"It wasn't there when I got downstairs from the last delivery."

He rubbed his face, muttered an Italian oath. "Who would steal such a piece-o'-shit bike?"

"I don't know."

He cocked his head at me. "I bet you forgot to lock it! You didn't lock it, did you?"

I thought about lying, changed my mind. "No, I didn't lock it."

"Sammy. *Sammy.*"

"I know, I know."

"You gotta make good for that bike."

I knew this would happen, and I also knew the old prick was enjoying it. Might he have sent someone to steal it, so his faithful employee could get stuck for the price of a much-needed new one? I wouldn't put it past him.

"How much?" I ventured.

He rubbed the back of his wrinkly neck. "I dunno . . . forty bucks?"

"Forty bucks! It's a twenty-year-old bike!"

"Sammy—"

"You said yourself it was a piece o' shit!"

"Yeah, but it *worked*, didn't it? And I have to *replace* it, don't I?"

"*I'll* replace it, okay?"

He hadn't thought of this possibility. His already narrowed eyes became razor slits. "Where you gonna get a bike?"

"Leave it to me."

"All right, but it's gotta be a bike that can do the job."

"It will be. Don't worry about it."

"Don't get mad, Sammy. You gotta be responsible in life, know what I mean?"

This was the perfect lesson for a fallen young Catholic, absolutely flawless. I'd sinned by watching a stripper, and for my instantaneous penance, I was hit with oil-stained pants and a stolen bike.

We turned off the lights and stepped outside. I helped him pull down the burglar gate.

"You want a ride home?"

"No, I don't want a ride home."

I walked off without saying good night. The oil stains on my pants were going to be hard to get out. Maybe I should present Napoli with a cleaning bill, as long as I was being dunned for the bike. If my mother were still alive she'd know how to get the stain out, but she was dead, and it was times like this that I thought of her.

Were people in heaven able to watch us down on earth? My mother wouldn't have liked to see me ogling a stripper. That would have made her suffer, and that brought up another point— would God let his good little souls in heaven suffer by witnessing the deeds of their sinful loved ones down on earth? Or did they just play their harps and hang out with each other in a blissful state of grace, ignorant of the sinning being done by their survivors down on earth?

I needed advice. I needed comfort. I needed a shoulder to cry on, but whose? My father's?

Well, it was worth a shot. He was bound to be at Charlie's Bar, as he always was on Saturday nights, not to mention Mondays, Tuesdays, Wednesdays, Thursdays, and Fridays. Charlie's Bar became my destination.

It was past 1:00 a.m. when I entered the joint, a place I'd only ever been to in search of my old man. Charlie's was a dingy, grimy gin mill that was more like a slovenly friend's finished basement than a licensed saloon. It had fake wood paneling in the halls, and bar stools with fake leather seats.

But Charlie McMahon was real, a burly, gray-haired retired fireman who worked the stick six nights a week, serving the working-stiff locals. He didn't seem to like his customers very much, but for some reason he liked my father, probably because they were both Irish, and for that reason he was always friendly to me.

"Sammy! What the hell happened to your pants?"

"Pizza box leaked on 'em."

"You still workin' for that miserable guinea?"

Apparently he'd forgotten that I was half Italian. "Yeah, well, it's a job. . . . My old man around?"

"He came and he left. Looked kinda tired. You guys doin' all right, Sammy?"

I shrugged.

"He misses your mother somethin' awful."

The hell he did. "So he went home a while ago?"

"Maybe half an hour."

"All right, I'll see you around, Charlie."

"Wait. Sit. Have one on the house, you had a rough night."

Before I could object he set a longneck Budweiser in front of me, dripping foam. "Happy days, kid."

"Thanks."

Why did he want me around? Maybe because it was so damn depressing in there. Three or four middle-aged guys were sitting at the other end of the bar, shell-backed men solemnly staring into the foam at the bottom of their beer mugs in search of that elusive key to happiness. What a place to look for it!

At least I was young—underage, in fact. Even if I just sat there without saying a word, I'd bring some vitality to those dismal early morning hours. Charlie went to the other end of the bar to refresh the shell-backs' drinks, and that's when she walked in and sat down next to me.

She didn't even look at me at first. Charlie came over when he was through at the other end, and he seemed less than delighted to see her.

"How's tricks, Fran?"

"Lousy."

He asked her what she wanted, and his eyebrows went up when she told him to make her a white wine spritzer. Charlie's usual customers were beer and whiskey people, the women included, and it was easy to read the unspoken thought in his head: *who does this broad think she is?* He made her the spritzer with cheap Gallo wine from a gallon jug, took her money, and went back to the other end of the bar. She sipped her spritzer, made a face at it, and set the glass on the bar. At last she looked at me, and I knew she'd been drinking heavily before she got here.

"What are you starin' at?"

She was right. I'd been staring at her. "I'm sorry. I didn't mean to stare."

"It's rude. Don't do it."

She was around thirty-five, not bad looking but frazzled, the way women often get when their marriages go wrong and they're stuck with kids. Her dark blond hair was cut in a stylish shag, and she wore stone-washed jeans and a brown leather jacket. She took out a pack of Kools, shook one into her mouth, and looked at me again. "You got a problem if I smoke?"

"No, ma'am."

"Don't *ma'am* me! You want one?"

"I don't smoke."

"Good for you. You'll live longer." She lit up, inhaled deeply, breathed it out through her nostrils. "What the hell happened to your pants?"

I didn't want to tell her, but I had to. I had to talk to *somebody*, and it came spilling out of me as if a dam had burst—the pizza delivery, the stripper, the leaking pizza boxes, the stolen bike. By the time I finished talking she'd smoked the Kool down to the butt and crushed it out in an ashtray. "So you gotta pay for the bike, huh?"

"Well, I have to replace it."

"What a prick. I always thought that Napoli was a prick, and now I know for sure."

She signaled for another spritzer, plus a beer for me. She smacked my hand away when I tried to pay. Charlie served us in silence and gave me a look that could have been either an encouragement or a warning. Then he returned to Lonely Guy Corner.

Fran lit another Kool. "First time you ever saw a stripper, I'll bet."

"Well . . . yeah."

"First time you ever saw a naked woman in person, right?"

She smiled at me like a lawyer who knows the answer before he asks the question. There was no point in trying to lie to her. My face felt hot as I nodded.

Thankfully, her smile did not evolve into a laugh. She nodded, downed the rest of her spritzer, shook her hair, and looked me in the eye. "Would you like to see another one?"

My scalp tingled. Fran stared at me as rudely as I'd stared at her minutes earlier. This was it. This was absolutely and without a doubt the moment no man can be ready for.

"Yes," I finally replied, but was my frantically beating heart really in it? I didn't know. I couldn't know. All I did know was that I wasn't ready to be alone that night. Fran seemed neither pleased nor surprised by my reply.

"Drink up," she said, "and let's get out of this dump."

We didn't say good-bye to Charlie. She walked out of the place and I followed her like an obedient, fearful pooch.

I was frightened. While I'd been in Charlie's I'd felt safe, but suddenly I felt like a hostage, walking the night streets with Fran, even though nothing was stopping me from getting away. In fact, it seemed as if she'd forgotten all about me. She was two full strides ahead of me, and picking up speed. All I had to do was stop walking, but I didn't do that. I couldn't do that. This was the first woman I'd spent any time with since the death of my mother, and I wasn't ready for it to end.

I wondered if she'd known my mother. I doubted it. Fran didn't seem like a churchgoer to me. I hurried to catch up to her. She was breathing hard.

"Are you okay, Fran?"

She stopped walking, turned to glare at me. "How do you know my name?"

"I heard Charlie say it."

"He never spoke my name!"

"Yes, he did! How else would I know it? I don't know you. I never saw you before!"

She seemed as if she was about to start crying. She covered her face with her hands, took openmouthed breaths between her palms. She was hurting. I didn't know what to do. My mind raced with possibilities, one of which was to tiptoe away, then sprint the half mile to my own house. But I didn't do that. I couldn't. It would have been like abandoning the wounded.

"Would you like to know *my* name?" I offered at last.

"No, I would not," she said, keeping her face covered. "I have no interest in knowing your name."

"Okay, I won't tell you."

Fran seemed relieved to hear this. She kept her hands over her face but at least her breathing slowed. The night was loud with crickets. It was early October. Fran began to chuckle.

"Stupid crickets," she said.

"Why are they stupid?"

"Because winter's comin', and they don't even know it, 'cause it's been so warm. The first frost is gonna hit, and they'll all be dead."

"Yeah, but *they* don't know that. It won't be so bad. It'll just happen to them, and that'll be that."

At last, Fran's hands fell from her face. For the first time all night she stared at me with wide-open eyes.

"What are you," she asked, "a *philosopher*?"

I shrugged. "It's true, isn't it?"

"You're goddamn right it's true. . . . How old are you?"

"Seventeen."

"Seventeen, and already you understand somethin' like that. Man, some bad shit must've happened to you, huh?"

If she was waiting for an answer, she wasn't going to get one. I just stared back at her, listening to the crickets.

"Sometimes I wish I was a cricket," she said softly. "Be nice not to know what's coming, you know?"

"I know."

Fran stared at me for another moment. Then her eyes narrowed, and she grabbed me by the elbow.

"Come on," she said, "we're not far now."

Anybody who might have been watching us at that point could have taken Fran for an undercover detective hauling in a suspect. But it was nearly three in the morning. Nobody was watching us.

Minutes later she led me up the three steps to her front door and into her house, and only then did she release my elbow with a shove that was almost dismissive. The house was boxy, cramped, low-ceilinged, the kind of place that made you want to run outside and gulp air. Fran ripped off her jacket, tossed it on the floor. "Sit down, I'll bring us a drink."

I sat on a dark green couch. Fran fetched a bottle of Jack Daniel's and two glasses. I'd never drunk whiskey before, but this did not seem like the time to bring that up. Fran poured with a heavy hand. We clinked glasses, and then she said:

"To my wonderful husband, who walked out on me and our two boys like it was nothing."

Fran's head went back like a Pez dispenser as she downed her drink in one gulp. Then she let out a laugh, the least happy laugh I'd ever heard.

I was shocked. A husband! The looming sin of fornication was about to be compounded with adultery! All I could do was sit and stare at Fran, who poured herself another drink and downed it the same way.

"Come on, drink up," she scolded, "you're fallin' behind!"

I did as I was told. Catholics are good at that, even when the wrong person is giving the orders. The stuff went down like liquid fire. Fran went to refill my glass but I covered it with my hand.

"You're married?"

"Ah, not really. Not for long. The bastard finally moved out and got his own place. He's got the boys this weekend. One weekend a month he takes the boys, and I have a little time to myself. Only thing is, I forgot how to be alone. Ain't that somethin'? I don't know how to do it anymore." She laughed that horrible laugh again, a sound more like crying than crying itself.

I stood up. "You want me to go?"

"No. Don't. Please. Hang out. Just . . . hang out awhile."

There was an angry vulnerability to her voice. She hated herself for this weakness, hated me for revealing it. She got to her feet and grasped my elbow as she had before, but this time the grip was different. Not a domineering woman bullying a shy young man, but a blind person in desperate need of help to cross the street. She carried the whiskey bottle in her other hand. We headed upstairs, Fran clinging to my elbow as if she expected me to break into a run.

But that wasn't going to happen. My desire to flee was gone. I was going to see this thing through, wherever it took me, wherever it took her. "Where's the bathroom?"

"Here."

She pushed a door open, pulled a light cord. "I'm at the end of the hall, when you're through."

It wasn't clean. There was stuff growing in the mortar between the floor tiles and there were deep brown water level rings etched into the toilet bowl. Then I saw three toothbrushes in a plastic cup, two of them with *Star Wars* handles, and remembered that the woman I was about to fuck was a mother. I lifted the toilet lid with my foot, took a piss, flushed with my elbow, and then headed down the hallway.

A night-light shining from an open doorway caught my eye. I stepped inside and realized this was Fran's sons' room. I had no business being here, but I had to look around.

They had bunk beds with a little wooden ladder leading to the top one. There was a *Jaws* shark poster on the wall, and I stepped on something that turned out to be a Spider-Man action figure. There was a framed photograph on the wall, and as my eyes adjusted to the moonlight I saw that it was a shot of Fran and her sons on some kind of amusement park ride, captured by a fixed-focus camera as the thing plunged down a man-made waterfall. The boys looked to be a year or two apart, maybe six and seven years old. Everybody's hair was blown straight back, and their mouths were wide, wide open in what looked to be shouts of absolute joy. You look at a picture like that and figure the people in it will never, ever be unhappy.

"Where the hell are you?"

Fran's voice startled me. I left the boys' room and went down to the end of the hall, where a dim, flickering light beckoned. I entered this room and saw that the light came from a thick green candle on Fran's bedside night table. The whiskey bottle stood next to it. Fran's clothes were all over the floor, dropped where she'd stripped. She was in bed, under the covers up to her neck.

I stood at the foot of the bed like a doctor on a house call. "I went to the wrong room."

"You idiot. Come on."

With trembling hands I took my clothes off, but not carelessly. I made a neat pile of it—shoes on the bottom, shirt on top. I guess I wanted to be ready for what I suspected would be a rapid exit—grab all my stuff, and get the hell out of there.

I stood naked in the candlelight, not hard, not soft, awaiting yet another invitation. Fran ripped back the covers and revealed her white-skinned self. It was a startling sight, my second naked woman on the same night, but nothing like the sight of Mandy, or whatever her real name was.

I was drunk, but I understood at once the reason for the candle. Any other kind of light would have been too harsh on Fran's thickened midsection and floppy breasts.

"Get in bed," she said wearily, as if we'd been married for twenty years.

I crept onto the bed, and lay beside Fran without touching her. Fran got up on one elbow to look at me, and managed a smile. "Well, at least you're a little bit excited."

It was true. I was slowly hardening. She reached over and petted it as if it were a friendly collie, and it stood strong.

I was thinking about Mandy. She was probably asleep somewhere, totally unaware of her role in getting the pizza delivery boy laid for the first time. It would have been nice to talk with Mandy, just talk somewhere. If I'd gotten down the stairs faster, it might have happened. We could have gone for a cup of coffee at the Empire Diner on Francis Lewis Boulevard. I could have made her laugh, explaining why my pants were covered in pizza oil. I figured strippers could use a good laugh, that there wasn't much in their line of work to laugh about.

I never would have gone to Charlie's, never would have hooked up with Fran, never would have been poised on the brink of this thing that now had to happen, whether I liked it or not.

Fran took control. I thought we might kiss first but that wasn't on the agenda. Fran went down and took me in her mouth in a way that was far from gentle. I couldn't believe it was happening. I didn't even know that people did things like this. Masturbation was all I knew about sex. I felt my hands bunch into fists and wondered if I should be stroking her hair or doing *something* with my hands—anything but making fists!

What did I know? I had never kissed a girl, never hugged a girl, never seen a pornographic film. I hoped that instinct would carry me, but so far that didn't seem to be happening.

Fran's head rose. She wiped her mouth with the back of her hand. "Did you like that?"

"Yeah," I lied.

I was actually glad it hadn't been pleasurable. I would have shot too soon, and somehow even I knew enough to know that women didn't like that.

Fran stretched out on her back. "Come on, let's have it."

The time had come. I climbed on top of her, ready to meet my fate, but I was having a hard time with the angles.

Fran lifted her head, like an annoyed sunbather when a passerby accidentally kicks sand on her. "What the hell are you doing?"

All I could do was breathe. It jutted from me like the prow of a schooner, but my ignorant knees were planted on the outsides of Fran's thighs. Good for wrestling, bad for sex.

"Hey. How are you gonna fuck me from there?"

She sounded like a baseball coach scolding a boneheaded player for throwing the ball to the wrong base.

"Well. Uh . . ."

"Get your knees on the *inside*, for Christ's sake!"

I did as I was told, for my own sake, not Christ's, and with Fran

pulling me toward her it happened, a swift, efficient, unemo-
tional event that ended even before I was through pumping, as
Fran suddenly decided she'd had enough of it and shoved me
away. I nearly went off the bed but managed to hang on somehow, clutching the edge of the mattress and pulling myself back
aboard beside Fran, who'd rolled away to the other side, tangled
up in the sheet. We were both breathing hard, the air ripe with
whiskey. Whatever we'd been doing was over, now and forever.

"You okay?" she asked the wall.

"Uh-huh."

"Sorry it couldn't have been with someone special, kid."

And then she was crying, softly and quietly, like rain on cotton.
I tried to touch her, but she curled herself into a ball, like one of
those roly-poly armored insects that protects itself this way, but
Fran's only armor was her rage, and that, suddenly, was gone.

"Fran?"

"Shhh. Give me a minute. Just be quiet."

I did as I was told. I wondered what time it was. The windows
were black with night, but dawn couldn't have been far away. On
the other hand, it was hard to imagine the sun ever rising again.

"Find me my robe, would you? It's on the floor somewhere."

I was glad to have something to do. While I was looking for
the robe Fran sat up in bed, blew out the candle, and took a
drink straight from the whiskey bottle.

"You want a swig?"

"No, thank you."

I handed her the robe. She stood to put it on, sat back down,
and seemed to calm down. I sat at the foot of the bed, awaiting
instructions.

She took another swallow of whiskey. "You can leave now, if
you want."

There was nothing I wanted more, but I needed more than
just her permission. I needed her blessing, a blessing in this far
from holy place. "I'll stay if you like."

"Why?"

"Maybe you want to talk."

She managed a weak smile. "You're a nice boy, aren't you?"

"I don't know."

"Sure you are. You go to school, you've got a job, and now you've been laid. Too bad it wasn't with your girlfriend, huh? Somebody you're really crazy about."

"I don't have a girlfriend."

"Don't bullshit me."

"I'm not. I don't have a girlfriend. I've *never* had a girlfriend. I've never . . ."

Fran's eyes were bleary. She seemed to be wobbling, as if she were on a raft at sea. "Never *what?*"

"Never even kissed a girl."

Why was I telling Fran things I could barely tell myself? I'll always wonder about that.

She stared at me, struggled to focus. Her eyes narrowed with determination. She crept toward me, reached around for the back of my neck, pulled my face toward hers, and suddenly stopped. She let me go, retreated to her end of the bed.

"No," she decided, ending an argument with herself. "A kiss is special. It's okay that I was your first fuck, but a kiss is special. That you should have with someone who matters."

She took another drink from the bottle.

"I don't think you should drink anymore."

"I won't. I'm done now." She screwed the cap on the bottle, as if to prove her sincerity. Her consonants were slurring and her eyes were at half-mast. I was sure she was going to pass out, and then what was I supposed to do? Take an easy exit? That wouldn't seem right.

She wobbled, seemed ready to pitch face-forward off the side of the bed, and then suddenly she straightened up with an odd alertness, a matter of will over whiskey.

"Get dressed," she said. "We have to do something."

I did as I was told. It took me less than a minute. She got off the bed, tied the robe around herself, stepped into a pair of slippers, and led the way downstairs.

"Do what?" I asked, but she wouldn't say. I followed her out the front door. The sky was going gray with the first light of dawn as we crossed that tiny, dew-soaked lawn to a tin shed at the edge of the property. Fran struggled with the shed door, which finally slid open with a rusty groan. I could see that it was jammed with gardening equipment—rakes, shovels, an old-fashioned push mower.

Did she want me to cut her lawn, at five o'clock in the morning? I would have done it for her, but that wasn't what she wanted. Fran reached into the shed and tugged hard at something that seemed reluctant to budge. The metal walls boomed and banged as the thing she struggled with made its way out of that tangle of junk, and suddenly it was free and clear, out in the open. Breathing hard, Fran set it before me. "Here. This is for you. You said you needed one, didn't you?"

It was a rusty old bicycle, probably ten years old, maybe even older. It had a faded blue frame, wide wheels, and flat tires.

"Oh my God."

"It was my husband's. Look at the seat. Stupid fucker carved his name right there in the leather. See?"

I looked. On the back of the seat the name BOB had been scratched into the leather, probably with a penknife.

Fran chuckled. "What a dick! Who the hell carves his name into a bicycle seat?"

"I can't take this bike, Fran."

"Yes, you can. Bob didn't want it. The boys don't want it. It's all yours. There's nothing wrong with the tires, they just need air. Been years since Bob rode this bike."

I felt paralyzed standing there, holding on to that bike as Fran shivered against the morning chill. She stroked my hair in a way that was almost affectionate.

"You take it, and you tell your boss to go fuck himself."

They were the words I needed to hear. I walked the bike to the sidewalk, with Fran at my side. She stopped at the end of her path.

"Go on, now, get out of here, I gotta get some sleep before my boys come home."

She kissed my cheek and pulled back for a last look at me. I had to say something, and what I said was, "Thanks for the bike."

I was deliberately specific in my thanks. I didn't want her to think I was thanking her for sex. Even I knew that would have been rude. She said, "Don't mention it," and walked back into her house without so much as a backward glance.

How much of this night would she remember? Would she remember giving the bike away? I knew I couldn't return it. How could I return it? It would be like trying to return my virginity.

There was an all-night gas station on Northern Boulevard, and that's where I headed. They had an air hose that cost a quarter and in no time at all I had the tires pumped up. I climbed aboard the bike and rode it home, savoring the predawn sounds, the end of the crickets and the start of the mourning doves. It was a decent bike with better balance and a better glide than the one that had been stolen. Old man Napoli was going to come out ahead on this deal.

When I got home I put the bike inside our garage and locked the door. I went into the house and could hear my father snoring. He didn't even know that I hadn't been home all night. I knew he'd sleep until at least eleven o'clock, and I wanted to be sure and get up before him to deliver the bike to Napoli.

I didn't want my father to see the bike, didn't want him to ask any questions. I didn't want him to know anything about the night I'd just had. I just had to hope that Charlie McMahon wouldn't tell him anything about me tipping a few with Fran, but I wasn't too worried about that. Charlie looked like a man who had secrets of his own.

My father was still asleep when I left the house, rode the bike to Napoli's World Famous Pizza, and presented it to my boss.

He was stunned. "Where's you get this bike?"

"A broad I fucked last night gave it to me," I thought of saying, but instead I opted for, "I told you I'd get it, and I did."

"By God, you sure did, Sammy."

"God didn't have anything to do with it, Mr. Napoli." I leaned the bike against the side of his building. "Now we're even."

'You're a good boy, Sammy."

"One more thing. I quit."

He was stunned. He thought I was kidding. I assured him I was not kidding. He offered me a raise. He offered to pay me forty bucks for the bike. I told him it wasn't about the bike, or the money.

I left him standing there outside the pizza parlor, clutching Fran's husband's bike as he yelled at me until I was out of earshot. I went home and slept for twelve hours.

CHAPTER TWELVE

Jake listens to my story without a word of interruption. He puts a steadying hand on my shoulder and says, "Quite a night."

"Yeah, you're right about that."

"Think she still lives here?"

"I wouldn't know."

"Only one way to find out."

And before I can stop him Jake is jogging across the street, bound for the front door of the place I entered a virgin and exited a confused man all those years ago.

"Jake, stop!"

He ignores me. He climbs the three steps to the door, rings the bell, and stands there waiting. I run to catch up with him, and when I get there—it seems to take years!—the door opens and an old lady in a loose nightgown is standing there.

It's Fran, all right. Her hair has gone salt-and-pepper, mostly salt, and she's gained at least fifty pounds, but those angry eyes are absolutely unmistakable, peering out of a moon face. She looks at Jake as if he's just pissed on her doorstep.

"Hello, ma'am."

"What do you want?"

Her voice is both whiny and demanding, as if her vocal cords have been marinating in bile since the last time I saw her. She keeps her gaze on Jake and barely gives me a glance. I doubt she would recognize me anyway, a kid she fucked in the dark and chased away before dawn, but you never know.

"My father and I are lost," Jake says. "Could you tell us the way to Holy Cross High School?"

"It's around the corner." Fran lifts an arm to point, the flesh between the shoulder and the elbow loose and swinging. When she brings her hand back down, I see that it grips a cagelike contraption, which Fran's other hand is already gripping. It's a walker, a four-legged aluminum walker. The first woman I ever had sex with is crippled. Somehow it would have been easier to learn that she was dead.

"I'm sorry we made you come to the door," Jake says.

"Yeah, I just had a hip replacement. Lots o' laughs. Anything else, kid?"

"No, ma'am. You have a nice day."

We turn to leave, and Jake is all but whispering when he asks, "Is that her, Dad?"

"Yes, it's her."

"*Wow. . . .*"

Then suddenly Fran's shrill voice seems to pierce my back instead of my ears, as if she's thrown a dart:

"Wait! Get back here!"

Oh my God. She's recognized me. It's taken a moment for the penny to drop, but she's picked me out of the rubble of her past, and now she wants a word with the boy-man who never came back for seconds.

Together we trudge back to Fran's stoop. She's still at the doorway, clutching the walker as if it owes her money.

I look her right in the eye this time, figuring I have nothing to lose. If she wants to yell at me, I can take my penance like a man. Fran studies my face, then Jake's.

"I shouldn't let you in my house," she begins cautiously, "but I have a table I want moved and I'm thinking you two can do it for me."

"We'd be delighted," says my son, who gives Fran a moment to back up in her walker before entering the house and beckoning for me to follow. Resigned to whatever's going to happen next, I follow my son into the dwelling I have never once returned to, even in my dreams.

Fran obviously lives alone. The place hasn't been painted in a long time and there's a faint odor of urine in the air. There's a bedpan in plain sight, on the floor beside the threadbare couch, the same one Fran and I sat on before heading up to her bedroom.

Fran's heavy body shuffles along, preceded by the walker. What the hell had happened to her? Back in the day she was slim, or at least trim, a woman on the brink of middle age doing her best to fight the clock. But as always the clock wins, even if the fight goes the full fifteen rounds.

"Follow me," she says to Jake, the exact words she used with me when it was time to go to her bedroom. But Fran's stair-climbing days are clearly over. I notice that there's a cot in the corner of the living room. Fran is stuck on the first floor of this lousy house for the rest of her wretched life. The walking contraption makes squeaking sounds as we follow Fran to the kitchen, where she gestures with a jerk of her chin at a battered Formica-topped table.

"I want that table on the other side of the kitchen, against the wall," she says. "The chairs, too. You think you can handle it?"

We can handle it, all right. Jake takes one side of the table and I get the other, and in less than a minute we have the table and chairs where Fran wants them.

"Anything else?" Jake asks.

Fran shakes her head. "That's it for now. My sons would have done this for me, but they're both useless. They take after their father that way."

"I'm sorry to hear that," Jake says.

"Not as sorry as I am to say it. Notice my lawn? They've been meaning to cut it for about a month now. They *mean* to do a lot of things for me that never get done."

Suddenly she's staring at my face, and I'm staring right back. It's hard to believe that I have a history with this woman, that if she hadn't taken whatever precautions she took we could have had a child who'd now be closing in on his thirtieth birthday.

"Do I know you?" Fran asks, almost gently.

I swallow, long and hard. "I don't think so."

"You from around here?"

"Used to be."

"You're from around here and you don't know where the high school is?"

"I've been gone a long time."

The three of us stand there for a few moments in silence, looking at each other. Fran eases herself into a kitchen chair and says, "I hope you guys aren't waiting for a tip."

"No, ma'am," Jake says.

Fran points toward the door. "You can let yourselves out. Slam the door behind you, it's self-locking. And here's a tip. Don't get old." Her eyes mist up. "You hear what I'm saying? Don't get old."

We mumble our good-byes and let ourselves out.

Jake is calm, but I'm hyperventilating to the point where I could use a paper bag to breathe into.

"Jake. I cannot believe you did what you just did."

Jake is shaking his head. "She just might be the saddest person I've ever seen."

"She was sad thirty years ago, too."

Jake catches my elbow, pulls me to a stop. "We can't just leave."

"What do you want to do?"

"The least we can do is cut the grass for her."

He says it plainly, as if this idea is the most obvious thing in the world.

"Are you serious?"

"Come on, Dad, don't think about it. Let's just *do* it."

It's an amazing idea, a crazy idea, a beautiful idea, an idea I never could have had. My boy has a heart, and it's in the right place.

The same old shed is on the side of Fran's property. It's in a state of near collapse, but the sliding door still opens. The same long-neglected tools are still in there, including an old-fashioned push mower and a crusty old pair of scissor-type hedge clippers. I pick up the clippers and make a few practice chopping motions. I find a can of Three-In-One oil and squirt some on its axis.

"Might as well do the hedges while we're at it," I say. "Go ahead, kid, take the mower. The lawn's all yours."

I can see that Jake is looking forward to it, like a kid about to ride his first roller coaster. He's a city boy. He's never cut a lawn before.

Jake has to lean his full weight on the mower to make it move through the high grass. The lawn is thick and mulchy, and I know he's going to have to cut it, rake it, and cut it again to do the job right. Meanwhile, I'm hacking away at the hedges, trying to restore the rectangular shape I imagine they once had.

We work for at least ten or fifteen minutes before Fran appears at the door in open-mouthed shock. "What the hell's going on here?!"

"We're helping you out," Jake says.

Fran raises an admonishing finger. "I didn't ask for this. I'm not paying for this!"

"Don't worry, we're not charging you," Jake assures her.

Fran is freaking out. She's breathing hard as she says, "You are both trespassing. I'm going to call the police and report you for trespassing!"

Jake doesn't know what to say. I set the hedge clipper down, walk to the base of the steps, and look up at Fran, who is not used to people doing anything nice for her. Unlike Blanche Dubois, she has never relied on the kindness of strangers.

But I am no stranger, and it's time for her to know that.

"Lady," I begin calmly, "you and I spent a night together a long time ago. You might not remember it because it only happened once and we'd both had a lot to drink, but I sure remember it because it was the first time I'd ever been with a woman."

Fran puts her hand to her throat. She doesn't quite trust me, but she senses that I am not lying. She hangs her head like a sinner.

"I went a little crazy when me and my husband split," she says, staring down at her slippers. "I don't remember much from those days."

"You gave me a bicycle."

She looks at me in shock. "I *did*?"

"I was working deliveries for Napoli's, and somebody stole my delivery bike, so you gave me your husband's old bike."

"Christ! I always thought somebody stole that bike!"

"No. You gave it to me. Got me out of a jam."

"What's your name?"

"That's another thing. You wouldn't let me tell you my name."

"Tell me now."

I tell her. The hand at her throat moves to cover her mouth as her eyes widen. Then she drops her hand and says, "You're Mary Sullivan's boy!"

"That's right."

Jake turns to me. "Your mother's name was Mary?"

I can't answer him. All I can do is return Fran's stare. Her eyes are moist, and she grips the handles of her walker as if she's about to blast off into space.

"I don't remember that night," she says gently. "But I'm sure I wasn't very pleasant company for you."

"I was no picnic, either. My mother had just died. It wasn't an easy time for either of us." I turn and gesture at Jake, who's resting his hairy chin on the lawn mower handle.

"This is my son, Jake. It was his idea to do the yard work."

"Thank you, Jake."

"You're welcome."

"We'll finish up and leave," I say.

"No!"

Fran's voice is like iron, the voice I recall from our night together. "You finish up, and then we'll have lunch."

"Oh, you don't have to—"

"I'm making lunch," Fran says, and without another word she's back inside, slamming the door behind her.

Jake looks at me. "Looks like we have lunch plans."

"Looks like."

An hour later we're all seated around the Formica table Jake and I moved for Fran, eating grilled cheese sandwiches and drinking iced tea. Outside, the lawn is twice-mown and raked, and the privet hedges have been hacked into rectangular shapes. I've even spaded the soil around the base of the hedges, to give the place a touch of class. Jake and I have filled four big black plastic bags with clippings and trimmings, neatly lined along the curb for the garbage man.

I fear that Fran will want to talk about our bumbling, stumbling night together, but luckily she doesn't. There's nothing much to say, really—we both know it was a drunken collision between two desperate people. Truth is, Fran seems far more interested in Jake than she does in me. She reaches out and strokes his hair.

"Your grandmother had hair like this," she says. "Same beautiful shine."

Jake stops chewing. "Really?"

"Oh yes. Shame you never knew her. What a woman she was!" Fran turns to me. "I'd say she was just about the most . . . *religious* person I ever knew."

I swallow some grilled cheese, nod. "She was big in church activities, yeah."

"That's not what I'm talking about. I'm talking about the way she *treated* people. It's not as if I even knew her well. I wasn't much of a churchgoer. But when my husband walked out on me, who do you think showed up at my door with a casserole?" She smiles at the memory of it. "It was one of those Italian dishes, with that weird black vegetable Italians like so much."

"Eggplant parmigiana," I say.

"That's right! That was it! Something I could never make myself. And she didn't make a big *deal* out of it. She just said, 'I hear you're having some trouble, so I made extra.' That's the kind of person she was."

Jake is absolutely transfixed by Fran's words. He now knows more about his grandmother than I have ever told him.

"Nice thing to do," Jake says.

"It certainly was." Fran turns to me. "Heart attack, wasn't it?"

"Yeah."

Fran strains to remember more. "Wasn't there something unusual about it?"

I force myself to shrug. "Only that she was young. Just turned thirty-nine."

Her brow remains knotted for a moment, then relaxes. Luckily for me Fran was a casual Catholic whose memory has obviously been ravaged by years of boozing.

"Well, if there's a heaven, she went straight there, I can tell you that," she says. "Really a saintly person." She smiles at Jake, frowns at me. "Can't say I thought the same of your father. Little bit of a brute, wasn't he? Whatever became of him, anyway?"

She doesn't know. She stays in this house, trapped by her crumbling hips, so she doesn't know what goes on in the neighborhood.

"He died a few years after my mother," I finally say.

"He did? From what?"

"Heart attack."

"*Both* parents had heart attacks?" Fran says. "Jeez, that doesn't bode well for you, does it?"

"I try not to think about it."

"I'd get a checkup, if I were you."

"I'll think about it."

"I can't believe I didn't know about your father dying! Not that I ever hear anything much. I don't exactly get around these days. . . . Listen, I'm sorry I said that nasty thing about him."

"It's okay. You're absolutely right. He could be a brute, all right."

I can sense Jake's excitement. He's stumbled into this mother lode of information about his ancestors, and he's going to make the most of it.

"What made him a brute?" Jake asks.

"Jake, I—"

That's as far as I get. Jake holds a hand up to silence me, without even looking at me. "I was asking Fran, Dad."

I shut my mouth. Fran can't help cackling with glee as she says, "He liked to mix it up once in a while at Charlie's Bar."

Jake's eyes widen. "My grandfather was a barroom brawler?"

Fran nods, gulps iced tea. "I once saw him knock a guy out with one punch. And it wasn't as if he was a big man, your grandfather. Had to stand on his tiptoes to reach the other guy's chin!"

Jake and Fran are laughing out loud. I feel as if the walls of this house are closing in on me.

"We've got to get going," I say. "I promised Jake I'd show him the house I grew up in."

Fran shakes her head. "I still can't believe I didn't know about your father passing."

"We sort of kept it quiet. There wasn't a wake or anything."

"No wake!"

"He wanted to be cremated, and then we scattered his ashes at sea. He was in the navy when he was a kid."

"He was a character, all right. I'm sorry you lost him."

"Me, too."

Fran insists on accompanying us to the door. She shakes hands with me, but takes Jake in a full embrace. He has to jackknife his body to allow for Fran's walker.

"You're a nice boy. Stay that way."

"I'll try," Jake says. It's dawning on me that all my exes—Doris, Margie, Fran—like Jake a hell of a lot more than they ever liked me.

"Thanks for doing the yard work," Fran says. "Gonna call my sons and tell 'em it's done, and while I'm at it I'll tell 'em to go to hell." She shuts the door behind us, and it seems fitting that the last word I'll ever hear her speak is "hell."

I'm walking, but I can't feel my feet. I feel dizzy, as if I've just given blood.

"That," I tell Jake, "was the most surreal experience of my life."

He doesn't seem to hear me. There's a dreamy look on his face as he asks, "Did your mother really have hair like mine?"

"In fact, she did."

"How cool is *that*? I inherited my grandmother's hair! Can you tell me more about her? Was that eggplant dish one of her specialties?"

"Let's sit awhile," I say as we come upon a wooden bench at a bus stop. I sit down, but Jake is too restless to join me. He paces back and forth, like a fighter eager for the bell.

"Dad, why did Fran say there was something unusual about your mother's death?"

"Jake—"

"She was trying to remember it, and you got all nervous."

"Jake. Listen to me."

"I'm listening."

"I can tell you some more things about my mother, but first you have to understand why it's taken so long for me to . . . get around to it."

"All right."

"Are you sure? Because this is serious stuff."

"How serious?"

"Very serious."

"Just tell me, Dad."

"I don't think you understand what I mean when I say *serious*. This is something I've never told anybody, not even . . . myself."

"Dad. What the hell happened?"

A bus stops in front of us. The driver opens the door and waits for us to board, shakes his head when we don't, and pulls away. I take a deep breath, absorbing mostly bus fumes.

"Well, I pretty much killed my mother, is what happened."

CHAPTER THIRTEEN

Jake stops pacing and sits beside me, gazing at me in total disbelief. In the past twenty-four hours he's seen his father go from embittered tabloid journalist to unemployed loser to confessed murderer. Could I be telling the truth? For the first time all weekend, my son seems frightened.

"Dad. Come on."

"You heard me."

"What'd you do, shoot her? Stab her?"

"Nothing that obvious."

"Poison?"

"Nope."

"Jesus, Dad, what the hell are you saying?"

"I'm saying I have to tell this story my own way, and it's probably going to take me a little while because I've never told it before, *ever*, to *anybody*, so you just sit there and don't interrupt and maybe, just *maybe* I can do this thing."

Jake sits as quietly as a bird watcher. Overhead, a mockingbird sings in the branches of a silver oak tree. I let him go through his repertoire of imitations before clearing my throat and beginning the tale of something I've kept buried for more than thirty years to a boy who's only been alive for seventeen years. It is a story of death that is dying to be told, and once I start telling it, I cannot stop.

Mary DiFrancesco Sullivan was a quiet person, a somewhat stout woman who just wanted to be a wife and a mother—or, looking back on it, maybe just a mother.

Then again, maybe she just wanted to be a saint. And if you want to be a saint, it's going to mean trouble for any mere mortals who happen to live with you.

The funny thing is she didn't like trouble. She hated conflict, hated shouting and loudness of any kind. That's one reason she didn't like going to the movies, because they were always so loud—the screaming, the booming music, the explosions. The only movie I ever remember her admiring was *The Song of Bernadette*, which tells the story of the young girl who discovered the magical healing waters at Lourdes.

We actually had a bottle of water from Lourdes in the house. My mother dabbed it on my forehead whenever I had a fever. My father said it was tap water, and that he wished he'd thought of a scam that sweet.

Ahhh, my father.

Danny Sullivan was one of the loudest and most confrontational people in the world. Nobody could understand how he and my mother ever hooked up. In my mind I always figured that he must have repeatedly hollered out his proposal, and she agreed to marry him if he would promise to lower his voice.

That's a cartoony version of what might have happened, but even cartoons contain a germ of truth. She was a sheltered Italian girl who'd never been far from home, while my old man had seen quite a bit of the planet's watery surface during his two hitches in the navy.

He made his living as a subway motorman, but my old man never really left the navy. Around the house he was always using terms like "shipshape" and "swab the deck," and the fact that I was never in any branch of the armed services probably galled him. If I'd been drafted and killed in Vietnam he would have cherished my memory, but the war ended before I turned eighteen and he was stuck with the reality of a living, breathing, moody teenager instead of a corpse that could not disappoint him.

One Sunday afternoon when I was about five years old my father fell asleep watching a football game on TV. He looked so comical lying there on the couch—hair askew, socks halfway off his feet, hairy belly exposed—that I couldn't help giggling at the sight of him. Just then my mother appeared with his usual Sunday lunch on a tray—a longneck bottle of Budweiser, and a tuna salad sandwich on Wonder Bread. She was a wonderful cook, but this was the sort of food he preferred to eat. She looked at him, turned to me and said, "Sure gets quiet around here when he's asleep, doesn't it?"

We both covered our mouths to muffle our laughter. Nobody had to say a word about it, but in that moment, we became secret allies against the head of the house, a man we both suspected was a bit of a buffoon.

When it came to everyday life, just about everything went his way—where we went on vacation, what colors the rooms were painted—until it was time for me to attend school. That's when my father found out that his wife not only contained a spine— she contained a spine that did not bend a millimeter on issues that mattered to her.

The old man wanted me to attend public school, free of charge, but my mother insisted that I attend a Catholic school. Personally I was indifferent to the issue but fascinated by the way she calmly and quietly stood her ground while he ranted and raved about what a waste of money Catholic school would be. He'd go on and on about it, and when he'd pause for breath she'd all but whisper matter-of-factly, "He's going to Catholic school." She almost sounded bored when she said it, and he didn't know how to handle that.

All those years he'd thought he was in charge. Now he knew that he wasn't. It was just that up until this point, his decisions hadn't interfered with her passions. She didn't mind conflict when one of her passions was at stake.

To make matters worse for my father, he was faced with an opponent who refused to behave as if a conflict was even going on. It drove him crazy. He literally pulled at his hair in frustration. The night it all came to a head I hid at the top of the stairs, a terrified five-year-old whose future was the subject of a raging battle going on downstairs.

"What the hell do you want him to be?" my father roared. "A *priest?*"

"No," she said. "I just know that Catholic school will be better for his soul."

"His *soul!*"

"You heard me."

"What's the *real* reason, Mary? Come on."

"I just told you the real reason. Also, he won't have to face a negative element in Catholic school."

"Oh, you mean niggers?"

"Danny! That's a *horrible* word."

"Really? What's worse, Mary, saying a word like 'niggers' or taking your kid out of a perfectly good school system to *avoid* them?"

"We are not having this conversation."

"Oh yes, we are. Listen to me. This is the world, woman. People are people. They flood in and out of my subway cars every day and let me tell you, you might as well get to know them all, *especially* the black ones, because he will be dealing with them, one way or another. They are not exactly an endangered species."

"Oh God, Danny, the way you *speak!*"

"I speak plainly, free of bullshit. You should try it some time. You're sheltered, Mary. You sing in the choir and you bring food to sick parishoners because you think it buys you points in heaven—"

"I do these things because I *like* doing them!"

"Fine. Great. But I notice that all the people you help are white Catholics who believe in the same hocus-pocus as you."

"My faith is *not* hocus-pocus!!"

"Your answer to our son's education certainly is! Abracadabra, hocus-pocus! Stick him in Catholic school, and nothing bad can happen to him!"

"Do you *want* bad things to happen to him?"

"I want *life* to happen to him! I don't want somebody telling him to say a prayer and light a candle when he should be figuring out ways to solve his own problems!"

They were silent down there for a few heartbeats, and then my mother cleared her throat and said, "Hear what I say, Danny. Sammy is going to St. Aloysius School in the fall."

"We'll see about that."

"We certainly will."

I had to run to my room because my mother was coming up the stairs to go to bed, while my father slammed the front door on his way to Charlie's Bar. When he came in that night, he slept in the spare bedroom for the first time. It wouldn't be the last time.

She was a true believer, my mother, attending the eleven o'clock Mass each Sunday and the seven o'clock Mass every morning during Lent. I went with her on Sundays, but she was on her own during Lent.

My father never went to church at all. She never even tried to get him to go. All her willpower was focused on one issue, the school issue, and at last he caved in. It was the first marital battle he'd ever lost.

The night before I was due to enroll at St. Aloysius, he did a strange thing. He'd been spending his spare time scraping the outside walls of the house to prepare it for a paint job. Now, at the dinner table, he announced that he was ready to start painting, and he wanted my mother to pick a color.

He was giving her a choice! Nothing like this had ever happened before!

My mother was both stunned and suspicious as she thought it over. He even gave her the sample sheets provided by Benjamin Moore, so she could study the little circles of paint before making up her mind.

She pored over the sheets for an hour. At last she decided she'd like the house to be painted robin's egg blue. The previous color had been yellow.

"You sure that's what you want, Mary?"

"Yes, Danny. Anything but that terrible yellow."

"You got it, girl."

He stayed behind the next day when we went to St. Aloysius. The enrollment process took most of the morning, and when we got home he was up on a ladder with a bucket, painting our little clapboard house. We stood and watched him, stunned at the sight. Suddenly his once-in-a-marriage offer made sense.

"How do you like that, Sammy?" my mother said. "Your father got even."

He certainly had, and it was a master stroke, both literally and figuratively.

There he stood on the ladder, almost gleefully spreading bright yellow paint on the clapboard walls. He'd put a couple of empty cans in the curbside garbage pail, and I could read the labels: canary yellow. It was probably the brightest shade they made.

My mother looked at our rapidly yellowing house, took a deep breath, and began walking toward the ladder. My father glanced over his shoulder at us, but didn't miss a stroke. I was so anxious that my heart felt as if it might pound right out of my chest. Would he pour the paint on her head? Would she pull the ladder away from the wall and make him fall?

This was it. They were going to kill each other, and I was going to be an orphan!

God, I had so much to learn about marital conflict. Sometimes you blow up on the spot, other times you let things marinate. My mother, I was learning, could marinate with the best of them. All she did when she got to the base of the ladder was ask my father if he needed any help.

"From who, you?" he asked, not taking his eyes off his work. "Forget it. You'd paint the Stations of the Cross all over the house. We'd have people genuflecting as they passed by."

"Whatever you say, Danny," she said pleasantly. She turned to me and winked. War had officially been declared at the Sullivan household, and it was us against him.

I didn't like that. I didn't like it at all. For the first time, I wished I had a brother, or a sister—somebody to be a true ally in this house where the uneasy peace we'd always known was gone for good.

I had to wear a green blazer with the school insignia on a patch over my breast pocket, and whenever my father saw me wearing it he'd throw me a mock salute.

"Closest thing you'll ever get to a uniform!" he'd say.

The school cost about five hundred bucks a year, and he loved reminding my mother about how many times he had to make the subway trip from South Ferry to The Bronx to make five hundred bucks. It was actually a bullshit complaint, because by this time she'd taken a job as a receptionist at a medical center and was paying the tuition out of her own pocket.

The years passed. I graduated from St. Aloysius and moved on to Holy Cross High School. By this time I was working after school and weekends to make my own money, so I could pay for my books and my lunches. Everything seemed to be going pretty well, except that I was going to burn in hell for masturbating so much.

Yes, indeed. The catechism we studied in religion class said it was "seriously sinful, when deliberately indulged in."

A great bit of information, eh? The sort of thing I never would have been taught, had I attended public school. And I believed it. I believed I was indulging in something that was seriously sinful.

That didn't stop me from doing it, every chance I had. I wasn't trying to be evil. On top of my raging hormones I just needed a little something to help me cut the tension in the house, and nothing worked better than masturbation. I was losing my soul, and there wasn't even anybody I could talk to about it.

I kept going to Sunday Mass with my mother, but I stopped receiving Holy Communion, because I knew I was not in a "state of grace." While everyone around me got up to take the magical wafer on their tongues I sat there alone among the pews, like a leper. My mother wanted to know what was wrong. Then she *demanded* to know what was wrong.

I would not say. I was shy to the point of mortification, and for the first time ever my mother and I were butting heads.

It was killing me. By this time conflict with the old man was a living state, like arthritis—I barely even noticed it anymore. But all it took was one sad-eyed look from my mother, and I was on the floor.

We grew further and further apart. She upped her own dosage of church, going every weekday morning to the seven o'clock Mass, Lent or no Lent. I still went with her on Sunday mornings, but one Sunday morning in September of my senior year I decided that routine was about to change.

I was nervous about what I had to do, so nervous that I'd jerked myself off both the night before and on the morning of my big announcement, and during the morning session I actually heard the church bells pealing for the ten o'clock Mass. I was both drained and nervous when my mother appeared at the door to my bedroom half an hour later to tell me to get ready for "the eleven."

She was already dressed, a vision in black. The dress was snug on her because she'd been gaining a lot of weight, but it was still her favorite going-to-church dress. It made her look like a widow. Wishful thinking, I guess.

"You want to start getting ready," she said. It was what she'd said to me on a hundred Sunday mornings, but not until now did I realize what a strange sentence it was. She was telling me what I wanted to do. How can anyone, even your mother, tell you what you *want* to do?

She couldn't—not anymore. I pulled the covers to my throat, took a deep breath, and let it fly. "Mom. I'm not going."

She stood her ground, stunned but undeterred. I hoped she'd go away, but she didn't.

She stared at me. "Are you sick?"

"No."

"Then why aren't you going?"

"Because it's all bullshit."

She let out a cry I can still hear in nightmares, an inhuman sound, the wail of an animal caught in a steel-jawed trap. Down the hall, I could hear my father snoring. He went out drinking every Saturday night just so he could stick it to my my mother by sleeping late and nursing a hangover well into Sunday afternoon.

My mother stared at me in wide-eyed disbelief, as if I'd morphed into someone else, an absolute stranger, or maybe something even worse than a stranger . . . her husband.

She put a hand on the wall for support. "What exactly is bullshit?"

It was stunning to hear her use the word, even in this context.

"All of it," I replied.

"Church?"

"Yes."

"Prayer?"

"Absolutely."

"God?"

"There is no God."

She turned the color of cement. I hadn't really meant what I'd said about God, but it was too late. The harpoon had found its mark, right through her heart. She even put her hands to her chest, as if she meant to grab the wooden shaft and yank it out, but instead she let her hands fall to her sides and gave me a smile both sad and pitying.

"I'm very sorry to hear you say that," she said calmly, and I could see that her strength was returning. It was remarkable, almost scary that someone who'd been jarred so thoroughly could rally so fast. She was looking at me in a way she'd never looked at me before.

She was looking at me the way she looked at my father.

"Oh, Samuel," she said in a voice that was soft but not gentle, "I've done all I could, but now my worst nightmare has come true. You have become your father."

My scalp tingled. "Hey, Mom—"

"I fought it as hard as I could, but I can't fight it anymore. Go ahead and be what he is. Forget the church. It's too difficult a life, isn't it? The time it takes, the discipline . . ." She sighed deeply. "I just wanted you to have a rich life. I didn't think it was too much to ask, or expect."

"All right, all right, I'm coming with you."

"Why? So you can sit there and sulk? Sit there like a stone, refusing to receive Holy Communion? What's the point?"

"Let me get dressed—"

"No." She held up a hand. "You don't understand. I don't *want* you there. I *forbid* you to come with me."

I could not believe what I'd just heard. Blood pounded in my temples. The world was collapsing all around me, as I stared at this stranger who used to be my mother.

"Mommy?"

"Go back to sleep for a few more hours. I guess that's all you're good for, anyway." She patted my foot, like a doctor comforting an invalid. "Sure, take the easy way. Be like your father. Don't respect anything. Make fun of the things people believe in. Lie in bed all day and pleasure yourself with your hand. You seem to be good at that."

She knew. *She knew!* My faced was burning. I wanted to pull the blanket up over my head, but I felt paralyzed. All I could do was lie there in bed while my best friend in the world became my mortal enemy.

She patted my foot. "I'm taking you out of Holy Cross. No point attending a school you don't believe in, is there?"

"Mom! I'm sorry!"

"No, you're not. What a waste of time it's been, trying to guide you. I should have realized it was hopeless long ago. Well, you know what they say—better late than never." She looked at her watch, forced a chilling smile. "Speaking of late, I'd better get going." She leaned over and pressed cold lips to my forehead in what was unmistakably a farewell kiss.

"I'm ashamed of you, Samuel. I never thought I could be, but I am."

She turned and left the room. I was trembling. I got out of bed and began pacing around in my underwear, thinking I could walk off the trembles, but this was a rumble that came all the way from the core of my being. It felt as if my head was going to burst. I heard her footsteps going downstairs. In another few seconds she'd be gone. My bedroom window overlooked our front path. I opened it, leaned on the windowsill, and waited for her to appear.

There she was, directly below me. I didn't know what I was

going to say, but I had to say something. All the rage and frustrations of my seventeen years had become twisted into one hard, ugly knot, which fit rather neatly into the slingshot of my mind. It was time to let it fly.

"Hey, Mom. Up here."

She stopped, turned, looked up at me with what appeared to be mild curiosity. I could have spit on her from there, but that's not what I did. If only that was what I'd done!

What I did was to clear my throat and say, slowly and clearly, "I wish you were dead."

I was jolted by the sound of my own voice, but there was no way to unsay what I said, no way to pretend I didn't mean it. At that moment, I meant every word of it. My mother's eyes widened, and then she was smiling at me in a horrible, knowing way.

"I'm sure you do, Samuel," she replied. "Shame you don't believe in God anymore. You could pray for me to die."

She winked at me, kissed her fingertips, and blew me a kiss before turning to resume her walk to church. Anyone watching this scene from across the street would have thought it was a mother and son exchanging loving words on a Sunday morning. I watched her go until she reached the end of the block and turned the corner, and then I knew exactly what I had to do.

I started packing to get out of that madhouse, once and for all.

I had no idea of where I was going, but I had to be out before my hungover father woke up and before my fanatical mother returned. I had maybe an hour.

Where could I go? I'd never been anywhere. I had a little over five hundred dollars in the house, saved up from all my odd jobs, and I figured that would be enough to take me someplace far from Flushing.

Plans raced through my head, like desperate ghosts chasing each other. I'll rent an apartment (where?) . . . I'll get a job (doing what?) . . . I didn't know. How could I know? I was seventeen years old. All I could do was focus on the job at hand, which was to get all my stuff together and hit the road, *any* road, in any direction. The mission was all about motion, not destination.

I had to get a suitcase from the spare bedroom where my father slumbered. The curtains were closed. It was dark and hot, reeking of his sour beer breath. He continued his openmouthed snoring while I yanked the biggest suitcase I could find out of the closet, causing a minor avalanche of clothes and shoes that did not wake him.

I packed rapidly, taking only what I considered to be the essentials, but I still had to sit on the suitcase so I could get it closed. I hefted the thing—it was heavy, but I figured I could carry it to the bus stop if I got it up on my shoulder. I rolled all but twenty dollars of my money into a bankroll, stuck it in a sock, tied a knot in the end of it, and shoved it into the zipper pocket of my Windbreaker. Then I slipped the twenty dollar bill into my pocket, and made sure I had exact change for the bus. At last, I was ready to go.

My father was still snoring. Mass was still in session. I was going to make it, going to do this thing. I hefted the suitcase and started for the stairs. It was going to be a brand-new life for me, away from the two of them. I'd call them later today, or maybe tomorrow, or maybe never. The main thing was, I'd be out of it. Never again would I be stuck in the middle of the madness.

I got down the stairs and already I was breathing hard from the weight of the suitcase. I figured maybe I should open it up and leave some of my stuff behind, lighten up.

No, I decided—no more delays. Catch your breath, pick up the bag, and go.

And that's what I meant to do, with every fiber of my being, except the phone started ringing as if it meant to jump off the hook. On the fifth ring I heard my father answer the upstairs phone in his gruff-sleepy voice, which I knew very well, followed

by a cry of despair I didn't think could possibly come from a
man like him.

My mother dropped dead on the way to the communion rail
that morning, less than an hour after I told her that I wished she
was dead. She was not yet forty years old, but she was overweight
and her heart had had enough.

That's what everybody said, anyway. I was the only one who
knew better.

A doctor standing behind her on the communion line did his
best to revive her, but he was a podiatrist, and apparently anything north of the ankles was unexplored terrain for him. He probably couldn't have done anything anyway. She was, as the priest
distributing communion wafers put it, "dead before she hit the
floor."

More than that, she was dead before the final communion
wafer could be placed on her tongue, and there were more than
a few whispered laments in and about the church over this. Not
that my mother hadn't died in a state of grace—if there was a
perfect parishoner, she was it. But that last wafer on her tongue
would have been the cherry on the sundae, the golden pass to
fling the Pearly Gates wide open for her arrival. Another ten or
fifteen heartbeats, and she might have made it.

The phone call to our house had come from the pastor, who
told my father that his wife had collapsed on the way to communion. He grabbed me and the two of us literally ran to church.
He'd pulled on last night's clothes and reeked of dead cigarette
smoke, and he was literally whimpering as we burst into the
church. I'd been there the Sunday before, of course, but this was
probably my father's first time inside a church since his wedding
day.

My mother was stretched out on her back, right where she'd
fallen. Somebody had placed a pillow beneath her head, and a

priest's vestment was draped over her body. There was an odd grin on her face, as if God had whispered the all-time joke into her ear just before stopping her heart. Her eyes were open, gazing straight up at the ceiling, through it, beyond it.

"Oh, Mary. Ohhh, Mary, what happened?"

Tears began to flow from my father's eyes, but not mine. Everybody thought I was in a state of shock, but that wasn't it. I was a murderer, and murderers don't cry.

And through the shattering, stunning, beyond-belief grief I couldn't help marveling at the power of this woman. In the last moments of her life, my mother had managed to defy all odds and get both me and my father to go to church.

An ambulance took the body away. My father and I went home to get ready to do all the things you do when a member of your family dies. My father was so completely out of it that he never even asked about the giant suitcase I'd packed, even though he practically tripped over it on his way up the stairs.

From then on, it was all a blur—the arrangements with the funeral parlor, the burial out on Long Island, the visits from casserole-carrying neighbors . . . How strange it was to be on the receiving end of sympathy casseroles! Through it all, I never told my father the fatal words I'd spoken to her before she went to church that final day. I never told anybody, until now.

Jake stares at me as I reach the end of the story, the way people look at a priest after a truly heartfelt sermon.

"Jesus, Dad. That's pretty . . . operatic."

"Let me say it now, if I've failed to mention it before, Jake— masturbation is not a sin."

"Never thought it was."

"In fact, it's probably the leading prevention of violent crimes."

Jake grins, shakes his head. "You okay?"

"Pretty good, considering that I killed my mother."

"You didn't kill her!"

"Were you listening to me? Did you hear what I said to her? I told her I wished she was dead. Minutes later, she died."

"I say shocking shit to Mom all the time, and she's still alive."

"What kind of shit?"

"Like, 'I refuse to take any more fucking cello lessons.' Things like that. I may even have told her to drop dead once or twice."

"That's different. 'Drop dead' is an *expression*, something you say when you're angry. What I said was mean and cruel and . . . *deliberate*."

"She said some pretty nasty things to you, too."

"Not as bad as what I said."

"Dad. You're wrong. You're blaming yourself for no reason."

"I think there's a reason."

"Is that why you dropped out of school?"

"I dropped out because none of it made any sense to me anymore."

"I can relate to that."

"My father had no problem with it. He thought I was going to enroll at the local public school. He got the tuition back and left it all to me."

And as I speak those words, I remember claiming my own tuition refund from Peter Plymouth, just yesterday. My God. History repeats itself yet again in the Sullivan family.

"Hang on, hang on," Jake says. "Your father left it up to *you* to find a new school and enroll there?"

"Correct."

"So you just didn't bother enrolling?"

"That's about the size of it. By the time he found out what I'd done, I was a copyboy at the *New York Star*. Got a taste of ink, and that was that. Had my first byline when I was eighteen, and two years later I was a full-time reporter. No way I was ever going to sit in a classroom again."

"How'd you get the job at the *Star*?"

"I . . . sort of knew somebody there."

"Who?"

"It doesn't matter. Point is, I went and did it."

Jake slumps back on the bench, awed by what he's heard. "The balls on you, Dad!"

I have to admit, it's a good thing to hear. "Yeah, I guess it did take balls. It was also a stupid thing to do."

"Why?"

"Because my life could have been different. It could have been better."

"You think?"

"Sure. With the right education, I could have gone another way, instead of wasting my life cranking out crap for the *New York Star.*"

"Yeah, but I never would have been born."

"Excuse me?"

"You'd never have been a newspaperman, and you'd never have gone to that movie premiere, and you'd never have met Mom."

This kid of mine, and the things he comes out with.

"I guess you're right about that."

I'm actually feeling a little better. It feels good to unload my secret, the kind of good you feel when nausea finally passes and a light, cooling sweat breaks out all over your skin.

Jake pats my shoulder. "Everything happens for a reason, Dad."

"Is that so? Maybe I'll understand it better when I'm your age."

"I'm not just saying this stuff because I'm your son. You've been beating yourself up for a long time, and you should stop."

"How?"

"I don't know. But you deserve a break."

My face is wet. Tears are rolling down my cheeks. I cannot believe how hard my son is working to make me feel better. He actually wipes my tears with the back of his hand.

"You're quite a guy, Dad. You did amazing things with your life, when you were just a kid. A kid without a high school diploma!"

"Hey. That doesn't mean *you* don't need one."

"I know, I know."

"I *do* have an eighth grade diploma from St. Aloysius. And I won the English medal, if memory serves. Even then I could serve up the bullshit pretty good."

"Pretty *well.*"

"Yes, that's correct. I was just testing you. Glad to see they taught you some useful things at that school."

I smile at Jake, who shakes his head in wonder.

"Your father must have been pretty impressed with you."

"Nah, he barely knew what was going on in my life. We pretty much just coexisted in the house after my mother died. We ate in front of the TV to break the silence. I'm sure he was relieved when I moved out."

"Why?"

I sigh, shrug, rub my eyes. "He probably suspected that I'd upset her badly just before she died."

"No way!"

"Deep down, I think he blamed me for what happened."

"You should have told him what you told me! He'd have understood. It's too bad you didn't clear the air before he died."

My hands are shaking. I squeeze them together to calm them. Another bus stops and the driver opens the door for us and waits, until Jake waves him away.

"Thing of it is, Jake, the guy's still alive, as far as I know."

CHAPTER FOURTEEN

Jake's eyes widen and then sparkle as his face breaks into an astonished grin. "My grandfather is *alive!*"

"Well, he might be. I haven't seen or heard from him in a long time."

"So he *didn't* have a heart attack!"

"Last I knew he had the heart of a bull, along with the stubbornness of one."

"Dad. You lied to me."

"I'm sorry. I don't know how many apologies I can make to you, but every time I think I'm done, there's always one more."

"You lied to Fran, too. You told her he was buried at sea!"

"I can live with lying to Fran."

Jake is too amazed by the news to stay mad at me. "How long since you last saw him?"

"Since . . . well, the day you were born."

"He came to the hospital!"

"Yes, Jake."

"Whoa! So he *saw* me! He actually *knows* about me!"

"Yes, he . . . yes."

"So he knows Mom, too!"

"Yes, they've met. They weren't exactly each other's biggest fans."

"Holy shit. This is *amazing!*"

"Listen, he *might* be dead. But I never got a phone call from anybody asking me to claim his body, and I'm his only blood relative."

"Besides me."

"Sorry, Jake, sorry. That's right. Besides you."

"Or maybe he remarried, Dad. If he remarried and died, his wife could have buried him."

"Believe me, he did *not* remarry. If Danny Sullivan is alive, he's by himself. At least I hope so, for the sake of women everywhere."

"Danny Sullivan," Jake says, savoring the name. "Sounds like a tough Irish middleweight!"

"Funny you should say that. He did a little boxing when he was in the navy, plus the Saturday night fistfights at Charlie's Bar."

"Dad—"

"Don't even dream it, son."

"We *have* to."

"No, we don't. We've all gotten along for a long time without seeing each other."

Jake spreads his hands. "You wouldn't have told me about him if you didn't want to see him. And anyway, you already promised to show me the house. Did you mean it? Or was that just another lie?"

Jake's got me, and he knows it. He gets up, takes me by my elbow, and literally helps me to my feet. "Come on, Dad, it's time. Let's go. Lead the way."

And just like that we are on the way to my father's house, for the first time since I was a teenager.

Clearly, this is not shaping up to be one of our usual rent-a-movie and Chinese takeout weekends.

I'm walking a lot more slowly than I normally walk, savoring the sights. I've walked these streets a million times, but almost everything seems different. The sidewalks are new, and there are clumsy additions to some of the old houses, gobbling up the little bits of lawn that had been left, and there's lots of chintzy aluminum siding where once there was wooden clapboard.

But there's also something missing, and I suddenly realize what it is—it's kids. There are no kids out playing in the streets, like in the old days. They're all inside with their computer games, or having conversations with one another online, or sending each other text messages on their mobile phones.

The air grows heavier the closer we get, because my old house is only a few blocks from Flushing Bay. My knees are starting to quake. As a young reporter for the *Star* I'd climbed tenement steps and banged on doors in the city's worst neighborhoods, and never once did I feel so much as a tingle of fear. I felt invincible back then, and besides, I had nothing to lose.

Now I have things to lose. A son. My pride. My sanity, or what's left of it.

Jake senses my fear. "You okay, Dad?"

"I'm just doing the math. If he's alive, he's seventy-nine or eighty."

"Maybe he moved to Florida."

"No, Jake. My old man wasn't the type of person to budge. If he's alive, he's here in Flushing."

"Why'd you tell me he was dead?"

"You'll see when you meet him. *If* you meet him."

"I already met him, in a way."

"Well, yeah. Like I told you, he came to the hospital the day you were born, and that was the last we all saw of each other."

"I'll bet this has something to do with Mom."

"Since you brought it up . . ."

"What happened?"

"Well, it's your name."

"My name?"

"Your last name. Your mother insisted that her name went in there along with mine, so she wouldn't get 'wiped out,' as she put it. My old man took one look at the 'Perez-Sullivan' last name on the card over your bassinet, and he went nuts."

"Come on."

"Swear to God. He actually barged into the nursery with a black Magic Marker and crossed out the 'Perez' on the card. The nursery's supposed to be a sanitary area, and here's this lunatic with no gown and no mask, scrawling away. Somebody called security, and it took three guards to drag him out of the hospital."

Jake chuckles. "That's pretty funny."

"Yeah, well, your mother didn't think so. When I told her what happened she said, and I quote: 'The less our son has to do with that man, the better.' "

Jake is no longer chuckling. "That sounds like her, all right."

"Oh, she meant it. That was the end of it."

"You never saw him again?"

"Never saw him, never spoke with him." I sigh, long and hard. "It's less dramatic than it sounds, Jake. It's not as if we had a strong relationship going before the bassinet thing. Sometimes people just let go of each other. He didn't call us, and we didn't call him. And the years just passed."

Jake stops walking and takes my arm. His eyes are bright with tears that have not yet spilled over.

"I hope you don't let go of me," he says.

I take him in my arms, hugging as if we're both falling from the sky and sharing one parachute.

"Never happen," I say. "Never." And I hope to Christ I am telling the truth.

And as we hold each other, a funny thing happens, right there on that crooked little street in Queens. I can feel strength flowing from my son right through my arms, across my chest, and straight down my legs, where the quivering of my knees suddenly stops. I pull back from my son, wipe the tears from his eyes with a gentle knuckle.

"All right, then, Jake. Let's go see if this old bastard is still breathing."

The clapboard house is still standing, though the yellow paint is peeling and faded. Jake points at it from half a block away. "That's got to be it. Am I right?"

"You are right."

"Think he's alive?"

"We'll know soon enough."

A tall privet hedge blocks our view of the front lawn, but as we approach we can hear digging sounds, the scrape of steel against stone, and as we reach the front walk there he is on his knees, in jeans and a green T-shirt, prying up a chunk of cement with a crowbar.

He's got his back to us. His thick hair has gone completely white, the radiant white of a healthy old man, and it's cropped close to the scalp. All around him are pried-up chunks of the short cement path that used to lead from the front door to the sidewalk, and then I see a sledgehammer, which he's obviously used to smash the cement path to smithereens.

Sledgehammers and crowbars. So much for my premonitions about a feeble old man.

He wiggles the crowbar from side to side, loosens a chunk of cement, pulls it free with a groan of satisfaction, and chucks it aside. Now the entire path has been removed, down to the dirt. My father gets to his feet, and claps his gloved hands together to knock off the dirt. He turns toward the sidewalk and freezes at the sight of us standing there.

Except for the totally white hair, he hasn't changed very much since the day Jake was born. He's still as lean as a leopard, his big blue eyes twinkle with mischief, and his bare arms are ropy with sinew and muscle.

"So, Dad," I begin. "How are you, anyway?"

He stands there and stares at me, squints at me, as if maybe his eyes could be playing tricks on him in the wake of the enormous physical effort he's just expended to demolish the cement path.

But he quickly realizes I'm no mirage. He pulls off his gloves and tosses them to the ground, like a hockey player ready for a fight.

"Holy shit," says Danny Sullivan, in a voice many decibels quieter than the voice I remember from my childhood. Still looking straight at me, he points a finger in Jake's direction. "My grandson?"

"Yeah."

"Come here, kid."

A wide-eyed Jake obeys my father, stepping up to him and stopping before him as if a medal is going to be pinned to his chest. Instead, my father reaches out and gingerly touches his cheek, then his chest, then his arms, as if Jake is an oil painting, a work of art that is not quite dry. A smile that's half a smirk creases my father's face. "You're taller than your old man."

"A little."

"You happy about that?"

"I guess so. I hadn't really thought about it."

My father turns to me, smiling broadly now, and I see that he still has his teeth. They gleam a golden yellow in the early afternoon light.

"How about that?" he says. "The Spick-Mick is taller than you!"

Political correctness was never one of my old man's strengths. Jake has grown up in a hothouse of it under Doris's roof, so I'm somewhat astonished to see that he's all but doubled over with laughter at what his paternal grandfather has just called him. My father offers a hand to shake with Jake, then pulls the boy into a headlock. "Your father let you drink beer, kid?"

"Yes, sir."

"Call me Danny. Should we go inside and have a cold one?"

"Unless you want to take me to Charlie's Bar."

"Ho-ho!" My father laughs out loud. "Charlie's Bar! How do you know about Charlie's Bar?"

"I've heard some things," Jake deadpans.

"Well, kid, I'd love to take you, but Charlie's Bar burned to the ground about five years ago. So what say we go inside and wet our whistles?"

"Okay by me, Danny."

My father keeps Jake in a headlock on the short walk to the house. Giggling like he did when he was five years old, Jake has to walk hunched over so's not to break my father's grasp.

I'm still standing on the sidewalk in a state of shock. When they get to the door, my father turns to me. "You can come in, too, if you're thirsty."

The three of us sit at the old kitchen table. The wooden chairs have gone rickety with the years, the same chairs we sat on when my mother was alive, and fighting the good fight for my soul.

My father has kept the walls freshly painted and the house is surprisingly clean, but all the furniture and appliances are the same stuff I grew up with. This tiny, boxy house is like a well-kept museum, with an eighty-year-old curator.

He's taken three longneck bottles of Rheingold beer from the refrigerator, and we all drink straight from the bottle. Nobody proposes a toast. My father wipes foam from his lips with the back of his hand and says to Jake, "Still got that double last name going?"

"Hey, Dad—"

"I'm just asking! I'm not allowed to ask?"

Jake nods and says, "My last name is Perez-Sullivan."

My old man winces, quite theatrically. "It's a hell of a mess."

"Why do you say that, Danny?"

"Well, Jacob—do they call you Jacob?"

"I prefer Jake."

"Good! Well, Jake, look at it this way. You've got two last names, right? Now let's say you fall in love with a girl whose feminist mother also refused to surrender *her* last name. You marry, you have a kid, and that kid's got *four* last names. I mean, where does it end? A generation later it's *eight* last names, then *sixteen*. Christ Almighty, what the hell's the phone book gonna look like fifty years from now? It'll be two feet thick!"

I duck my face so Jake can't see me smiling, but it doesn't matter. He's actually laughing out loud over his grandfather's perceptions.

"Good point you got there, Danny."

"Well, it's just common sense, isn't it? At some point you gotta stand in front of the bullshit wagon, put your hands up and say, 'Enough!' "

He delivers this rant to Jake, but of course it's intended for my ears. I never liked the fact that my kid had two last names, but like so many fathers of my time I let it slide, let the bullshit wagon run right over me.

Jake gets to his feet. "Danny," he says, "is it okay if I take a look at my father's old room?"

"You do whatever you like." My father points toward the staircase. "Second door on the left. Toilet's the third door, in case you need it."

Jake leaves. My father and I drink in an excruciating silence I feel compelled to break. "Charlie's Bar burned down?"

"Few years back. Charlie forgot to turn off a space heater one winter night after last call."

"Anybody killed?"

My father laughs. "Always the reporter, eh, Sammy? No, nobody was killed. But the last bar in Queens that refused to serve 'light' beer was gone forever, I'm sorry to say."

"How's Charlie?"

"Dead. Cancer got him about a year after the bar burned down."

"Must have been rough on you, losing a friend like that."

"Yeah, well, you get to be my age, you're gonna attend some funerals. . . . Did you ever darken Charlie's doorway?"

Was this a trick question? Or did he really not know about the night I went in there looking for him, and wound up getting laid for the first time?

"I was underage," I finally say.

He nods, shrugs. "Well, it's too bad we never hoisted one together at Charlie's."

It feels funny to know that the place I first got laid out of is gone. Why hadn't Fran mentioned it? A little bit of my history is ashes, and I'm tempted to tell my father about it, but what for? Why bother? He hardly knows anything else about me, so why should he know this?

My father gulps more beer, clears his throat, and gestures toward the stairs Jake has just climbed. "What's with the hair and the beard? Your kid starring in *A Passion Play*?"

"He likes it. I figure it's better than a tattoo."

My father shoves his shirtsleeve up toward his shoulder, revealing a blue tattoo of an anchor with chains beneath faded letters that read U.S. NAVY. "What, may I ask, is wrong with a tattoo?"

"Please don't show him that."

"Why not?"

"Dad—"

"All right, all right." He rolls the sleeve back down. "What's it been, fifteen years?"

"Seventeen, Dad. Almost eighteen. Since the day Jake was born."

"Christ!" He shakes his head. "You know, I thought you might've picked up the phone to give me a call on 9/11, just to let me know you were alive."

"Funny, I was waiting for you to call me on that same day."

"I guess we were both wrong."

"I guess."

"How come Doris didn't come with you for this little reunion?"

"We've been divorced for thirteen years."

"It didn't last, eh? What a shock."

"I guess it just wasn't a marriage made in heaven, like you and Mom."

My father sits back, studies my face, drinks more beer. "You happy since you split?"

"No."

"How about Doris?"

"Probably not."

"So nothing changed, except you've been shelling out for two apartments all these years, and shuttling the kid back and forth."

"That's one way of looking at it."

"Tell me another way."

"Two people could not get along. If they'd stayed together, the misery would have eaten them alive."

"You're miserable anyway."

"It's a different kind of misery."

"Bullshit. Misery is misery. All in all, you might as well have stayed together. It worked for your mother and me. It's not as if we had the perfect union."

"Mom was good enough to drop dead on you, old man. It would have been interesting to see how things would have shaken out if she'd lived. My gut tells me you'd have wound up in a furnished room in Kew Gardens."

He tightens his big-knuckled hand around his beer bottle. "Watch who you're calling an old man."

There is true menace in his voice. We have not so much as shaken hands, and suddenly it looks as if our first physical contact might be his fist flattening my nose. As family reunions go, this one could use a little work.

I swallow some beer and say, "Been a long time since you painted the house, I notice."

"It's next on my list, after the front path."

"Got a color picked out?"

"Same as last time. Canary yellow. Benjamin Moore, the best stuff around. Got eight gallons in the garage."

I shake my head in wonder. "It's so nice how you uphold traditions, Dad. Mom's dead, but you're still going with that color she despised."

"You got a problem with it?"

"I'm just amazed at how long you can stay spiteful. You picked that ridiculous color because you were so pissed off about me going to Catholic school."

"I picked that color because I like it. Yellow, like buttercups, like sunshine. You got something against buttercups and sunshine?"

"Paint it with polka dots, for all I care. Mom's dead. You can't hurt her anymore."

"What the hell is that supposed to mean?"

"Enough, Dad. This was a mistake. We'll drink up and get the hell out of your life."

"Suit yourself."

I drain my bottle, set it down, and start to chuckle.

"What's so funny?"

"I'll tell you what's funny. My son thought maybe you'd remarried. Nobody who ever knew you would think such a thing."

"I've had plenty of chances."

"Yeah, sure. Women just line up for the chance to be miserable with you, don't they?"

"Not lately. They did for a while. But I only ever loved your mother."

It's almost a paralyzing thing to hear, and for a moment or two I can't move, and I can barely breathe.

Can there be any truth to what he's just said? And if there is, how different might his life have been if my mother had lived? Maybe time would have healed their wounds. Maybe they would have grown into each other, a pair of lovable curmudgeons spending too much time together, griping away on their trips to the mall. Maybe it could have worked. Anything can work, if love is real . . . right?

"You loved her, Dad? Is that what you said?"

"In my own lousy way, yeah. Don't get me wrong here. She was a pain in the ass and a religious fanatic. She liked getting her own way. I liked getting *my* way. And poor you, always stuck in the middle. Did I ever apologize to you for that? If not, I apologize now."

"Don't bother. Doris and I did the same thing to our son."

"Well, there you go. Maybe we all do it. Maybe there's no such thing as compatibility. Not if your last name is Sullivan."

Just then Jake bops back into the room, shattering the mood as he sits down, grabs his beer bottle and takes a swig. "Who's that girl on that poster in your room, Dad?"

"Poster?"

"Her name is Debbie Harry," my father says. "A singer. Your old man was obsessed with her. He pleasured himself on many a night, staring at that poster."

The two of them laugh out loud at my expense. I can feel my face burning. "The Debbie Harry poster is still hanging in my room?!"

"I haven't touched a thing since you left. Go take a look."

"I don't need a look."

"Go ahead. You seem tense. Go relax yourself. Jake and I will respect your privacy."

Jake tries to suppress a giggle.

I roll my eyes. "Jesus, Dad!"

"All right, all right, it was just a joke. A bad joke."

A silence falls over the table, so severe a silence that the ticking of the kitchen clock seems to get louder with each successive second, ominous as a fuse burning toward a bomb. Jake can feel it, too. He's struggling for something to say, and at last he says it.

"Danny," he begins, "how come you smashed up the path to your house?"

"He's going to build a moat," I say. "Fill it with pirhana. Keep everybody away for good."

My father ignores me, turns to Jake. "It was in lousy shape. I've been meaning to replace it for years. Finally getting around to it, replacing it with something that'll last."

He's deceptively optimistic, my old man. He's eighty years old, and determined to build a path that will last another fifty years. Why? Who will walk on it, besides the mailman? Who comes to visit this hard-bitten, angry old man?

My father leans closer to Jake, as if to confer with a conspirator in a shady deal. "I'm not pouring cement this time. Ohhh, I've got a beautiful plan for that path."

Jake seems truly interested. "What's the plan?"

My father looks left and right before answering, as if an outsider might be trying to eavesdrop.

"Cobblestones," he all but whispers. "Gonna build a beautiful cobblestone path."

I laugh out loud. The two of them stare at me.

"What's funny?" my father asks.

"You. You're funny. You'd never spend money on *rocks*. You hate spending on *food!*"

"Who said anything about spending money?"

"What are you going to do, steal them?"

"What I'm gonna do is none of your business, unless you decide to stick around, in which case you can help me."

"We'd love to help," Jake says. "We've got no plans whatsoever."

"Jake!"

"Come on, Dad! What have we got to lose?"

"Make up your minds," my father says, "because we've got to do this thing at fifteen fifteen."

I turn to Jake. "That's navy talk for three fifteen."

Jake rolls his eyes. "I figured that out, Dad."

I'm really not liking the sound of this project. "Why do we have to do it exactly at that time, Dad?"

"Because," my father says, cackling like a pirate, eyes twinkling like a pair of sapphires, "that's when the tide is at its lowest."

CHAPTER FIFTEEN

My crazy father changes from work shoes to calf-high rubber boots and digs out some old work gloves for Jake and me. Step one in whatever the hell we're doing is to load the busted-up cement chunks into the back of his station wagon, which I'm astonished to see is the same old clunker he was driving when I moved out.

"This dinosaur still runs?"

"Lubrication, my boy. The right lubrication and the motor stays shipshape forever." He lays a tattered blanket down on the flatbed part of the trunk, and another blanket on the backseat of the car. Then the three of us begin to load the cement chunks.

"Easy, now," he cautions. "Lay 'em down gently. That's it, Jake."

"Where are we taking this stuff, Dad?"

"We're dumping it."

"Where?"

"You'll see when we get there."

I'm not crazy about that answer, but I am pleased to see that my son digs right into the work, bending and hoisting and loading as if he's done back-work all his life. He was the same way with the lawn-mowing at Fran's, diving right into the job. It's hard to know how city kids will handle manual labor, and this is a sweet surprise.

"Load it evenly," my father says. "Use the backseat, too. Got to distribute the weight."

When the last chunk of cement is loaded the three of us pile into the front seat, and nobody has to tell Jake to sit in the middle. He understands that he is our generational buffer, the reason things are going as smoothly as they are.

The car starts up with a roar. My father puts it in reverse and begins inching his way out of the driveway. "Now I've got to drive slowly, so's not to bust a shock with this load," he says. "So be patient. We're not going far."

We crawl along the streets of Flushing as if we're carrying a nuclear missile. My father turns to Jake. "How's school?"

Funny thing to ask, considering it's a question I never got when I lived with him.

"I got kicked out yesterday," Jake says.

My father looks to me to see if it's the truth. I nod, I shrug. He turns back to Jake.

"Jesus Christ, what did your mother say? She worships at the altar of formal education, doesn't she?"

"She doesn't know yet."

"Don't tell me. You were at a private school, am I right? Very white, very expensive? One or two token blacks just to give the yearbook a little bit o' pizzaz?"

"You got it, Danny."

"What'd you do, punch a teacher?" he asks, almost hopefully.

"I wrote something they didn't like."

My father makes a snorting sound. "For *that* they threw you out? Words on a page?"

"Yep. Also, I refused to apologize for what I'd written."

"Good lad. So what's next for you?"

"I'm really not sure, Danny."

"I still know people at the Transit Authority. I was a motorman, you know. I could get you in, but you'd need a high school diploma, or whaddayacallit, the equivalency certificate."

"He's not going to work for the Transit Authority, Dad!"

"I know he's not. He *can't*. He's not qualified. But don't piss on it, son. Good union, good medical, good dental. My pension check comes every month."

"I'm sure it does."

"It's more than you're gonna get from that newspaper you write for."

"I'm not there anymore."

"What the hell you talkin' about? I was readin' one of your articles just yesterday."

"I got fired just yesterday."

"*Ho*-lee *shit!*"

My father looks from Jake's face to mine in wide-eyed disbelief at these two losers in his car.

"Don't worry, Dad," I assure him. "We're not moving in with you. This is just a visit."

He gets his eyes back on the road, and then he begins to chuckle.

"What's so funny, Dad?"

"You wanna know what's funny? You *really* wanna know?" He thumps himself on the chest. "*I'm* the best-educated person in this car. Me. I actually got my diploma, from Franklin K. Lane High. Worst school in all of Brooklyn, maybe the world, but they gave me a sheepskin, all right, and that puts me ahead o' you guys with your high-priced schools!"

He's laughing out loud, and so is Jake, and then, moments later, so am I. My father's sense of caution abandons him for a moment as we dip into a pothole, and the bottom of the car gets scraped with a horrible sound that I just know involves a spray of sparks.

Jesus Christ, what if the gas tank ignites? What if the car explodes, killing the three of us and sending chunks of cement in all directions like so many missiles? What would the headline be in the *New York Star*, and what in the world would Doris say?

We head slowly but surely toward the murky shores of Flushing Bay. When I was a kid my father occasionally took me fishing here, and I don't remember hooking anything that was alive. Once I snagged a skeletal umbrella, nothing but ribs and a handle, and another time a rusted hubcap, and that was pretty much the extent of my catch.

There's a chain-link fence running along the length of the street above the shoreline. We ride along this lonely stretch of road for a few minutes until suddenly we reach a section where the fence has been flattened, either by vandals or an out-of-control car. My father stops the car here, and we all get out.

"There's no parking here, Dad. Didn't you see the signs?"

"Don't worry. Nobody ever comes through here, except by accident."

A wildly overgrown hill leads down to the gray beach, mucky and messy at low tide. My father periscopes the area, checks his watch and smiles. "Perfect timing. It is now fifteen oh three. We'll need ten minutes to get rid of the cement, anyway."

We follow his lead as he takes a chunk from the car and rolls it down the hill. Before it can hit bottom, the foliage swallows it up.

"Dad. I'd say this is illegal dumping."

"I'd say you're right, which is why it'd be smart for us to do this fast."

We're caught up in it now. The three of us grab cement chunks from the car and toss them down the hill, where they vanish whisperingly into the undergrowth.

"We're not hurting anything, Jake," my father says. "It's not as if anybody had plans for this area. It's a goddamn dump, whether we dump here or not."

"I hear you, Danny."

"Jake," I say, "please understand that we *are* doing the wrong thing here, whether my father wants to admit it or not. He just doesn't want to pay for private carting."

"Private carting!" my father laughs. "Sure. Some guinea outfit that takes the stuff away, and dumps it right where we're dumping it, only in the middle of the night. At least we're doing it in broad daylight. It's more honest that way."

"Oh, we're honorable people, Dad."

"Hell, you can go to confession on Sunday and wipe the slate clean. Oh, wait. I forgot. You don't go to church anymore, do you?"

I swallow hard before answering. "I'm a fallen Catholic like you, Dad, which pretty much means that I've gone from believing in everything to believing in nothing."

While we've been arguing Jake has been getting rid of the cement chunks. He rolls the last one down the hill and says, "That's it, Danny."

"Good lad!" He turns to me. "Well, I may be a fallen Catholic, but I believe in cobblestones, if that means anything to you. So what say we go and get 'em?"

He leads the way through the broken fence and down to the beach, a crooked, slippery walk through waist-high weeds with thorny seed pods that cling to our pants. The beach itself is ripe with sewage smells, more muck than sand, with the tips of plastic bottles jutting out all over the place. There's also a half-submerged supermarket shopping cart sticking out of the muck. What the hell is *that* doing there? Salvador Dali would have to drop acid before he could paint a scene like this.

We follow my father's strident footsteps. He's on a mission, impervious to the ugliness of it all.

"Not exactly the Hamptons, is it, Jake?"

Jake doesn't answer me, but strides ahead to walk shoulder to shoulder with my father. My father pats his back. "How's your mother these days, Jake?"

"She's okay."

"Still afraid of being mistaken for a Puerto Rican?"

"She corrects people who get it wrong."

"I have to admit, I was always amused by that. *I'm Spanish, not Puerto Rican!* Like there's something wrong with being a P R."

"Oh yeah," I say, "listen to the great civil libertarian."

"You got that right."

"Dad. Please."

My father stops and turns to face me, a gloved hand flat against his chest to indicate how I have wounded his pride. "For twenty-eight years I opened the doors of my subway trains for anybody who wanted a ride. Blacks, Puerto Ricans, Chinese, Indians . . . *everybody* rode with me. Homeless people slept on my trains on winter nights. Never threw a soul off for any reason, unless they got violent, in which case I tossed 'em with my own two hands."

He smiles at Jake. "It was all in the timing, kid. You shove 'em through the open doors, hard enough so they hit the opposite wall. By the time they recover and try to get back on, the doors close in their faces. I especially enjoyed doin' that to those Wall Street assholes when they got all liquored up and full o' themselves."

He holds up a finger. "Never called a cop, not once. Handled all my own problems. I admit that I'm a little bit proud of that."

"Jesus," I say, rolling my eyes.

"*Awesome,*" Jake says, keeping his eyes trained on a man who's clearly becoming his hero.

We resume walking. Jake and I have to veer toward higher, harder ground, because the beach is getting muckier. Safe within his boots, my father ignores the muck, though he sinks to his ankles with each step.

Suddenly he stops walking. He joins us on higher ground, checks his watch and smiles.

"Fifteen fifteen on the nose," he says. "The tide is now at its lowest. Now look. Look where I'm pointing."

He points out toward the horizon, maybe twenty yards out. A mysterious, uneven ridge of some kind bulges ever so slightly from the surface of the muck, like a row of rotted molars.

"See it? See the tips of those rocks sticking up? They're only visible at dead low tide, which is what it is now."

He turns to us with a triumphant smile. "Cobblestones," he says. "The foundation of an abandoned pier, or some damn thing. Whatever they are, they're mine! *All mine!*"

He starts to laugh insanely, as if we've come upon Captain Kidd's treasure. He even does a little bit of a jiglike dance on the sand. "We load 'em up, we take 'em away. Gonna have me a cobblestone path, that's what I'm gonna have."

"Dad. You can't be serious."

"Why not?"

"This is *stealing*."

"It is? Who the hell are we stealing from?"

I think it over. "One way or another, I know that this is city property."

He laughs out loud. "City property? You think the city knows there's an old broken-down pier here on Flushing Bay, a pier that's been forgotten for a hundred years?"

"I don't know. Probably not. But I have a feeling that if they *did* know, they'd have problems with a guy taking it away one stone at a time."

"Well, then, son, do me a favor and don't tell them. These stones have been underwater since before any of us were born. It's time they saw the light of day once again. It's a sin, leavin' them to waste away down here. It's time they were *useful* again."

I turn to my son. "I really don't think this is a great idea, Jake. We should go."

Jake's eyes widen in disbelief. "Dad, come on. We *have* to do this."

"Why?"

"Because if we leave, Danny'll try to do it by himself, and it could kill him."

"That's right," my father says. "I'm doing this with or without you. Me, a senior citizen. It's a lot of stones and quite a bit of climbing, and if I drop dead in the process it'll be on your head."

Just what I need—to be responsible for the death of another parent. My father knows he's got me. He grins at me, and tugs on his boots to make sure they're up as high as they can be. "Now I'm going out there and pullin' these things from the muck. You either carry 'em up to my car, or you don't. It's as simple as that."

He squelches his way into the muck, his feet leaving holes that quickly fill with black water. Piss clams squirt into the air, jarred by his footsteps, and I'm amazed that anything is able to live in this stuff.

My father reaches the ridge, bends over and pulls out a stone, which he carries back to us, cradled against his chest.

It's an ugly thing, ragged with seaweed and coated in muck. When he reaches us my father pulls off the seaweed to reveal it as a rectangular-cut cobblestone, bearded with barnacles.

"Look at that beauty," he says. "Ten, maybe twelve bucks if I was to buy it."

He hands it off to Jake, who takes it in his gloved hands and stares at it in wonder. "Why do you suppose they had a pier out there, Danny?"

My father shrugs. "Who knows? Maybe this was a pretty place back then. Maybe people docked their sailboats here and had lunch in a nice restaurant, before it all turned to shit."

"Wow," Jake says. "Imagine!"

"Lay it down in the car the same way you did with the cement," my father tells him. "Don't carry more than one at a time. And watch you don't slip on the hill, Jake."

"Gotcha, Danny."

It's as if they've known each other for years. Jake heads off with the first stolen stone. My father looks at me, wipes a speck of muck off his nose with the back of his glove.

"Your son is in. How about you? You in?"

I tug the gloves on. "I'm in. You knew I was in. You guilted me into it."

"Yeah, I knew that'd work."

He heads back to the long-lost pier, pulls out another stone and carries it back. This one has even more seaweed on it than the first one, plus a cluster of mussels that clings to it like a bunch of grapes. He tosses it on the sand. "Find yourself a piece of driftwood and scrape it as clean as you can. No sense hauling crap we don't need to the house, is there?"

Without waiting for an answer he returns to the mother lode, while I look around for a piece of wood to scrape the stones clean.

It quickly becomes an assembly-line process—my father plodding out to the muck and uprooting the stones, while Jake and I scrape them clean and carry them to the car. This bizarre Sullivan family reunion is in full swing.

I can't resist sticking it to my son. "See the kind of work you wind up doing when you leave school, Jake?"

"Yeah, Dad, I see."

"Imagine doing work like this for the rest of your life."

"Don't have to, Dad. Remember, I have a plan."

"Oh yes, your big plan."

"I never said it was a *big* plan. Just a plan."

"You ready to tell me what it is?"

"I only want to explain it once, so I'm waiting until tomorrow, when I can tell you and Mom at the same time."

"Jake. Come on. Tell me."

"Dad. Be patient. I'm a little busy here, helping my grandfather steal a pier." He won't say anything more about it.

Soon we fall into a rhythm, timed so well that each time my father returns with a stone, one of us is there to take it. There is no way to stay clean. The stinking muck is all over our forearms and the bellies of our shirtfronts.

Again, I am struck by what a good worker Jake turns out to be. Soon his speed and enthusiasm upset the rhythm of the process—he gets up and down the weedy hill so fast that he "laps" me, and then the two of us are standing there waiting for my father's deliveries.

"Admit it, Dad," Jake says, "this is kind of fun."

"Oh yeah. What could be more fun than helping your grandfather commit a maritime crime?"

"You worry too much, Dad."

"That's because my father doesn't worry enough."

"You worry enough for *all* of us."

By this time we've loaded dozens of ancient cobblestones into the aged station wagon. They're heavier than the cement chunks were, far more dense, and the car sags under their weight.

"Dad," I tell him as he chucks the latest stone on the sand, "we can't take many more. The tires are starting to bulge at the bottom."

He's not even breathing hard. "All right," he says. "Tide's coming in anyway. Another ten minutes and it'll all be underwater. That's the last one for you, Jake. Wait for us up there."

"Okay, Danny." Jake takes the driftwood stick and quickly scrapes the stone clean, then hoists it and makes his way toward the hill.

My father watches him go. "That kid of yours is all right, you know."

"I've always thought so."

"He's not afraid of work. People either want to work, or they don't. That's what it's all about, in case I never mentioned it to you."

"I don't think you ever did, but better late than never."

"What the hell are *you* gonna do about a job?"

"I'll think of something. I'm not afraid of work, either."

My father hesitates. "If you need a few bucks—"

"Dad. That's not why we came out here today."

"I know, but remember I offered."

"You've been reading my stories, huh?"

"What do you mean?"

"You mentioned that you read my article yesterday."

He swallows. "Yeah, I read the *Star*. Maybe it's not the greatest paper in the world, but you made it better than it would have been."

I'm shocked by the compliment, or whatever it was he just gave me. It's the first time he's ever said anything about my work.

His face is pink as he turns to go back to the muck. "Two more stones—one for you and one for me, all right?"

"Sure, Dad. No sense going up there empty-handed."

"Yeah, that's right." He stops and turns to me. "You know, maybe some o' me got into you after all."

He lugs two more cobblestones to the beach. We clean them and hoist them, and then together we carry them to the car. He struggles to balance the rock against his belly as he works his way up the hill. "Christ, this isn't easy, is it?"

"No, Dad, it's a bitch. Aren't you glad Jake and I dropped by today?"

"You have no idea."

When we get to the top we see that Jake is leaning against the car, chatting to a big uniformed man in a forest ranger–type hat. Everything he's wearing, including the hat, is the same shade of shit brown. Jake seems as if he might be concerned, but he doesn't look frightened. In two days he's gone from honor student to dropout to juvenile delinquent. Tomorrow being Sunday, maybe I'll take him to church to rob the poor box.

"Oh, fuck me upside down," my father startles me by saying, "what in the hell have we got here?"

"Calm down, Dad."

"All right. I'm calm. But you listen to me. First thing we do is load these stones into the car. They *belong* to us. This moron doesn't even *exist* until all the stones are loaded. *Then* we'll talk to him."

"Dudley Do-Right might not like being ignored."

My father's nostrils widen like those of a balky horse as he exhales with contempt. "I'm not interested in what he likes," he says, squaring his shoulders for the final approach to whatever the hell is going to happen next.

CHAPTER SIXTEEN

My father sticks to his plan. He breezes right past the man in the hat, pulls the car door open and loads his cobblestone onto the backseat pile. I blindly follow, clacking my cobblestone down next to his. My father turns to the guy as if he's noticing him for the first time.

"Well, good afternoon, there!" he booms. He pulls off his muck-soaked gloves, and for a moment it looks as if he's going to shake hands with the guy. But he doesn't. He tosses his gloves into the car, pushes back his hair, puts his hands on his hips and faces the guy, almost defiantly. "Something we can do for you?"

"Are you the owner of this vehicle?" the guy asks, in the maddeningly calm, almost bored tone of someone who knows he's got the weight of the government behind him. This guy's got a big, pigeon-shaped body, a butterfat face, and half-dead eyes. He might be thirty, he could be forty, and if he's got a wife the chances are excellent that she's thinking of somebody else when he's on top of her. Then again, he's probably still living with his parents. If there's a textbook face for the Mama's Boy, I'm looking at it.

His name tag says ORVIETO, and I know right away that we are in a bit of trouble. He's clearly an Italian who didn't have the brains for the police department or the balls for the Mafia, so he's wound up with this ridiculous Parks Department job. He probably patrols the forgotten Queens coastline day after day in search of some violation, *any* violation, and at last his pathetic prayers have been answered. He's finally got himself some action. He's snagged a trio of cobblestone pirates.

But he's taking it by the book, a step at a time, beginning with this question about vehicular ownership. My father proudly pats the hood of his station wagon.

"I am indeed the owner," he says. "A hundred and eighty thousand miles of faithful service, she's given me."

"There's no parking allowed here, sir."

"I'm sorry. I was not aware of that."

"The signs are posted all along the road."

"My eyes are not what they used to be."

Orvieto hunches down a little to peer inside the car. The mucky, barnacle-encrusted cobblestones make for a bizarre sight. "What are you transporting inside your car, sir?"

"Nothing."

"Nothing?"

"At the moment, I'm not *transporting* anything. I'm standing still, and so is my vehicle."

The Irish are known for their love of wordplay, and my father is no exception, but he is picking a terrible time to break balls. Jake purses his lips to keep from laughing out loud, and all I can do is stand there as my father proceeds to make a bad situation even worse.

Orvieto stands up straight, forces a grin. "All right, I'll rephrase the question. What have you got inside your car?"

"That's better! Cobblestones."

"Cobblestones?" Orvieto asks, genuinely surprised.

"Yes," my father says. "Some people know them as Belgian blocks."

"Where did they come from?"

"Bounty of the sea!" my father exclaims, pointing toward the beach the way Moses might have pointed toward the Promised Land. "They've been buried in the muck and mire of this bay for God only knows how long. I couldn't bear the waste of it, so I decided to salvage them."

"Salvage?"

"Yes. It means, 'to save from being wasted,' or words to that effect."

Orvieto stares at my father through cop-narrow eyes. "I know what 'salvage' means," he says evenly. "But what you're doing isn't salvaging. What you're doing is stealing."

Now everything's out on the table. Jake crosses his arms and stares at his feet. My heart is hammering away, but my father has managed to make himself look genuinely aggrieved.

"*Stealing!* In all my life, I've never stolen so much as a stick of chewing gum!"

"Well," says Orvieto, "there's always a first time."

"Exactly who have I stolen from?"

"The City of New York, sir."

My father turns to look at me, as if daring me to tell him I'd told him so, but I say nothing. This is his show, and for now, his son and grandson are merely passengers on this rapid ride to hell.

"Officer," my father says to Orvieto, "let's face it. The city of New York had no earthly idea that these stones were out there, buried at the bottom of an old forgotten pier. The only reason *I* knew about it is because I'm a lonely old man who prowls these beaches, thinking back to my youthful days in the navy. I served my country, you know. Two hitches in Dubya Dubya Two, and believe me, I was in the thick of it. A Jap submarine sank my ship. Seven hours I bobbed around in that cold, cold sea, staring at the stars, praying the rescue ship'd get there faster than the sharks. Were you in the service, Officer?"

Orvieto sighs, shakes his head. "No, I wasn't."

"Well, it was a different time. People believed in things. And all these years later, I can tell you with my hand over my heart that I *still* believe."

He sweeps his hand toward Flushing Bay, an almost blissful smile on his face. "Know what I believe? I believe the sea was tryin' to give something back to me. She nearly took my life in the war, so now, all these years later, she's makin' it right with the gift of these stones. What do you think?"

Clearly bored by it all, Orvieto pulls a pad and a pen from his jacket pocket and steps right up to my father. He's easily half a foot taller, not including the hat. "I think you're full of shit, old man."

My father looks up at Orvieto's calm, chubby face, which now wears a cruel little smile, a smile that becomes the target for the punch.

It's a textbook roundhouse from my old man, and it lands with a shocking crunch on the mouth of Parks Department Officer Orvieto, who collapses as if all his bones have suddenly turned to jelly.

"Jesus!" Jake exclaims, his eyes as big as baseballs.

My father stands there, fists poised defensively, as if he expects his opponent to retaliate. But Orvieto does not respond. He is out cold.

"Call me an old man, will you?" my father murmurs, more to himself than the unconscious man he's just clocked.

Orvieto has slid straight down into a seated position, his back against the side of the car. He looks as if he could be taking a yoga class. Amazingly, his hat is still on his head, though now it's a little crooked.

He's absolutely still, and it dawns on me that my father might have killed him, and I'm trying to figure out the potential consequences: a manslaughter rap for my father, five to fifteen, which at his age could be a life sentence, and what about Jake and me? Would we be considered accomplices, just for being there? Or would the jury believe that we were sucked into this cobblestone caper, when all we meant to do was drop in on my dad one Saturday afternoon for the first time since Jake was born?

It would all depend on how good a lawyer I could hire, and without a job I couldn't afford the worst Queens Boulevard lawyer in the Yellow Pages, and just as these calamitous thoughts are racing through my mind Orvieto's eyelids begin to flutter and my heart soars with hope.

"He's all right," my father says, his fists still clenched. "Lucky for him I pulled that punch."

I turn to my father and Jake, who stand side by side. I put one hand on my father's shoulder and the other on Jake's. It's like a touch football huddle, and the time has come for me to call the next play. "Dad, please, calm down. Jake, are you all right?"

"I'm better than that cop," Jake says.

My father sneers. "He's no cop. He's some bullshit Parks Department flunky whose uncle got him his pathetic ball-breaking job."

"Dad, listen to me. When this guy comes around, *I'm* doing the talking, okay?"

"Look at him!" my father exclaims. "Some tough guy! No gun! No handcuffs! What's he gonna do, poke me with his pen?"

"He's got a walkie-talkie, Dad, and if he calls for help we're dead. Okay? So I'm begging you—let me take it from here. Trust me, all right?"

My father looks me in the eye and hesitates before reaching out and patting my cheek. It's the first time he's touched me today, and the first time he's ever touched me in such a gentle way. When I was growing up we shook hands on birthdays and Christmas, and that was pretty much the extent of our physical contact. Funny that my first-ever portion of paternal affection should come in the midst of a felonious assault that could put my father behind bars. It's also kind of funny that I've got tears in my eyes.

"All right, kid," he says softly. "It's your game now. Get us out of this mess."

I take a moment to blink away the tears and focus before turning to squat and face Officer Orvieto, who's making little groaning noises. He opens his eyes, coughs, clears his throat, and spits a gob of red mucus on the pavement. His lip is swollen, but I don't think my father broke any bones or loosened any teeth.

"Are you all right, Officer?"

He stares at me but says nothing, his tongue probing his wounded lip.

I reach out and straighten his hat. "Are you aware of everything that's happened?"

"I was assaulted."

"Okay, good. You remember. That's a sign that you haven't been badly hurt."

He makes a woozy gesture with his hand. "You'll all have to come with me, the three o' youse."

"Well, I'd like to talk to you about that. Do you ever read the *Star*? The *New York Star* newspaper?"

He's puzzled by the question, but he nods. I pull my press card from my back pocket and hold it to his face. "I'm a reporter with the *Star*. Been there a long time. And believe me, this is the kind of story we really love to tell."

Orvieto manages to sit up a little straighter. "*What* story?"

"The story of how an eighty-year-old man got into trouble for taking something that nobody even knew was there. A cranky, eccentric old man—a *war* hero, mind you—picking through the muck at low tide, minding his own business, when suddenly some cop decided to give him a hard time."

Orvieto points past me at my father. "He is in the wrong here."

"I'm sure he is, if we're going strictly by the book. That's why it's such a good story for my newspaper. It gives the readers a little something to talk about, argue about. Because let's face it, Officer Orvieto—who in their right mind would think my father has done anything wrong with this little scavenging expedition? Gathering up rocks that nobody even knew were there, rocks that would have stayed buried in the muck until the end of time?"

Orvieto opens his mouth to speak, but lets it close without saying anything.

"It wouldn't be just one story," I continue. "I could turn this thing into a crusade, especially if you arrest me and my son along with my father. Three generations of one family, disgraced over a bunch of slimy old rocks. And let's not forget the tale of the tape."

Orvieto hesitates before asking, "What the hell is that?"

"You know, like they do the day before a prize fight. Pictures of you and my dad, side by side. Heights and weights, and all the other vital statistics. You're what, six-two, maybe two-twenty? My father goes maybe five-seven, one-fifty."

"One forty-seven," my father corrects me. "I'm still a welterweight, same as I was in the navy."

"There you go," I say, not breaking my gaze from Orvieto's eyes. "You've got seven inches and seventy pounds on the guy, not to mention he's fifty years older than you." I lean in a little closer before adding, "And he dropped you with *one punch.*"

At last, Orvieto gets the picture. His face flushes and he takes a deep breath.

"See, people love reading about the little guy who triumphs against the odds. What we've got here is your classic David and Goliath story, with a lot of funky elements thrown in—a crazy old man and an overzealous cop, waging war over a bunch of rocks from the bottom of a polluted bay."

This isn't like the hustle I pulled on Headmaster Peter Plymouth about the story I was threatening to write. Everything I'm telling this asshole is *true*. This is a good story, and I'd be delighted to write it up, if I still had a job at the paper.

I can't help laughing. "Shit, I haven't even mentioned what the TV news would do with a story like this. Ever had a TV crew show up at your house, unannounced? They start filming before you even know what the hell's going on. That's why almost everybody looks ridiculous on television. Jesus Christ, we could all wind up on Letterman! He could do a Top Ten list about the Cobblestone Caper!"

I hear Jake and my father chuckle over that, but Orvieto does not. He's gathered himself sufficiently to rise slowly to his feet, and even allows me to help him up by the elbow.

"The cobblestone caper," he murmurs, shrugging his way out of my grasp. "Very funny."

"Well, you know how they like to make fun. My point is that if this story gets out, only one person really gets hurt, and that person is you. So ask yourself—is it worth it?"

Orvieto stands there returning my stare, volt for volt. He's a little taller than me, so I'm looking up at him, but I'm really rolling now, and I'm not intimidated. I look left and right and even dare to put a hand on his shoulder before speaking again.

"Level with me—this is just a temporary job for you, isn't it?" I say. "I'll bet you're trying to join the police department, aren't you?"

Bingo. I've hit the bull's-eye. Orvieto swallows. "I'm on the waiting list."

"Okay, fair enough. No shame in that. But do you honestly think that New York's Finest are ever going to call up the guy who was at the heart of the famous Cobblestone Caper?"

I've just played my trump card. Either it'll work or it won't. Orvieto pulls on the brim of his hat, dusts the dirt off his ass, and struts slowly all the way around the car, peering inside at the cobblestones. He stops in front of my father, as if considering whether or not to throw a punch, but then I see that his hands are clasped tightly behind his back, as if they've been cuffed.

"What do you have to say to me, old man?"

Those words again! If my father throws another punch, it's all over. But he manages to restrain himself. He gazes down at his muddy boots, takes a deep breath. "I'm sorry I lost my temper, Officer."

"Look at me when you say it."

My father lifts his head and looks right at him, with the eyes of an abandoned puppy. "I'm sorry I lost my temper."

"Officer Orvieto."

"Officer Or-vi-*eto*. You're Italian, aren't you? I like Italian people. They have a true passion for living. My wife was Italian, rest her sacred soul."

Orvieto stares at him for a moment before moving to Jake and eyeing him from feet to face. Then he comes back to me and nudges me aside, so he can reach inside the car.

He takes out a cobblestone. His hands are so big he can actually clasp it in one hand. He looks at the stone and he looks at my father, and I wonder if Orvieto plans to bash my father's skull in. But instead, he goes to the busted fence and spitefully shot-puts the cobblestone down the hill, where we dumped all those cement chunks.

Then he turns to us, claps the muck off his hands, and says, "Get the fuck out of here, and I mean this minute. And do *not* come back."

Obedient as schoolboys, the three of us pile into the car. We all understand that we must remain silent until we start rolling. My father starts the car and puts it in gear.

"Christ, we're ridin' heavy," he whispers as we begin to roll. "Sit as still as you can. One bump and the whole carriage'll collapse."

We roll along until Orvieto and his hat are a speck in the rearview mirror. Then the road curves and he's out of sight, and the three of us begin to whoop and holler and laugh as if we've just pulled off the Brinks job.

"*Masterful*, my son!" my father exclaims. "What you did back there was masterful, although I wasn't thrilled about being called crazy."

"Was that a bunch of bullshit, about the Japs sinking your ship?"

"Total bullshit."

"Thought so. Good touch, though."

"I thank you."

Jake puts his head back and howls, then pats my knee. "Unbelievable, Dad," he says in a voice choked with pride. "That was just amazing."

I roll down my window to breathe in the salty, briny air. "I did what I had to do," I say. "That's all. Christ, but I need a drink."

"We all do," my father says. "But let's get this red-hot cargo home first!"

Jake puts his arm around my neck for a quick hug, my father beeps the horn for no damn reason, the cobblestone cargo reeks like a sewer, and in the midst of the madness I suddenly realize that this, right now, is far and away the happiest moment of my life. And if anybody had told me yesterday that I'd be having my happiest moment tomorrow, I'd have told that person he was completely insane.

CHAPTER SEVENTEEN

When we get to the house my father pulls the car right into his little garage and closes the door after it.

"Gonna leave it in here for a few days. Just in case that mountie has a change of heart and decides to come lookin' for me."

"Should I unload the stones?" Jake asks.

"No, Jake, my boy, you've done enough. I won't need the car for a few days, anyway. Let's go inside."

We follow my father. I can't wait to be out of the garage. It's tiny and dark and creepy. Lined up along one wall are all those cans of canary-yellow paint. The garage connects straight to a little laundry room with a sink and the very same old Maytag washer-dryer setup my mother used.

I realize for the first time that after my mother died, my father had to take care of all of the household tasks. How did he do it? Nobody taught him, and he wasn't the type of person to ask for help. While the two of us lived together my clothes were washed and folded (but never ironed), groceries found their way into the house, and meals appeared on the table—not great meals, a lot of fried meats and plenty of sandwiches, but meals nonetheless. We didn't starve. We were clean. Life went on.

I should have admired him for that, but I never did. Only now does it amaze me that a man who'd never before performed any domestic chores somehow managed to do all of them. He didn't crumple up and die, didn't let despair destroy him. He just put his head down and did what he had to do.

"Strip to your shorts," my father says to Jake and me. "I'll do a wash. You guys can't go back to town like that, they'll throw you off the bus."

We do as he says, handing over our muck-spattered shirts and pants. He strips down as well, and while the three of us are washing up at the sink Jake sees his tattoo.

"Whoa! Awesome, Danny!"

My father flexes his arm to make it wiggle.

"You're a lot of help, Dad."

"Aw, relax, the boy's not gonna run out and get one." He pats the tattoo. "Jake, I woke up with this in the Philippines, and I still don't know how it happened. That's pretty much the way it is with tattoos, not to mention women."

Jake laughs as my father loads the washing machine and pours in a tiny amount of liquid detergent. He was always telling my mother she used too much soap.

"By the way, we've got seventy-one cobblestones," Jake informs us. "We *had* seventy-two, until that cop threw one down the hill."

"A pathetic show of strength," my father says. "He was trying to get his balls back. I'd say he didn't succeed."

"So at ten bucks apiece," Jake says, "that's more than seven hundred dollars' worth."

Danny grins at him. "Not bad for an hour's work, eh?"

"Not bad at all."

Jake never, ever talks about money. It's always been an abstract thing to him, and suddenly it's come into focus, thanks to my father.

"Well," I can't help saying, "I'm guessing that the fine for what we did, had I not opened that cop's eyes, would probably have been around five hundred bucks. And they would have confiscated the stones. That would have made for a net loss of twelve hundred dollars. Keep that in mind while you're calculating things, guys."

My father gets the washing machine going and turns to me, the two of us in our skivvies. The hair on his chest is white and his abdomen is as flat as a pearl diver's. I'm sucking in my gut, but there's no way to hide all those years I've spent behind a desk.

"For God's sake, Sammy," my father says, "can't you for *once* just enjoy what happened, instead of worryin' about what *might* have happened?"

"Yeah, Dad," Jake adds. "Enjoy the moment."

I'm shocked that my son would say such a thing, that the two of them would gang up on me. "I thought I *was* enjoying it."

"Yeah," my father says, "you were enjoyin' it, all right, for about eleven seconds. Then you had to go and think about it. Stop thinkin' about it, already. Think you can do that?"

"I'll give it a shot."

He reaches into a laundry basket, pulls out some clean T-shirts and tosses them to Jake and me. "Your clothes'll be clean in a little while. What say we order a couple o' pizzas, and sit around the kitchen table tellin' lies?"

"I'd love that," Jake says.

"Okay by me."

"Fine, then," my father says. He pats my belly. "Now put on that T-shirt already, so you can let your gut go slack."

He leads the way from the laundry room to the kitchen, through a narrow corridor where I used to roll my toy trains back and forth on the yellow linoleum strip. It's the same old linoleum with a darker, deeper path worn down the middle, but the walls of the corridor are different.

Once bare, they are now covered with pictures—framed photographs of my mother, my father, and me. It's odd, because there were no photos of any of us on display while my mother was alive. Since her death and my departure, my father has created this shrine.

"Holy shit!" Jake exclaims.

"Welcome to the Sullivan family photo gallery," my father says with mock severity.

There's a baby picture of me asleep in a crib, and a picture of me on a swing, being pushed by my father. I'm maybe two years old, skinny and sullen, in a too-big blue-and-white striped T-shirt and ridiculously baggy short pants. My bangs have been cut in a straight line just above my eyebrows, like Moe of the Three Stooges. I'm clinging to the chains as if I expect to be launched into space while behind me my frowning, black-haired father prepares to give me a push.

Jake roars with laughter at my haircut.

"The ol' soup-bowl-on-the head trick," my father explains. "Saved a fortune in barbershop fees with that one."

"You made me look like an idiot, Dad!"

"Small price to pay. Look at this one, Jake. This is the one that got the whole thing rolling, so to speak."

It's a wedding day photo—my father in a tuxedo, my mother in a white dress, standing on the steps of some church on a cloudy day. Neither of them is smiling.

"Your grandmother, the former Mary DiFrancesco," my father says gently.

Jake studies the picture as if he's waited all his life to see it. "She had intense eyes, Danny."

"Yes, Jake, everything about her was intense. Guess that's why she's no longer with us."

I'm beginning to understand why we never hung pictures in our house when I was a kid. They're all too depressing. Sad, suspicious faces in every shot.

Except one.

"Whoa!" Jake exclaims. "Is *that* my grandmother?"

My father nods. "Rockaway Beach, 1951. Before we were married. Before she started piling on the pounds."

I never would have recognized her. My mother is a slim young thing in a red one-piece bathing suit, standing on the sand with one knee playfully jutted against the other. Her glossy black hair hangs to her shoulders, hair that is much like my son's, as Fran pointed out earlier today.

She's got a pair of sunglasses in her hand, which she's obviously taken off for the sake of the picture, and she's beaming at the camera with a smile that's every bit as bright as the sun she's squinting against. My father stands behind her, lean and moody and dangerous, arms crossed against his chest.

"Yeah, I remember that day," my father says. "It was a Friday. Know how I remember? Because we ate hot dogs for lunch, and Mary realized what day it was, and made me rush her home and get her to a priest."

"Why?" Jake asks.

"Because in those days, Catholics were forbidden to eat meat on Fridays. It was a mortal sin. If you ate meat on a Friday and you died without confessing that sin, you went straight to hell."

Jake snorts in disbelief. "Come on, Danny!"

"I'm tellin' ya, kid, that was the rule."

"She *believed* that?"

"She did indeed, Jake, with all her considerable heart and soul."

"But that's *insane!*"

"Insanity is a major part of the Catholic faith, my boy. They changed the rule years later, but on that day it was a race to save her soul. We ran off in our beach clothes and didn't stop until we reached the door to the rectory. She banged and banged on the door until at last a sleepy priest finally appeared.

"Imagine that—you open the door, and here's this half-hysterical girl in a bathing suit, begging forgiveness for having accidentally eaten a frankfurter. The priest himself couldn't believe it! He made the sign of the cross, told her not to worry about it, and slammed the door without saying good-bye. He was plenty pissed off, I can tell you. Who knows? He was probably pleasurin' an altar boy when Mary came knocking."

Jake laughs out loud, and so do I. My father shakes his head. "Poor Mary. They had her but good, those rascals. She never even thought it odd when the church changed the no-meat-on-Friday rule, and she didn't think it funny when I suggested that it happened because the fish merchants of the world had failed to meet the pope's asking price for a renewal of the meat ban."

"You know, Dad," I say, "you would have made a great news-paperman."

"Tell me something I don't know."

The last frame in the gallery catches Jake's eye. It's a small one, and it encloses not a photograph but a tarnished medal of some kind, with a faded blue-and-red-striped ribbon.

"What's this, Danny?"

"That's the eighth-grade English medal, which your father won," my father replies matter-of-factly. He puts his hand on my shoulder and gives it a squeeze. My soul is tingling. I cannot believe he has done this.

"He's always been good with words, your old man, as I came to know by his gift for back talk. Come on, then, let me call Napoli's and order a coupla pies."

I'm stunned. "Old man Napoli is still in business?"

"Nah, he died a long time ago. The family sold out to some greaseball from the other side, and the new owner kept the old name."

My father phones in the order and then we sit around the table, guzzling beer while we rehash the drama of the cobble-stone caper. My father's spirits are all but soaring.

"Tell me, Jake," he says, "what in the hell were you and that half-assed mountie discussing before your father and I arrived on the scene?"

"The weather, mostly."

My father cackles. "Beautiful!"

"He kept asking me what I was doing there, and I kept telling him, 'Waiting for my partners.' "

"You didn't!"

"What else could I say?"

"Didn't he want to know about the stones?"

"Yeah. I told him they weren't my property, so I could not comment upon them."

"Oh, Jesus," my father says to me, "I'm afraid we may have the very first lawyer in the Sullivan family!"

I can't help laughing along with my father. Jake isn't laughing, though. His mood has suddenly shifted, as if he's the only one in the room who's just heard bad news. He drains his beer bottle, sets it down, folds his hands on the table, and leans toward my father.

"Danny," Jake says, "you have to help us. My father thinks he killed your wife."

CHAPTER EIGHTEEN

The room falls so silent I can hear the hum of the sixty-watt bulb that hangs over the kitchen table. My father looks as if he's not sure he's heard what he thinks he just heard. He turns to me. "What's the boy talking about?"

I can't say anything. I can't even move. This is Jake's movie, and I don't have any lines.

"What I'm talking about is something that happened on the day she died, right before she went to church," Jake says. "My father refused to go with her that day. He told her he didn't believe in God. He said it was all bullshit."

My father looks at me. "You told her that?"

Blood seeps back into my brain, enabling me to nod.

"Did you mean it?"

Can I speak? I can try. "At the time, yeah," I manage to say.

"Ho-ly shit."

"I'm sorry, Dad."

I start to say more but my tongue slumps down in my mouth, like that of a fighter who can't answer the bell. Jake puts a hand on my shoulder. Then, calmly, almost clinically, Jake relates the rest of the story, the way a court reporter would read back the testimony of a witness. When he gets to the climax, he puts no great emphasis on the words "I wish you were dead." He just says them.

Then he clears his throat. He's through being a reporter. He is my son again.

"Danny, my father thinks he's a murderer. He's been carrying this around for a long time. Please help him."

My father's hands are covering his face. I figure he must be crying behind those fingers, but when he takes his hands away he's pale but dry-eyed.

He looks at me. A sad smile tickles his lips, a bittersweet smile for both the lost years behind us and the found years ahead.

"You poor kid," he breathes. "Carryin' that around all this time. Now listen, you hear? You *listen* to me."

He reaches over to clasp his hand on top of mine, the callused flesh of his palm rough against the soft skin on the back of my hand.

"You didn't kill your mother. *I* didn't kill her, either, by the way. She killed herself, and not just because she ate too much."

"Dad—"

"Listen to me, *listen* to me. Your mother didn't know how to get mad. When things bothered her, she put on a show like nothin' was wrong. She never yelled, she never let it out. Which would have been fine, if she really *was* calm, but she wasn't. It all boiled around inside her. She was a difficult, stubborn, opinionated person, and before you say 'Look who's talkin',' think about this— didn't you find it unusual that your mother had no friends?"

I'm stunned to hear him say that. "Sure she did! She had loads of friends!"

"Name one."

I open my mouth, close it, think about it, and realize he's right.

"She had *admirers*," my father says. "That's an entirely different thing. You can admire a person without liking her, can't you?"

He doesn't expect me to answer this question. Anyway, my silence is an answer.

My father leans back, gulps some beer. "How can you have a friend if you can't tolerate an opinion other than your own?" he asks. "The answer is, you *can't*. So what the hell can you do? Where can you turn?"

I clear my throat and say, "The church."

"Bingo! Sorry. Terrible pun, but you understand what I'm sayin'. The Catholic church lays it all out for you. No need to argue about anything, or question anything. They tell you what God wants you to do, and you do it. A perfect world for a woman like your mother."

"But not you."

"No, not me. Not by a long shot. See, your mother helped everybody who needed help. She liked the weak. But I'm pretty strong, as you might have noticed. She had a hell of a lot of trouble with anyone who was as strong as she was, and believe me, she was *strong*."

"Not *that* strong, Dad. I told her I wished that she was dead, and an hour later she was."

My father shrugs. "So?"

"Are you saying that was a *coincidence*?"

"Are you saying it *wasn't*?"

"How could something like that be a coincidence?"

My father makes erasing motions with his hands in midair, as if to clean a blackboard cluttered with gibberish. "Wait. Stop. Let me get this straight. You believe that you had the *power* to *will* your mother's death, is that right?"

"I wouldn't call it a power."

"Oh, that's good. Because you see, Sammy, human beings do not *have* such powers. Maybe God has that power, *if* there's a God, but let me ask you this—if there's a God, and if he's good, why would he strike down one of his top soldiers here on earth just because her masturbation-happy son wanted it to happen?"

I'm weeping now, quietly and steadily. "I don't know."

"You don't? Well, luckily, *I* do. He would only strike *her* down to punish *you* for that nasty thing you said."

He spreads his hands. "Where was *her* punishment? She dies beautifully, perfectly, *in God's house!* Think about that! No pain, no lingering, unlike most poor bastards who die a little bit at a time with their lousy ailments. No goin' back and forth to hospitals year after year, with surgeons takin' her away a piece at a time. No goin' bald from chemo, no bullshit visits from relatives tellin' her how good she looks while she's wastin' away . . .

"Instead, she goes straight to heaven. She's got a harp and wings and eternal happiness. Meanwhile, you drag yourself around for thirty years with this barrel o' guilt strapped to your back. Now do you see why I never set foot in that lousy church? I just couldn't stand all the dirty tricks they use to keep everybody in line! Guilt, on top of more guilt! What bullshit!"

He turns to Jake. "Did you know that they believe in something called Original Sin? Ever heard of that one, Jake?"

"No, sir."

"It means you're born with a sin on your soul, a sin carried over from when Adam and Eve ate the forbidden fruit in the Garden of Eden, and you can only wash it away through baptism, and babies who die before they're baptized go to a place called 'limbo.' That's neither heaven nor hell. I'm guessing it's a lot like New Jersey. Have you ever heard of such lunacy?"

Jake is laughing too hard to answer. My father turns back to me.

"You're the one who suffered, Sammy, not your mother," he says. "I'll say it again—if anyone got punished, it was you. Not her. *You.*"

By the end of his speech, he's almost whispering. Jake is transfixed by every word of it, and looks as if he wishes he'd been taking notes. I can barely hear myself as I ask, "Do you think God wanted to punish me, Dad?"

He actually chuckles at the question. "I'm not sure I actually believe in God. I'm just layin' it out for you in the only two ways you can look at it. Either God meant to punish you, which in my book makes him a pretty spiteful son of a bitch, or it was all just a coincidence."

He winks at me. "My money's on coincidence, Sammy. And I think it's time you started bettin' that way, too. Your mother was fat. She was also, as Jake pointed out, intense. Fat, intense people tend to have fatal heart attacks. That's the way it goes."

I draw the longest breath I've drawn in years. My lungs feel bigger. There actually seems to be more room in my body for air, for blood, for life.

One of the wackiest stories I ever wrote for the *New York Star* was about a sixty-something woman from the Bronx who'd struggled with a weight problem all her life. No matter how seriously she dieted or exercised, she remained grossly overweight. Then at last it was discovered that she had a sixty-eight-pound benign tumor in her abdomen, which doctors estimated had been growing for more than thirty years. Thirty years! They removed the tumor, and she was fine.

I got permission to interview her at her hospital bedside. She was sweet and forthcoming, and looking forward to a "normal" life for the first time in years.

I even got a look at the tumor, a pink, floppy-looking thing that resembled a giant half-deflated beach ball. The photographer I was with took a few shots of it, then excused himself to go and vomit.

The story didn't make sense to me. Why did a doctor have to diagnose this gigantic growth? How could this woman have carried that thing around for so long without knowing or even *suspecting* it was there?

She shrugged at the question. "Because I've always had it," she said simply. I didn't fully understand what she meant until now, right now, here in my father's sanctified kitchen. He has just lifted this ten-ton growth from my soul, this thing I've always had, and I'm feeling almost giddy. I fight the urge to jump up and shadow-box. My father is grinning at me. He knows he's gotten through. I take a swallow of beer, and it's like a drink from the Fountain of Youth. I grab my son and take him in a bear hug.

"Jake. Thank you for this road trip."

"You're welcome, Dad."

"If you learn anything from my life, learn that it's important to be careful in the things you say and do."

"I will, Dad."

"But not *too* careful," my father chimes in.

I release Jake from the bear hug. "Jesus, Dad, what are you telling your grandson?"

"That wasn't sexual advice," my father says. "By all means wear a condom at all times, maybe two. I'm talkin' in general here." He gulps beer, puts his bare foot up on the table. "Did we or did we not have a bit of an adventure today?"

"We sure did."

"Nothing a *careful* person would have experienced, though, was it?" He clinks his beer bottle against mine and Jake's.

"Here's to Officer Orvieto," he says. "I know I'll sleep soundly tonight, knowing he's on the job."

"Great cop," Jake says. "A tribute to the men in brown."

My father laughs at that one, and I realize that Jake has downed three or four beers and is half in the bag.

"Hey," I tell him, "go easy. We've got to deal with your mother tomorrow."

"To Doris!" my father says. "The woman who gave me this splendid grandson!"

"Yeah," I say. "She gave him to you, all right. Come tomorrow, she may kill him."

"Aw, Dad," Jake says, "you really do worry too much. Please stop worrying, 'cause—"

"Because you've got a plan. I know. You've told me a million times, so please, don't make me wait any longer. What the hell is this *plan*?"

"You'll hear all about it tomorrow."

"Jake—"

"To-*mor*-row," Jake insists, and the way he says the word sends my father into a beery rendition of "The Sun Will Come Out Tomorrow," with my son joining him on the second chorus.

But suddenly Jake stops singing. He stares at me, sensing from the look in my eyes that there is more to know about his father, one more story to be told. He also knows that this is the day to ask me whatever there is to ask.

"Hey, Dad," he begins, "why did you freak out when you saw that crucifix before?"

I can't say I'm surprised by the question. I told him I'd tell him about it later, and here we are, later.

My father stops singing and goes pale. He puts his beer bottle down and says to Jake, very softly, "What crucifix?"

"We stopped by his old high school and there's this giant crucifix out in front. Dad could hardly look at it. I thought he was going to get sick."

My father turns to me, looking truly weary for the first time all day. "You might as well tell him," he says. "This is a night for the truth. He might as well know what you and I know, Sammy."

I can feel myself trembling. "Dad," I begin, "even *you* don't know the whole story about the crucifix. I'm the only one alive who knows the whole story of the crucifix."

The truth of it hits me as I speak these words. My father's eyes widen in shock. I guess I always thought I would take this story to the grave with me, but suddenly it's time to share it.

My father picks up his beer, takes a bracing swallow, puts a hand on Jake's shoulder. They're both looking at me with the eyes of children who are about to hear a ghost story, eager and reluctant at the same time.

My father turns to Jake. "You sure you want to hear this story, kid?"

Jake nods. "Yeah, I do. I might as well hear everything, after all these years of never hearing anything."

My father grins at Jake. "Smart," he says, and then he turns to me. "Go ahead, Sammy."

"Dad. Are you sure *you* want to hear this?"

"Yeah. Yeah, I want to know the whole story, whatever it is. Come on, man, we're listening."

His voice is quaking. I've never heard my father's voice quake before. He's afraid. He should be.

CHAPTER NINETEEN

My mother first read about it in the *Tablet*, the weekly newspaper for the Archdiocese of New York. It seems that a janitor in a small church in Scranton, Pennsylvania, was mopping up one morning when he happened to notice red stains on the floor beneath the life-sized crucifix at the altar. Looking up, he saw that the wooden Christ figure was bleeding from the nail holes in his feet.

A miracle. And just like that, Scranton turned into Jerusalem as Catholics from all over the country flocked to view this miracle.

Of course my mother wanted to go and see it. My father thought she was out of her mind. We took a two-week vacation to a Pocono Mountains resort each summer during the last week of July and the first week of August, and that was the extent of the Sullivan family travels. An old navy buddy of my father's owned the place, so we got a discount on our cabin. My father fished, my mother struggled to cook our meals on a bottle-gas stove, and I formed fleeting friendships with the children of other vacationers around a large swimming pool with a cracked cement floor. Then we returned home to Flushing for the remaining fifty weeks of the year, and no other family trips were ever even discussed until the Bleeding Jesus hit the headlines.

Our church was organizing an overnight trip to Scranton—a chartered bus there and back, plus one evening at a Howard Johnson's Motor Lodge, buffet dinner and buffet breakfast included. My mother would leave on Friday morning and be back late Saturday afternoon. The cost was fifty dollars. She had the money, her own money.

Now it was Thursday night. We were at the kitchen table, eating macaroni and cheese, and my mother wanted my father's approval. He was dead set against it.

"Mary. This is ridiculous."

"Not to me it isn't, Danny."

"Why do you want to see this thing?"

"It's a miracle in our lifetime."

"It's a scam that's going to be found out, sooner or later."

"Oh, Danny. You have no faith at all, do you?"

"Not in things that don't deserve it. Somebody's workin' an angle here, I can just feel it."

My mother shook her head. "It's so sad. If *you* can't explain it, it has to be a fake."

"And if *you* believe it, it has to be real."

"You would have laughed at Lourdes, Danny."

"I'm laughing at Lourdes right now, Mary. Everybody who goes there in a wheelchair comes home in the wheelchair. Who gets healed?"

"There's such a thing as *spiritual* healing, you know."

"Yeah, I know. That's where the priest says, 'Don't you feel better now?' just as the collection plate comes around."

By this time my mother had her hands over her ears. When he was through talking she lowered her hands and said, "I'm going to Scranton and I'm taking Samuel."

"You're *what?!*"

"You heard me."

I was shocked. This was the first time I'd heard that I was going to Scranton.

"Your supper for tomorrow night is in the freezer," my mother continued. "Preheat the oven—"

"Whoa, whoa! Why are you dragging the kid along?"

"I think he should see this."

"Mary. Don't turn your obsessions into his obsessions."

"Danny—"

"Sammy," my father said, leaning into my face, "do you want to go on this trip?"

I was twelve years old, and I was in a terrible jam. The truth of it was that I wanted to attend a school dance that was being held on Friday night. I'd never been to a dance before, and all the kids in my class were going to be there, including Margaret Thompson, and I'd been lying awake nights thinking of ways to ask her to dance.

She was the prettiest girl in my class, maybe the prettiest girl in the world. She had green-blue eyes and perky ears and blond hair that she wore in pigtails, and a giggly laugh that just about made me swoon. All the guys liked her, and I knew they'd all be asking her to dance.

She barely knew I was alive. Once she asked if she could borrow my eraser, and when she returned it to me her fingers brushed the palm of my hand, and I damn near fainted.

Would I pass out if I tried to dance with her? I didn't know, but I was willing to try. At least I thought I was.

Then came the Bleeding Jesus of Scranton, and suddenly my mother wanted me to go with her. The only good thing about that was that I'd miss school on Friday. The bad thing was that I'd miss the dance. The worst thing was that no matter what I wanted to do, I didn't want to disappoint either of my parents, and that was an impossibility.

My father had me locked in his gaze. "Don't look at your mother. Look at *me* and tell me—do you want to go on this trip?"

I swallowed, put my fork down. "Well, there's this dance at the school tomorrow night."

"There you go!" my father said. "He wants to go to the dance, like any normal kid!"

My mother looked at me. "Samuel. There'll be plenty of dances."

"Oh, for Christ's sake!" my father roared.

"And I really don't want to travel alone, Samuel."

"*Alone!*" My father snorted. "You'll be with your own kind! A bus full of Holy Rollers, going to see a phony miracle!"

She ignored the insult, didn't even look at him. She was smiling at me in a way that was both motherly and seductive. "It's up to you, Samuel," she said softly. "You choose."

My head was pounding. I wanted to break a window, run outside, scream at the sky. My father was glowering at me. My mother looked at me as if she'd known what my answer would be all along.

And she did, of course. I couldn't let her go alone. I couldn't disappoint my mother. I couldn't do what I really wanted to do, any more than I could flap my arms and fly to the moon. "I'll go with you, Mom."

My father threw down his fork and got up from the table. "A hundred bucks shot, instead of fifty," he all but snarled on his way out the door.

"It's not your money, Danny!" my mother called after him, but I doubt he heard her. She was stroking my cheek the way she did whenever I was a very good boy.

I was the only child on the whole damn bus. The passengers were mostly women and almost entirely elderly. Canes and crutches filled the overhead racks, and the reek of Ben-Gay arthritis cream was enough to make my eyes tear. Every seat on the bus was full, with the exception of two in the back, which were being used to transport folded-up wheelchairs.

One old man named Harry Campbell wore jet-black sunglasses. He was stone blind. Why was he making the trip if he couldn't even see the bleeding crucifix?

"He has faith," my mother explained. "He has the faith to believe in a miracle, even if he can't see it."

He has fifty bucks, my father would have said. He has fifty bucks for the bus and the motel.

I had to hide a smile, thinking of what my father would have had to say if he were along for the trip. It would have been a lot less spiritual but a lot more amusing.

Maybe that's why my mother wanted me to come with her so badly. I would be a teenager in less than a year—the sap was rising, the hormones were brewing. Maybe she sensed that her grip on my soul was loosening, and that a trip like this would strengthen it. Maybe, maybe, maybe. . . .

Our motel room had two narrow beds, a bureau, a window overlooking the highway we'd just come off, and a bathroom with a shower, but no tub. There were two glasses on the bathroom sink, wrapped in plastic pouches. There was a paper band around the toilet seat that was supposed to assure us that the thing was clean, that our asses would be the first to make contact with it since the gray-haired Irish maid we'd passed in the hallway had given it a swipe with a disinfectant-soaked cloth.

My mother put our small overnight bag on the bureau, and then we stretched out on the beds for a little rest. Everybody from the bus would be gathering downstairs in about half an hour, and then we would all walk to the church to bear witness to the miracle.

We lay there staring at the ceiling, a checkerboard of perforated white tiles. I wondered what we'd be having for dinner. I was thinking ahead, past the miracle. I had never been to a buffet. The thought of it was a lot more exciting to me than a bleeding Jesus.

"Samuel?"

"Yeah, Mom?"

"I'm glad you're here with me. Are you glad you're here?"

"I guess."

"We're very lucky to be seeing what we're about to see. People all over the world wish they could be here."

"Uh-huh."

"Samuel?"

"What?"

"I want to apologize for your father."

I didn't like what she'd just said, or the way she said it. "Apologize for what?"

"What I mean is . . . I'm sorry he's not a better man."

I sat up on the bed, staring straight into her shining eyes. This was the sort of thing she never could have said in our house, or in that rickety cabin in the Poconos. She was telling me she was sorry she'd allowed Danny Sullivan to be the father of her child, instead of someone worthier of the role than the wisecracking, beer-swilling lout she'd permitted to impregnate her.

It was a hell of a thing to hear, especially in a boxy little room like the one we were in, so close to the Pennsylvania Turnpike that the whine of traffic was as constant as a heartbeat.

What could I say? I felt sorry for her and furious at her in equal measures. If she had that kind of scorn for my father, how could she feel about *me*, the fruit of his loins?

No—no, I was wrong about that. She was looking at me with what appeared to be unqualified love. She obviously didn't think of me as a part of him—and after this special road trip together, I'd be hers more than ever.

"Samuel. Have I upset you?"

"I'm okay."

"I'm not criticizing your father. He's a certain type of person, that's all. He's not much like me . . . or you."

I wasn't going to respond to that. I was starting to think about the dance I'd be missing, and the way my father wanted me to go to the dance. It was enough that my mother had gotten her way and hauled me along on this crazy trip. It wasn't necessary for her to tear him down. So I remained silent, staring at the perforated ceiling, wondering why there were holes in those tiles and why my parents couldn't get along.

My mother rose from her bed. "We should go downstairs and join the others. Do you have to go to the bathroom first?"

I did have to go. I snapped the paper band off the toilet seat, took a piss, washed my hands and face with a tiny bar of motel soap, and then I was as ready as I'd ever be to see the Bleeding Jesus of Scranton, Pennsylvania.

It was a three-block walk to the church, but it took us the better part of an hour, at a crutches and wheelchair pace. Inevitably my mother wound up leading the blind man with the jet-black glasses, his bony hand clutching the crook of her elbow, and though a local church guide had been sent to lead us it was obvious to all that my mother was the one in charge.

She appointed (or should I say anointed?) me to push one of the wheelchairs, containing what was left of a once-vigorous woman named Helen Paulsen, who claimed to have been a member of the U.S. Olympic swim team during the 1920s. She blamed her decrepit hips on all those years of kicking her way up and down swimming pools, but she had no regrets—God was good, she said, God will look out for me.

God, and the pension left to her by her late husband, who'd been a member of the Steamfitters Union before lung cancer claimed him.

"Oh, Samuel," she said, looking straight ahead as I pushed her along the sidewalks of Scranton, "it is so *awfully* good of you to push me this way."

For some reason Mrs. Paulsen, a lifelong resident of Flushing, had acquired a half-assed British accent.

"I don't mind, Mrs. Paulsen."

"And aren't you a lucky lad to be taking part in this thrilling expedition?"

You'd have thought we were hacking our way through a jungle on our way to find Dr. Livingstone. She turned her head to look at me. "I said, aren't we lucky—"

"Yes, ma'am, we sure are lucky to be here."

"Why, you're the only child on the trip! Are you aware of that?"

I was aware of it.

The church was a small gray building with a plain metal cross out in front, over the front doors. Buses with logos from all over the Northeast were parked along the curb, and a steady stream of people was flowing in.

They were prepared for it, too—a makeshift ramp had been built to cover half the stone stairway leading into the church. I joined a line of wheelchairs at the ramp and slowly pushed Mrs. Paulsen into the cool, incense-smelling church. To my right, my mother was leading the blind man up the steps. We inched along at an identical pace, side by side. My mother winked at me, her partner in this mission of mercy.

It was now five o'clock in the afternoon. All the kids from my class were at home, getting ready for the dance. I was pushing a cripple, on my way to watch a statue bleed.

We shuffled toward the altar, where flashbulbs popped. Mrs. Paulsen rocked from side to side, unable to contain her excitement. A pale priest with a butterfat face but a slim body stood in front of the altar, smiling benignly at the approaching hordes. He wore rimless glasses that seemed to be buried in the flesh around his eyes. I could smell the Vitalis that held his thinning, slicked-back hair in place.

"Keep moving, please," he said softly, to nobody in particular. At last we were in front of the altar, where our shuffling steps came to a halt before the strangest sight I had ever seen.

A huge cross stood behind the altar, bearing a life-sized wooden Christ figure that was held to the cross at the hands and feet by nails that seemed to be the size of railroad spikes. The figure must have been made from some kind of fruit wood, a dark brown color that had never tasted paint or varnish. The only real color was the bright red liquid that dripped from the holes in Christ's feet into a golden bowl that had been placed on the floor below.

I didn't know what to feel. I suppose I should have felt afraid—I mean, how creepy was *this?*—but before I could feel anything, here came the voice of my mother, all but choked with joy, describing the sight to the blind man who clutched her elbow:

"He's bleeding from his feet . . . there, a drop just fell . . . Oh, Mr. Campbell, it's an amazing sight . . . the blood falls into a little golden bowl on the—there! Another drop just fell from his feet! It's very bright red . . . absolutely beautiful . . ."

Mrs. Paulsen turned around to look at me, her eyes brimming with tears. For a moment I thought she might spring from her wheelchair and run up to embrace the dripping Christ figure, but instead she just smiled and said, "Thank you, *thank you*, Samuel, for bringing me."

"You're welcome," I replied automatically, and a moment later we were moving to make way for the crowds behind us. There was no time to get a really good look at the crucifix, so it all seemed like a dream. We moved past the altar and hooked around toward the back of the church—wheelchairs to the left, ambulatory people to the right. Silent nuns stood at the corners of the church with collection baskets, into which everybody dropped paper money and coins. My mother had given me a dollar to contribute, which I dutifully donated.

We would all meet out front to begin the walk back to the motel, and our already-paid-for buffet dinner. My mother had the dreamiest look I'd ever seen on her face. She was literally happier than I'd ever seen her—or had I ever seen her happy at all before?

I was troubled, though. I had questions I wanted to ask, questions I didn't want Mrs. Paulsen or the blind man to hear. I would have to wait until later.

Dusk was coming, and with it a chill in the air. I helped Mrs. Paulsen put a shawl across her shoulders before beginning the push back to the motel. My mother was a big woman, but suddenly she seemed as light and graceful as a ballet dancer. Her feet seemed to barely touch the ground, and I half expected her to take wing and fly back to the motel, with Mr. Campbell hanging on like a pilot fish.

"Oh, Samuel," she said, bending to kiss my cheek, "wasn't that just *amazing*? Aren't you just . . ."

She paused, struggled to find the right word, found it at last ". . . tingling?"

"Yes, Mom," I lied. "It was amazing."

"Are you hungry?"

"Yes." At least I was telling the truth about that.

"So am I," she said. "Hungrier than I've ever been!"

She looked wide-open, innocent, joyous—all the ways she could never be in my father's presence.

I thought that maybe I shouldn't ask her the things I wanted to ask her. I didn't want to wreck this perfect experience for her. But I was a kid, and I was curious, and in the end I went ahead and did it.

At least I waited until after we'd eaten.

The motel buffet was a lot more dazzling to me than the Bleeding Jesus, a long row of metal pans heated from below by flaming cans of Sterno. There was lasagna (overcooked, not nearly as good as my mother's), southern fried chicken (tasty but a bit greasy), creamed corn, french fries, breaded flounder fillets (for Catholics who still adhered to the no-meat-on-Friday ban, even though the pope had lifted it), and string beans (straight from the can, and limp as a priest's handshake).

There were also bowls of cold stuff on offer—potato salad, sliced beets, coleslaw, and sliced dill pickles. Everything had a large metal spoon in it, and you just helped yourself.

I stuffed myself with chicken and creamed corn, while my mother must have fired down half a dozen fish fillets drenched in tartar sauce. It was hard to tell exactly how much she'd eaten because the fillets were boneless, while I had a mountain of chicken bones on my plate that testified to my greediness.

Everybody stuffed themselves. Apparently nothing stokes an appetite better than a good old-fashioned miracle. The conversations were loud, almost raucous, as if we'd all just been to an exciting ball game. The motel staffers cheerfully refilled the food pans as they emptied. The Bleeding Jesus was bringing in the kind of business this small town had never known before. For a little while I was glad to be here, and then I was jabbed by thoughts of the dance. Would I ever have worked up the courage to ask Margaret Thompson to dance? This was a question I'd never be able to answer. Who would be holding her in his arms, instead of me? That was a question that would torment me all night.

When we'd laid waste to the main meal, out came the desserts—chocolate cakes and cherry pies, gallon containers of chocolate and vanilla ice cream, plus chocolate and butterscotch sauce in squeeze containers, whipped cream in cans, rainbow sprinkles, and a huge jar of maraschino cherries.

My mother built us the biggest ice cream sundaes I'd ever seen—three scoops apiece, topped by whipped cream, sprinkles, butterscotch sauce, and maraschino cherries. We were certainly getting our money's worth from the Bleeding Jesus package deal. The crowd got even louder during dessert, probably from the sudden sugar rush. It was almost like being at a pep rally. In the midst of the noise and halfway through my sundae, I chose my moment.

"Hey, Mom, can I ask you something?"

"Of course you can, sweetheart."

"How come Jesus wasn't bleeding from his hands?"

The smile fell from her face. A bit of whipped cream on her upper lip was giving her a white mustache, but I didn't think this was the time to mention it. Instead, I plunged ahead with more questions.

"I mean, shouldn't he be bleeding from his hands, too? There are holes in his hands, aren't there?"

"Of course there are."

"But the hands weren't bleeding. And what about the crown of thorns on his head? The thorns made Jesus Christ's head bleed, didn't they?" I swallowed. "Well, the head of the wooden Jesus wasn't bleeding," I said in a voice that had suddenly become a whisper. "I just don't understand . . . why it wasn't bleeding in those other places."

My mother detected the whipped cream mustache on her lip, wiped it off with a napkin, rolled the napkin into a ball, and tossed it on the table.

"Samuel. Why must you ask these questions?"

My scalp tingled, as it always did when I feared I was letting her down.

"Mom. You said I could ask."

"These are the sort of questions your father would ask."

Oh boy. Now I'd done it.

"Mom. I'm sorry I said anything."

"No, no, sweetheart, that's all right. I'm glad you're so . . . observant."

She didn't mean that. She reached across the table, patted the back of my hand. A smile returned to her face, but it was like the smile of a clergyman, bland and vague.

"I can't answer your questions, Samuel. I can't say why the head and the hands aren't bleeding, because I don't know why. I also don't know why his feet *are* bleeding. You see? That's the way it is with a miracle. We can't understand it. We can only appreciate it."

"Okay, Mom."

"Does that make sense?"

"Sure," I lied.

"I'm very glad you're here with me."

"Me, too, Mom," I lied again.

"Now, this is a night to celebrate, so let's finish our sundaes and go back for more. How does that sound to you?"

Later, up in our beds, we lay on our backs, bloated with food. The waistband of my pajamas bit into my belly and I wondered if the hum of highway traffic would lull me to sleep or keep me awake.

I'd never slept in a room with my mother before and it felt strange. She was groggy from the feast and lay staring at the ceiling, a dreamy look on her face.

"Samuel."

"Yeah, Mom?"

"What do you want to be when you grow up?"

She'd never asked me anything like this before. The question frightened me a little. I didn't want to disappoint her.

"Uhhh . . ."

"It's all right if you don't know. It's perfectly all right if you don't know."

"Well . . ."

"I just want you to know that I think you're a very special boy. Can you think of any other boy in your class who could have appreciated this experience the way you do?"

"No, Mom."

That was the truth. Most of the boys in my class were baseball players, roughnecks, troublemakers, and some of them were just plain crazy. Marvin Kelly's specialty was turning his eyelids inside out so that the red showed above his bugged-out eyeballs. He'd do that to himself and then hide in the girls' cloak closet, waiting for someone to open the door and shriek with terror. Craig Jancovic was an albino with white hair and pink eyes who once caught a big beetle in the schoolyard, rubber-banded it to a firecracker, and blew the creature to smithereens.

And the wildest kid of all was a dark-eyed terror named Alonzo Fishetti, who came to school each day as if he were doing the nuns a favor. At twelve he was already shaving and flirting relentlessly with the girls. He didn't seem to mind getting hit with the yardstick, or any other punishment they could dream up for him. Fishetti became a legend one afternoon when he climbed out of our second-story classroom window and began walking on the ledge, intending to go around the corner to the other side of the building. That's where the girls' bathroom was, and that's where they were changing their clothes for a basketball game. Fishetti figured he could get a good look at half-naked girls through the window, but halfway there he lost his balance and fell to the ground, breaking his ankle. He didn't even cry. He just lay there on the macadam, lit up a Camel cigarette, and waited for help to arrive.

I never did things like that. I never even *dreamed* of doing things like that. I was a good boy. That's what the nuns always wrote in the "comments" section of my report card—a good boy, polite, well behaved.

But I didn't know what I wanted to be when I grew up, and before I could say anything more, my mother spoke.

"I wanted to become a nun."

Her words jolted me. She didn't even sound like herself, maybe because she was crying. She rolled on her side to face me, blinked back tears.

"You did, Mom?"

"I certainly did."

"What happened?"

"Your father happened."

I swallowed, tasting something disagreeable from the buffet feast brewing deep in my guts. "You mean you fell in love with Dad, and decided to get married?"

She didn't answer me right away. "Well," she finally said, "something like that."

"But if you'd become a nun—"

"I never would have had you. That's true, Samuel. Obviously things worked out for the best."

She didn't mean it. My own mother was telling me that if she had her way, a second chance to do it all again, she'd want to spend it as the Bride of Christ. I was the only person in the world she could share this with, and the only person who shouldn't have been hearing it.

I stared up at that unbelievably ugly perforated ceiling. It was like the night sky in reverse—black dots instead of white for stars, a white background instead of a dark one.

"Samuel."

"Yeah, Mom?" I figured she wanted to apologize for what she'd just said, but I was wrong. She cleared her throat, hesitated.

"If you should decide to become a priest . . . well, that would be all right with me."

I sat up and looked at her, my blood tingling. She was beaming at me, her eyes bright and hopeful, and through my shock and confusion it did dimly occur to me that maybe, just maybe, this was the real purpose behind our trip to see the Bleeding Jesus of Scranton.

"You want me to be a priest, Mom?"

"I didn't say that. I want you to be whatever you want to be. *If* you wanted to be a priest, I would be . . ."

She couldn't find the right word. "Happy?" I guessed.

"Pleased," she decided. "Pleased for you, and the life you would lead."

I lay down again, stared at the ceiling. For the first time ever I began thinking about the life of a priest—saying Masses, distributing communion wafers, going to people's houses for Sunday dinners . . . hearing confessions! What would that be like, sitting in a dark box to hear people tell me their sins!

And what about those white collars that always seemed to be choking the men who wore them? Every priest I'd ever seen seemed to have the edge of that collar biting into his neck fat, like the collar of a dog being restrained by his master. That particular detail of the priestly life seemed to be the worst of all—I'd be forever digging my forefinger into my collar, pulling it away from my Adam's apple to get a few unblocked breaths of air. Could I live with that? Could *anybody*? Apparently, they could.

"I don't know if I could do it, Mom," I blurted.

"Oh, sweetheart, you don't have to know! You have years and *years* to think about it."

I didn't want to think about it. I didn't want to think about *anything*. I guess I just wanted to be a kid.

It was getting late, but I wasn't sleepy. I realized that by this time the school dance was over, and I couldn't help thinking about which of my classmates had gotten to dance with Margaret Thompson. By missing the dance I feared that I'd be completely out of the running for the winning of Margaret's heart. That thought saddened me beyond words. All I could do was sigh.

My mother heard me. She sensed my anguish but completely misunderstood it.

"Samuel, please stop worrying. Forget I said anything. Don't even think about being a priest."

"Mom. If I became a priest, I couldn't get married, could I?"

"That's right, Samuel."

"So I couldn't have children, could I?"

"No, you couldn't."

"I might want to do those things, Mom." *Even though you didn't want to!*

"Of course you might, Samuel. You'll make all those decisions when the time comes."

She wasn't being sincere. Her words were like the warning on a cigarette package, something she was forced to say by law. She'd planted the seed she'd wished to plant, far from the wrath and mockery my father would certainly have rained down upon the life path she was suggesting for me with all her considerable will and might.

"Samuel. Let's try and get some sleep. We've got another big day tomorrow."

"Okay, Mom."

She rolled over and within minutes, she was asleep. She'd said what she wanted to say, so she could conk out with a clear mind.

But I was wide-awake and anxious, lonelier than I'd ever been—lonely in advance over the life my mother had mapped out for me. A priest? Who in his right mind could possibly want to be a *priest*? Beyond that, something else was troubling me— the fact that my own mother didn't seem bothered by the idea that she would never have grandchildren. Wasn't the desire for grandchildren a normal thing? Weren't old people always taking photographs of their grandchildren out of their wallets and boring anyone who'd listen with tales of these wondrous youngsters?

Well, that was fine for the rest of the world, but as far as my mother was concerned the Sullivan line would end with me, and that was all right.

I looked over at the stranger in the next bed, her shoulders heaving with each breath she took. I was sad. I was lost. A weird feeling was gnawing at me, and it took a minute to figure out what it was. At last, it came to me. It was a brand-new feeling, one I'd never experienced before.

I missed my dad.

It felt as if I'd been asleep for five minutes when my mother shook me awake. She was showered and dressed, and cheerfully announced that the buffet breakfast was being served in fifteen minutes—just enough time for me to shower and dress.

We stuffed ourselves again, and this time there were pans of scrambled eggs, pancakes, link sausages and bacon, as well as tubs of oatmeal and Cream of Wheat and small boxes of every cereal they made at Kellogg's. My mother must have eaten a dozen pancakes, drowned in butter and maple syrup, while I couldn't stop myself from gorging on the link sausages. If we'd stayed at the motor lodge for another night or two I'm sure that somebody from our group would have suffered a gluttony-induced coronary.

We were all packed up and ready to leave, our stuff stowed safely in the bus. The plan was to make one more visit to the Bleeding Jesus, return to the bus, and head home. We paired up as we had the day before, my mother leading the blind man while I pushed Mrs. Paulsen.

I was woozy from the food, from a lack of sleep, and from the almost indescribable weirdness of it all. I needed the wheelchair almost as much as Mrs. Paulsen did that morning. I actually clutched its handles to maintain my balance.

My mother, on the other hand, looked as if she'd just swum the length and breadth of Lourdes, and emerged from the waters brimming with hope and happiness for the sweet, blue-skied future. She probably could have given Mr. Campbell a piggyback ride to the church, stoked as she was by her faith and the miracle we were about to witness yet again.

The line leading inside was longer and slower this time. The cool weather had turned—the sun was hot, making me feel even dizzier. I didn't realize I was leaning my full weight on the wheelchair handles until Mrs. Paulsen suddenly tipped back and did a "wheelie," her dangling legs kicking the ass of the wheelchair pusher ahead of us. She shrieked, and I quickly set her down on all four wheels and apologized to the tall, skinny guy we'd bumped. He was cool about it, and then I apologized to Mrs. Paulsen.

"Oh, don't worry, Samuel, I'm fine."

A tight claw on my elbow—my mother had me in her grip from the adjacent line for the ambulatory, her total mortification burning like hell's fire in her eyes.

"Was that supposed to be *funny*, young man?" she hissed.

"Mom! It was an accident!"

"Kindly be careful, and remember where we are."

"I'm sorry. . . ."

But I wasn't sorry. I was sick of this whole thing, and dying to be out of there. The last thing I needed was another look at the Bleeding Jesus. I also knew that everybody back at school on Monday would be telling me about what a great dance I'd missed, and how I should have been there, and that was going to kill me.

I was tempted to turn the wheelchair around, push Mrs. Paulsen back down the ramp, and then let her go rolling down the long, steep sidewalk. Talk about a Holy Roller! And how many of those waiting out there would have rushed to save her, at the price of their precious places in line?

We inched our way into the church. The heat was worse indoors, as the place was not air-conditioned. Rotating fans pushed the steaming air around without cooling anyone. I was sweating right through my shirt, but my mother seemed remarkably cool. Mr. Campbell took off his glasses to wipe sweat from his face, and I saw with horror that he was not only blind—he had no eyes at all. His eyelids covered the sockets like sunken drumskins, and I wondered how such a thing could have happened to him. Had he been born that way, or had some disaster robbed him of his eyes? Thankfully, he put his glasses back on to hide the horrible sight. . . .

A sudden bumping sensation—while staring at the blind man's empty eyes, I'd once again rammed Mrs. Paulsen into the wheelchair pusher in front of us. This time, he was not quite so understanding. He turned to me with his hands on his hips, rolled his eyes, and sighed in exasperation.

"Do you *mind*?" he said, clearly a queen. "I mean, it's getting a bit *boring*."

I apologized all over again, to the man and to Mrs. Paulsen. I dared to look at my mother, who was shaking her head.

"I suppose that was another accident, Samuel?"

My cheeks burned with shame, and suddenly, in the midst of all this, we were upon the Bleeding Jesus and the smiling priest with the butterfat face. It was the same scenario as the day before, but something was different. Everything seemed to have slowed down. It was as if the line had stopped moving, and we had all the time in the world to drink in this miracle, unlike the fleeting passage of the day before. So much had happened to me since we were here last—two buffet meals, and two remarkable revelations. My mother wished she'd become a nun and not a wife or a mother, and she wanted me to be a priest, just like the man in black who stood there with his hands behind his back, guarding the Bleeding Jesus.

I was more interested in that man than I was in the miracle. He seemed peaceful and smug, and for no good reason I wanted to do something to jolt him, snap him out of his superior state of calmness.

A red velvet rope hung in a protective loop before the crucifix, and it might as well have been a barbed-wire fence. Nobody went near it. It was strictly a symbolic thing to keep the believers at a respectable distance.

It made sense. It was only natural that everybody would want to touch the Bleeding Jesus, to see if its flesh was warm, to let it heal the maladies within their bodies, known or unknown. But if you let one person touch it, you'd have to let *everybody* touch it, and then what would happen? The red velvet rope was there for our own good.

And the hell with that.

I released the handles of Mrs. Paulsen's wheelchair, walked around it, and stepped right over the lowest part of the rope's loop. A collective gasp rose from the masses, as if I'd just stepped onto the surface of the moon.

"Son," the priest said, calmly but firmly, "get back in line."

My mother wasn't nearly so calm. "Samuel!" she hissed. "What do you think you're *doing*?"

I igorned the both of them, took a step toward the Bleeding Jesus. My mother called my name again, and it sounded as if she was a mile away. Again, I ignored her.

I was staring at something that seemed kind of odd. Up close like this, I could see that there was a horizontal line in the wood above the Christ figure's bleeding foot, right across the shin, maybe six inches above the nail. Then I saw vertical cuts running down from the edges of the horizontal cut, which met at another horizontal cut just above the ankle. Together the lines formed a rectangle in the wood, a rectangle that could not be seen from the other side of the velvet rope. It was as if somebody had made cuts with a thin-bladed saw, then sanded them smooth to hide them. Why?

A hand gripped my shoulder—the priest with the butterfat face had a grip like iron. "Son, please, get back in line."

It wasn't really in me to disobey a priest, but I had to. I shrugged my way out of his grip, knelt before the Bleeding Jesus, grabbed at his shinbone, and pulled.

A chunk of wood came off in my hand, clean-cut on four sides. My mother screamed. I still had the chunk of wood in my hand as the priest grabbed me from behind and pulled me away, but of course it was too late.

Within moments, the entire church was aware of what had happened, the news traveling like a lightning bolt from the crucifix all the way back to the last person in line. They rushed the altar like a human tidal wave.

"Fake!" somebody screamed. "It's a fake!"

People were pushing each other, punching each other. I wrestled my way out of the priest's grasp, still holding the block of wood. Suddenly it was knocked from my hand by my mother, who then grabbed my wrist and pulled me away from the mob, past the altar, and toward a red-glowing exit sign beyond it. Her other hand gripped the elbow of the blind man, who kept asking as he stumbled along: "What happened? What happened?"

We dragged behind her as she found the exit door, and the three of us plunged outside. It was an emergency exit door, so when it slammed behind us there was no handle on the other side, no way to get back inside. We stood there in an alley full of crates and garbage cans.

"What happened?" the blind man asked again, his breathing jagged with terror. My mother wouldn't answer him. She stroked his back, the way you'd calm a dog frightened by thunder. I was jolted by a sudden concern—Mrs. Paulsen! What was going to happen to her inside the church, with nobody to guide her?

"Mom," I said, "I'd better go get Mrs. Paulsen!"

It was as if she hadn't heard me. She continued stroking Mr. Campbell's back, staring accusingly at me all the while.

"Mom?"

"Ohhh, Samuel." She shook her head, sighed, rolled her eyes to the heavens. "Samuel, what have you done?"

I couldn't answer her. I'd exposed a fraud, but I'd let her down. She'd always told me to tell the truth, but apparently *revealing* the truth was an entirely different thing.

I couldn't believe it. She was angry with me, disappointed in me! We stood staring at each other in that alley, her hand still mindlessly stroking the blind man's back. "What happened?" he continued asking, his patience as limitless as the heavens above. "Please tell me, Mary, what happened?"

CHAPTER TWENTY

The perpetrator of the Great Hoax of the Bleeding Jesus of Scranton turned out to be the butterfat-faced priest himself, Father Joseph Bielinski. Like Jesus Christ himself, the priest had been a carpenter's apprentice when he was a boy. And like countless Catholics, he was dismayed by the loss of faith and the drop in attendance at church.

So he'd taken it upon himself to create a miracle in his own sleepy parish. Late one night, he carefully cut that chunk of wood from the Christ figure's shin. He hollowed out the area and installed a rubber pouch filled with a red fluid that turned out to be Karo sugar syrup mixed with a red dye. He drilled a tunnel through the wood from the base of the shin cut to the nail holes, and through this tunnel he snaked the narrowest of plastic tubes, which was connected to the blood pouch like an intravenous drip. The tube slowly fed the fake blood through the nail holes, a tiny drop every ten seconds or so. Father Bielinski glued the shell of the shin back in place to hide the whole apparatus, sandpapered the edges, and that was that—until I ripped the thing off and exposed the fraud to the world.

Now I knew why the Christ figure couldn't bleed from the holes in his hands. The crucifix was in a Y shape, with the hands higher than the forearms. Father Bielinski may have been in the miracle business, but he needed the force of gravity to make it happen. Even a miracle worker can't make fake blood flow upstream.

Our bus left for New York three hours late. Somebody else had wheeled Mrs. Paulsen to the bus—I was glad to see she wasn't hurt.

But she wouldn't look at me. *Nobody* would look at me. I had fucked up the whole trip. I had single-handedly shot down a miracle, dashed their hopes for a richer, more meaningful life. We drove away from that church like people fleeing from a burning city, the bus driver threading his way among police cars and ambulances.

People were being bandaged by Red Cross workers, right out there on the sidewalk. I saw head injuries, and white bandages stained with blood—*real* blood. I saw an old lady being carried on a stretcher, an oxygen mask clamped to her whiskery face.

It was my fault she'd gotten hurt. It was my fault that *everybody* was hurt, or unhappy. If I'd left the Bleeding Jesus alone, none of this would have happened. It was my first real sip from the bottomless cup of guilt I would continue to drink from for the rest of my life.

"I'll have to soak those overnight."

The voice of my mother, speaking to me as she stared out the bus window—last row, last seat. The blind man was asleep beside her, his head on her shoulder. I sat across the aisle from them.

"Soak what, Mom?"

"Your pants. Your *good* pants. To get that . . . *redness* out of them."

I looked at my pants. There was a slash of fake blood on my thigh. I dared to touch it, and it felt crusty from the dried sugar syrup.

"Samuel. Don't touch it."

"I'm sorry, Mom."

"What a mess," she said, shaking her head. "Oh God, what a mess!"

"It'll wash out."

She turned to me at last, her eyes twin balls of brown fire. "I don't mean that. I mean the terrible thing you've done."

I tried to swallow. It felt as if a tennis ball was lodged in my throat.

"Me!"

"Why did you step over that rope? Who said you could touch the crucifix? Didn't you hear the priest tell you to stay away from it?"

All I could do was breathe. People on the bus were looking at my mother, admiring her as they loathed me. She closed her eyes, sighed as deeply as any human being has ever sighed.

"Your father," she moaned. "Your father is going to have such a field day with this."

And then she remained as silent as a stone for the remainder of the longest bus ride of my life.

But she was dead wrong about my father.

He was there to pick us up at the church parking lot. Of course by the time we got there the whole neighborhood knew what had happened, via word of mouth—no CNN in those days. We'd gotten out of Scranton fast enough to keep me from being identified as the boy who'd revealed the disgrace of the Bleeding Jesus, but everybody in Flushing knew I was the one, and that included my father.

He stood outside the bus with his hands in the back pockets of his jeans, looking as if he'd been waiting there since we'd departed. We were the last ones to get off the bus.

"You guys okay?" he asked.

He was being really decent, this guy my mother was sorry had been the one to sire me. He should only know how she felt about him! It was tempting to shout this terrible truth to him, but I didn't. I just stood there while he rubbed my hair with one hand and took his wife in a gentle embrace with his other arm.

My mother wept. I'd never seen her cry before, never even imagined she could do such a thing in his presence. He tucked her face against his chest to deprive the rubbernecking crowd of their pleasures.

"Get the bag, kid."

Our bag was the last one in the luggage compartment, all the way in the back. The driver was waiting for me to get it, a dirty look on his face. He knew I was the reason he was three hours behind schedule. I had to climb inside the compartment to get our bag, and was gripped by a fleeting but terrifying thought— the bus driver was going to slam down the luggage lid with me still inside, and drive off to some remote area to kill me! And what's more, he'd be doing it with my mother's permission, as well as her blessing!

But no. I scurried in and out with the bag. The bus took off with a great wheeze of diesel fumes, and then we Sulllivans got into our car and went home.

My father drove slowly. He kept checking on my mother, as if she were made of porcelain and might shatter if he hit the brake too hard. "Mary."

"Not now, Danny."

He looked at me on the backseat and winked, a wink that promised everything would be all right. But he was promising something he couldn't deliver. "Look, Mary, I just want to say—"

"I have never, ever felt so terrible in all my life."

"Come on."

"I mean it."

"What about when your parents died?"

"This is worse. *Much* worse."

"Oh, come on, Mary!"

My father didn't know what else to say, and I didn't know what to feel. I tried to imagine my parents dying, and couldn't think of anything worse than that. Yet here was my mother, pretty much saying that she'd rather have a false Bleeding Jesus dripping away in Scranton, Pennsylvania, than the two people who gave her the gift of life.

My dad tried to hold his tongue, but he just couldn't. "I tried to warn you," he said gently. "This whole thing had a bad stink, right from the start."

"Danny. You've got to talk to him."

"Who?"

She jerked her thumb over her shoulder without looking at me.

"Oh, you mean our son! Talk to him about what?"

"The terrible thing he did."

My father laugh-snorted. He could be very dangerous when he made that sound. He was like a ram backing up and lowering his horns for battle when he made that sound. "Hang on now, woman. You're upset with Sammy for revealing a *fraud!*"

"Don't call it a fraud! If Samuel hadn't done what he'd done, everything would have been all right!"

She was practically screaming, and when she stopped we just sat there in the jarring silence. My father was breathing hard. He was not bracing himself for battle. For the first time ever, he seemed to be afraid of his wife. Until now, she'd been an amusing religious eccentric. Now, suddenly, she'd pole-vaulted over the line, into the sand pit of total insanity.

His hands tightened on the steering wheel. He looked at the stranger beside him, then at the child behind him. This time, he did not wink at me. He shook his head from side to side, as if in mourning for the loss of something precious, a loss he should have seen coming, a loss he should have done something to prevent. But what? What could he have done?

"You talk to him, Danny," my mother said. "Explain to him that people can't just go around touching things that aren't theirs."

"Mary. Calm down."

"I'm tired, Danny. I'm very tired."

"I know you are. Let's just get home."

"Yes, home. I want to go home."

"Shhhh, shhhh . . . we're almost there."

My mother went straight to bed without even saying good night to us. My father and I were rarely the only two people awake in the house, and neither of us was comfortable with it. He went to the refrigerator and came to the kitchen table with a bottle of Rheingold beer and a glass. This puzzled me. My father never drank from a glass. He sat down, and told me to sit with him.

"How old are you now, Sammy?"

He was serious. He didn't know. Every year or so he asked me how old I was, like a census taker.

"Twelve."

"Well, hell, I'd say the time has come for your first cold frosty one."

He poured beer into the glass and pushed it to my side of the table. I couldn't believe it. Every time he popped open a beer for himself, my mother sighed and her nostrils went wide. And he wasn't breaking the law, the way I was about to! What would she say if she saw me with a beer in my hand?

I kept my hands on my lap. The room reeked of hops, corn, and barley. It was so quiet I could hear the bubbles popping in the head of foam.

"Dad. I'd better not."

"Come on. I was ten when I had my first taste."

"Mom wouldn't like it."

"Sammy, your mother is already as upset as she can be. Nothing you or I do can make it worse. Now lift that glass."

I obeyed him. He clinked his bottle against my glass.

"Drink."

I filled my mouth with beer. I didn't like the taste. It seemed grimy and bitter, but I swallowed it, then gulped down the rest and slammed the glass down as I thought a hardened drinker would. My father chuckled, took a swallow from his bottle.

"What do you think, kid?"

"Not very good."

"You have to get used to it."

"If you have to get used to it, what's the point?"

He laughed out loud. "Good question." He leaned back in his chair, took another swallow of beer. "You didn't do anything wrong, kid."

"Mom thinks I did."

"Your mother is wrong, dead wrong."

"She doesn't think she is."

"She never thinks she's wrong. It's what makes her so much fun to be around."

"Nobody on the bus would talk to me."

"Nobody on that bus has anything worthwhile to say, Sammy. They're crazy people."

"Mom's not crazy!" I all but cried, wanting to believe my own words.

"Shut up!" my father hissed. "Whaddaya want to do, wake her?"

"She's *not* crazy! Don't say she's crazy!"

"No, no, of course she isn't! Point is, you shouldn't have been on that trip in the first place. You should have gone to the dance."

He reached across the table and rubbed my hair, awkwardly, as if he'd read in a magazine that this was a good thing to do when your child is upset.

"This is gonna pass, Sammy. Not for a few days, maybe, but it'll pass, and remember—*you didn't do anything wrong.* If I'd been there and seen somethin' funny about the crucifix, I'd have done the same thing."

Bullshit, I thought, and then I excused myself to go to bed.

"Don't tell your mother about the beer!" he chuckled as I

headed for the stairs. It was a moot point, as far as I was concerned. What were the chances that my mother and I would ever again be on speaking terms?

I stripped down and got into bed without bothering to brush my teeth. I was exhausted. I fell asleep as if I'd been drugged, and I thought I was dreaming when I opened my eyes and saw a woman in a flowing, breeze-puffed nightgown approach my bedside. An angel? The Blessed Mother?

No. It was *my* mother, smiling at me as if nothing terrible had happened. She knelt at the head of the bed, stroked my hair.

"Samuel? Samuel, I forgive you."

I should have been angry, but I couldn't even think that way. I was grateful to be on her good side, no matter what kind of lunacy it involved. So instead of telling her to get out of my room, I did the only thing I thought I could do. I thanked her.

She kissed my forehead, and then her brow knotted in alarm. "What's that smell on your breath? Beer?"

I lacked the strength to make up a tale. "Dad shared his beer with me."

Her back arched with a jolt, St. Sebastian absorbing yet another arrow. But she didn't have the strength for a fight. She rose to her feet and left my room as mysteriously as she'd entered it. The whole thing felt like a dream, but it wasn't.

A cawing, shrieking blue jay woke me in the morning. It was Sunday. In a few hours we'd be getting ready for church. Church! It didn't seem fair to have to go again, after having spent Friday and Saturday in church, but routine was routine, and we did what we had to do.

My father urged us not to go. "Haven't you had enough for a while? And besides, you ought to let this thing die down."

He might as well have been standing on the edge of the ocean, begging the tide not to come in. My mother smiled at him as falsely as she could.

"Would you rather he stayed here and got drunk with you?"

My father looked at me, his betrayer.

"I didn't say anything!" I cried. "She smelled it!"

He shook his head, rolled his eyes, and headed out to Charlie's Bar for the first cold frosty one of the day. My mother and I set off walking to the eleven o'clock Mass at ten minutes to the hour, as we had for as many Sundays as I could remember.

But of course everything was different. There were murmurs and whispers as we passed people . . . "That's the boy . . . he's the one . . ."

My mother didn't say anything. She kept her head as high and proud as a show pony's, but her jaw was clenched as we took our usual seats.

A hard poke to my rib cage—I turned and saw Alonzo Fishetti, the toughest kid from my class, the crazy one who'd fallen from the second-story ledge and broken his ankle while trying to spy on the half-dressed girls. His ankle was still in a cast, and he dragged it like a peg-leg pirate when he walked. Even his jet-black hair looked dangerous, soaked with lotion and combed straight back to reveal a dazzling widow's peak. His eyes were a little too close together, separated by a beaky nose. He was the crow, and I was the worm.

"Hey, Sullivan. Did you really pull that statue's leg off?"

This was the first time he'd ever spoken to me. I was honored and intimidated. I shrugged, cleared my throat. "Just a piece of it."

He smiled, patted my shoulder. "Cool!" he said. "Most definitely a cool thing to do."

I couldn't believe it. Nobody had ever accused me of being cool before, and this was coming from the toughest, coolest person I knew! He winked at me.

"Great shit, Sullivan. I didn't think ya had it in ya."

This was the ultimate—approval from Alonzo Fishetti! For the first time ever, I felt like one of the guys! I had to say something to him, but what? I thought about it and cleared my throat before speaking.

"How was the dance, Alonzo?"

"Ah, I didn't go. How'm I supposed to dance with this fuckin' ankle?"

With that he dragged himself out of church, probably to go outside for a smoke. I'd never felt so honored, never heard anyone dare to say "shit" and "fuck" in church, and beyond all that I was elated to know that at least one boy, Alonzo Fishetti, did not get to dance with Margaret Thompson while I'd been away.

"Who *was* that horrible boy?" my mother demanded. For a moment there, I'd forgotten that she was sitting beside me.

"Just a kid from my class."

"What's his name?"

I told her. She made a knowing sound in her throat, a clucking sound. "Ahhh yes, the Fishettis. His father ran off when he was two years old. His mother has had quite a few . . . *boyfriends* over the years."

I was shocked to be hearing something like this from my mother, but of course it made sense. In any act of charity, a person learns all about the weaknesses of those being helped. I guess the Fishettis rated a casserole or two over the years, to take the sting out of whatever misery Alonzo's mother's chaotic love life created. In her own inimitable way, my mother had just called Alonzo Fishetti's mother a whore.

The Mass began, and there was a low communal moan as Father Peter Vallone made his way to the pulpit. He was a big, fat, dumb priest whose sermons seemed to last for months and never made any kind of point. He probably had attention deficit disorder back in those days before it was diagnosed, and for this reason he was the best priest to confess your sins to. You could tell him you'd murdered five people and by the time he gave you your penance, he'd have forgotten this sin and given you two Our Fathers and two Hail Marys to wipe your soul clean.

But there was a new determination to Father Vallone on this day. He seemed both focused and angry as he stood before us, his chubby hands gripping the sides of the pulpit.

"We all know about this terrible thing that happened in Scranton, Pennsylvania," he began, and a movielike murmur ran through the crowd. Hundreds of eyes were upon me. My mother gripped my wrist. If Father Vallone singled me out, I knew I would die of mortification.

"Yes, yes, a terrible thing. A priest cut open a Jesus figure, much like this one"—he gestured at the plaster-cast crucifix behind him—"and stuck a balloon filled with blood inside the leg, to make it bleed from the nail holes in the foot. Well, maybe it wasn't exactly a *balloon*. It was probably something thicker than a balloon. Maybe it was a rubber pouch, like a hot water bottle. Maybe it was made of plastic. Maybe . . ."

Father Vallone's tangents could take his flock to the ends of the universe. Usually they put us to sleep, but not today. Today we were all listening as this man exhausted the physical possibilities of the reservoir that held the fake blood. He was just explaining how the pouch could have been made out of an old bicycle inner tube when an unbelievably loud voice interrupted him:

"Get to the point!"

It was as sudden and shocking as a clap of thunder. People literally cowered at the sound of it, no one more than me as I looked to my right and saw that the words had come from my mother, who now stood on her feet, glowering at Father Vallone.

The priest stared at her in wonder. "Are you all right, Mary?"

He knew her well. Much of his girth had been put there by meals my mother had cooked for him.

She ignored his question. "Will you please just say what you mean to say?"

Father Vallone had never been in a jam like this. He'd been spouting lazy, unchallenged sermons for so long that he'd probably forgotten that some people were actually listening. And he'd sooner have expected the Jesus figure behind him to leap off the cross and perform a tap dance on the altar than hear words like these from St. Aloysius's number-one parishoner.

The priest looked around helplessly, then back at my mother, his jaw slack with embarrassment. "Uhhh . . . well, jeez . . . all I mean to say is that this terrible thing—"

"*What* terrible thing?"

A murmur ran through the crowd. People were looking at each other and at my mother, who was still on her feet. She seemed to be growing taller as she awaited her answer.

Father Vallone cleared his throat, brought a handkerchief to his mouth, wiped something off his tongue. "The terrible trick Father Bielinski played on his flock."

"Why was it so terrible?"

"Come now, Mary—"

"He was trying to bring a little bit of faith back to the people! I don't think that's such a terrible thing! Who did he hurt by what he did?"

"Mary, your own son is the one who—"

My mother made erasing motions in midair to shut him up. "I've spoken with my son about it. That's my business. So let me ask you again—who did the priest hurt by what he tried to do? Everybody was happy. Everyone *believed.* He didn't do it for money, or for fame. He did it to help people!"

The murmurs rose to a pep-rally level. A woman yelled, "Sit down, Mary!" but she was quickly shouted down. Father Vallone seemed paralyzed at the pulpit. He literally did not know what to do.

But my mother did. She squeezed past me and made her way straight to the altar. Nobody stopped her as she climbed the steps to the pulpit and gestured dismissingly for the priest to step aside, which he did, almost gratefully. My mother adjusted the pulpit microphone to her height as Father Vallone stood behind her, busted down in rank to altar boy. It was my mother's show now, and there was no stopping her.

"The Bleeding Jesus of Scranton *is* a bona fide miracle," she announced. "If we judge what people do by their intentions, then Father Bielinski is not a sinner. He brought us all together. He reinforced our faith in a godless time."

She pointed at me, and I stopped breathing.

"My son is sorry he ever touched the Bleeding Jesus, but really, what did he reveal? A fraud? No! He revealed the work of a good man in desperate times, a man who wished to bring attention back to the things that matter. Hear what I tell you, people! Father Bielinski is *not* a scoundrel!"

She smiled, raised her hands toward the heavens.

"He is a hero!"

I was growing faint, and had to tell myself to start breathing again. This was my mother, someone I'd once known as the gentlest, quietest person in the world. But she'd shed that skin, molted into something else . . . a woman on a mission.

And then the most remarkable thing that ever happened in a Catholic church happened, more remarkable than statues that bleed or weep or tap dance. Everybody at the standing-room-only eleven o'clock Mass at St. Aloysius got to their feet and gave my mother a standing ovation.

I didn't know what to feel, where to look, what to do. Father Vallone cut bait on the rest of his sermon and went straight to the distribution of communion wafers.

Everybody came up to receive. It was incredible. My mother had infused that crowd with a jolt of faith no clergyman could have mustered. I half expected people to ask for her autograph as we left the church, and as we stepped outside the flash of a camera bulb went off right in my face, not hers.

"Thanks, kid!" said the photographer, a skinny man with a Lucky Strike cigarette dangling from his lip and a press card jammed in his hat band. This was my introduction to the publication that would later play a major role in my life, the *New York Star*.

"Now gimme one wit ya muddah!" the photographer said, and before either of us could object he took a step back to widen his shot, flashed away, saluted us with a grin and not another word before trotting away, leaving us to face a slim, serious, balding man who looked more like a priest than what he actually was—a true-blue reporter for the *New York Star* named George O'Malley. At forty years of age he was a father of six, a rhythm-method Catholic with the dubious title of Religion Editor.

He introduced himself to us and apologized for the photographer's crude behavior. He wanted to talk to me about the Bleeding Jesus, but my mother forbade it. He wanted to talk to my mother about it, but she told him to go away. He didn't seem particularly disappointed by her refusal, and I understood why the next day. He'd already gotten what he needed, having been inside to hear all of my mother's rant, which he quoted extensively in his story.

But I was the big news of the day. My startled face was on the front page of Monday's *New York Star,* under a headline reading:

EXCLUSIVE PHOTO!
THE BOY WHO UNCOVERED THE CRUCI-"FIX!"

Now everybody who didn't already know about what I'd done knew about it. The kids in the schoolyard waved the front page in my face, jeering and laughing with a glee the nuns could do nothing to stop. Luckily for me Alonzo Fishetti told them to knock it off, and that ended the teasing more abruptly than gunfire would have. At one point in the school day Margaret Thompson came over to me while I was using the classroom pencil sharpener. I'd never been this close to her. She smelled wonderfully sweet, like a rose grown in a pot of sugar.

"Sammy?"

"Oh, hi, Margaret." Trying to act casual, though my hand trembled so much that I could barely turn the handle on the pencil sharpener.

"Are you all right?"

"Sure."

She smiled, shrugged. "Sorry you missed the dance," she said, and then she was gone, leaving me to turn that sentence over in my head a million times to try and figure if she was just being polite, or if she meant it.

And then a funny thing happened, a thing that kept this story going when it otherwise might have died a swift and quiet death. My mother had actually enjoyed being quoted in George O'Malley's story, and telephoned him the day after it ran to arrange for an interview. She had something big to tell him, and she wasn't kidding.

She was establishing the Father Joseph Bielinski Defense Fund, the proceeds of which would go toward keeping him from being excommunicated from the Catholic Church.

This was it, then, the ultimate showdown—Mary DiFrancesco Sullivan versus the Vatican.

Our phone never stopped ringing. Letters came to the house, some containing checks, many containing cash. Cash! How pure, how simple were the people who stuffed cash into envelopes and dropped them in the mail, with full faith that they would go to the right place!

Their faith was justified when it came to my mother. Every cent of the money went into an account for the disgraced priest at our local bank.

Father Bielinski phoned our house every night for a week after the story broke, a soft-spoken man we technically had never even met. The strength with which he had grabbed me to try and pull me away from the Bleeding Jesus didn't match the soft, defeated voice I heard over the phone.

"Is Mary Sullivan there, please?"

He didn't have to identify himself. I knew who was calling. Before I could even say anything my mother was there, taking the phone from my hand and gesturing for me to go up to my room, out of earshot.

At supper a few nights later she dropped the bombshell while my father was cutting into his steak. "He's going to stay with us for a few days."

My father looked at her, poked a slab of meat into his mouth. "Who?"

"Father Bielinski."

My father set his knife and fork down. "Mary. Have you lost your mind?"

"He has nowhere else to go. It's the least we can do for him."

There was no fight left in my father. My mother was no longer a worthy opponent for him—she was a mental patient to be handled with the weary patience of the men in the white coats. He rubbed his hand through the bristles of his crew-cut hair and looked at me with tired eyes before turning his defeated gaze toward his wife. "When's he getting here?"

"Tomorrow night."

"Where's he gonna sleep?"

It was a good question. My father slept in the spare bedroom so often now that he didn't intend to lose it, especially to a disgraced priest.

"In the garage," my mother said. "We can fix up that old cot of yours. We'll keep the car in the driveway while he's here."

"How long did you say he's staying?"

"As long as he likes."

"I thought you said it would only be for a few days."

"Then why did you ask?"

"Oh boy, Mary. Oh boy. I'm not hangin' around for this."

He wiped his mouth on his napkin, rose from the table, and left the room. My guts were in free fall. My father was leaving us!

How could my mother just sit there, spooning mashed potatoes into her face?

"Mom!"

"It's all right, Samuel. Your father's just a little upset."

"He's leaving us!"

"He'd never leave us. Finish your meal."

I couldn't choke down another bite. Minutes later my father reappeared in the kitchen, carrying his old duffel bag from his navy days. He wore a black-and-red-checkered woodsman's jacket, far too warm for a night light this.

"Where are you going?" my mother calmly asked.

"Deer hunting with Charlie McMahon."

Charlie had a cabin far up in the woods in upstate New York. Once a year or so my father joined him on a hunting expedition, but never for an overnight trip, and never this abruptly.

My mother forced a laugh. "Really? When were these plans made?"

"About eleven seconds after you announced that the priest was coming here." He turned to me. "I'll be back on Sunday night, Sammy." He turned back to my mother. "By that time, he'd better be gone."

Without another word he left the house, slamming the door. My mother finished her mashed potatoes, set her fork down.

"This could actually work out quite nicely," she said, more to herself than to me.

CHAPTER TWENTY-ONE

The next night Father Bielinski was dropped off in front of our house by someone driving a black car, a car that barely came to a stop to let him out before rolling off into the night.

The butterfat look had drained from his face, as if he'd been fasting since the scandal broke. He had the ageless look of a priest—he could have been thirty, he could have been fifty. He didn't have the conventional dock poles to mark the normal passages of life—wives, children, grandchildren. His only dock pole had been the priesthood, and now that was gone. He was a man totally unmoored and adrift in the world.

Father Bielinski carried a small brown suitcase that may very well have contained all his worldly possessions. He wore his black priest clothes, save for the white collar—I imagined it being ripped from his throat by an angry bishop in a defrocking ceremony.

He stood out there like a lost child until my mother took him by the hand, led him inside, and sat him down at the kitchen table. There was no need for us to introduce ourselves—everybody knew who everybody was. My father was way up in the woods with Charlie McMahon, so we could all relax.

Relax? Maybe that's not quite the word for it. A tremor seemed to be coming from the priest's body, radiating from his core, as if there was a motorized apparatus where his heart had been. He didn't want anything to eat. All he wanted was a cup of black coffee. When he lifted the cup, it chattered against the saucer. He seemed exhausted.

"Thank you for having me," he said.

"Thank you for being here," my mother replied.

"Everybody else has been so . . . *harsh*," he finally decided.

"They certainly have." My mother patted the back of his hand. "Everything is going to be all right."

The priest forced a smile. He probably didn't believe her but he appreciated the gesture. "Thank you, Mary."

"You just relax and forget about everything for the next few days."

"I'll try."

He was tired. He wanted to go to bed. We took him out to the garage, where my mother and I had set up the cot. My mother showed him where the bathroom was and gave him a towel for his morning shower.

"Do you like bacon and eggs, Father?"

He grinned. "Love 'em."

"That's what we're having for breakfast."

"Great."

"Do you need a toothbrush, soap . . . ?"

"I'm all set. Thank you." He took my mother's hands in both of his and held them as if he needed the warmth. "I'll never forget this, Mary."

He let go of her hand, shook mine with surprising strength. "Go to bed now, you two, it's late."

"Yes, Father," we said together.

We left him in the garage. I was in my bed reading ten minutes later when my mother appeared in my doorway.

"You know, Samuel, this would be a good time for you to apologize to Father Bielinski, before he falls asleep."

I sat up in bed. "Apologize?"

"It'll only take a minute."

"Mom, I—"

"Just do it for me, Samuel, please."

I crept downstairs in my pajamas. The house was dark but there was a stripe of yellow light at the bottom of the door connecting the laundry room to the garage. For the first time in my life, I knocked on a garage door.

"Come in."

Father Bielinski was stretched out on the cot, still in his day clothes. He was barefooted. He'd set his shoes on the floor, neatly, each with a rolled-up sock inside it. He was a precise man, as I'd known from his work on the crucifix. The bare bulb in the garage ceiling burned brightly. Moths bumped into it, bounced off, came back for more. Moths would make great Catholics.

He'd been reading a Bible with what looked to be a leather cover. He marked his place with the book's built-in red ribbon, set the book on the floor, adjusted his glasses, and seemed startled to see me.

"Samuel! Hello."

"Hi, Father." I swallowed. "I want to apologize to you."

"Apologize?" He seemed surprised.

"Yeah," I continued. "I'm sorry for what I did to the crucifix."

He chuckled, sat up on the cot. "Samuel. Let's get something straight. *I'm* the one who did the wrong thing. All you did was reveal my sin."

This was the first time I'd ever heard the word "sin" spoken in regard to any of this business. It chilled me to think of a priest capable of sin. If this was so, what hope could there be for the rest of us?

I fought off a shiver and said, "Mom says you didn't do anything wrong."

He nodded. "Your mother is a very nice person. But she's

wrong about that, Samuel. I should not have done what I did. My intentions were good, but the deed itself was wrong."

I felt my eyes well up with tears. "I shouldn't have done what I did, either."

"Well, you couldn't have done what you did if I hadn't done what I did, could you?"

I was tired, dizzy, confused. "I guess not, Father."

He sighed, stroked my hair. "Samuel, I would gladly accept your apology if you had done anything wrong. But you didn't. I did. All right? Are we clear on that?"

"Yes, Father."

"I cut open the leg and planted the blood sack to create a false miracle. I acted alone. Nobody encouraged me to do it. Do you understand?"

It was like confession in reverse, the priest spilling his guts to a child. It was a little creepy. He could tell that I wanted to be out of there, but he wanted an answer.

"Do you understand?" he asked again.

"Yes, Father. . . . Are they going to let you be a priest anymore?"

He forced another smile. "I can't answer that. I've been suspended from my duties, for the time being. Please don't worry about that. Let's just look forward to a fine breakfast in the morning. Are your mother's bacon and eggs as good as they sound?"

"Yes, Father."

He stretched out on the cot. "Well, then, I'm going to dream about them all night, and then in the morning the bacon and eggs will be like a dream come true."

He winked at me. We shook hands, and I turned to go. By the time I reached the door, he called my name. I turned and saw that he was crying, but his voice was steady.

"Your mother is right about one thing," Father Bielinski said. "I *did* mean well. Do you believe that?"

"Yes, Father."

"Well, that means the world to me, Samuel, the world." He wiped his eyes with the heels of his hands. "Life gets very complicated sometimes, young man. I was trying to make it . . . *simpler.* Does that make sense?"

"I guess so."

"Thank you, Samuel. Thank you for listening, and God bless you."

I was dismissed at last. I went back upstairs, where my mother stood at the doorway to her bedroom.

"Did he accept your apology?"

"He said I didn't do anything wrong. He said *he* was the one who did the wrong thing."

Her face broke into a blissful smile. "What a wonderful man," she said, more to herself than to me. "Good night, Samuel."

We both went to bed. The house was absolutely silent, and would remain so through the night, without my father stumbling home in the wee hours. He was far, far away in the woods, trying to kill deer with Charlie McMahon.

I awoke to smells of frying bacon. It was Saturday morning, and we always had great breakfasts on Saturday mornings. I came downstairs to find the table had been set for three, with our best dishes and silverware. We'd never had a houseguest before and I could see how these special touches might make it a fun thing, despite all the turmoil.

Crisp strips of bacon were laid to drain on paper towels. It was a beautiful, sunny day. My mother was scrambling a big pan of eggs, fluffy and yellow as only she could make them. The kitchen clock said it was ten minutes past eight.

The torment in my mother's eyes was obvious: do you let a priest sleep, or do you wake him up to eat as you'd awaken a civilian? She wrestled with it, made a decision.

"Samuel, go and wake Father Bielinski. Tell him breakfast is ready."

I was glad to do it, pausing to knock on the garage door. He didn't answer. I knocked again, harder, hard enough to push the door open, a door that had always had a weak latch. The last thing I wanted to do was barge in on a priest's privacy, but I couldn't catch the door in time, and it swung open, and then the whole world turned upside down and inside out, right there in our tiny garage in Flushing, Queens.

Father Joseph Bielinski was hanging from the highest beam in our garage, but this was no ordinary suicide. This had to have been the sequence of events, some time in the wee hours of the morning:

He'd gotten up and made the bed, the blanket taut and tucked in all around. He'd taken off all his clothes, folded them neatly, and stacked them at the foot of the cot. He'd brought a loincloth with him, really just a wide cream-colored scarf, which he wrapped and tied around his narrow waist, and then he pressed a crown of thorns onto his head (Had he woven it himself? And where had he carried it? In his little brown suitcase? How do you pack a crown of thorns?).

Bleeding from the thorns, he found an old soda crate in the garage and stood it on its tall side, right beneath the beam. He also found a broomstick, and unscrewed the broom head from it. With the broomstick in one hand and a length of three-strand rope in the other, Father Bielinski climbed up on the soda crate.

Ours was a low-ceilinged garage—his head was probably nudging the beam as he tied the rope around his neck, and then around the beam. Then he put the broomstick across his bare shoulders and dangled his hands over each end of it, locking his widespread arms in place no matter what happened next.

What happened next (and last) was that Father Bielinski kicked the soda crate out from under his own feet. He dangled, he strangled, and there he hung on that bright, bright morning when I showed up to call him for breakfast.

It's funny how you notice things. Through the shock and horror of it, I couldn't help registering that the garage light was still on, that it had burned through the night. This was one of the things that drove my father crazy—leaving a light on unnecessarily. It's a good thing he wasn't around to see this. . . .

I heard myself giggling, or making a giggling sound that had nothing at all to do with humor. Maybe it was the first step toward madness. The second step arrived in the form of my mother, bustling into the garage with a cheerful morning greeting that died in her throat at the sight of the dangling priest.

"Sweet Jesus," she breathed. "Sweet Jesus . . ."

We stood beside each other, staring at Father Bielinski. A horrible, horrible odor filled my nostrils, and then I saw that the priest had shit himself in the final moments of his life. It ran down his leg and onto the floor in a steady drip, much like the drip of fake blood that had gotten him into so much trouble.

But the blood that flowed from his thorn wounds was real. He had done it. This time, Father Joseph Bielinski had actually done it.

He had created a Bleeding Jesus that shed genuine blood. And my mother and I were the only people in the world who knew about it.

I don't know how long the two of us stood there staring at the dangling priest. I had stopped making that giggling sound, and could hear my mother's heavy breathing. She stepped right up to the corpse, and saw something jutting from the waist of the loincloth. It was a note.

She read it, crossed herself, and handed it to me. The handwriting was small and neat.

"Mary, Sammy, thank you for caring. Yours in Christ, Father Joseph Bielinski."

She took back the letter and stuck it in the pocket of her apron. Then she looked up at Father Bielinski again, shook her head, and looked at me. She didn't have to say it. Her eyes were more accusing than words ever could have been. Forget the fact that the man himself had absolved me of responsibility for all that had happened—my mother's eyes said otherwise. This was all my fault. I was a bad boy.

"Mommy. I'm sorry."

She nodded, looked back at the priest, and put her hands on her beefy hips, the way she always did when facing a challenge.

"You're going to have to help me take care of this, Samuel."

Take care of it? Take care of *what?* The man was dead, wasn't he?

"What are we going to do?"

"He can't be found like this."

"He can't?"

"Absolutely not."

My mother went to my father's tool cabinet and found a pair of gardening shears. She set the soda crate up on its edge, stepped up on it with startling agility, and cut the rope. Father Bielinski fell like a puppet whose strings have been cut, but his arms were still spread wide, held in place by the broomstick as he landed in a puddle of his own shit. My mother remained perched on the soda crate for a moment like a giant dove before stepping nimbly to the floor.

"All right, Samuel. We've got to work fast now."

She gently removed the crown of thorns from Father Bielinski's head and set it aside. She pulled the broomstick out from across his shoulders, allowing his bony arms to fall to his sides. Then she stretched him out on the cement floor, very gently, as if he were still alive.

The rope was still around his neck. I couldn't stand the sight of it.

"Aren't you going to take the rope off, Mom?"

"No, that stays."

Her instructions to me were clear and precise, as if she'd had weeks to prepare them. I was to fill the bucket under the laundry room sink with warm soapy water and bring it to her, along with the "rag bag" where we kept tattered old clothes and torn towels. I did as I was told, and then she gave me a five-dollar bill and sent me to the Grand Union supermarket to buy a box of plastic trash bags.

"Make sure they're the heavy-duty kind, Samuel."

"Okay."

"And don't tell anybody what's happened here."

It all became horribly real to me on the walk to the supermarket, out there in the normal world. It was a dazzling day, a beach day, a picnic day, and we had a dead priest in our garage.

Luckily I didn't see anybody we knew at Grand Union. I found a box of ten heavy-duty plastic bags and took them to the ten items-or-less lane, where a gum-chewing checkout girl smiled at me.

"Second box for half price," she said.

"Huh?"

"These are on special. If you buy another box it's only half price."

How good it was, how sweet it was to hear the voice of somebody outside the lunatic world I inhabited! I wanted to stay there at the cash register and listen to this girl talk to the customers all day long, but I couldn't. I was in the middle of a mission from hell.

"I think these'll be enough," I managed to say.

She shrugged, rang it up, handed me the receipt and my change. "Okay, sweetie, have a nice day."

A nice day.

When I got back to the garage the first thing that hit me was the reek of Pine-Sol cleanser. My mother was mopping the floor. She turned to look at me.

"It took you long enough," she said.

The dead priest was now fully clothed, shoes and all. He was lying on the cot. Except for the rope around his neck, he could have resembled a man who'd fallen asleep while reading a book.

My mother had stripped him, washed him, and dressed him. I'm sure she'd worked without worry that someone might come along, because my father was far, far away and we never had visitors. My mother did a lot for needy people, but she did it on their turf. Charity may begin in the home, but as far as my mother was concerned, it was always an away game.

The dead priest seemed to be smiling. She'd washed away the bloodstains from his thorn wounds. She was washing the last of the shit from the floor when I walked in. She leaned the mop against the garage wall. "Give me the bags."

I handed them over. She took one and filled it with the rags she'd used to clean up, as well as the soiled loincloth and the crown of thorns. The last thing to go in was the disposable mop head. She sealed the bag, then dropped it inside another bag, which she sealed even tighter.

"Now listen, Samuel. Go back to Grand Union and drop this in one of their big garbage Dumpsters. They're behind the store."

I took the bag from her and stared at her, slack-jawed.

"We can't have it near the house," she said impatiently. "It's *evidence*. Do you understand?"

"Yes, Mom."

"Go. Don't take so long this time. And don't let anybody see you."

How was I supposed to keep anybody from seeing me? Was I expected to turn into the Holy Ghost?

I should have been scared, but I was too stunned to be anything but numb. I hurried to the supermarket. The plastic bag seemed to be gaining weight with every step I took. I went around back, where there was a row of giant Dumpsters. How the hell did my mother know about these Dumpsters?

They reeked of rotted vegetables and rancid animal fats. I stood on tiptoe to lift a Dumpster lid and tossed the bag in. It made a hollow kettledrum sound as it hit bottom. The Dumpster must have been empty. More garbage would cover up the bag in the course of the day.

I felt a hand on my shoulder. A young Puerto Rican in dirty workman's overalls was scowling at me.

"Hey. Whatchoo doin', man? This ain't no dump!"

I was petrified. "I just . . ."

"Come on, man, say it!"

"Our garbage cans are full. My mother told me to bring it here."

He let go of my shoulder, shook a finger in my face. "I'll let it go this time, but don'tchoo dump here no more."

"Oh, I won't. I promise."

"And tell your mother what I said."

"I will. . . ."

I walked away fast. Once I reached the sidewalk I broke into a run, which carried me all the way home. When I got to the garage the windows had been opened and a breeze blew through the place, weakening the Pine-Sol stench.

My mother was fussing around with the dead priest on the cot. She'd placed his hands over his lap and was now stepping back to view her scenario, cocking her head to assess it, like a woman arranging pillows on a couch.

Pleased with it, she turned and looked at me. "Did you do it?"

"Yes, Mom."

"Good boy. There's just one more thing."

She took the bare wooden broomstick the priest had used to crucify himself and began screwing the broom head bristles back onto it.

"Your father would notice if this was missing," she said. "You know your father."

She finished the task, stood the broom in its usual corner. "Okay, Samuel. Now we're ready."

"Ready for what?"

"I'll tell you all about it while we eat."

That's right. With the dead priest in the garage, we sat and had our bacon and eggs. Grease had congealed on the bacon and the scrambled eggs were crusty, but we ate them anyway, because it was a sin to waste food.

I was so stunned by all my mother had done while I was out disposing of evidence that I'd forgotten to tell her about the Puerto Rican who caught me using the supermarket Dumpster. Now it felt as if it were too late to tell her. Besides, what could we do about it? Go back and retrieve the bag? No way.

While we ate, my mother revealed her plan.

It was really quite simple.

"You didn't see anything, Samuel."

"I didn't?"

"I'm the one who found Father Bielinski hanging from the ceiling. I cut him down and tried to revive him, but it was too late. I put his body on the cot. It's as simple as that."

"What about all that other stuff?"

"There isn't any other stuff. By the time you showed up, I'd already cut him down."

My mother was many things, but until this moment she had never been a liar. This was terrifying to me, in a way more terrifying than the crucifix suicide itself.

What could I say? My mouth had gone dry. I had to swallow to speak. "Mom . . . that's not how it happened."

"As far as we're concerned, that's exactly how it happened."

"But the crown of thorns, and the other stuff—"

"Samuel! There *isn't* any other stuff." She lifted the phone.

"Remember what I said. It's important that we tell the same story, in case anyone asks you anything, including your father. *Especially* your father."

She waited for me to nod, then dialed 911.

The police showed up, a uniformed cop and a detective, and so did an ambulance. My mother stuck to the story she'd forged, and the cops had no reason to doubt her. They never asked me a single question.

The ambulance guys took the noose off Father Bielinski's neck. Then they put him in a body bag, zipped it shut, put it on a rolling stretcher, and took it away.

I was glad when he was out of our garage, but upset that his brown suitcase was still there. I wanted every trace of him to be gone.

The cops were wrapping things up. Almost casually, the detective asked my mother, "You cut him down, but why didn't you take the noose off his neck?"

"I didn't want to tamper with any evidence," my mother replied.

The detective seemed surprised. "Didn't you try to revive him?"

"Oh yes, but I knew he was dead."

"How'd you know that, ma'am?"

"He was ice-cold."

The detective stared at her for a long moment. "Did he leave a note?"

"No, sir," my mother lied.

The detective's eyebrows went up. I prayed that he wouldn't look at me, or my trembling knees.

"No note? That's kinda odd. You sure? You looked all around?"

"There is no note, Detective."

He looked at the uniformed officer, who shrugged.

"All right, then," the detective sighed. "Be forewarned, the press will be all over you. Lucky for you it's Saturday morning. Most of the reporters in this city got hangovers right about now."

My mother forced a sly chuckle. "Lucky isn't exactly the word I'd choose for a day like today, Detective."

Within hours the phone was ringing off the hook and reporters were knocking on our door. My mother and I holed up in the house, ignoring everybody. They didn't leave until dark. The phone rang until midnight.

"Mom?"

"Yes, Samuel?"

"Why did you lie to the detective about the note?"

"Because it's precious to me. The police have no business reading Father Bielinski's final words."

We went to the eleven o'clock Mass as always on Sunday morning, and this time a dozen newsmen were outside St. Aloysius, shouting questions at my mother as we arrived and left. They got pictures, but no words. My mother wouldn't even look at them.

The story had hit the Sunday papers with a splash, but the only one to worry about was George O'Malley's in the *New York Star*. He had a friend in the coroner's office who told him about some "mysterious puncture wounds" on the dead priest's head.

What could have caused them? The coroner did not know, and would not speculate. I started to worry about the garbage bag I'd dumped at Grand Union. If anyone poked through it they'd find the crown of thorns, and put the puzzle together.

I don't remember much about the Mass that day, except that Father Bielinski was never mentioned during the sermon. His name only came up in the list of the dearly departed we were told to pray for. Everybody stared at us but they left us alone.

As we were leaving church I saw George O'Malley among the newsmen standing in front of the church. He waved to me, and I waved back. My mother smacked my hand. It was the first and only time she'd ever hit me.

When we got home I couldn't hold it any longer. I told my mother about the Puerto Rican workman who'd caught me dumping the garbage bag at Grand Union. I expected to be yelled at, but she didn't do that. Instead, we both got on our knees and prayed.

"What are we praying for, Mom?"

"That nobody finds that bag."

Together we said ten Our Fathers and ten Hail Marys so that the plastic bag containing the dead priest's shit-stained loincloth and crown of thorns would make it all the way to the city dump in Staten Island, undisturbed, to eventually be buried under untold tons of garbage.

Amen.

Late that night we heard Charlie McMahon's car pull up in front of the house. I looked out my bedroom window and saw my father laughing with Charlie as he struggled to get his duffel bag out of the car. A dead deer was strapped to the hood of Charlie's car. I wondered who'd shot it, Charlie or my father. I'd seen enough death for one weekend. I prayed that when Charlie drove away, he'd take the deer with him. Sure enough, he did.

"Thank you, God."

I heard my father slam his way into the house. My mother was downstairs, waiting for him. She was going to tell him the same story the rest of the world believed about Father Joseph Bielinski. There was no reason for him not to believe it. I was beginning to believe it myself.

The kids at school didn't ask me about the suicide. Maybe the nuns had instructed them not to. Only Alonzo Fishetti had the guts to come up to me in the schoolyard.

"Guy musta been fuckin' crazy, huh, Sullivan?"

Alonzo, you have no idea.

My mother turned the proceeds of the Father Bielinski fund over to his church in Scranton, with instructions for them to do as they wished with the money. I graduated from St. Aloysius school that year and the following year went on to Holy Cross High School, an all-boys' school.

I never danced with Margaret Thompson, never asked her out.

When my mother died George O'Malley wrote an obituary about the staunch defender of the Bleeding Jesus of Scranton, and the way she stuck up for that suicidal priest, and the way she died in church, in line to receive Holy Communion. He sent me a letter saying if there was anything he could do for me, please let him know.

I let him know the day after I quit my pizza delivery job at Napoli's. I phoned George and told him I needed a job. He invited me to visit him at the *New York Star* office, where he offered me a job as a copyboy.

I quit school and took the job. Within six months I had my first bylined story. I was a promoted to reporter by the time I was twenty. I was George O'Malley's big find, something he could crow about. They said I was a natural newsman.

Of course I was. After all, I was the kid who'd exposed the hoax of the Bleeding Jesus of Scranton, Pennsylvania.

My mother wanted me to become a priest. Instead, I became a tabloid newspaperman. I guess there's really not all that much difference. It's all about getting people to believe in stories that demand an enormous leap of faith.

Funny thing was, I couldn't tell anyone my biggest story of all, until this crazy night with my son and my father at our old kitchen table.

CHAPTER TWENTY-TWO

By the time I'm finished talking my father and my son look almost windblown, as if they've been taken for a ride across a desert on an open wagon. Jake can just stare at me.

"My God," he finally says, peculiar words indeed to be hearing from the son of an agnostic and a fallen Catholic. Something else is going on with my father, something I've never seen before.

He is weeping, and making no attempt to hide his tears, which make his eyes seem bigger and bluer than ever. I think he is crying because he's just learned that his wife wanted to be a nun, and that she thought he wasn't good enough to be my father, but I am wrong.

"Sammy," he says, "can you forgive me?"

"Forgive you for what?"

"For not . . . being strong for you."

I'm shocked to hear him say this. "Dad. You're the strongest person I've ever known!"

He wipes his eyes with the back of his hand. "Usually, yeah. But those few times, I really fucked up, Sammy. I should've been strong enough to keep you from going on that ridiculous trip to Scranton. And then I should have been strong enough to stay here, instead of goin' hunting with Charlie, leavin' you here with your mother and that crazy priest."

"It doesn't matter, Dad."

"Oh, it matters, all right."

"Not anymore. What happened, happened. I feel better just talking it all out. I feel . . . good."

I realize I'm telling the truth. I do feel good, maybe not James Brown good, but better than I've felt since the day I was born, and that's something.

"Funny, you look good," Jake says. "You look . . . I don't know. Younger."

"Thank you, son."

"I want to thank *you*, Dad."

"For what?"

"For disobeying your mother's wishes and not becoming a priest so you could go on to become my father, that's what for."

"You're welcome."

Jake hesitates before adding, "I'm glad I was born, and I'm glad you're my father."

It's an amazing thing to hear. Jake speaks the words as if he's reading them off a plaque. I turn to my own father and repeat those exact same words. We all gather in the middle of the kitchen for a triple hug, brief but sincere.

And now it seems that there's just one more thing I need to know from my father. I take a sip of beer for courage.

"Dad," I begin, "please tell me. Why in the world did you marry Mom?"

For the first time ever, my father has a sheepish look on his face. "Why do you think? She was pregnant."

I choke on the beer. Jake is suddenly behind me, patting my back, kneading my shoulders. "Easy, Dad. You'll be all right."

I watch my father open a fresh beer and take a long, leisurely swallow.

"I never knew," I finally manage to say. "Never even suspected anything like that."

Of course I didn't. My mother, engaging in premarital sex? It was hard enough to imagine her taking part in postmarital sex!

My father shakes his head. "You got it in your skull that she was a saint. She wasn't. The only saints are the statues. It's an impossible challenge for anyone with blood and bone. And let me tell you—before the church *really* grabbed her, your mother could be a hell of a lot of fun. What the hell are you smilin' about, Jake?"

"Oh, nothing. It's just that my mother was pregnant when Dad married her."

"Yes, I knew that," my father says. "I can count to nine." He laughs out loud, hoists his beer bottle. "Here's to the Sullivan males! A potent bunch, if nothing else! You be careful out there, Jake, or you'll be pushin' a stroller before you're twenty!"

He and Jake clink beer bottles and drink.

Somehow I guess I've always had it in my head that nobody's life is as complicated as mine. Now, suddenly, I can see that I'm just a link in a chain of messes. It's not exactly a comforting thought, but it does make things a little less lonely.

I grasp Jake by the forearm. It's time for the question I always thought I would take to my grave, but it's clear that I must ask it now, right now.

"Jake. How badly have I hurt you?"

I'm looking right into those green eyes of his, like two seas. And right now the seas are calm.

"Dad," he says, "I always knew you were trying your best. That's what counts."

It's the greatest thing anyone's ever said to me. My father respects the moment by hoisting his bottle and gently saying, "Hear, hear."

My lips are quivering as I turn to my father. "You don't hate me, Dad?"

"What a question. Of course not. You're too busy hating yourself for anybody else to have a chance at it!"

He grins at me, winks at me, and is startled when I reach over and grasp his forearm. I'm the link between these two people, and while holding their arms I'm flooded by the same sweet, gooey feeling I used to get after confessing my sins to a priest. Back then, that feeling lasted for about five minutes. I'm hoping for something longer this time.

My father pulls out of my grasp. "Enough of that already, unless you plan to buy me a corsage."

Just then the front doorbell rings. The pizza has arrived.

"I got it, Dad," I say, and he doesn't object. He's still a little weepy-eyed, and doesn't want the delivery boy to see him this way.

Jake comes to the front door with me, where a dark-haired, skinny kid who could have been me thirty years ago stands there holding two boxes containing the pizzas—strong boxes, corrugated cardboard that doesn't bend or leak. Where were these boxes when I was delivering for Napoli's?

"What do we owe you?"

"Comes to twenty-five fifty."

I give the kid thirty bucks and tell him to keep the change. He mutters his thanks and walks off, and then I happen to see his bicycle at the curb, and my heart drops. I hand the boxes to Jake and tell him to take them inside.

"Where are you going, Dad?" He seems worried about me, afraid to leave me alone.

"I just want to talk to this kid for a minute."

Jake smiles with relief. "Pizza delivery boy shop talk, eh?"

"Something like that. Get started, don't wait for me."

Jake goes to the kitchen and I run after the delivery boy. He's just boarding the bike when I startle him by grabbing it by the handlebars.

"Hey! What the hell you doin', man!"

"Could I just see this bike for a second?"

"My *bike?*"

A big basket has been welded to the handlebars and the frame has been painted black, but the cracked leather seat is the original, and there they are, the letters BOB etched into the back of it. This is Fran's ex-husband's bicycle, still in service.

I start to laugh, still gripping the handlebars. The kid looks scared.

"Mister—"

"Do you believe in miracles, kid?"

"Huh?"

"Miracles. Do you believe that miracles happen?"

Clearly, nobody has ever asked him this question before. He has to think about it. "No," he finally decides. "No, I don't."

I can see that he's one of those sad, serious kids who works harder than he should for a boss who doesn't appreciate it. He also thinks I'm nuts.

"Mister, I gotta get back."

"I know you do." I release the handlebars. "I used to have your job, delivering for Napoli's."

His eyebrows rise. "No foolin'?"

"Swear to God. Like thirty years ago, maybe more, when the *real* Napoli owned the joint."

"Jesus, it's been around that long?"

"Yeah, and so has this bike. This was my delivery bike."

"You're shittin' me."

"I'm not."

I show him Bob's name on the back of the seat. "You want to hear the story about this bike?"

"Sure."

I tell him everything that happened to me that night—the bachelor party and the stripper and the bicycle theft, and losing my cherry to Fran, and the way she gave me her ex's bike. The kid listens to my story the way you hope kids will listen to stories, but I guess that makes sense, one old delivery boy telling a war story to another. By the end of my tale he's smiling, his teeth a radiant white.

"Great story," he says, "but I'm not sure I'd call it a miracle."

"You wouldn't?"

"Nah. It's just an old bike that's still around." He climbs aboard, spins the pedals around to getaway position. "Take it easy, man."

"What's your name?"

"Paul."

"Paul what?"

"Paul Fishetti."

Oh man. This can't be, but on the other hand, it can't be anything else.

"Is your father Alonzo Fishetti?"

"Hey! How'd you know that?"

"I went to school with him a long time ago. He was the coolest kid in the class."

Paul laughs out loud. "*My* father was cool? Gimme a break!"

"I'm telling you!"

"Bullshit!"

"What's he doing these days?"

"He's a plumber."

"Yeah? What else is he up to?"

"He watches TV and he argues with my mother. . . . What was so cool about him?"

I tell him how his dad used to sneak cigarettes in the schoolyard, and how he busted his ankle that time he fell from the ledge.

Paul is fascinated. "Why'd he climb out on the ledge?"

"He wanted to peek into the girls' changing room. Wanted to get a look at Margaret Thompson. We were all in love with a girl named Margaret Thompson."

Paul puts his head back and howls. "Oh man," he says, "that is pretty wild."

"What is?"

"Margaret Thompson."

"What about her?"

"She's my mother."

Paul is beaming now, and suddenly I can see his mother in his face—the perky ears, the hint of green on the outskirts of those brown irises, the playfulness. I have to grip the handlebars again to keep from falling.

"You okay, mister?"

I catch my breath, straighten up, release the bike. "You got brothers and sisters, Paul?"

"Yeah, there's four of us."

"You the oldest?"

"Youngest. My brother Richie's wife just had a kid."

So there it was. Margaret Thompson, the great unrequited love of my life, married the toughest kid in the class, and now she's a grandmother.

I want to ask Paul all about his mother, of course, but you can't ask a boy if he thinks his mother is pretty, and if she's turned fat and embittered I really don't want to hear about it.

But there's one thing I *do* want from this kid, and I amaze myself by actually asking for it.

"Listen, Paul. Mind if I take a little ride on your bike?"

He looks at me as if I've lost my mind. "A *ride?* Are you serious?"

"Just around the block. Come on, I'm not going to steal it."

He looks at his watch. "I'm already late gettin' back, man."

I hand him a ten-dollar bill. He sticks it in his pocket and says, "Don't change the gears, they're all fucked up."

I jump aboard the bike and started pedaling as if I've just robbed a bank.

"Just around the block!" Paul yells at my back. My shirt billows like a sail as I pick up speed. It still rides straight and true, Fran's ex-husband's ex-bike, so I am able to take my hands off the handlebars and hike my arms to the sky on the straightaways.

I have things on my mind and a million responsibilities, but I have never, ever felt so goddamn free.

I'm good to my word, returning the bike to Paul after one turn around the block. He climbs aboard and races off to Napoli's.

"Tell your parents Sammy Sullivan says hello!" I shout, but I doubt that he hears me.

Back in the house my son and my father are working on their second slices.

"What the hell took you?" my father asks.

"Just having a little chat with the delivery kid," I reply. I could tell them more, but I don't want to. I've emptied out all my secrets today, shared all the stories I've got to tell, but this one's all mine.

We polish off both pizza pies, and though we don't speak much while eating, it's not an uncomfortable time. We're three soldiers in the same foxhole, chowing down to stay strong for whatever's coming next. And we would do anything for each other.

My father gets our clothes from the dryer. Jake and I get changed, and I realize we should get going to rest up for tomorrow's big battle.

My father accompanies us to the sidewalk, along the dug-up trench that soon will be a cobblestone path. He tells us he's going to wait until next weekend to lay the stones, and Jake tells him he wants to help. Just like that, they have a date for next Saturday morning.

"Gonna teach him about stonework," my father says. "A trade that could come in handy, now that his formal education is over."

"Actually, Danny," Jake says, "I'd like to think that it's just starting."

He grabs Jake in a rough embrace, full of giggles and tickles. "See you next weekend, kiddo."

"Okay, Danny."

My father turns to me and extends a hand. I grasp it just as I used to all those birthdays and Christmases ago, and we both squeeze hard. My father releases the pressure first and I think it's over, but as I'm slipping from his grip he startles me by pulling me against him in the same kind of embrace he's just shared with Jake.

"Be strong tomorrow when you see Doris," he whispers in my ear. "Don't do what I did. Be there. Don't bail out."

"I won't."

"What do you think this plan of Jake's is all about?"

"I have no idea."

"If you like it, back him up. Back him up all the fucking way."

"I will."

He releases his grasp, pulls back to look at me. "It was good to see you," he says, and I think I'm imagining it but in fact I am not when he presses his dry lips to my cheek in what could only be called a kiss.

"I'm sorry we lost all those years, Dad."

He shrugs. "I'm glad we've got whatever's left." He thumps himself on his bony chest. "I ain't plannin' on checkin' out any time soon, I can tell you that."

He turns and goes back inside while Jake and I, brimming with beer, walk toward what I hope turns out to be Francis Lewis Boulevard, and the stop for the Q-76 bus. We both have to stop and piss into somebody's hedge on the way, and in the midst of it Jake's cell phone goes off and of course it's his mother, saying she'll be catching an earlier train than she was scheduled to take and will be home tomorrow by noon. High noon, you might say.

We find our bus stop. You'd think a father and son might have a lot to say to each other after such a day, but you'd be wrong. We are all talked out, and I am in a state of awe over the way this magical day has unfolded.

My son has saved me. There's no other way to look at it. Suddenly I realize there's one more thing to say, one more thing to do.

"Jake, we have to stop in the Village before we go home."

"The Village? What for?"

"You'll see."

We reach Matt Umanov's guitar shop on Bleecker Street half an hour before closing time.

"Oh no, Dad."

"Pick out the one you want."

"You don't have to do this."

"Did you hear what I said? Pick out the one you want."

"Are you sure?"

"Just promise me you won't set it on fire."

Jake confers with a bushy-haired clerk before selecting a honey-yellow acoustic guitar, made in Spain. It's just under seven hundred dollars, including the guitar case, and it's far and away the best money I've ever spent.

"Dad. I don't know how to thank you."

"Funny, I was going to say the same thing to you."

But there's no way I can thank him for what he's done for me. I'm out of the cage I've lived in for so long, and the liberty is absolutely intoxicating. Anything seems possible now. Who knows? I might even be able to have a real relationship with a woman. My son put the wings back on my shoulders, and so what if I can't really fly? The trick isn't getting airborne. The trick is dreaming that you can do it. It's good to dream, even when dreams remain nothing but dreams.

At Christopher Street we board the Number 1 local for the ride uptown. Jake cannot wait. He takes out his guitar and begins playing it, his hair hanging over his eyes.

"Go ahead, kid," I tell him. "Just think of it as a cello turned sideways."

I sit across from Jake and watch his fingers introduce themselves to the strings, like the hesitant moves of an infatuated boy holding a girl for the first time.

He gains confidence by the moment. By the time we reach Twenty-eighth Street, he's strumming it with ease. At Columbus Circle, he begins to play "Yesterday." It's a heartfelt rendition, all the more beautiful for its uncertainty. He finishes the song, and a few people actually applaud. The train stops at Seventy-ninth Street, and a man tosses three quarters into the open guitar case on his way out. Jake looks at me in wonder.

"Congratulations, son. You just turned pro."

We are exhausted by the time we get back to the apartment. For the second straight night we flop on top of the bedspreads, fully clothed. Jake gently strums his guitar, which has already become his old friend. In minutes we'll both conk out.

But first, Jake says something I will never forget. "I like Danny," he tells me. "He's a good guy. He's amusing. But you're the better man."

The better man.

I want to ask him what he means by that. I also want to take a last shot at asking him about this plan he's got for tomorrow, but I'm too late. The little cobblestone thief is snoring away.

I wait until his sleep deepens before taking the guitar from his embrace and locking it up in its case. I pull off his boots and cover him with a blanket. His face is smooth and his brow is relaxed. He looks the way he used to look, long before anything bad ever happened to him. Once again, my boy is king of the monkey bars.

"You lied to me *again*, Dad."

I'm shocked to hear his voice. I thought he was in a deep deep, sleep. His eyes are closed, but he is wide-awake.

"What did I lie about?"

"Your childhood." He smiles, keeping his eyes shut. "You told me you had a dull childhood."

CHAPTER TWENTY-THREE

We have never before had hangovers together. Yet another new experience on this most memorable of weekends.

It's ten-thirty when I awaken, ninety minutes until Zero Hour with Doris. I open my eyes and immediately squint them against the morning light. My tongue is dry and my head is pounding. It's a mild hangover, a beer hangover, and I know what to do to get rid of it.

"Coffee," I say out loud.

"Great idea," Jake moans into his pillow.

I'm a little stiff as I get up to make it. My long-dormant muscles are having a hangover of their own, from the gardening and the cobblestone stealing.

We drink the coffee black and scalding hot. We do not have to discuss the day ahead. We both know that we'll be facing his mother together, showing up at her place shoulder to shoulder, like a pair of hired guns. And at some point, Jake will pull the trigger and unveil the master plan for his future.

Jake's eyes are puffy, but I figure the coffee and a shower should straighten him out. We're a little bit shy with each other, and I guess that makes sense. We know so much more about each other than we did twenty-four hours ago. It's almost as if we've finally been introduced, after nearly eighteen years.

Neither of us is hungry. We're both anxious but eager to get through the task ahead.

"You want to shower first?"

"Whatever you say, Dad."

I happen to have a great shower. The water hits you in a needle spray that's both pleasure and penance for whatever you did the night before. Jake always takes a good long time in my shower, and this time is no different. He comes out with his hair slicked straight back, the ends of it touching his collarbones. "God, that felt good."

"I think I've got clean underwear here for you."

"I'll find it. You'd better shower, Dad, it's past eleven."

He wants to be there by noon. He doesn't want to put it off for a single minute, and suddenly I realize that I don't, either. Enough already. It's time for Columbia University professor Doris Perez, Ph.D, to find out what everybody else already knows.

I strip down, go to the shower, and take the needle spray full-force in my face, as hot as I can stand it. Then, slowly, I turn the temperature knob until the water is warm, then tepid, then cool, then cold. It's my own private hangover remedy, and I recommend it highly to anyone who does not have a heart condition.

Minutes to high noon. We are walking to the apartment on Eighty-first Street. Jake is carrying his bulky blue laundry sack, while I'm carrying his guitar.

"You okay, Jake?"

"Never better."

"Never better, he says. We're about to break some pretty rough news to your mother, and all I can say is that I hope you know CPR."

"She won't need it," Jake says. "This isn't going to kill her."

"She may kill *me*."

"I won't let that happen, either, Dad."

When we get to the building I'm ashamed to feel my knees tremble. I catch Jake by the elbow, just as he's about to climb the stoop. "Maybe you should see if she's home first, before I come in."

"No way she's home yet. We're a little early. And you know that's she's always a little late."

"I feel kind of funny going in there without her . . . permission."

"I'm giving you *my* permission. I live here, too. Come on."

We climb the four flights to the apartment. Jake gets the door open and says, "After you, Dad."

I have not set foot in this place since Doris and I split. On the rare occasions the three of us have hooked up since then, it was always in a public place, and I never thought I'd be back.

But I'm back. I step over the threshold into the very dwelling where Doris and I began our thing on that drunken night so long ago.

"Must feel weird for you, huh, Dad?"

"Weird isn't even the word for it."

I feel as if I've entered a fortune-teller's parlor. Doris always had a lot of books and paintings and gewgaws, but now it's totally out of control. There's not an inch of shelf space or wall space that isn't covered, crammed, packed, or stacked. Most of this stuff looks both fragile and irreplaceable. This has gone beyond collecting, and straight into the realm of storage.

"Christ," I say, "your mother does have a tendency to accumulate, doesn't she?"

"Yeah, it's in her nature. She surrounds herself with stuff to make her feel safe, I think. But I'm not sure it works."

An ancient gray cat with milky-blind eyes and bald spots on his back limps into the room. Jake squats to stroke him. "Come here, Jasper."

I'm stunned. "That's *Jasper*? He's *still alive*?"

"Well, barely. We had Max put to sleep about a year ago, and we should do the same with this guy, but Mom keeps putting it off."

I remember the two cats darting in front of me on my first night with Doris. Now one of them is dead, and the other one's darting days are long past.

"You know, this cat was here . . ." I shut up, let the sentence dangle.

"The very first night you were with Mom," Jake says matter-of-factly. "Well, that makes sense. He just turned twenty, believe it or not. He's a tough old bastard."

I squat beside Jake and stroke Jasper's head. He's staring at me, but I'm sure he sees nothing. He yawns in my face, exposing crooked yellow fangs.

"Christ, that *breath!*"

"Yeah," Jake chuckles, "it's pretty bad. Like he's rotting from the inside out. He hasn't got long now."

My stomach sinks at the sound of a key in the door. It opens, and in walks Doris, carrying a small black suitcase.

How long has it been since I've seen her? Three years? Five years? I can't even remember. Her hair has gone totally gray, and she's done nothing to color or highlight it, and it still tumbles down her back the way it always has. She wears black boots that make a clacking sound on hardwood floors, black slacks, a black sweater, and what can only be called a cape across her shoulders— black, of course, a silken thing that floats behind her when she walks.

Doris has always been aware of her own sense of drama. When she enters a classroom at Columbia the students are intimidated by the sound of the boots and the sight of the cape, as if Zorro has just arrived to teach them advanced Spanish literature. She takes a few steps inside before she notices me squatting on the floor, stroking the cat.

"Oh my *God*."

"Hello, Doris," I say. 'It's good to see you." This isn't quite the truth, but I suspect it'll be the last lie that'll be told today.

Doris is absolutely stunned. For a moment it looks as if she's thinking about calling the cops. Instead, she puts on her glasses, which I notice are bifocals.

"You got older," she says, examining me through the upper halves.

"Yeah, somehow I couldn't get around it."

"Gained some weight."

"Correct again. Nice to see you've got that same keen eye for detail."

She continues to stare at me as Jake gets up and gives her a kiss on the cheek.

"Hi, Mom. Did you have a good time at the conference?"

"As good a time as one can have in Schenectady," she murmurs, turning at last to look at her son. Her eyes widen in alarm. "My *God!* Your *arms!* What happened to your arms?"

Doris grabs Jake by the elbows and turns them to inspect his inner forearms, which are covered with dozens of small red scratches. She obviously thinks he's been shooting heroin, that two nights in my lackadaisical care have turned him into an intravenous drug user.

"It's nothing, Mom. Just a few scratches from barnacles."

"*Barnacles!*"

And I figure what the fuck, and dive right into it.

"We were helping my father steal cobblestones from Flushing Bay at low tide," I explain helpfully. "They were covered in barnacles." I hold out my forearms. "See, I got scratched, too."

Doris looks at me as if I've lost my mind. "Hold on, hold on. You went to see *Danny*?"

"Yes, that was part of the weekend festivities."

"Why?"

"Why not?"

"Because he's not exactly the sort of person Jacob should get to know!"

"I disagree, Doris. I figured it was time he met his grandfather, before it was too late."

"Oh, this is just *dreadful!*"

"Calm down, Mom," Jake says. "We had a good time."

"*Stealing cobblestones?* That's your idea of a *good time?*"

Doris is flying now. She shuts her eyes and holds her hands out defensively. "I don't even want to hear the details, but you say you were stealing cobblestones with Danny?"

"Not really *stealing,*" I say. "They were stuck in the muck. Nobody even knew they were there. We just took them."

"Kindly select the correct verb, Sammy. You said you *stole* them. Now you simply *took* them. Which is right?"

"We *acquired* them, Mom," Jake says helpfully. "You happy with that verb?"

Doris opens her eyes, which are burning bright. She's looking right at Jake. "Do you see now why I've kept you away from that man all this time?"

"Not really, Mom."

"What if you'd been caught? What if you suddenly had a crime on your record?"

Doris turns to me. "Did you think of that, in the midst of your cobblestone frolics? He'll be applying to colleges soon! Do you realize what a criminal record would do to his chances? One stupid little thing like this cobblestone stunt, and the course of his life is changed forever!"

"We didn't go out there to steal cobblestones, Doris. It was just a little task that came up in the midst of our family reunion."

"Ohhh, Sammy."

"Take it easy, Mom."

Doris turns back to Jake. "Well, now you know your grandfather. But you cannot tell me that you actually *like* this man."

"Danny? He's great. He's a pisser. And he likes *you*, Mom. He actually proposed a toast to you."

Doris doesn't seem to be getting enough air. She lets her head fall, pushes her hair back. "Danny Sullivan! Of all *people!*"

"I heard about what he did to my name card in the nursery. Pretty funny."

"Oh, you think that was *funny?* Obliterating my name? Contaminating a germ-free zone by barging into the nursery like an absolute *lunatic?*"

"He's a passionate guy, Mom."

Doris lifts her head, rolls her eyes heavenward. "All right, then, Jacob, tell me. I might as well know everything. Tell me all about these . . . cobblestones."

"Danny found a bunch of cobblestones at low tide, and we helped him carry them to his car. Some dopey Parks Department cop tried to stop him, so Danny flattened him with one punch, and then Dad talked the guy out of arresting him. Aw, Mom, it was *amazing*. Talk about teamwork! You should have been there."

The words hit Doris like a barrage of bullets. I don't know how she is still standing, but she is. "You're telling me that your lunatic grandfather actually struck a policeman."

"Well, not really a policeman. Some jerk in a uniform who works for the Parks Department."

"Jacob, listen to me carefully, now. I don't want you going near that grandfather of yours, ever again."

"I'm going out to Flushing next Saturday to help him put down a cobblestone path."

"No, you are not."

"Mom. I'm going. That's all there is to it."

Doris thinks this is going to be the big issue of the day. She can't even hear the night train coming down the tracks. She suddenly realizes she's still holding her suitcase, and sets it on the floor. I remain squatting, stroking Jasper.

Doris says to me, "Leave that cat alone and tell me why you're here."

The time has come. I give Jasper one last pat on the head before pushing at my knee to get to my feet. While I'm doing this, Doris foot-pushes her suitcase off to the side, where it comes to rest against Jake's guitar case. Before I can speak, Doris beats me to it.

"What's this?"

"Dad bought me a guitar."

"A guitar?" Doris shakes her head. "That's a purchase you may regret, Sammy. You don't want to know what Jacob does when he grows tired of a musical instrument."

"I know about the cello, Doris. He's promised me he won't incinerate the guitar."

She's startled that I know about the cello. She's about to say something else, but then she notices Jake's big blue bag. "What is *this*?"

The time has come at last. And before I can speak, Jake beats me to it. "That's my stuff from school."

"Stuff?"

"From my locker."

Her face darkens. "Jacob?"

"I got kicked out of school, Mom."

She puts a hand over her mouth, as if to block a scream. She's actually trembling, and it looks as if she's struggling to keep from attacking him.

"I got fired from my job," I say, if only to distract her rage from Jake. Her other hand goes up to her mouth, and her eyes are wide-open above the hands, the eyes of the girl in the horror movie who sees the monster coming coming toward her and can't do a thing about it.

Doris staggers backward until the backs of her legs bump the sofa cushions, and then my ex-wife collapses on the couch, landing on her ass in the middle of it, arms and legs spread like a sky diver. But she has no parachute. Instead, the cape billows behind her head, slowly settling as it loses air. Doris lets out a scream that comes all the way from her ankles and sends Jasper fleeing in what could be the final sprint of his life.

Jake runs to get his mother a glass of water. She's still screaming when he brings it to her, knocking the glass from his hand and then leaping from the couch to smack my face.

I see stars as I hit the floor, and I'm vaguely aware that Jake is engaged in a physical struggle with Doris. I look up and see that he's trying to embrace her, while she pushes at his chest.

"Mom, *please!*" he says, but Doris wails away, as if she's just been told that her only son has just died in a car crash. And maybe that would have been easier for Doris to take. There's no disgrace in a car crash.

It feels like hours but it's only minutes before Jake calms her down and gets her to sit back down on the couch. All the while Doris is making whimpering noises, sounds of mourning for her son's lost future. I get up off the floor and find some paper towels to mop up the water and pick up the pieces of broken glass. Doris is quaking, literally quaking, as if the temperature has just plummeted fifty degrees, but actually the room is quite warm. Jake takes her hands in his and squeezes them.

"Mom. Everything's going to be all right."

She waits for a gust of shivering to go through her before asking, "Why did this happen?"

Jake takes his essay from his back pocket and hands it to her.

"Read this, Mom."

She adjusts her bifocals before settling in to read it. She just keeps staring at the pages, long after she's finished. She's had time to read it three or four times before finally saying, "How ridiculous. Didn't they realize you were being ironic?"

"No, I wasn't. I meant every word. They wanted an apology, and I refused."

Doris neatly folds the pages and hands them back to Jake. "I'll straighten this whole thing out tomorrow."

"Mom. There's nothing to straighten out. Even if they let me back in, I wouldn't go."

"Jacob."

"Mother . . ."

They glare at each other, neither surrendering an inch, and I suddenly remember the way they used to clash when I lived with them. He was barely old enough to walk when he began standing his ground against his mother, refusing to eat cauliflower, refusing to go to bed, and even in the midst of this crisis I have to marvel over the power of the stubbornness gene.

These two are fully capable of an all-day standoff, and to break it I say to Doris, "Don't you want to know why I got fired?"

She doesn't answer, but she does look at me, which is encouraging.

"The headmaster called me up and said it was an emergency. Obviously, he tried to reach you first, and when he couldn't he moved on to the secondary parent. My boss wouldn't give me an hour off, so he fired me because I went to the school without his permission."

Jake is stunned. "Holy shit, Dad, it was *my* fault you got fired!"

"Don't worry about it, Jake. Best thing that could have happened to me."

"Enough," Doris says. "We've got a slightly bigger problem than your dubious journalistic career here." She points at me. It is literally the finger of blame. "You could have taken care of this, but you deliberately fouled it up so you could stop paying for school."

"Not true. I've been writing those checks for years. Why would I wait to bungle it up in his senior year?"

"Because you're spiteful."

"Mom. Dad didn't do anything wrong."

"Ohhh *God*, why is this happening?"

"For an agnostic, Doris, you're talking to God an awful lot."

She gives me a laser look through eyes narrowed to slits. "You've had a hell of a weekend, haven't you?"

"Yeah, Doris, a lot has happened. Speaking for myself, and without going into detail, all I can really tell you is that I hate myself a lot less today than I did on Friday."

"Ohh, how *wonderful* for you. Your son's life is in tatters, but the main thing is, you feel better about yourself."

"Thanks to Jake," I add.

"I feel better about myself, too, Mom," Jake says. "This was a really good weekend."

She ignores him, keeping that laser look trained on me. "Fuck you," she says. "Fuck you and whatever twisted impulse it was that made you want to turn our son into a high school dropout."

"I never had any such impulse. Come on, Doris, do you know me at *all*?"

"I don't believe I do. And you don't know me, either, and so what? That's all ancient history! The main thing is that our son is a *high school dropout!*"

"Dad dropped out of high school, and he's done all right."

I roll my eyes, bring them back down in time to see that Doris's mouth has dropped open.

"You weren't supposed to tell her, Jake."

"Is this *true*?"

"Yes, Doris, it's true. Everything you're hearing today is true, true, true."

"You told me you went to City College!"

"Well, honey, it was the eighties. I said a lot of things when I was trying to score."

"Ohhhhh my God!"

"You keep summoning God, Doris, and the big guy might just show up."

She spreads her arms, hands stretched toward the heavens. "What else?" she asks the ceiling. "What *else* has happened?"

"Well, on the bright side, Peter Plymouth gave me a seven-thousand-dollar refund."

"And you gladly took it."

"I'll split it with you, Doris."

"Hang on to it. You'll be writing checks for Jacob's new school."

"No, he won't," Jake says. "I am not enrolling anywhere else. I have had it with school."

The words seem to linger in the air, like skywriting. Doris can only stare at Jake, who stares right back at her.

"I've got a plan, Mom," he continues. "I haven't even told Dad yet because I wanted to tell you both about it at the same time."

Doris forces a cruel laugh. "A plan, eh? I can't wait to hear it, Jacob. Do you intend to take some kind of menial job with your glorious eleventh grade education?"

"No, Mom, I don't."

"Are you going to just hang around the house? Sleep until noon every day? *That* I would not tolerate."

"I wouldn't want to do that."

"Well *what*, then?"

Jake looks at his mother, then at me. There should be a drum-roll for what he's about to say, whatever it is, but it's out so fast that it's almost an anticlimax.

"I'm moving to Paris."

Doris makes a snorting sound of disbelief, a sound I can't help echoing with a similar sound of my own. *This* is his big plan, the plan he's refused to reveal for the past two days? It's a little far-fetched. In fact, it's outright crazy.

"*Paris?*" Doris shrieks.

"Yeah. It's something I've wanted to do for a long time."

Jake says it as if it'll be a nostalgic return to the banks of the river Seine. Strange, coming from a kid who's never been more than a few hundred miles from New York City.

Doris is holding her head at the temples. "Why in the world do you want to do this?"

"I've read a lot about it, and it seems like a cool city. Also, I've been studying French for years. Might as well make some use of it."

Doris has to find a way into his plan, a way to temper the lunacy of it, and suddenly it comes to her. The hands fall from her temples. "What I think you're *saying* is, you want to go to *school* in Paris."

Jake rolls his eyes. "No, Mom, that's *not* what I'm saying. Not everything in this world begins and ends in a classroom. Sometimes the *world* is the classroom."

"But, Jacob, without a *structure*—"

"I just want to live there, okay? I"ll make my own structure."

"Doing *what?*"

"Reading. Writing."

"Writing *what?*"

"Stories. Poems." He pats the guitar. "Maybe some songs."

"Ohhh, I *see*," Doris says. "Like your hero, that ridiculous Jim Morrison of The Doors." She shoots a withering look at me, the one who introduced our son to the music of the hard-drinking, ill-fated Lizard King, found dead in a bathtub in Paris at age twenty-seven.

She turns back to Jake, wise at last to his intentions. "You want to mirror the Morrison experience, is that right?"

"Well," Jake says, "everything but the fatal bath part."

I can't take any more of this. "Hey, Jake, come on. What's this really all about?"

"It's not *about* anything, Dad. I've wanted to do it for a long time, and now I can."

"*How* can you do it?" Doris asks. "It takes money to do such a thing, a lot of money. You'll need an apartment, plus food, plus travel expenses. . . . *I* won't pay for it, and on this issue I'm sure your father feels the same way."

"You don't have to pay for it. Neither do you, Dad."

Doris forces a laugh. "Oh, I see. Are you going to hitchhike across the Atlantic?"

"I turn eighteen in three weeks."

The statement seems to come out of nowhere. Doris and I look at each other to see if the other one understands it, but we both come up blank.

"Yes, you *do* turn eighteen in three weeks," Doris says. "We'll get a cake and candles and have a party for you, if you like, but what does any of that have to do with this insane notion you have about moving to *Paris?*"

"I want my money. And when I turn eighteen, I can have it."

Jake looks at Doris, then at me, and finally at both of us. "I'm entitled to my money, and there's nothing either of you can do to stop me from getting it, goddamnit."

So *this* is his plan, a plan that's landed in our laps like a meteor. I didn't see this coming, and I know Doris didn't, either. She puts a hand to her throat, shakes her head. She turns to me, and all I can do is shrug. What can we do? The kid remembered. We'd always thought he'd been too young at the time to remember, but he remembers, all right.

"And please don't tell me I can't afford it," Jake says, "because I know better."

He grins at us. I'm caught by conflicting feelings. I don't know whether to shake his hand and congratulate him, or belt him in the mouth for outsmarting his parents.

"Jake," I say, "I have to hand it to you. You are one crafty bastard."

"Thanks, Pop."

Doris is silent. Her mouth is shut, and her lips have disappeared. They may never reappear again.

What was I saying before, about money being an abstract thing to Jacob Perez-Sullivan? I guess I was wrong. He understands it, all right, and now he's eager to get what he believes is rightfully his.

He's smarter than his two parents put together. Kinder, too, but that really doesn't take much. And now he's ready to take off with the fortune he earned before he ever even knew what money was.

Chapter Twenty-four

It was a regular morning at the playground, a morning like all others. Jake was barely four years old, an adorable kid in blue-and-white-striped OshKosh overalls and red sneakers, racing around from the sandbox to the swings to the monkey bars. Winter was just losing its grip, and the warmth of the sun had him prancing around like a pony in a field of clover.

The world was all his, and rightfully so. If you can't be king when you're four years old, when *can* you be king?

I was having a hell of a time keeping an eye on him, but it was a delightful task. My boy just couldn't stop laughing. If there was any such thing as pure happiness, I was looking at it.

The place was crowded, as it always was on sunny days. Suddenly a well-dressed thirty-something man clutching a clipboard rushed into the playground, a man who was clearly on a mission.

Any adult who enters a New York City playground without a child immediately sets off a pervert alert, and there was nothing subtle about this guy. He was actually inspecting the male children, one by one. He'd crouch down in front of each boy, study his face, and quickly move on to the next.

Suddenly he was looking right into the face of my son, who was busy filling a pail with sand. The potential pervert lingered there, instead of moving away. I got to my feet and hurried over, ready to kill the man if necessary, but before I could say a word he turned to me and said, "Is this your son?"

Sweat was dripping from the guy's sideburns. He did nothing to hide his desperation.

"Yes, he's my son. What's it to you?"

"We'd like to hire him."

"*Hire* him?"

The guy pointed to a grassy field beyond the playground, where a cluster of people stood amid reflectors and light stands.

"We're shooting a print ad for Wilson's Grape Juice. I'm the art director, and our model just called in sick, so if I seem desperate, please forgive me."

"You want my son to be in the ad?"

"Yeah. He's got the look."

"What's the look?"

"It's in his eyes. Bright and cheerful, plus he's handsome. It'll take about an hour and it pays five hundred bucks." He glanced at his watch. "Say yes or no, please, because the clock is running and I'm trying not to go into overtime."

My instinct was to turn him down. I didn't want to turn Jake into a trick pony. I wanted him to be a kid for as long as possible.

"I'll pass," I said.

"A thousand," the art director said.

I was still reading the contract while the makeup lady was touching up Jake's cheeks. He was delighted to be in the midst of whatever this adventure was, charming and cheerful to the staff. His partner in the ad was an adorable red-haired girl with pigtails. They each had to hold up boxes of fruit juice while posing cheek to cheek and smiling from ear to ear. Jake took it upon himself to put his arm across the little girl's shoulders, delighting the art director, who was good to his word. The shoot took less than an hour, and right there on the spot he wrote out a check for a thousand dollars to Jacob Perez-Sullivan.

"Your kid saved my ass today," he said, handing over the check. "Ever think of making the rounds with him?"

"Never."

"Think about it," he said, shaking my hand. "I wasn't bull-shitting you before. He'd get work. He's got the look. Not many kids have it."

When we got home Jake excitedly told his mother all about the man who'd taken his picture in the park. Puzzled, Doris turned to me for an explanation. I knew from her face that there could be trouble, and when I told her Jake was going to be in a grape juice ad, Doris flew into a tirade. How *dare* I do this with-out discussing it with her? I told her there hadn't been any time to discuss it, that the whole thing had happened abruptly and was all over before I'd even had a chance to phone her.

I pointed at the notebooks on her desk. "Besides, you were translating poetry. Even if I'd called, you never answer the phone when you're translating poetry." She knew I was right. When Doris was in her Ivory Tower, the world outside did not exist. Still, she remained righteous.

"There is no excuse for what happened."

"Oh, Doris, just this once, *please*, give me a break."

"We *both* know you've done the wrong thing."

"Here," I said, slapping the check down on her desk. "Is this so wrong? Want me to tear it up?"

Her eyes widened at the sight of the sum. Doris was paid some-thing like twenty-five dollars a month by a Spanish-language mag-azine for her poetry translations, which never took less than three days to complete. She inspected her four-year-old son's check and was unusually quiet for a few minutes. "What is this product our son is selling?"

"Grape juice. Not liquor, not booze, not drugs, just grape juice. Unless you've got a problem with Cesar Chavez and the migrant farm workers, I really don't see what's so sinful about this money."

"Well. We could start a college fund."

"Exactly. My *God*, Doris, don't tell me that you and I are about to *agree* on something!"

She called for Jake to come to her, and enfolded him in an embrace. "I'm sure the juice is full of sugar," she said. "But I think I can live with that."

"Hallelujah."

"But don't *ever* do anything like this again without consulting with me."

"I won't," I promised. "We're arguing about nothing. This was probably a one-shot deal."

I was a little bit wrong about that.

The print ad came out and was a huge success. Jake literally looked like the happiest kid in the world, and the grape juice company got in touch with us about having Jake audition for a TV commercial.

Doris green-lighted the project, and Jake blew them away at the audition. He starred in grape juice commercials with talking parts that made him a mini-celebrity. *People* magazine included him on their Kids To Watch list, speculating that one day Jacob Perez-Sullivan might branch over to acting in TV sitcoms, and maybe even feature films.

Success has its price. I had to burn a lot of my vacation days to take Jake to work. Doris rarely had the time or the inclination to take part in this side of Jake's career, the hauling and fetching, though she did write elaborate excuse notes for the days he had to miss school ("Please excuse Jacob Perez-Sullivan from school today. He has a rare opportunity to take part in an advertising campaign for a fruit beverage that has been getting glowing evaluations from the Department of Consumer Affairs . . .").

Kids can get cranky with all those hours under the hot lights, waiting for art directors to make up their minds about lighting and camera angles, but Jake was usually pretty good about it. I actually loved being there with him because I wasn't at work and I wasn't at home. Work had always been stressful, and now home was just as bad. The clock was ticking for Doris and me. We were trying to keep up appearances for Jake's sake, but it was only a matter of time before we split.

I was sleeping on the couch and getting up before Jake did each morning so he wouldn't know about it. I was an early riser, but still I lived in fear that one morning Jake would wake up before me, find me sprawled on the couch, and demand to know what was going on.

I was ready with a string of lies: I was coughing all night, and didn't want to wake your mother . . . I wanted to read for a while last night, and I didn't want the light to keep your mother awake. . . . Your mother and I have absolutely nothing in common and nothing to share, so we don't wish to participate in the most intimate and trusting thing two people can do, which is to fall asleep side by side. . . .

Oh, buddy boy, what can I tell you? The sperm cell swims eagerly toward the egg, totally oblivious of the way the shooter and the catcher truly feel about each other, or don't feel about each other. You got your start in a climate rich in health and vigor and everything else you need but not love, buddy boy, not love, and I'd apologize for that if I thought it'd do any good, but it wouldn't. . . .

An argument on the shooting set snapped me out of my daydream. We were in a studio on West Forty-eighth Street, the set for a print ad. Jake was seated at a kitchen counter, between a bottle of Wilson's Grape Juice and a big bowl of grapes that the art director was not happy about. It seems that these grapes had a grayish pall to them, and were not nearly "robust" enough to suit his artistic eye.

The photographer wanted to get on with the shoot, saying what do you expect, it's the middle of February, this is out-of-season fruit so it's going to have an out-of-season dullness to it. The art director said it's not an out-of-season *ad*, it's got to look *right*, goddamnit, and in the midst of what was about to turn into a shouting match the makeup man—a maniacally energetic gay guy who'd dusted a springtime rosiness onto Jake's cheeks— came up with a solution.

He mixed some sort of purple makeup powder with vegetable oil, poured the resulting fluid into an empty spray bottle, put the grapes on a sheet of newspaper and spritzed them. The result was startling. The grapes were not only purple, they shone with the kind of sunny goodness the fruit juice label promised to anybody smart enough to drink the stuff.

Using a pair of tongs, the makeup man put the grapes back into the bowl. The photographer applauded, and the art director called the makeup man a genius.

"Hey, it's *just* a paint job," the makeup man said, and then he turned to Jake. "Do *not* touch these grapes, young man, and for heaven's sake don't even *dream* of eating them, or you'll wind up in the emergency room."

Jake grinned. "How'm I supposed to eat them if I can't even touch them?"

"Wise guy." He winked at Jake, turned to the crew, strutted off like the hero he was. "All right, people! Problem solved!"

The shoot went well, and when it was over the grapes—still wet and reeking of whatever that purple stuff was—were thrown straight into the trash barrel. Jake and I headed for the subway, trudging through the winter slush.

"Dad."

"I'm listening."

"It's wrong to waste, isn't it?"

"It sure is."

"They wasted those grapes, didn't they?"

"Well, yeah, in a way they did, because nobody ate them. But on the other hand, the painted grapes made the picture look better than it would have if they *hadn't* painted the grapes. See what I mean?"

"Uh-huh."

"Don't feel bad about those grapes. They served a purpose, even though they went in the garbage."

"Dad?"

"Yeah?"

"How come Mom never comes with us to the studio?"

The hairs at the back of my neck prickled. I took a deep breath, the giveaway that I was about to tell a lie. "Your mother's got a busy schedule these days."

"She doesn't have any classes today. It's Friday."

"Well, she's grading papers."

"She never grades papers until Sunday."

"Jake. She has things to do. She just couldn't come with us today."

"She never comes with us anywhere anymore."

"That's not true! And remember, she takes you to your cello lessons."

"*You* never come to my cello lessons."

"Buddy boy, I *do* have a job. If I don't show up once in a while, my boss tends to get upset."

Jake ignored what I'd just said. "Doesn't Mom like us?"

I stumbled on the slippery subway steps, grabbed the handrail to keep from falling. "Jake. What a question!"

"Doesn't she?"

"Your mother loves you, Jake. You know that."

"Does she love *you*?"

We'd reached the subway platform. The uptown Number 1 train roared into the station just then, giving me time to compose myself in the wake of this dreadful question. We got on the train and settled into our seats. Jake was all earnest-looking in his thick winter coat and hat, staring at me as he waited for his answer.

"Of course your mother loves me, Jake. And I love her."

There was no strength in my words, absolutely none. My heart was colder than my slush-numb feet.

"You never kiss her," Jake said.

I forced a chuckle. It had a horrible sound, like laughter in a funeral parlor. "Sure I do!"

"I've never seen you kiss her."

"We kiss in private, in our bedroom."

"You don't sleep in the bedroom."

How long had he been holding *this* in? How the hell did he know? I didn't have to ask.

"I was thirsty one night and I got up to get a drink and I saw you on the couch."

He'd gotten himself a drink of Wilson's Grape Juice, packed with Vitamin C and fortified with essential nutrients. We always had plenty of that stuff around, free of charge.

I swallowed, long and hard. Jake's gaze was steady, relentless. Did he want the truth, or did he want comfort? I opted for comfort. It would be easier on both of us. "Sometimes I can't sleep, so I get up to read, but I don't want to wake your mother. So I go to the couch with my book, and sometimes I fall asleep reading."

"The light wasn't on, Dad."

"What light?"

"The reading light by the couch. You were just asleep there, in the dark."

Jesus Christ. "I didn't want to wake up your mother by going back to bed in the middle of the night, so I just stayed on the couch. It's no big deal, Jake."

He stared at me like a trial lawyer who knows the witness is lying, and can do nothing about it. I had to say something to break that terrible stare. "We usually eat dinner together, don't we?"

This gave him something to think about. "Yeah. . . ."

"When you're in a play, we always go together, and what about when we take weekend trips upstate? Aren't we all together then?"

It had been a long time since we'd taken a weekend trip, but he seemed to be buying it.

"Yeah." A tickle of a smile appeared on his face. "I guess we are."

"Sure we are!" I was encouraged by my own false enthusiasm. "Listen, when we get home, we'll all have dinner together, and maybe there'll be a good movie on TV that we can watch."

"Mom doesn't like the movies we like."

"Well, that's all right. The main thing is we'll eat together, and we can tell her all about the painted grapes."

His face lit up. "Can I tell her?"

"Sure. It's all yours, champ. You tell her."

We came home to an empty house. It was nearly eight o'clock when Doris trudged in with a shoulder bag full of books. The sight of this was supposed to tell us she'd spent the day at the library. Maybe she had, or maybe she'd spent the afternoon humping one of her colleagues. I didn't really care, either way.

By this time I'd begun a stupid fling with a copygirl from Hoboken that took place one night a week, during Jake's cello lesson. Her youthful enthusiasm soon gave way to whiny complaints about the limits of our relationship, to which I could only reply: "What relationship?" She knew my situation, knew I wasn't about to make any kind of move that would jolt my son. She "wanted to write" and heard I was a good person to learn from, and that's how it started—the crusty old rewrite man with the heart of gold, showing the budding journalist the way.

But my heart wasn't gold, and her dreams of a journalism career were tarnished by a nightmarish lack of talent. She could not put a sentence together. If the English language could speak for itself, she'd have found herself facing assault charges.

I was always eager to catch that train out of Hoboken, to get home in time to tuck my son into bed. The fling only lasted a few weeks, and when I broke it off in a coffee shop near the *Star* she was as relieved as I was. She stared at me long and hard before saying, "You think you're doing your son a favor, but the price he'll pay goes up every day."

I was stunned by her words. For one thing, it was a startling perception. For another, it was the most coherent sentence she'd ever come up with. Maybe I was a better mentor than I'd thought. . . .

Anyway, Doris entered the house after a day of reading and/ or fucking, and luckily Jake was taking his bath, so I had a chance to fill her in as she poured herself a glass of white wine.

"Doris. He's asking all kinds of questions."

"He has an inquisitive mind."

"He was asking why we never kiss, and why I was sleeping on the couch."

Now I had her attention. "What did you say?"

"I told him we kiss in private, and I like to get up and read at night so I won't disturb you."

Doris nodded approvingly, one conniver to another. "Not bad."

"I also reminded him that we eat dinner together. "

"Except on the night he has his cello lesson." She had a catlike grin she saved for times like this. "Where is it you go on cello nights, Samuel?"

"The library, just like you. Now listen. We've got to jolly it up a little bit tonight, you hear me? I'll order in Chinese. That always puts him in a good mood."

Fifteen minutes later we were seated at the table, passing around Chinese food cartons. In the midst of it all was our son, clean and chirpy from his bath, his wet hair slicked back so that his ears protruded in a way that was almost unbearably adorable. He was happily chattering away about his day, but when he got to the story of the painted grapes Doris put her chopsticks down and looked accusingly at me.

"What a horrible thing to do. That's false advertising!"

"No, it isn't, Doris. The grapes were out of season. They just needed a little sprucing up."

"It seems very wrong to me."

You'd have thought that the paint job was my idea. Jake looked from his mother to me. His ears seemed to be trembling. I struggled to remain calm.

"Doris," I said, "they aren't advertising the grapes, they're advertising the *juice.*"

"Nonetheless, it's a canard."

"Ooh, a *canard.* Is that the big word of the night? Let me look it up so I can think of something snappy to say."

"You needn't look it up, it simply means—"

Every Chinese food carton jumped as Jake's small fist slammed down on the table.

We looked at him in shock. His lips were quivering, and his eyes were blurred with tears of fury.

"Can't you two *ever* stop fighting?"

It was a question, a plea, a cry for decency. Doris and I looked at each other, two reasonably intelligent people who'd greatly underestimated the perceptivity of this human being we'd come together to create. What a strategy we'd lived by. Feed him, clothe him, send him to school, keep him busy, and he'll never detect the underlying tension in this home, will he?

Not much he wouldn't. And even if he weren't a bright boy, he would have known. Kids detect marital misery through their skins, not their brains, the way animals know when to run from an earthquake before the seismograph even detects the tremors.

But when you're a five-year-old boy living in the midst of marital turmoil, there's no place to run. All you can do is sit there in your Spider-Man pajamas and listen to your parents go after each other in an argument over a bowl of painted grapes that has absolutely nothing to do with a bowl of painted grapes.

The sudden silence was excruciating. Jake's words struck like meteors, and it's as if Doris and I were waiting for the dust cloud to settle, but that could take years, so I blustered my way through the dust, flying blind as I said, "We're just having a little disagreement, Jake."

He gave me a withering look. "Bullshit," he replied, and it was the first time we'd ever heard him use a vulgar word.

Doris gasped as if she'd just been knifed in the chest. "That was uncalled for, Jacob!"

He ignored her. "It's not just a little disagreement. You guys fight all the time."

"Not *all* the time," I said, but there was no strength in my words, none at all. I was just throwing them up the way an over-matched boxer throws up his arms to block a barrage of punches.

But there were no more punches. Jake's attack was over. The anger was gone from his tears. Now his eyes were wet with sorrow and his face was pale. Smudges of that rosy makeup stood out on Jake's white cheeks. It took a lot of washing to get them off, and Jake had failed to do it in the bath. He looked like a heartbroken clown.

Shouldn't one of us have gotten up to hug the boy? Doris and I just sat there, staring down at our plates. We had been outed. The fraud of our lives was no longer a secret. Jake understood the situation, maybe even better than Doris and I understood it. His childhood had just come to an abrupt end on that miserable winter night, and even Chinese food couldn't fix that.

He didn't want the rest of his chicken lo mein and pork fried dumplings. He picked up his plate and set it on the floor, where the cats appeared out of nowhere to devour the food.

This was strictly forbidden by Doris, but she realized this was not a night to enforce the house rules. If Jake were to have pulled a pack of Marlboros out of his pajama pocket and lit up, Doris probably wouldn't have objected.

Me, I'd have asked him to give me a cigarette. And a blindfold. For the first time in my life I actually wished I were dead, and even that wouldn't have been quite enough. Lousy as I'd been as a husband and a father, my death would have traumatized Jake and made things worse for Doris.

No, I didn't wish that I were dead. What I wished was that I'd never been born.

But I was, and so was Doris, and somehow we got together and because of that Jake was born, this sweet, bright five-year-old who got up from the table to kiss first his father and then his mother on the cheek, politely, like a child from an upper-class British family bidding his parents good night before the governess takes him up to bed. Doris tried to hug him, but he kept his arms tight to his sides and tensed up, like someone trying to break a wrestling hold. He took a few steps toward his room and then whirled around to face us, like a gunslinger expecting an ambush.

"You're going to get a divorce, aren't you?"

There was no place to run, no place to hide, no place to die. I tried to speak, but my words, whatever they might have been, perished in my throat. Doris wasn't doing much better. She took off her glasses, rubbed her eyes, squeezed the bridge of her nose, and put the glasses back on before speaking just one word:

"Eventually."

What a way to put it. Yes, my boy, your parents' marriage is a dead thing, but there's no rush to bury it. The divorce is just something we'll get around to, like new carpeting in your room.

I was ready for Jake to throw a tantrum, burst out crying, but he didn't. This was no shock to him. He'd absorbed the shock of it bit by bit over the years, all on his own, piecing together the all too obvious puzzle of his parents' collapsed marriage (collapsed? Had the structure actually ever stood in the first place?)

without letting on to either of us. This is something unhappily married parents just don't get. They're not the only ones keeping up a facade. The kids do it, too, and it's absolutely exhausting.

No wonder Jake looked tired. His eyes seemed as flat and cold as the eyes of a shark. No light. No hope. Nothing.

"I'm going to bed now," he said to both of us, or maybe to neither of us.

"We'll tuck you in," I said.

Jake chuckled, and he was right. What a ridiculous offer, like offering a Band-Aid to a man whose throat has been slashed. He held up a hand to keep us both at bay. "I'll tuck myself in," he said, turning to go once again.

Suddenly, he turned to face us one more time, arms folded across his chest. He looked like the world's youngest lawyer.

"You guys," he said, "are like the grapes."

Doris looked at him in wonder. "Baby?"

"Your marriage," Jake said, almost impatiently. "It's like the grapes. Just a paint job."

He went straight to bed.

I really don't know why I didn't die that night. Doris and I couldn't even talk about it. We cleared away the food and went to Jake's room to find him sound asleep, stretched out on his back as if he were on a beach somewhere. He wasn't faking sleep. He was dead to the world. He'd just put down the burden he'd been carrying for so long, and now at last it was time to rest. There were heartaches and traumas to come, but not tonight. Tonight there was only the oblivion of sleep.

But not for his parents. I went to bed with Doris for the very last time that night. We lay on opposite edges of the bed like castaway enemies forced to share a life raft, sighing and crying over this monumental mess.

Toward dawn Doris passed out, but I didn't, and at first light I moved to the couch. I didn't want Jake to catch me in bed with his mother. On top of everything else that had happened, the last thing he needed was false hope.

There was remarkably little to say about it in the weeks that followed—Jake had pretty much said it all that night. He'd actually accelerated the divorce process. Doris and I probably would have stewed and simmered and grumbled at each other until Jake went off to college, and who knows? By that time, we could have been too old and weary to split. Jake had fanned the spark of truth into a flame that burned down the facade, once and for all.

I started looking for an apartment, and two months later I was out of there. It was a relief to me, and a relief to Doris, and probably to Jake as well. We'd all be better off than we'd been before, except for one thing.

That special light was gone from Jake's eyes. He could still laugh and kid around the way he used to, but there was usually an underlying sarcasm to it, biting and bitter. And it wasn't until the light was gone that I was able to figure out what it had been.

It was the one emotion that was simply unteachable, and totally undefinable until it was gone.

Joy.

Without that special light, Jake had lost "the look" that got him noticed in the first place. His career began and ended with the grape juice campaign. I took him on some more auditions, but nothing panned out. He was all washed up at age five. He inevitably retreated into himself, having learned that the world is not such a magical place, after all.

But those commercials Jake had already starred in ran and ran and ran, long after the divorce was finalized, long after the light was gone. When the residual checks finally stopped rolling in there was more than a hundred and fifty thousand dollars in the bank account of Jacob Perez-Sullivan, to be held in trust for him until either his eighteenth or twenty-first birthday, a date to be determined by both his parents—or, in the event of the death of one parent, by the surviving parent. I don't know what the ruling was if we were both dead.

Doris took care of the trust fund. I had no idea of what it could be worth by now, with more than a decade's worth of interest. Jake had never once mentioned the money to me in all those years since his career had crashed and burned. I figured he didn't know about it.

But he knew, all right. Maybe he came across the trust fund paperwork the day he dug around in his mother's drawers to find our wedding license. He'd bided his time until the day his English teacher gave that impromptu writing assignment.

In a flash, Jake saw the stars align in his favor—the controversial writing assignment, his mother's absence—and poked at the little pinhole of light until it was now the big, wide-open gate to what he wanted. Total, absolute freedom from everything and everyone he's ever known.

Quite a plan. A hell of a plan. Son of a bitch.

Doris and I can't even say anything for a minute or so. We just look at our son standing there facing us, confronting us, breathing hard but evenly, arms folded across his chest and one booted foot placed defiantly ahead of the other.

Doris clears her throat. "That money is supposed to be for your college education."

"Aren't you getting the picture, Mom? I'm not *going* to college. I'm not even going to finish high school."

"Ever?"

"I don't know yet. But for now, this is what I'm doing with that money. And believe me, it'll be more of an education than any college could offer."

"Sarah won't like this. Have you thought of that?"

"We broke up, Mom. And anyway she's too busy humping Pete Hogan to care about anything else."

"Oh, Jacob!"

"It's true. Don't ever mention her name to me again."

Doris's face softens. "Is that what this is all about? You've been betrayed, and your heart is broken, so you want to run far, far away?"

"Oh, come *on*, Mom. That's not it, and you know it."

Doris is literally quivering. "You're frightening me, Jacob."

It's the first time I've ever heard my ex admit to being scared about something. She's got a powerful personality, and some might even consider her to be a bit of a bully, but right now she's totally intimidated by her own son. In a way, I guess it makes sense that the only person who can make her feel this way is the person who came out of her.

"I'd hate to think that I frighten anyone," Jake says. "I'm just telling you how I feel. Remember, you two are the ones who got that whole thing started with the TV commercials. That wasn't my idea, was it?"

He taps himself on the chest. "But *I'm* the one who *made* those commercials. *I'm* the one who got teased in the school yard for three years, because those fucking commercials kept running. Think that was *fun*? Do you think I *enjoyed* that?"

Doris and I are silent. He'd never complained about being teased, at least not to me. And then it hits me that until now, my son has never really complained about anything, despite all the bad things that have happened to him.

"*I* did the work," Jake continues, "and *I* suffered, and I've waited thirteen years to get what I've got coming, and I can't imagine any reason in the world why I shouldn't have it. It's *my* money. It isn't anybody else's."

"College," Doris all but whispers.

Jake sighs, shakes his head. "I could never go to college the way you'd want me to, Mom. I never liked school very much."

"But you love to *read!* You love *books!*"

"Yeah, I do. That won't change. You don't have to go to school to read books. I'll take a bunch with me. You and Dad can each make a list of what you think I should be reading."

"Won't be much overlap on those lists," I can't resist saying.

Jake smiles. Doris ignores me and plows ahead.

"You're an *honor student!*" she sputters.

"Yeah, I was an honor student. That was just to keep you off my back, Mom."

He sighs, weary with it all. "And now I say—enough, already. All the guys in my class kept talking about where they wanted to go to college, and it was driving me crazy. Harvard, Yale, Princeton, Brown. Blah, blah, blah." He shakes his head. "The last thing I'd ever want to do is go and *live* at a school. Jesus! There'd be no *relief* from it! I'd feel like I was in class twenty-four/seven! I'm not about to waste forty-five grand a year for something I don't even want, especially when it's *my money!*"

He's shouting by the end of his statement. Doris literally puts her hands over her ears and tilts her face to the floor. I try to put a comforting hand on her shoulder, but she shrugs it away.

"How about if *we* pay for it?" Doris offers.

"How about if *nobody* pays for it, Mom?"

"Calm down, Jake," I say.

He momentarily shuts his eyes, composes himself, resumes speaking. "I just want to do this thing, *my* thing," he says softly. "I've never really *been* anywhere or *done* anything that wasn't somehow connected to my *formal education.* Everything's a part of the *big plan.* . . . Well, the hell with that. This is *my* plan, and I can only pull it off if I'm far, far away from everything and everyone I've ever known. I'm not saying it'll be easy, but it's what I want."

Doris lifts her head, her eyes red and teary. "Why?"

Jake shrugs. "Maybe I'm just tired of being a hothouse flower, Mom. I'd like to be a dandelion, you know? I want to see what it's like out there in the weather, feel what it's like to taste the rain."

"For how long?"

"I don't know. Six months, a year . . . the point is, I've been thinking about this for a long time, and now I can do it without turning to anyone for help. It's my money, and *I . . . am . . . going.*"

Doris dabs at her eyes with a handkerchief, shakes her hair, and juts her chin. Whenever she does this, she is braced for battle. "Actually, you will need our consent."

"Excuse me?"

"The money. It's yours when you turn twenty-one, not eighteen. Not unless your father and I give our consent."

"You'll do that," Jake says. "I know Dad will."

"Don't be so sure," I say. "I have to think about it."

Jake goes to his mother, and dares to caress her cheek with a gentle hand.

"Mom," Jake says, "I'm *begging* you. I've been an obedient son, even when I thought your demands were ridiculous, and I don't think I've ever asked for much, or given you any real trouble."

"Jacob. Need I remind you that you burned a two-thousand-dollar cello on the roof of this house?"

"Because you gave me no other choice. Please, *please* don't put me in another corner. I'd hate to think of what I'd burn this time."

Jake falls to his knees before his mother and clasps his hands together in what would appear to be prayer.

Doris lets her head fall and shuts her eyes. Again I go to her and place a comforting hand on her shoulder. This time, she does not shrug it off. The shoulder feels bony. Doris is tired. She is not a kid anymore, and can't go fifteen rounds the way she used to.

"Please, Mom," Jake all but whispers. "Please, please, *please* don't fuck this thing up for me."

Doris turns to me with imploring eyes. She wants to know what I think. She *really* wants to know what I think. Suddenly, this is my ball game.

I remember what my father had to say to me about being there for Jake. I am there, all right, with my son, at his side, not running off to the woods the way my father did, not failing him, not . . . *bailing out.* I take a deep breath, weigh it all up in my heart and my brain. They confer, and the decision, a unanimous one, comes straight from my soul.

"Doris," I say, "we've got to let him do this thing."

CHAPTER TWENTY-FIVE

It is almost as if Jacob-Perez Sullivan, four days past his eighteenth birthday, has gone into the Witness Protection Program. His beard is gone, and his hair is cut even shorter than mine. We owe this miracle to his beloved grandfather, Danny Sullivan, who'd given Jake some valuable advice while the two of them constructed that cobblestone path together a few weeks earlier.

"When you hit the road, Jake, you ought to clean up your appearance," my father advised. "Shave and a haircut, man. Last thing you want to do these days is resemble a terrorist. Good-lookin' kid like you, they'll be cavity-searchin' you at every port just for the fun of it."

Nothing Doris or I could have told him would have resulted in the cleanup. The change in Jake's appearance is so dramatic that I can't stop staring at him as the three of us make our way through JFK Airport.

It's our second family outing in less than a week, after years of never doing anything together. Our first outing wasn't your typical divorced-family-getting-together-for-old-times'-sake gathering.

The three of us had gotten together to kill the cat.

* * *

It was long overdue. Poor old Jasper was blind, and probably deaf. He couldn't eat, he moaned in his sleep, and you could see his skeleton through his coat. He was twenty years old. It had been a hell of a life.

The veterinarian's office was in the basement of a brownstone on West Eighty-eighth Street. I carried Jasper in an old pet carrier box, while Jake walked arm in arm with Doris. It was a beautiful sunny day, a great day to die or a terrible day to die, depending on your point of view. Is it better to die on a rainy day, since the day is a washout anyway? Or is it better to die on a sunny day, to go out on a cheerful note?

Jake and Doris were actually in tears as we entered the place, a small, dingy room rank with smells of alcohol and animal fur. The vet was a small, gnomeish man with round eyeglasses, a full head of white hair, and an appropriately mournful face.

He embraced Doris. She'd left a lot of money here over the years, and this would be her final payment. Maybe that's why the vet looked mournful. He clasped his hands together, like a priest about to address his congregation. "Are we ready?"

Doris nodded. She lifted the lid of the carrier case to stroke Jasper's head one last time. "Good-bye, old friend."

I turned to Jake to see if he wanted a final farewell. He shook his head, wiped his eyes.

"I said goodbye to him back at the house, Dad."

I followed the vet into a closet-sized room with two chairs and an examining table. I set the carrying case on the floor and lifted that all but weightless creature onto my lap. He meowed nervously. He may have been blind and deaf, but he could sense where he was, and he didn't like it. Unpleasant things had been done to him here.

The vet was busy preparing a syringe. He didn't seem quite so mournful now, with Doris out of sight.

"Who are you to Doris?" he asked.

"Ex-husband."

He couldn't help chuckling. "Well. This is an odd thing for you to be doing."

"We do things together once in a while for the sake of the child, you know? Birthdays. Graduations. Executions."

His eyes narrowed. "You're a funny guy, eh?"

"Depends on who you ask, Doc."

Jasper was squirming on my lap. I stroked his head. He licked my hand. Oh boy.

The vet was ready. "Now listen. Just hold him the way you're holding him. I promise you he won't feel a thing."

"Just make sure you get him and not me, Doc."

He chuckled, held up the syringe. A drop of poison hung from the tip of the needle. "This wouldn't be enough to kill a man of your size. Might make you sick for a day or two, but that's all."

"Take careful aim anyway."

The vet gave Jasper's head a perfunctory stroke, a wordless eulogy. Then he pulled up a fold of the fur on Jasper's back, stuck the needle in there, and pumped in the poison.

Jasper perked up in my lap, cocking his head as if he'd heard someone calling him from another room, or maybe another world.

"Just hold him," the vet said. "Stroke him. He'll be asleep in less than a minute."

Jasper shut his eyes and rested his head on top of his paws. A surge of current seemed to run through his body, and then he was still, absolutely still.

"Okeydoke," the vet said, turning to write something in a notebook. "Set him on the examining table. I'll do the rest."

"Let me take his collar off first."

I removed the collar, a strip of worn yellow leather that held a metal tag with Jasper's name and address. What a pathetic thing for a cat who never left the apartment, except to visit the vet's! I laid Jasper's bare body on the examining table. It was all over.

"What happens to him now?"

"He'll be cremated. Would you like to have the ashes?"

Here we go, I said to myself. There's always a fucking angle.

"How much?"

"A hundred dollars."

I was no longer a *New York Star* reporter, but this was the kind of thing that made me want to reach for my notebook and go to town. "What do I get for my C-note?"

The vet seemed offended by my slang. "Well, you get Jasper's remains in a small urn, plus a certificate saying these are his remains."

"I see. That way, we know it's authentic."

The vet stares at me before answering. "That's right."

"What's the urn made out of?"

The vet adjusted his glasses. "Believe it's some sort of metal."

"You don't *know* what kind of metal it is?"

"Why is that so important?"

"Because you should know what the hell it is you're selling to people before you bang 'em for a hundred bucks. And while we're on the subject, let me ask you this—are all of your animals burned separately, or is it one big bonfire?"

"I beg your pardon!"

"I don't want to shell out a hundred bucks to wind up with the remains of some stranger's dead Doberman pinscher mixed in with Jasper's ashes."

"Sir. Let's remember something here. This isn't even your cat."

"That's right, it's my ex-wife's cat. But she's in a very vulnerable state right now, and if you go to her with this ridiculous offer she'll jump at it, and I don't want that to happen. So let's just forget the ashes deal, pal. Don't even offer it to Doris."

He shrugged. "As you wish."

"Oh man, what I *wish* is that I could catch the rascals who probably chuck these dead animals in the river and then scrape out the bottom of their barbecue grills to fill up urns and sell ashes to grieving pet lovers! That's what I wish, as long as we're talking about wishes!"

By this time I was practically yelling. The vet looked as if he was ready to dial 911. I held up an appeasing hand. "I'm going, man, I'm going."

He didn't follow me back to the waiting room. Doris and Jake were sitting there, reading magazines. They looked up at me as if hoping I had a miracle to report—that the vet had injected Jasper not with poison but with a miracle elixir that had turned him back into the bold, beautiful kitten he once was.

I wanted to believe that, too. There was nothing to say. All I could do was burst into tears.

They took me to a nearby ice cream parlor, where I ordered the biggest hot fudge sundae on the menu. I ate every bit of it, hogging it down with all the grace of a junkie sucking on a crack pipe. People stared at me, but I didn't care. They didn't know what it was like to have a cat die on your lap.

On the way out, I remembered something. "Shit, Doris, I left the carrying case at the vet's. Want me to go and get it?"

"What for?" Doris replied, and maybe that was the saddest thing that happened all day, the idea of knowing without a doubt that you will never have another pet. Maybe it's not quite the same as knowing you'll never have another child.

But without either of those things, what is left?

Anyway, this trip to the airport is promising to be every bit as emotionally turbulent as the cat murder. But so far, it's going all right—remarkably well, in fact.

It's a ridiculous thing to say about an eighteen-year-old, but he actually looks ten years younger, which would make him eight years old, but that's not how I mean it. This isn't about his hair. It's about the light that's back in his eyes for the first time in so long.

I was wrong about the light in the eyes. It *can* come back, if you believe in miracles, and you don't have to believe in God to believe in miracles. You just have to believe in each other. Maybe it's the same thing. Maybe it's a better thing.

"Have you got everything?" Doris asks.

"Absolutely everything," Jake patiently replies.

We've been over the checklist countless times. His tightly packed canvas bag contains his clothes and his books. The carry-on bag contains his first-ever passport, his ticket to Paris, the reservation for his hotel on the Left Bank, insurance papers to cover medical emergencies anywhere in Europe, a blank notebook, five pens, the book he happens to be reading at the moment (Leonard Gardner's *Fat City*—one of my choices, I'm proud to say), a twenty-four pack of Trojan lubricated condoms, five hundred U.S. dollars, and a bank card that will enable him to get money from cash points wherever he goes. Jake will stay at the hotel until he finds himself an apartment.

He's letting me carry his guitar, which he's learning to play with astonishing skill. Those cello lessons paid off after all, lubricating Jake's transition from one stringed instrument to another.

Doris has deposited thirty thousand dollars into Jake's checking account, but the trust fund is still quite healthy. The remaining amount, after the withdrawal, stands at $157,543 on departure day.

Moneywise, I'm doing all right myself. After I was fired from the *New York Star* the union lawyers went to bat for me and wangled eighteen months' worth of severance pay, plus medical coverage. Management tried to *un*-fire me, claiming Derek Slaughterchild lacked the authority to do what he'd done, but it didn't hold up in arbitration. I had been fired, all right. There were witnesses who hated Derek as much as I did, and they were delighted to testify to what they'd seen and heard. I'm sure it was no coincidence that a few weeks after the ruling, Derek was fired, and I'm told he wept like a baby while he packed up.

So here I am, on a year-and-a-half-long sabbatical at full pay. Not only that, but I have no more tuition or child support payments. If I wanted to I could get on the plane and go with Jake.

But I wouldn't do that to him. This is *his* time. I know it, he knows it, and so, at last, does Doris.

Jake is straining under the weight of his bag, but as usual he won't let me help as we make our way toward Air France.

"Look at this," he says, reaching into his pocket. "Danny gave it to me."

He pulls out a rectangular box. It's about the size of a deck of cards, encased in brown leather.

"Open it, Dad."

Inside the box is an old compass, with a black enamel face and raised white letters indicating north, south, east, and west. Its needle quivers as we continue walking, ever sensitive to direction.

"How cool is *that?* It's from when Danny was in the navy."

"Extremely cool," I agree, trying to ignore a twinge of envy over the fact that this family relic is skipping a generation to land in my son's hands. But the twinge quickly passes. I am happy, very happy for my son. I close up the compass case and hand it back to him.

"Danny says that when in doubt, always head north."

"I'll trust that he knows what he's talking about."

When we reach Air France, Jake checks in his big bag and answers the ticket agent's routine questions as if he's heard them a million times before. Doris and I stand on either side of him, letting him handle the whole thing. As the agent affixes a tag to Jake's bag she seems to notice Doris and me for the first time.

"I assume the child is traveling alone," she says.

"I wouldn't call him a child if I were you," I reply.

We begin the walk to Jake's departure gate. I've sworn to myself that I'm not going to cry, but it's a vow I may wind up breaking. Doris seems to be holding up all right, but it's hard to tell. She's the one who's lived with our kid all these years, so she's the one whose day-to-day life is going to change drastically. I realize I know nothing about her personal life, outside of how it relates to our son. I wonder if she has a boyfriend. Maybe now she'll remarry. She's about to get her first true taste of what it is to be alone.

As for me, I'm okay by myself for now. For the first time in my life I'm alone without being lonely.

Suddenly I'm in the grip of a powerful memory that hasn't paid a visit in a long time. It's something that happened one autumn day when Jake was about two years old, and the three of us went to the Metropolitan Museum of Art. Jake wasn't crazy about the idea of a museum visit, but we appeased him with a promise to take him to a nearby playground afterwards.

Doris kept us both there longer than we wanted, staring at painting after painting as if she meant to memorize every brushstroke. It was late afternoon, almost early evening when we finally came out and brought Jake to the playground, which was now empty except for us. The kid was cranky, and so was I. Doris and I began arguing, and when we came up for air we suddenly we realized that our son was nowhere in sight.

You don't even know where to begin in a situation like this. Doris ran frantically around the playground, screaming his name, while I raced outside the gates and began running down Fifth Avenue, looking wildly about for my son and his kidnapper. Then it hit me that the kidnapper might have taken Jake the *other* way, so I reversed direction and ran a few blocks uptown, stopped, sensed the hopelessness of my mission, and hurried back to the playground, praying I'd see Jake nestled in the arms of his mother.

But she was standing there alone, still screaming his name to the sky. She turned to me, tears streaming down her face.

I looked at my watch. Twelve minutes. Jake had been missing for twelve minutes. By now he could be halfway to Brooklyn, or Jersey City, or any place else where a bridge or tunnel could accommodate a speeding car. Oh, they are *good*, those kidnappers! They wait for their moment, and they pounce. All they need is two selfish parents who'd rather argue with each other than watch their child, and Doris and I were those parents!

Doris collapsed into my arms. I told her we had to call a cop, *right now*, and as I was saying it a round metal lid on the ground of the playground went up, and Jake popped out like a happy gopher. This particular playground, it turned out, had a series of underground tunnels for the kiddies to crawl through. Jake found this out twelve minutes before we did, twelve minutes that aged each of his parents twelve years.

We ran to him and hugged him and wept uncontrollably, and now, for the first time since that day, we do the same thing as we reach the departure gate, me on his left, Doris on his right, the two of us hugging him before he disappears into this new tunnel that's going to take him away for a lot longer than twelve minutes.

He's got his arms around us. "It's okay," he says. "It's okay." Jake's eyes are wet but he's under control. He's had a lot longer to think about what he's doing than we have.

At last, we pull away from him. Doris can't even speak. I wipe my eyes, blow my nose. I don't know what the hell I'm going to say to my son, but suddenly I'm saying it.

"Always remember the bacon."

He seems puzzled. "Bacon?"

"Yeah. The smell of bacon on Saturday mornings, whenever I made us breakfast. You're going to have some lonely times, and when you do, you'll feel better if you remember the way the bacon smelled."

"That's good advice, Dad."

He hugs me, then hugs Doris. "I love you both very much," he says. I hand him the guitar, and then he turns and heads off.

He hands his passport to an apathetic-looking security person, who glances at it and waves him through. Jake doesn't even look back as he turns the corner, and I have to admire him for this. He's already said good-bye. He doesn't want to milk it, the way so many people do at airports.

Jacob Perez-Sullivan is on his way to the City of Lights, a place his parents have never been.

Doris Perez stands there with her arms folded, staring at where Jake has last been seen, like a fisherman's wife checking the horizon for the sight of a sail. I have a feeling she'll stay there all day if I don't do what I do next, which is to take her by the elbow.

"Doris. Come on. Let's go."

"Maybe we should stay until the plane takes off."

"If you want."

It happens about an hour later. We watch from behind as Jake's plane races down the runway and lifts into the sky without a bump.

"Look at that, Doris. He's finally getting what he always wanted."

"What's that?"

"He's flying. How 'bout that? Our son is finally flying."

We watch until the plane disappears into the clouds; then we begin the walk toward the exit at JFK, which has to be the world's ugliest airport—shitty carpets and ratty shops run by angry people, people who clearly would rather be elsewhere. I guess it would be depressing to work at the airport, watching people go off to places all over the world while you stand stuck behind a cash register, selling magazines and breath mints and airsickness tablets.

Doris is still weeping, but it's an aftermath cry. She's more or less under control.

"He'll be all right," I say. "He's a healer, you know?"

"A healer?"

"Yeah. If he can do anything to help a situation, he does it. Have you ever noticed? It's in his nature. On that crazy weekend that you were away, he did all he could to help anybody we came across."

"Don't remind me of that weekend."

"Be proud of him, Doris. He's a good kid. He'll be a good man."

"Well," she says, wiping her eyes, "what are *your* plans, now that you're out of work?"

"I'm out of work, but I'm still getting paid."

"How nice."

"I'm thinking of going back to high school and getting that diploma."

"You asshole," Doris says, but her heart isn't in it, because her mind is on Jake.

"Doris. He'll be fine."

"So you say."

"If he doesn't like it, he can always turn around and come back."

"He may never come back."

"Of course he will. We're his family—especially you, Doris. You've always been right there, in his face. Now that you're out of his face, he'll finally have a chance to miss you, and believe me, he will. Jake always liked Thanksgiving. I'm betting he'll be back for a Thanksgiving visit. Christ knows he can afford it."

"Oh *God*," Doris sighs as she suddenly hurries ahead of me. But her idea of hurrying is just a brisk walk for me, and it's easy to keep up with her.

"Have a little faith in him, Doris."

"Shut up. Just please, for *once*, shut up."

"Everything happens for a reason. Jake told me that."

"I'll *bet* he did." She shakes her head. "That weekend, that

weekend," she moans. "*Why* did I have to go away on *that* weekend? Why?"

"I can't answer that."

"I know you can't."

"But I *can* tell you that what happened would have happened
anyway, eventually. This isn't about one crazy father-son weekend, Doris. This is about a unique young man who won't walk
the path just because everybody else is walking it. You should be
proud of him."

"You really think so?"

"Yeah, I think so, Doris. I learned a lot on that weekend, but
the best thing I learned is that Jacob Perez-Sullivan is a good person. He's got a good core. You put it there, Doris, and maybe I
did, too. So I think maybe we didn't mess up so badly, after all."

Doris startles me by falling into my arms for the first time, perhaps, since that terrifying day in the playground when we
thought our son was gone for good. I once saw a photo of one of
the Japanese pilots who bombed Pearl Harbor shaking hands
with one of the Americans who dropped the big one on Hi-
roshima. Two old warriors, fifty years later, showing there were
no hard feelings. That's Doris and me, hugging at the airport.

"I *am* proud of him," she says.

"So am I."

The hug evaporates, and we continue our walk toward the
exit. The three of us had taken a car service to the airport, but
now we'll have to get in line for a cab.

But I'm not quite ready to leave. I feel a little bit dizzy, and the
very idea of getting into a stinking New York City yellow cab
makes me feel nauseated.

I tell Doris I'm not feeling right, that she should go ahead
without me. She actually seems relieved. We've had a decent
time today, and spending any more time together could only
wreck it.

Doris goes off to the cab line. I get myself a Coke, find myself a seat, and sip it slowly to settle my stomach, happy to watch people and planes come and go. I don't have any appointments. Nobody expects anything of me. My ex-wife is heading home, and my son is in the sky, and I have absolutely no place to be.

And then it hits me how wrong I am. There's someplace I want to be, all right, and I get up and begin the journey my bones knew I'd be making before my brain did.

CHAPTER TWENTY-SIX

The Train to the Plane carries me to the subway system, and from there it's easy to get to Flushing. It's a warm day, even though we're halfway through October. Autumn doesn't really exist anymore in New York. It seems that we go straight from summer to winter, air-conditioning to steam heat, with no room in between to open the window and breathe fresh air.

I actually work up a sweat on the walk to the house, where the cobblestone path my father and my son have built is a sight to behold. They didn't use any mortar—the stones are set down deeply in the dirt, holding each other in place. Over time they can only become more deeply and tightly set, so what would be the point of cementing them?

I walk over the stones on my way to the front door. They are freckled with little white circles, rims of calcium that are the remains of the barnacles my father could not scrape away completely. Will those circles be there forever, or will time, rain, and footsteps wear them away? I'd like to think they'll be there forever, mysterious little markings for the mailman to puzzle over on his daily deliveries. . . .

Before I reach the front door I'm jolted by a scraping sound on the other side of the house. I look up and notice that the clapboards out front are pretty much down to bare wood, and that the lawn and shrubbery are covered with paint flakes, like yellow snow. I walk around to the back of the house. My father is up on a ladder, scraping dead paint off the clapboards. His hands and face are peppered with paint flakes. He does not wear a dust mask. I wouldn't expect him to wear one. He thinks dust masks are faggy. A real working man breathes the air that's in front of him, and takes his chances.

I stand behind him for a while, waiting to be noticed. He's going at the clapboards hard and fast with a scraper, and when he's out of breath he takes a break, wipes his face with the shoulder of his T-shirt, and at last sees me standing there.

He doesn't seem in any way surprised. He takes a few deep breaths before saying, "Kid's plane get off all right?"

"Yeah. He's over the Atlantic as we speak."

"What are you doin' here?"

"I don't know, Dad. I really don't know."

He climbs down the ladder, tosses the scraper aside, and claps his hands clean. I figure he wants to shake hands with me, but he doesn't. He puts his hands on his hips and stands in front of me. He doesn't seem glad to see me, but he'd not unhappy about it, either.

"Jake really liked that compass you gave him."

"Yeah, it might just come in handy for him."

"You guys did a good job on the path."

"Yeah, he seemed to enjoy the work. Hell of a project. Lot of fussin' around to get the thing level. No two cobblestones alike, you know? But he didn't get impatient about it."

"That's good."

"Might as well tell me what the hell you came here for, Sammy."

I shrug, spread my hands. "Thought you might need a hand painting the house."

"Yeah, right. You didn't even know I was gonna paint the house today!"

"I had an inkling."

"The hell you did!" He laughs out loud, squeezes my shoulder. "Your son just took off for the other side of the world. You're feelin' a little lonely, so you went to see your old man. You can admit it, Sammy. It's not such a terrible thing."

My red face tells him what I don't have to say in words. But there is something I do have to say, and it comes out in a burst, like a bolt of lightning.

"Could I sleep in my old room tonight?"

He's stunned by my request. He's trying to act as if he isn't, but he is. "Sure," he finally says. "You certainly may. Provided you give me a hand with this paint job." He cocks his head, squints one eye. "Big job. There's all the clapboards, then the trim and the windows. Might need you to stay more than one night."

"I've got no plans, Dad. Believe me, I've got no plans."

There's a tickle of a grin on his face. "What about the color? You okay with the color?"

"Canary yellow? Well, like you said, Dad—buttercups and sunshine. Nothing wrong with buttercups and sunshine."

He digs out an old pair of gym shorts and a ragged T-shirt for me. I get changed and resume the scraping job, while he goes inside and makes lunch for us, cheeseburgers and french fries he heats up on a pan in the oven. We wash it all down with lemonade. No beer until later, when the day's work is done.

After lunch my father goes to the paint store to pick up a couple of new brushes while I finish the scraping job on the back of the house. When he gets back he examines my work with a critical eye, finding a spot or two of loose paint that I somehow missed. Other than that, he says, I have done a good job.

"You ready to start painting, Sammy, or are you too tired?"

"Of course I'm not too tired. Are you tired?"

"I don't get tired anymore, Sammy. Ain't got the time for it."

We're going to paint the front of the house first, he explains, because the late afternoon sun is shining on the back and that's the worst way to paint, in full sun. I already knew this, of course, because when I was a kid he'd tell me things like this countless times, but I don't let on that I've heard it before. Truth is, it's good to hear his advice again, the same way it's good to hear a golden oldie rock 'n' roll song you haven't heard in a long time. Like a visit from an old friend.

I bring the ladder around to the front of the house, and set it up at the highest peak. The plan is for me to work up on the ladder, while he paints whatever clapboards he can reach from ground level. It'll be three days' work for the two of us, easily. I feel warm and gulpy, knowing I'll be spending the next few nights in my old room. Later on I'm going to have to walk to Kmart to buy some underwear and a toothbrush. A razor, too. I can't borrow his razor, because he shaves with a straight-edge blade, and that thing always terrified me. . . .

My father comes out of the garage carrying a can of paint. He pries the lid off to stir the stuff, and it's a good thing I'm not on the ladder when he does this, because I would have fallen off at the sight of it.

It's Benjamin Moore exterior house paint, but it's not canary yellow. It's robin's egg blue.

I don't say anything. I *can't* say anything. My father doesn't say anything, either, about how he took all those cans of canary yellow and brought them back to the paint store to exchange them for this new color while I was finishing the prep work.

He doesn't ask my opinion about the new color. We both know whose favorite color this was, and there's no reason in the world to talk about it.

He stirs the paint with a flat wooden stick for five minutes before pouring some of it into a small plastic container and passing it to me, along with a brand-new three-inch paintbrush.

"I'm not being cheap with this stuff," he says. "I just don't want you goin' up there with a full can, in case you knock it over."

"Makes sense, Dad."

"I'm not sayin' you *would* knock it over, but anything can happen up on a ladder, you know?"

"Dad. I'm not offended."

"Can't screw around at these prices. Twenty-eight bucks a gallon! Not to mention the damn primer. And that's a *sale* price! Do you believe that?"

"I'll be careful, Dad."

Paint and brush in hand, I slowly climb the ladder until I am facing the peak of the house. I dip the brush into the paint, pat it on the inside of the container, and touch the wood with my first stroke. The stuff spreads beautifully and it's a lovely color, like the sky on Easter Sunday, obliterating the bare wood and the few remaining shards of yellow. The newly painted wood looks to me the way a soul is supposed to look after confession—clean and shiny and beautiful, ready to face the elements. I feel ridiculously happy about what I'm doing. Maybe I'll become a housepainter. There would be worse ways to spend my time.

I go back and forth with the brush, getting the paint deeply into the grooves of the wood, then dip the brush back into the paint container.

"Don't put it on too thick," my father says. "Gonna need two coats anyway."

"I know that, Dad."

"All right, then, I'll get started down here."

He begins to paint the lower areas, and we fall into the wordless rhythm of two workmen getting a job done. I know I am going to be tired tonight, a good tired, a delicious tired, and I'll fall asleep beneath my old Debbie Harry poster and dream blank dreams.

But first, I'll watch some TV with my father. Maybe we'll catch an old black-and-white movie, something with Humphrey Bogart or Robert Mitchum. There won't be much variety, because my father doesn't get cable. That's okay. If nothing good is on maybe we'll just eat Napoli's pizza and drink beer.

My daydreams are interrupted by the sound of his voice, directly below me.

"Jake's in Paris by now, isn't he?"

"Should be."

"I've never been to Paris. You ever been to Paris?"

"Dad. When would I have gone to Paris?"

"Maybe the paper sent you there to cover a story. You were never a foreign correspondent?"

"Please. The farthest the *Star* ever sent me was the Bronx."

This gives him a good laugh. "Hey, you wanna call him? Feel free to call him from here."

"He wants to wait a few days before he calls us. I think I have to respect that wish."

My father chuckles. "Kid's got balls, Sammy. You got 'em, too."

It's the nicest thing he's ever said to me. Actually, he says it to the clapboards directly in front of his face, not to me, but still, it's quite a thing to hear, and when you're not expecting words like that, they go right through you. I have to grip the ladder for a moment, until the tingle passes.

"Thanks, Dad," I manage to say.

"Sammy?"

"Yeah?"

"You're drippin' on me here. Try not to drip on your father."

"I'll do my best."

We work for a few more hours in silence, a silence my father breaks with a sentence that goes straight to my core.

"Well, anyway," he says, "she'd have gotten a kick out of this."

He says it as if the two of us had been having a long conversation about my mother, a conversation he wanted to wrap up.

I don't say anything. There's nothing to say. At last, it has all been said. The only sound is the sweet, whispery slide of paint-brushes over wood, a healing sound neither of us wants to vio-late.

We paint until dark, then step back to examine the front of the house. It gleams in the moonlight like a promise that will be kept.

My father puts a hand on my shoulder, and I'm shocked when he leans on me for support. He's tired. He's an old man. In the darkness he seems vulnerable, maybe even a little frightened. He stares at the house, nodding in what seems to be approval.

"Looking good, Sammy," he says. "Second coat'll take care of anything we missed the first time." Without taking his gaze off the house he gives my shoulder a squeeze. "We'll get there. Don't you worry, we'll get there."